"TELL
WHAT

"My name is Alexander, Alex, if you prefer." He sighed in exasperation, uncrossed his arms, and stood up, towering over Evelyn by nearly a head. "Be assured, Miss Wellington, I am not known for my temperance. A long bethrothal to me could very well ruin your reputation."

Evelyn considered the possibility. "I have never been betrothed to a rake before. Shall I have to see you very often when we are officially affianced?"

His fingers closed about the nape of her neck and she started, but he made no attempt to release her. "Every night, my dear, until I teach you respect."

His mouth closed over hers, and Evelyn shut her eyes and gave herself up to the kiss. It was a reckless, mad thing to do, but she wanted it, and it seemed only fitting to seal this insane betrothal with an equally insane kiss. . . .

REBEL DREAMS

Patricia Rice

AN ONYX BOOK

ONYX
Published by the Penguin Group
Penguin Books USA Inc., 375 Hudson Street,
New York, New York 10014, U.S.A.
Penguin Books Ltd, 27 Wrights Lane,
London W8 5TZ, England
Penguin Books Australia Ltd, Ringwood,
Victoria, Australia
Penguin Books Canada Ltd, 10 Alcorn Avenue
Toronto, Ontario, Canada M4V 3B2
Penguin Books (N.Z.) Ltd, 182–190 Wairau Road,
Auckland 10, New Zealand

Penguin Books Ltd, Registered Offices:
Harmondsworth, Middlesex, England

First published by Onyx, an imprint of New American Library,
a division of Penguin Books USA Inc.

First Printing, September, 1991
10 9 8 7 6 5 4 3 2 1

1

July 1765

Alexander Hampton, heir presumptive to the Earl of Cranville, pulled his snowy cravat loose and propped his polished buckled shoes on the captain's table in a definitely unlordly manner. Pouring a tumbler of rum from the bottle at his side, he regarded his companion with sardonic amusement.

"An old smuggler like you dares to lecture me on right and wrong? For shame, Jack. Hypocrisy is as dangerous a fault as stealing."

Uncomfortable in the uniform of captain, Jack Ruggles shrugged off the braided coat and soiled vest, and, in shirtsleeves like his employer, settled down for a long night's bout of drinking. "Smugglin's for them that got no better. You're a rich man now. You got no reason to risk yourself or your partners."

Hampton's dark face grew momentarily cloudy as he sipped at his drink and contemplated his unseen but still troublesome partners: the very proper Earl of Cranville and the very improper, Lord Rory Maclean. The ship lurched as it hit a swell broadside, but he scarcely noticed it. The lantern on the wall swayed and flickered, but his thoughts had retreated down a melancholy path and only the liquor burning down his throat held any reality.

"Since one of those partners was your companion in crime," Alex ruminated aloud, "I cannot believe he will frown too heavily on a little extra profit. Jacobite rebel that he is, he'd find it highly amusing to ignore the fat, lazy nabobs in the great British West Indies. It's their doing that the Yanks must pay such outrageous prices for sugar. I wonder they don't shoot the customs officers and take matters in their own hands. The merchants we deal with in the colonies have been raising holy hell about that Revenue Act since it passed last year. I can buy the sugar cheap from the French, sell it in the colonies at a decent profit, give the tax collectors their tariff, and we all still come out ahead. Where's the harm?"

Jack watched the bloody great lordling with suspicion. Hampton seldom actually sailed with his ships, so his presence gave evidence of some change of unusual nature. Jack found it hard to believe that the aristocratic gentleman was actually contemplating taking up smuggling. True, the man had a reputation as a rakehell, and there had been a time when his debts had been such that he had to flee the country in pursuit of his heiress cousin. That was a time Jack remembered with a shake of his head. Alex Hampton had a lot to account for and was capable of making a great deal of trouble, but smuggling wasn't his style.

"Aye, Rory might close his eyes for politics, but you forget the earl. He'd not take kindly to his heir's venture into crime. And he'd want no part of the profits."

Stretching his long muscular legs in their tight buckled breeches and stockings, Hampton tilted his chair back at a precarious angle as he carelessly tossed back the rest of the rum in his cup. Unadorned by wig or powder, his coarse black hair was tightly bound at the nape. His valet would have a choking fit if he could see him now. That was why he'd left the man behind in London.

The earl. The damned righteous, arrogant Earl of Cranville, holder of the title, estates, and purse strings. Alex owed his fortune to his cousin the earl, and to the earl's daughter, and to the daughter's husband, Rory Maclean. He wasn't quite certain yet whether to be resentful or grateful. He returned the chair to the floor and poured another cup.

"How do the colonists survive without the damned nobility breathing down their necks and telling them what to do? Isn't it about time his majesty considered giving peerages in America? The Duke of New York, the Marquess of Boston—look at all the younger sons that could be granted earldoms. Why, in no time we'd bring the savages under a noble yoke, and all would be as peaceful as it is in merry old England."

Jack snorted, finally recognizing Hampton's talk as a means of antagonizing his listener and relieving his boredom. He'd found the wrong drinking partner for that. Jack Ruggles wasn't known for his flights of fancy.

"There might be some to protest that, seein' as how the Yanks think they already own the land, but you're welcome to the task of claiming it. It makes about as much sense as smuggling."

Hampton grinned at this grudging reply he'd drawn from the older man. In the summer heat of the cabin his elegantly tailored coat had been a severe irritation, and he had already shrugged it off, deciding he might as well shoot his noble image all to hell. The flowing shirt and thin silk vest beneath didn't bind his shoulders as severely as the coat had, but he was restless and couldn't make himself comfortable as he sat back with his drink.

"You're dead set against the Indies, then? That's a shame. Think of what your percentage would be on profits like that." Despite his nonchalance, he watched the captain shrewdly. It wasn't just boredom that made him tempt the ex-smuggler like this. Disgruntled employees had been known to involve themselves in worse crimes than padding profits. The letter of complaint in his vest pocket crackled as he shifted in his seat.

Jack favored his employer with a scornful look. "I wouldn't want to come up against the Maclean should he ever find out I risked his wife's ship in such a scheme. Buy your own ship if that's the trade you seek. That bloody Revenue Act made it a fool's game. I don't want to be hauled up before no Admiralty judge."

Satisfied, Hampton found another topic to antagonize the old tar. "His wife's ship! How noble-minded my cousin's husband is. Alyson hasn't the vaguest notion which end of the ship goes forward, much less how many ships her grandfather left her. Women are a feather-headed, worthless lot, good for only one thing. Why in the name of Old Nick the Maclean insists on treating the fortune as hers is beyond my comprehension. By law, she can't own a thing, and rightly so, I might add."

Jack rubbed the rum from his mustache with the back

of his hand before taking another gulp. He couldn't trade the gentleman cup for cup, but the amount he had consumed already left him pleasantly relaxed as he reminisced about the lovely lady under discussion.

"The Lady Alyson is a fine, bonnie lass, as the captain would say. She needn't know which end of a ship is up. That's not for her to know. She's made the Maclean happy and given him two brawny boys. If he wants to call the ship hers, he has that right."

Alex agreed grudgingly. "Acquiring a fortune is one good reason for the chains of marriage, I daresay, but I'll be deviled if I can think of any other. Old age, mayhap. The earl in his senility might appreciate a winsome wench like Lady Cranville, but the man's been leg-shackled over half his life. You'd think he'd know better than to try it again. I'll be bound if I can find any reason to give a woman the power to carp at me night and day. Just think what a wife would have to say when I decide to go on voyages like this! I shudder to think of it." He shook his dark head in dismay and sipped at his cup.

"Aye, Dougall and Maclean both retired from the sea when they took wives, but I can't see they suffer for it. Whenever the Maclean gets the itch to sail, Lady Alyson goes with him. I wouldn't mind having a woman in my bed right now if I could find one willing to do the same."

Since his thoughts were on the same subject—the woman in his bed, not marriage—Hampton growled a reply. As much as he detested the wiles of deceitful women, he regretted not having a lightskirt aboard right now. Six weeks was a long time to go without a woman, particularly since he had a voracious appetite that kept his mistresses well sated. If he could only keep their material wants as satisfied as their physical ones, he wouldn't be quite so discontented with his bachelor state. But he'd be damned if he'd go into debt again to supply them with their expensive trinkets. Women might be a necessary evil, but he didn't have to support them.

Resolutely ignoring the uncomfortable pressure in his loins, Hampton refilled his cup and raised it in a salute. "Here's to our lovely colonial ladies, may they lift their skirts as freely as the London ones!"

Jack frowned at this disrespect, but he had no objection to another drink. Hampton would be in for a bit of a surprise when he met the Boston ladies.

Elegantly garbed in a navy silk frock coat and buff breeches of the latest London fashion, but with a head pounding like all the hammers of hell, Alex Hampton leaned his arms against the railing and watched the wharf below with a frown as the ship anchored.

He had never been to Boston before. He hoped this wasn't a typical arrival scene. He might have to recommend that Cranville Enterprises find other, less dangerous ports for their wares, if so.

A vociferous argument appeared to be going on between the plainly clad captain of a colonial sloop anchored further down the wharf and a gaudily garbed official on the boards. Two red-coated soldiers were stiffly trying to hold back a crowd of angry bystanders who yelled and screamed and drowned out any chance of understanding the argument. Hampton raised a dark brow at the motley assortment represented. There were well-dressed gentlemen in dark broadcloth and three-cornered hats who were quite likely merchants. He could see tradesmen in long jerkins and leather breeches, and a gang of ruffians in tattered shirts and worn sailor's garb. Despite their differences in station, they all yelled the same slogans and phrases and seemed to be in general agreement on the topic of the gaudily dressed gentleman's ancestry. Interesting.

He went in search of Jack. The sooner he got the cargo unloaded and his business transacted, the better off he would be. A few days in port with a willing whore while they loaded up again, and he could be on his way. In this heat, even the barren outposts of Cornwall looked appealing.

"What's the racket about down there? Are the natives always this restless?" Alex found the captain staring down at the crowd with a frown of concern.

"See that gent in the bright coat? That's the customs officer. It looks like he'll be tied up for a while. We can't unload until he approves our papers."

Hampton grimaced. "In that case, lower the plank.

I'm going ashore. I'll leave the unloading in your expert hands."

Jack gave his employer a sideways look but said nothing. Young gentlemen tended to get bored, restless, and impatient. He didn't know Hampton well enough to judge him otherwise. With a signal to his mate, he sent a sailor down to lower the plank. His own head ached enough in the sun's merciless heat. Hampton's ought to be ready to fall off.

Several of the mob turned to stare with suspicion at the tall, darkly handsome gentleman descending from the familiar frigate of Cranville Enterprises. Deciding his unpowdered hair and sophisticated London tailoring were a contradiction but not a danger, they returned to their shouting and forgot about him. Hampton elbowed his way through the crowd without interference.

He eyed the row of tidy brick structures along the wharf with total lack of interest. Somewhere amid those unimposing structures worked an expert troublemaker. He would locate the crotchety old gentleman, demand an explanation, maybe even have him sign an affidavit to the effect that it was all a mistake, and then he would find the nearest promising tavern.

As he trudged along the wharf searching for a name to match the letter in his pocket, he cursed the heat, the noisy mob, and the wretch who had forced him to make the journey to this forsaken hole. His partners had insisted the man was a merchant who could be trusted and that any complaint must be seen to personally, but he had serious doubts on that matter. He had personally overseen the loading of the ships in question. He had too much at stake to lose time or money on charges of this magnitude. He would have bloody well known if there were any illegal goods in that hold before they sailed. Someone was trying to stir up trouble, and he damned well intended to know why.

The warehouse was not difficult to locate. "Wellington Storage" was emblazoned in bold letters above the office door. From the size of the structure, this was no mean operation. No wonder his partners had insisted on investigating. Still, men were known to get senile. Or perhaps there was just some simple mistake. He was willing to let him off on that if it would shorten the time until he could reach the comfort of a cool tavern.

He stepped into the dusky interior without knocking. A long counter separated the office from the lobby, and he couldn't help but admire the neatness of the small room as compared to the dust-and-cobweb-infested offices he'd been in back in England. Of course, there was the minor difference of age, but it looked as if this building had been here for a decade or more if the ledgers lined along the wall were any indication. That was time enough to gather cobwebs and wharf rats and bury the counter in a quarter-inch of filth. He glared at the polished wood warily.

A clerk appeared from some hidden doorway. With only one small window over the high account desk, the room relied on a single lamp for illumination. Hampton could discern little of the clerk but slim height and an unusual smock. Peremptorily removing the letter from his pocket, he consulted the signature to verify his memory.

"I have come to see E. A. Wellington. Is he here?"

"I am E. A. Wellington. May I help you?"

The husky, almost sensual voice made him start, and he stared as the clerk strode forward into the light from the window. The sun sent a copper glint shimmering through glossy chestnut hair pulled back in a single black ribbon.

Alex stared at the waist-length hair held by that simple bow, then skeptically raked his gaze over E. A. Wellington's odd garb. Breeches and stockings appeared beneath the smock, but the shoes were much too small to be a man's. His gaze drifted upward, probing the contours of the flowing blue muslin without success, then settling on the smooth and unmistakably feminine features above a slender throat. Haughty eyes of some deep hue regarded him with dislike from beneath gracefully arched brows.

He met the dislike with coldness. "I'm not inclined to deal with females or underlings. I wish to speak with the E. A. Wellington who wrote this letter, and I wish to do it immediately. I haven't journeyed here from London to be fobbed off by charades."

The clerk stepped to the counter and removed the letter from his hand. She was above middle height, but not so tall that he couldn't look down on her lustrous hair. A woman with hair like that had no business confining it in a single ribbon. It could drive a man to distraction wondering what it would look like if the ribbon came untied and the thick brown tresses fell in disarray over her proud shoulders and down her narrow back. Damn, but maybe that was her intention. Alex held his lust in rigid reins and watched coldly as she regarded the letter.

She returned it to the counter and looked up to meet his furious eyes. "I am Evelyn Amanda Wellington, and I wrote that letter. I will assume you are not Lord Cranville."

Hampton's temperature shot up another few degrees. He had known men to quake in their shoes when he regarded them with less fury than he did this female now. His own cousin used to run at the sight of him, and even now regarded him with caution when he went into a temper. How dared this impertinent female keep up this game and make veiled insults?

"I am Alexander Hampton, Miss Wellington, if Wellington you truly are. Lord Cranville is a silent partner in Cranville Enterprises. He has no interest in the shipping line. That is my territory. Perhaps I would do better to ask to see your father."

Twin spots of red colored her high cheeks, and moist, generously shaped lips compressed above an obstinately square chin. "You may ask as you wish. He died last autumn, well before this letter was written. In any case, I always handled his correspondence when he was alive. If you have come to answer the charges in that letter, you will have to deal with me."

Evelyn straightened her shoulders and met the stranger's thickly lashed eyes with as much ferocity as she could summon. She was accustomed to dealing with blustering ships' captains, irate merchants, and lecherous delivery boys. She was not accustomed to the impact of furious square-jawed giants with eyes she would give gold for. Lud, but a person would have to be a saint to look into those eyes without quivering. She had to remember her anger before she could catch what he was saying.

". . . answer the charges! I came here to demand you

retract them before my partners believe I have taken up a life of crime. Cranville Enterprises does not and never will engage in the practice of smuggling. I, personally, have no desire to hang for French brandy. I trust you are prepared to give evidence of your charges."

"The best evidence will be the contents of your current shipment." Evelyn kept her simmering temper in check as she faced the arrogant stranger. That he had actually come in person to answer her letter threw doubt on the charges, but his scornful attitude rubbed salt in open sores. She was tired of being treated as less than a person because she was female. She could run this warehouse as competently as her father had, as she had in fact helped him to do these last years. This man had no right to look at her as if she were lower than a snail.

"Then find someone to send with me, and he's free to inspect every damned crate and keg addressed to Wellington Storage. Then I expect a written letter of apology to pacify my partners in this matter."

"It would be very surprising if the operation continued after that letter was received, but on the possibility that you kept the letter quiet and are not involved, I will accompany you. Give me a minute to find someone to mind the desk."

Moving toward the back room and untying her smock, Evelyn was startled into stopping by her visitor's irate reply.

"I refuse to take a fool female into the hold of a ship to faint at the first rat she encounters! Give me someone with a little experience and a stout stomach."

Evelyn turned to glare at the polished features of this London gentleman with his clipped, haughty accents and narrow mind. "I have been visiting the holds of ships since I was ten. How many years have you spent going into them, Mr. Hampton?"

That remark stung, and he had no ready reply but silence. Vowing to take her straight down into the bowels of hell if she requested, Hampton gave her a curt nod. "Very well, if that's your wish."

Satisfied she had pierced his thick hide, Evelyn removed herself to the back room, where she hastily took off her smock and pinned her hair up in a thick swirl. Generally she wore breeches only when she was working with the stock in back, but she saw no reason to change to go into a ship's hold. The men who worked down here were accustomed to her unusual garb. It made more sense than long skirts and laces, under the circumstances. She rather thought the arrogant man outside would have a different opinion, though.

Smiling maliciously at that thought, she called to Jacob to mind the front. His small face popped from behind the stacks to gaze at her quizzically.

"You're going to leave me here alone?" His boy's voice broke with incredulity.

Evelyn grinned and tugged at a long curly lock escaping from his ribbon. "You keep telling me you're eleven going on twelve. That should be old enough to stand out there and tell anyone who asks that I'll be right back."

Jacob jerked his head away from his sister's undignified caress. "I can do that, easy," he said scornfully.

When he accompanied Evelyn to the front room, however, he stared in a decidedly little-boy fashion at the stranger filling the small space on the other side of the counter. Unlike Uncle George's padded satin frock coats, this man's expensive attire clung naturally to wide shoulders and flared neatly at the waist. The immaculate lace at his wrist and throat bespoke wealth, the black satin bow at his nape reflected simplicity, but it was the short vest that held Jacob's attention. He hated vests. They clung and flapped around his knees when he ran, but this stranger's vest stopped at the hip. Surreptitiously Jacob tried to see if he wore a sword.

"Mr. Hampton, this is my brother, Jacob. Jacob, mind your manners!" Evelyn scolded as she turned to find him standing on his toes in an attempt to see over the counter.

The man's coldly chiseled features showed no amusement at her brother's obvious fascination, and she hurried out to accompany him from the office. "We are going to check on a shipment from Cranville Enterprises, Jacob. I should be back directly."

Hampton opened the door for her, but he seemed uncertain whether to offer a lady in breeches his arm. Scorning any hint that she might not be able to walk the wharf unaided, Evelyn solved his dilemma by striding toward the crowded ramp ahead of him.

A frown puckered her forehead as she observed the mob still screaming curses, but it wasn't an unusual sight anymore. Everyone's temper had risen these last months since the first rumors of Parliament's newest attempt to draw blood from a turnip. Things would go back to normal once sensible heads in his majesty's cabinet listened to reason. She couldn't believe an entire government could be so dunderheaded as not to realize that there weren't enough coins in all the colonies to pay what the Stamp Act required if it were put into law. Let the politicians rant and rave about the constitutional implications of passing such a tax. The practicality was all that concerned her.

As they reached the nearly impassable region between the ships, Hampton grabbed his slender companion's arm, and blocking her from the crowd with his larger body, made a path toward the ship's ramp. The wooden sides of the *Minerva* rose above them, and overheated, unwashed bodies closed around them. Alex cursed at having to escort a woman through such a scene, but she seemed unconcerned by the stench or the half-dressed state of some of the sailors. She appeared deaf to their obscenities. He had to keep from gaping in astonishment as she calmly walked up the loading plank as if it were a grassy hillside. The sight of her hips swaying in front of him turned his thoughts in a different direction, and Alex watched in fascination. Only a thin linen shirt and broadcloth breeches covered her trim figure, and Alex could easily discern every hill and valley of her supple curves. He was in no state for rational conversation by the time they reached the deck.

Evelyn glanced questioningly at him as Hampton jerked her arm and headed for the hold without speaking, but seeing the grim look on his dark face, she wisely held her tongue. The captain came hurrying toward them, but the man at her side waved him away with a peremptory gesture. A small tickle of fear stirred in her stomach as the power this man wielded began to register somewhere in the recesses of her mind. He owned this ship and dozens more like it. All these men were at his command. If he truly were a smuggler, he need only lock her in the hold and set sail. No one on board would dare question him.

Sending Hampton's tight-lipped visage a furtive look, she decided he looked quite ruthless enough to do that or worse. Lud, why hadn't she seen that before? Was she so enamored of those dark eyes that she had taken leave of her senses?

Feeling her begin to resist his hold, Alex sneered impatiently. "What's wrong? Having second thoughts about getting your elegant slippers wet?"

Since she wore sturdy leather brogans to protect her toes from dropped crates, pride tilted her chin higher. "I should think that you would be more concerned with your pretty gold buckles and silk stockings, Mr. Hampton. I'm dressed more sensibly for this expedition than you."

Muffling a curse, Alex handed his hat to a seaman and began to clatter down the steps into the darkness of the hold. The lantern hanging just inside scarcely gave enough illumination to see the steps. He found the flints and a second lantern and struck a light. Out of habit, he turned to hold his hand out to help his companion down. Despite her outlandish garb and sharp tongue, she was still female. He had been taught at an early age to respect the sex, and even though later years had proved women's treachery, his habits hadn't changed.

Despite her bold words to the contrary, Evelyn despised these excursions into the moldy confines of a ship's interior. She didn't like the stench, the creaking darkness, or the ever-present threat of rats. Even though she wore none, she had the urge to lift her skirts from the water and debris of the lower depths. Without conscious thought, she accepted Hampton's offered hand.

The contact almost shocked her into flight. Large, strong fingers wrapped firmly around her smaller ones, reassuring her with their warmth and smoothness at the same time that they made her insides do strange little dances. Surely she had held a man's bare hand before. There was no reason for these odd sensations. Try as she might, she could only recall her father's hand holding hers without gloves. When she would tug away, Hampton's fingers closed tighter.

Frightened, she glanced up at him again. In the uncertain light from the lamp she thought she saw an oddly mocking look upon his face, but it did not seem directed at her. He scanned the rows of barrels and crates until he found what he was looking for.

"Over there, Miss Wellington. Shall I call someone to begin prying them all open?"

She could read the familiar brand burned into the wood, but she shook her head. "Only the crates of porcelain, Mr. Hampton. And it might not be wise to open them under any eyes but ours. I, too, am averse to having my neck stretched."

He murmured something incomprehensible as he turned his gaze on the mentioned part of her anatomy. She caught him staring at her with the kind of warmth she had learned to avoid, and shaking her hand free of his grip, she strode determinedly to the cargo, searching for the symbol that would indicate a shipment from Staffordshire.

Still imagining what that lovely white throat would look like with a necklace of hemp around it, Alex shouted to one of the sailors hovering above. He should have found a whore first. He hadn't had a sensible thought in his head since he first laid eyes on this vicious termagant, and he disliked feeling like a fool.

"If all my men are under suspicion, Miss Wellington, then we had better take more than the suspected cargo," he replied in low undertones as two men clattered down to join them.

He pointed out an assortment of crates he wished removed, gave orders that the porcelain be treated with respect as it was a wedding gift, then calmly took the termagant's soft hand in his and started up. He ignored her tug of protest. By holding those very feminine fingers he could remember she was female even in the darkness of a ship's hold. Otherwise he might be tempted to strangle her.

On deck again he confronted a frowning Jack. The captain carefully avoided looking at the feminine figure clothed in men's garb and sought his employer's shuttered face. "You can't remove the cargo until customs approves it. There's still a ruckus down there that don't look like it will end soon."

Releasing Evelyn's fingers, Hampton walked to the rail and glanced over. The others followed suit. He pointed to the officious-looking gentleman in satin surrounded now by soldiers. "The man in orange is the one we need to see?"

Beside him, Evelyn muttered "rust," but he chose to ignore her correction. He intended to damn well settle this matter here and now and get as far from this temptation as he could go. He had never seen another woman like this one, and he hoped to God he would never see another. His hands literally itched to encompass that tiny waist, and the thought of those breeches buttons that close to his fingers made him shiver. His brain had evidently abdicated in favor of his loins.

When assured the man in orange or rust or whatever was the one he sought, Alex jammed his hat on his head and shoved his way back into the crowd below.

Evelyn watched with interest as Hampton shouldered his way to his goal. A head taller than most of the crowd and hiding a more muscular physique beneath his silks and laces than the tradesmen in their homespun, he had no difficulty defeating any protest to his arrogant path. The startled customs officer looked bewildered as Hampton caught his arm and began hauling him through the crowd, but Evelyn knew he was as much relieved as alarmed. Uncle George had never known when to keep quiet or how to deal with the results once his tongue was loosed. The soldiers would prevent the other ship from unloading, and without a target, the mob would eventually disperse. Hampton was doing him a favor. She shook her head in despair that a relative of hers could be so lacking in common sense. Thank goodness he wasn't a blood relative.

George Upton gave no sign that he recognized her as Hampton hauled him on board and ordered that he begin inspecting the cargo. He preferred not to acknowledge the fact that he had a niece who wore breeches. Evelyn smiled and leaned back against the railing while Hampton carefully chose the crates he wanted removed first.

Obviously accustomed to authority and expecting efficiency to match his own, he paid no heed to the fact that the customs officer and the captain were frantically flipping through the manifest to keep up with his selections.

When the first of the crewmen began hauling the crates down to the wharf, Hampton came to retrieve his unorthodox companion. The sight of her unexpected smile practically gave Alex heart palpitations. When she leaned back against the rail like that, he could see the distinct lines of her uptilted breasts beneath the windblown shirt. He would be able to see more were she wearing an evening gown, but somehow this tantalizing silhouette was more arousing. He had to be out of his mind.

This time, he took her arm and steered her toward the ramp. He didn't intend to stay in this rebellious port long enough to take a mistress, so admiring her firm flanks did him no good whatsoever. He was quite certain she wasn't the type to throw up her skirts—or roll down her breeches—for a few hours' dalliance. He would have to keep his thoughts firmly on the matter at hand.

Alex found that exceedingly difficult to do when he was once more left alone in the dark with Evelyn, this time inside the dry comfort of her warehouse with her little brother standing guard outside. The crates that had been hauled in were scattered about their feet, but all he could think of was taking her waist in his hands and discovering the multitude of possibilities in those enticing lips she covered unconsciously with the tip of her tongue.

Her seeming unawareness of his thoughts warned that she was innocent of passion, and grinding his teeth, Alex looked around the massive warehouse. "I'll need a crowbar to open these. Where do you keep them?"

Evelyn breathed a sigh of relief at this abrupt end to the tension that had been building between them. She couldn't help it if he were the most handsome man she had ever had the misfortune to come across. If he were any one of the hearty sea captains or effete aristocrats who graced her uncle's drawing room, she would already have the crowbar in her hand and be prying at the crates. If he even wore the garb of a soldier, she could despise him and would have no difficulty returning his rudeness.

Instead, he walked with muscular grace in the direction she indicated, and she could almost feel the strength in those hands as he returned with the tool to pry at the wood.

To her amazement, she realized she had already forgiven him of all charges of smuggling, and she waited with drawn breath to see the contents of the box. There were many other things she couldn't forgive him for, but they would cease to be a worry as soon as he was gone.

The lid flew open and Hampton swiftly removed the top layer of packing material. In triumph, he lifted the heavily detailed hand-painted porcelain. "Staffordshire, madam. Not brandy. Have you any further proof?"

Silently Evelyn knelt beside the crate and carefully set aside the lovely dishes on top. Removing the second layer of packing, she uncovered a gleaming row of bottled brandy. Lifting a bottle for his inspection, she raised a wry eyebrow. "Brandy, sir. Not Staffordshire. Do you need further proof?"

As he grabbed the bottle from her hand to inspect it, the commotion outside grew louder. Alex cast a glance through the wavy panes of glass in time to catch sight of a half-dozen red-coated soldiers marching this way. Hastily he hit the cork with his hand and replaced the bottle in its bed of straw.

"Let's get this covered before someone sees it." He grabbed a handful of the packing and began to cover up the contraband again.

Hastily Evelyn did the same. "What am I supposed to do with it? Every one of these crates marked 'Staffordshire' will probably be like that."

Lifting the lid, Hampton began to hammer it down again. "What did you do with the last shipments?"

"I had already shipped them before I realized what they were. I had ordered a set for my mother as a Christmas gift. That's how I discovered it. I don't normally inspect everything we receive."

"You suspected all the shipments after opening one crate?" He turned to stare at her with incredulity.

"No, two. I thought the first a mistake and ordered another. They came in while I was not here. By the time I came back to work, the other crates had been delivered, but mine was still here. It was the same as the first. That's when I sent the letter. I was furious. I not only did not have the gift I wished for my mother, but I was stuck with harboring two crates of illegal brandy. If they are found, I could be arrested. You don't know what it's been like here since they started rewarding spies and liars for turning in their neighbors to the Admiralty Court."

Her fury was evident in the flash of violet eyes. Alex turned away from her indignant expression, and shouldering the crate, walked down the rows stacked high with goods on the way in or out of this busy port. It wouldn't do to hide a crate of porcelain in the pile of flour sacks. That would show they had something to hide, should it be uncovered. He found a crate of Chinese porcelain and set it on that, then looked around. There was an empty space on one particularly high shelf. That would suffice.

Evelyn watched in astonishment as the elegant gentleman easily carried the crates, lifting them over his head to carefully set them on the highest shelf. Even if anyone found them there, it would not seem unusual to store porcelain out of the way of clumsy feet. Still, she could not keep the brandy forever. She eyed Hampton's richly garbed frame dubiously as he dusted himself off.

"What do we do now?"

"We get the hell out of here before someone wonders what I am doing lingering so long with you. Do you know where your shipments went? Where these will go?" Hampton began steering her toward the door with a mixture of anger and fear, not fear for himself but for her. Smugglers were not notoriously given to kindness toward those who turned them in. He would have to work carefully.

"I looked them up, but the names meant nothing to me. They were companies in various towns some miles from here."

"Can you get me a list?"

"Yes, but it will take some time." Even Evelyn began to perceive the precariousness of their situation if he lingered much longer. If their smuggler were anywhere about, he must wonder at the shipment being unloaded early and at the command of so important a person as the ship's owner. Their prolonged conversation might drive him to investigate.

"Then we'll need to meet again, preferably somewhere else. Any suggestions?" Alex could think of a few, but he didn't think she would appreciate the view from his bed in the tavern.

"My uncle's. I will see that you receive an invitation to dinner. I'll pass you the list when I can. No one could suspect us of colluding on a social occasion."

"Your uncle might. It's better if we claim no prior acquaintance other than that necessary to unload the ship."

"That's not a problem. My uncle will never know that I am the one inviting you. Trust me."

Her lovely ivory complexion was marred with a smudge of dirt, but Alex knew better than to touch it. Grimly he placed his hat under his arm and made a brief bow. "I will leave it to your discretion. It will take time to find out who shipped it from my end. The receivers are our best hope."

"I understand. Good day, Mr. Hampton." Evelyn said this in full view of the front office as he opened the door to escort her out. Only her brother and the clerk from another warehouse were in the room, but she felt the need for formality.

She breathed a sigh of relief as he departed. Finding the smugglers was going to be easier than dealing with one Alexander Hampton. She shivered at the thought of meeting him again. Was he always so angry?

2

"They say he owns half of Cranville Enterprises and is a close friend of Lord Cranville's. I cannot imagine such wealth, can you? Just the contents of the one ship in port now must be worth tens of thousands, and he must own dozens. Why, I saw bolts of silk in there that would make your mouth water."

Evelyn set her teacup down and gestured toward the package on the seat beside her cousin. "I really must be going. Mama insisted that I bring you some of those candies Mr. Hampton gave Jacob. They are really quite delicious, though personally I find the man perfectly odious. Flaunting his wealth and name in front of starving, unemployed sailors is the height of maliciousness."

Evelyn smiled to herself as she rose and reached for her hat. Her cousin Frances leapt to her feet in a flurry of silken skirts and laces and a cloud of scent. Generally her cousin's porcelain prettiness sported a pout of boredom when she was forced to converse with her bourgeois relatives. At the moment, she was all sunshine and roses, catching Evelyn's arm gaily and attempting to delay her departure.

"Faith, but you must not hurry so! We never have time for a good girlish chat. Sit and tell me more about this odious gentleman. Is he old? Is he ugly?"

Evelyn donned her hat and began to tie the ribbons. "Quite striking, actually. He has the longest eyelashes I've ever seen on a man. And the meanest mouth." She added that for her own personal satisfaction. She certainly wasn't going to allow anyone to think she was enraptured by a ruthless Tory. It should be quite amusing to see how the hateful man pried Frances' claws loose from his scalp. "Anyway, he is still unmarried, which shows that London women have much more sense than I ever gave them credit for. I really must be going. I'll see you later."

She hummed to herself as she left the house. She really had no idea of Hampton's marital or financial state, as it was of no concern to her, but it was all the information Frances required to set her on the prowl. At twenty, she was a year younger than Evelyn, but horrified at her spinster role. Evelyn could have told her the opinion of the available young men of town that kept her single, but she was quite certain Frances didn't wish to hear herself described as a spoiled, greedy Tory. Frances wasn't really quite that bad. It was just that she didn't belong in Boston right now. Even the wealthy aristocrats were beginning to look skeptically upon Britain's ruling party. Frances would be much better off back in London, where she had been born.

Of course, if Frances were not quite so thoughtless, she would have offered her cousin the use of the carriage to take her down to the wharf, but Evelyn was accustomed to the walk and did not object to the anonymity of the crowd. The Uptons' carriage was just one more sore point in a town where the grandest transportation was a good horse. On the worst days of the year Evelyn rode a rented hack down to the bay, but the rest of the time she rather enjoyed traipsing across the Common and gossiping with her neighbors, stopping at Faneuil Hall for fresh vegetables or to listen to the arguments of the men trailing out from some town meeting on the upper level. She felt quite at home in this milieu of men, and because they were accustomed to dealing with her at the warehouse, they often accepted her into their conversations.

With her father's death Evelyn had taken his place in more positions than the warehouse, however. As she hurried past the State House, a young man in dark broadcloth and rakishly cocked hat hailed her.

"Miss Wellington! Will we be seeing you at the meeting tonight?" He crossed the dusty cobblestones to stop in front of her, politely removing his hat as he admired the oval face turned toward him.

"I will try to be there later, Pilgrim. I suspect I will be commanded to my uncle's house for dinner first."

The young man looked concerned. "Then perhaps we should hold the meeting at the tavern. We have no wish to overburden your poor mother—"

Evelyn waved away his protest. "You don't know how much it means to my mother to be allowed to continue hosting these meetings. Please, do not consider moving it. I will be there as soon as I can, to take her place should she grow tired. You know the Sons of Liberty are always welcome in our home. My father would have wanted it that way."

The young man grinned. "He always preferred your mother's fare to the tavern's, and I must agree with him. But I fear our little committee will soon overflow your accommodations. In times like these it might be necessary to bring all the smaller groups together under one roof. You know we discussed it last time."

"I know, and then you will find it necessary to keep women out." Evelyn spoke with more irritation than sadness at the departure of this group whose politics fascinated her. "Stand forewarned, we will form a committee of our own, and you will never know what we are up to."

Instead of lecturing as some of the older men might have, he only grinned and returned his hat to his head. "Just don your breeches and join us, Miss Wellington. We'll be happy to have you."

She laughed as he strode off. 'Twas a pity she could find no romantic interest in Pilgrim Adams. He was a fine young man, even if his red hair and freckles made him look more clown than merchant. Unfortunately, she suffered Frances' problem in reverse. She had worked and played with all these young men since she had been in leading strings. They thought her one of them. It seldom occurred to them to come courting a woman they had exchanged argumentative blows with the day before. The few who had dared to approach her door with flowers in hand were men who believed she would stay home if she married, leaving them with the care of her father's profitable business.

Tightening her lips as she remembered those few disasters, she hurried toward the bay. She intended to teach Jacob the business just as their father had taught it to her. One day they would share equally in the warehouse and expand to other activities. Right now she wished there were some way of owning their own ship, but that would have to wait. No one would lend capital to a female. She would simply have to be satisfied with increasing the profits until she could buy one on her own. Or with Jacob. By the time she had saved that much money, he would be of age.

The royal summons to her uncle's dinner came in the middle of the afternoon. Evelyn glared at the message with a mixture of relief and annoyance. The day had turned out to be intolerably hot, and perspiration rolled down her back as she sat on her high stool pulling ledgers in search of the names of the companies ordering porcelain in the last year. Caught up in the detective work, she had traced all orders of Staffordshire porcelain back to 1762, at which point she found no more. Then she had traced all orders made by those particular companies. She was in the process of locating old correspondence for names and addresses when the message came from her uncle.

She glanced at the long-case clock on the wall. Four o'clock! Good heavens, Frances had taken longer than usual to win her father over, or had maliciously delayed the message until there was scarce time for her cousin to get ready. Whichever, she would have to be satisfied with the hastily scribbled notes in her hand.

Calling for Jacob and the hired man, Benjamin, to close up for her, Evelyn tucked the list into her deep skirt pocket and hurried out into the street. By the time she walked home her hair would be dirty and disheveled and she would need a bath. Heating the water and hauling the buckets would take another half-hour. Her hair would have no chance of drying. Perhaps she ought to just show up in breeches and smock to teach her uncle the results of ill manners.

Already tired and irascible and worried about the results of her research, Evelyn was in no humor to be treated as a dependent relative when she arrived at the Uptons'. The maid abandoned her in the hallway and she was left to discard her mantilla on the hall tree and to enter the drawing room unannounced. In deference to the occasion she had donned a lilac silk that flowed extravagantly behind her but did not require the use of the French panniers Frances favored. She was unadorned except for the lace frills of her sleeves and décolletage and made no attempt to mock the English fashion of piling her hair upon cushions and covering it with powder and plumes. Let the lordly Englishman scorn her lack of fashion. She had arranged her newly washed and still-damp tresses in a loose coil covered with a bit of lace and a lilac ribbon. If Uncle George complained of her plainness, she would tell him in no uncertain terms that she would wear breeches the next time he summoned her so late in the day.

She tried to keep from scowling as she entered the drawing room to find Frances clinging to Hampton's arm and gazing up into his sardonic face with a look of rapture. Foolish creature! Couldn't she see the mockery in the man's damnable eyes? He thought them all primitive amusements compared to his usual sophisticated company. Even Frances' elegant imported gown and fashionably coiffed hair adorned with matching pink roses would not impress a man like Alexander Hampton.

As she entered, his gaze turned to her, and she felt it rake consideringly over her modest silk and unpowdered hair. It must be like comparing a caterpillar to a butterfly, she surmised angrily. She did not have it in her to be grateful when he merely acknowledged her presence with a nod and returned to her cousin's conversation rather than making some insulting comment.

Obviously he had dressed down for the dubious honor of dining with colonials. He wore the same navy silk frock coat he had worn yesterday. His lace was newly cleaned and starched, but no more elaborate than for a business call. He had not even condescended to powder his hair, but wore it tied in a simple black ribbon. Uncle George must be choking at such arrogance.

As her Aunt Matilda finally detached herself from a querulous servant, Evelyn swiftly assessed the remainder of the company. At such short notice the guest list was small. There were the encroaching neighbors, the Stones, and her uncle's best friend, Thomas Henderson. Uncle George had been throwing her into the lawyer's company for several years now, but the feeling of antipathy between them was mutual, thank goodness.

She smiled at her aunt and submitted to that lady's questioning on the state of her mother's health. Anything was better than confronting either Hampton or Henderson.

Conscious of the insipid chatter of the silly peacock at his side, Hampton allowed his thoughts to drift elsewhere. The gracious smile Evelyn bestowed upon her aunt all too clearly revealed her affection for the older woman. What would it take for a man to elicit such a response? From the glare she had gifted him with, he was not likely to find out. It was a good thing they were agreed on the priorities of this situation. Now that he'd found that buxom tavern maid to ease his needs, he could deal sensibly with Miss E. A. Wellington. He'd get the list from her, place a few careful questions, hand his evidence to the Admiralty Court, and get the hell out of here before the straitlaced witch scratched his eyes out just for thinking.

Alex attempted to maintain a pleasant demeanor throughout dinner as the Henderson fellow occupied much of Miss Wellington's conversation to the exclusion of all else. Frances kept up a continuous bright chatter that needed only an occasional nod of his head or polite murmur to keep the words flowing, so he had ample opportunity to observe the table's other occupants.

The Stones he dismissed out of hand as nonentities. Matilda Upton seemed a motherly, kindly woman with no significant thoughts of her own. He had been shocked to discover that "Uncle George" was the same officious customs officer who had approved his cargo, but he could see the reason why Miss Wellington might not wish to acknowledge the relationship. The man was a pompous ass, so puffed up with his own consequence that the veriest pinprick would deflate him. Alex toyed with the idea of applying his notorious humor to the task, but refrained. In London he might make veiled allusions to toadeating frogs and garden-grub Yankees, but he felt certain they would not be appreciated here.

Except, perhaps, by the haughty blue-eyed female across the table. Doubtless she would have a number of insults to return in kind, and he wasn't at all certain that he wished to hear her opinion of him. Gad, but she had an incredible face! It was all high bones and sharp angles filled in with a gardenia-petal softness that begged to be touched. It wasn't a beautiful face by any means, but it was a strong one, and definitely striking. While most women painted already pale faces even whiter, she did nothing to conceal the lovely ivory-and-rose complexion. He wondered idly who had deemed it fashionable to look like a ghost. He much preferred Miss Wellington's natural color.

Until this time he had considered his cousin Alyson to be one of the loveliest women of his acquaintance. This woman in no way resembled Alyson, but still he couldn't keep his gaze away. Whereas Alyson was all soft, cuddly curves and vague smiles and instinctive gestures, this woman was tall and straight with clear eyes full of intelligence and a manner sparing of extraneous words or gestures. He began to find it amusing to continue the comparison: Alyson's contrasting shades of black and white to Evelyn's warm hues of rose and ivory and brown; Alyson's wandering thoughts to Evelyn's precise conversation. He had never realized how different two women could be, but he suspected the pair would be famous friends should they ever meet. They both distrusted him heartily, and rightly so.

Alex stifled a groan of protest as the women withdrew to allow the men their after-dinner brandy and cigars. He sniffed the brandy with suspicion, deciding it was of the same quality as the bottles in the warehouse, but there was no reason to believe it was smuggled. Certainly a customs officer would buy only from English merchants after paying all the appropriate tariffs. The tariffs were exorbitant, but since they were no longer at war with France, there was a brisk trade in the brandy market again.

Hampton reluctantly joined in the general discussion of the fairness of the king's policies in asking the colonists to pay part of the cost of the last war with the French. The cost of housing English troops in the colonies was undoubtedly high, he agreed politely, wishing to hell they would shut up and let him find Evelyn. All he wanted was that list and to get out of here. Politics had never been his strong suit.

But Upton was obviously interested in courting his favor, and he could guess why. Grimacing at the thought of peeling off those peacock feathers to bed a pigeon like Frances, Alex rudely declined a second drink and announced he was prepared to join the ladies.

Upton hurried to comply. As they entered the drawing room, Alex swiftly located Miss Wellington thumbing through a book of verse while listening to her aunt's conversation. Frances was artfully arranged at the spinet, rippling at some minor piece. She looked up to him expectantly, but he swiftly occupied the seat beside Mrs. Upton and appropriated the volume of verse in Evelyn's hand.

"Macpherson? Bah, he's a Scottish simpleton. I should think you would have more challenging literature to occupy your mind."

"And I suppose your tastes run to Fielding, Mr. Hampton?" The scorn in her voice indicated her opinion of this writer of lascivious novels.

Not at all pleased with being ignored but content that Hampton had evidently taken her cousin into dislike, Frances slid from her bench to lean daringly over their guest's shoulder, giving him the best advantage of her extravagant décolletage.

"Do you enjoy poetry, Mr. Hampton? My father is said to have one of the best libraries in Boston since the one at Harvard burned. Books are not easily come by here, you know. Shall I show you his library? Perhaps while you are here you will feel free to make use of it."

Hampton boldly eyed the voluptuous Upton asset he would most like to make use of but wisely refrained from mentioning the display. Instead, he rose abruptly, nearly plummeting Frances to the floor while holding his hand out to Evelyn.

"I will return Miss Wellington's vulgar taste in poetry to the shelves and show her some more useful literature, then. If you will excuse us . . . Come, Miss Wellington."

His peremptory commands were meant to be obeyed and Evelyn stared at him in astonishment and rising mutiny, but realizing this was the reason they had both suffered through this dinner, she rose and made a polite curtsy to her bewildered family. "If you will excuse us just a moment, I will show Mr. Hampton the library."

Alex almost grinned at the well-modulated fury in her voice, but he was already halfway across the room and no one could see the twitching of his lips. 'Twas a pity he dared not meet this Trojan again. Listening to her insults might certainly be more interesting than chasing rogues.

Once in the library, Evelyn hastily removed the folded paper in her pocket and passed it to the stern stranger who managed rudeness so well. "Here is the list of everyone receiving Staffordshire in the last three years. The same companies also seem to buy a great quantity of tea and regular shipments of port. The crates and kegs they are shipped in would be very similar to those containing silk, Madeira, and coffee and would represent a small fortune in duties. I won't go into the details of their transactions with some of our local shipping, but it is even more open to suspicion. I shall have to stop dealing with these firms entirely. I didn't have time to see if I could locate any correspondence containing names and addresses of the owners."

Hampton glanced at the list and shoved it in his pocket. He contemplated her worried expression with an odd pang of concern. Curtailing the companies she dealt with would undoubtedly reduce her income, and it would also give rise to the smugglers' suspicions. One choice was as dangerous as another. Why he should care what happened to her was beyond his knowledge, but since his honest cousin Alyson had arrived in his life, he seemed to have developed a nagging germ of conscience.

"You cannot afford to stop dealing with those companies and arouse their suspicions. You must assume them innocent until proved otherwise, and we need to catch both ends of the trade if they are guilty. That will take time. Continue your business as usual, Miss Wellington, and let me take care of the rest."

After all the work she had done to collect that list and practically prove her suspicions, he intended to dismiss her entirely! It was really just too much to bear. The long, hot day boiled over into seething fury, and Evelyn regarded him with venom.

"If you think I intend to casually hand you that list and forget everything that has happened, you are quite mad, Mr. Hampton. For all I know, you are part of the ring. If you cannot work with me on this, then I will have no choice but to turn the evidence over to my uncle and the courts."

"If you were a man, I could call you out for that, Miss Wellington." Angrily crunching the list in his pocket, Alex strode toward the door, but he couldn't resist one final word. Turning to eye her furiously straight stance in the center of the room, he added, "I am surprised that you have not already turned the evidence over to your uncle instead of relying on a suspicious character like me."

Evelyn's gaze faltered and her fists clenched at her sides as he struck a solid blow to the weakness in her defense. Gritting her teeth, she admitted, "I have heard my uncle make mention of several of those companies. I fear he may have some interest in them."

Alex's hand fell from the door latch, and he quickly traversed the room to stand in front of her, forcing her to look up to meet his eyes. "When were you intending to tell me that minor piece of information?"

He was furious, and rightly so, but she refused to flinch before the dark wrath of his eyes. "I wanted to know for certain that you intended to help me. You have given me little enough reassurance that you do not intend to walk back on that ship and sail away, leaving me to my own devices."

He deserved the recrimination, but that did not make it any easier to take. Her accusing violet eyes made him shift his gaze away. The sound of footsteps in the hall warned that their time was limited. "Find some intellectual book, Miss Wellington. Someone's coming. Where can we meet on the morrow?"

Evelyn hastily fled to the shelves, her fingers easily finding a favorite volume. "On the Common, in front of the school, at three."

The door swung open and Frances peered around the corner with a dimpled grin. "I hope I'm not interrupting anything?"

Alex favored her with a scathing glance. "Your cousin has the mind of a mule, Miss Upton. She'll never benefit from a man's learning. But then, a pretty girl like you needn't understand that, need you?"

Evelyn stifled a giggle as Frances tried to determine if she had been insulted or complimented. Deciding no man would insult her, she smiled gaily and came in to claim Mr. Hampton's arm.

"A woman need only understand what a man likes, Mr. Hampton. Evelyn has an unfortunate tendency to forget that upon occasion."

Alex heard the muffled noise from the slender figure at the shelves, and out of sheer maliciousness, he concurred, "How right you are, Miss Upton. I am certain you have never forgotten what a man likes." Smoothly he guided her out the door. "Your exquisite gown is a perfect example, my dear."

Hearing a book slam against a wooden shelf, he grinned to himself. A tied score, and the next round to be fought tomorrow.

3

Evelyn made a wry moue as she watched the tall, athletic grace of the man approaching along the summer-dry grass of the Common. He had evidently adopted the simpler style of male attire favored here, but even in a plain brown broadcloth coat and buff breeches it was apparent that he did not belong. The coat was cut away at the front to reveal the expensive embroidered short vest beneath. Instead of the ever-present cocked hat, he wore some new fashion with a narrow brim and high crown. Since he also wore boots, she assumed he had been riding. Apparently the English even had appropriate attire for that.

Hampton's stride revealed he was not precisely happy to be here, and as he came closer, she could see the grim line of his mouth indicating his opinion of her interference. Very well, if that was the way he wished to be, she could show him just how mule-headed she could be.

He halted in front of her and observed her crisp sprigged apron and straw hat with what she assumed was contempt as she held out her hand in greeting. "I see you have not sailed with your ship yet, Mr. Hampton."

Instead of making a curt bow over her hand, he lifted it with a malicious dark twinkle in his eyes. "No, Miss Wellington, I thought you might wish to be instructed on what it is men like." With that, he pressed a kiss to the back of her hand.

Evelyn felt the shock wave all the way up her arm, but she steeled herself against the odd sensations he appeared to deliberately strive to stir in her. Removing her hand, she informed him coolly, "Not unless you care to be equally instructed on what women prefer, Mr. Hampton. I can begin by telling you that to be publicly mauled is not high upon the list."

"Privately, then? I have this room above the tavern . . ."

If she had held one of her cousin's foolish fans, she would have hit him with it, but she was not so simple-minded as to strike him here in full view of half the town. As it was, she could feel the eyes of every occupant of the houses along Common Street striving to identify them, and a number of people crossing the grass in various directions slowed to observe their actions. She had thought it safest to meet him in public, but she was having second thoughts about the concept of safety. If half the town knew she was meeting him, how long would it be before the smugglers started putting two and two together? Or one and one?

"Mr. Hampton, I doubt that we have time for your notion of humor. By nightfall our names will be paired together if we continue to linger here much longer than is necessary to exchange polite greetings. Have you come to agree to work with me on this investigation?"

Alex had felt her shiver when he kissed her hand, and he watched her speculatively through her cool speech. Perhaps he had taken her measure wrong the other day. A woman who worked around men all day and was accustomed to their company might enjoy male company in other ways too. She was much more to his liking than the mindless maid who had filled his bed these last two nights, even if she had a tongue sharper than Maclean's sword. If the truth be told, he could learn to enjoy fencing with her if he thought he had any chance to unlace that enchanting bodice to find the soft flesh beneath.

"Heaven forbid that our names be paired together, Miss Wellington," he replied solemnly. "I am at your command. Shall we find a more private meeting place?"

Evelyn frowned, afraid he was not taking this at all seriously; yet he never smiled. She didn't like uncertainty, but that was all she felt in his presence. He could be a smuggler and a murderer for all she knew. But she could not handle this problem alone. She would have to trust him until he proved otherwise.

"There's a small barn outside the town gate where my

father occasionally stored goods. We still rent it, so I have every right to inspect it. I must warn you, it's a bit of a walk, but you cannot miss it. There's a broken wagon in the side yard. If we went there separately, none would notice. There's no one about out there to see."

Since the area indicated was little more than a mud swamp between the river and the harbor, he could understand why there would be no one about. She spoke as coldly as ever, and his mind told him she was totally devoid of any intent other than the one expressed, but he could not help that other part of him hoping for an ulterior motive in this privacy. Lifting his hat, he made a curt bow.

"In half an hour, shall we say?"

Relieved that he was so biddable, Evelyn nodded and walked in the opposite direction from the one he was taking. What they needed was a good long discussion of how they intended to ferret out the villains and bring them to justice. Her correspondence had produced a few illegible signatures, but they meant little to her. It would be necessary to track down the vague addresses on the invoices. Since most of their customers came and picked up their own merchandise, it wasn't necessary to have detailed directions. Usually bills were paid on the date of delivery so the unreliable mail needn't be called upon. It might be possible to follow one of the delivery wagons when it came to collect a shipment. She wasn't certain how to arrange the fine timing that would require, but it was a point worth taking. Perhaps Mr. Hampton would have a better idea. She didn't doubt his intelligence.

Later, cantering his rented mount up to the decrepit building that fitted the description he had been given, Hampton certainly did have better ideas. Investigating the barn's interior, he discovered the farmer had apparently decided to use what his renter had neglected. A fresh stack of hay lay piled in one corner. He had some very pleasant memories of haystacks, even if the results had not been so pleasant. He was a man of the world now. He did not expect any more than a little momentary physical pleasure from this particular stack.

Sunlight filtered through holes in the roof and between boards missing from the walls. Alex idly watched dust motes caught in a molten stream of gold. The air was warm, but not unpleasantly so, and he was half-tempted to discard his coat and hat and sprawl upon the hay for a quick nap. It had been a long time since he had been in anything so primitive as a barn, and he could not recall ever being in a barn so primitive as this. The ones on his mother's estate had been snug and airless. The breeze drifting through this drafty shack would never have been permitted at home.

Remembering the maid he had met with frequency in the warm security of his mother's hayloft when he was little more than a lad, Alex frowned and glared impatiently at the open door. One little half-witted maid had taught him the pleasures of the body as well as the deceit of the female sex. He had always been good at his lessons. He never forgot that one.

Women were for enjoyment, nothing more. Miss Wellington put on a lot of prim airs, but no proper lady would meet him in a place like this. He would let her lead the way. It should be amusing to see how she got around to what she really wanted. He certainly hoped she wasn't a marriage-minded female like her cousin. Marriage was definitely not in his vocabulary.

When Evelyn finally walked in, hot and tired and dusty, Alex was sitting cool and relaxed in his shirtsleeves on a comfortable bed of hay. Her scowl brought him promptly to his feet, and he made a polite drawing-room bow before her. "You will forgive my not offering you a ride. I assumed our intent was to meet in private."

Irritated that she had not had the sense to do the same, she once again withdrew her hand from his. "Quite correct, Mr. Hampton. Let us be done with this quickly. I have had time to consider several ideas as to how to trace the smugglers, but I am yet uncertain as to how to put them into action."

"As you said, let us be quick." She ignored his suggestive glance and, shrugging his shoulders, Alex continued, "I cannot tarry long despite the pleasure of your company, Miss Wellington. The smugglers must be found so I may return to England. Will you have a seat or must we remain standing?" He indicated the old blanket he had thrown across the haystack.

Evelyn regarded the tattered wool with disfavor, but Alex's tone offered a challenge she could not ignore. Wrapping her skirts carefully around her, she managed to gracefully maneuver herself onto a corner of the disreputable blanket. When Hampton threw his long masculine frame down beside her, she nearly jumped and ran. His sudden proximity actually made her shiver, and she tried not to notice how indecently large he appeared in sleeveless vest and no coat. His manner was a trifle too intimate for her tastes.

"I have not yet sent out notices that the shipment has arrived, but everyone is likely to have heard that the *Minerva* is in port by now. I thought we might have someone follow the delivery wagons." Evelyn tried not to show her nervousness as Hampton crossed his hands behind his head and casually lay back against the straw. She stared rigidly ahead so she could not see the rugged strength of his shoulders or watch the chiseled darkness of his face. Then he crossed his booted feet, and she could not help but notice the bulge of muscular thighs in tight breeches as they brushed against her skirts. This was inexcusable. She would have to get out of here. Stomach in ever-tightening knots, she waited for his reply.

"Excellent idea, Miss Wellington," Alex responded sarcastically. "The man following could pretend he was a dog and trot alongside the wagon for the fifty or one hundred miles it might take to its destination. No one would ever suspect a thing."

Heat and nervousness ignited simmering anger at his sarcasm. Without any thought at all, Evelyn turned and punched Hampton in his damned flat stomach. He grunted more in surprise than pain and caught her arm before she could flee in fury.

"What the deuce was that for?" Alex gripped her arm tightly, refusing to let it go when she tried to jerk from his grasp. If this were her idea of pleasure, he wanted no part of it.

"That was for being a stupid man with a sarcastic mouth, Mr. Hampton. I cannot believe I've risked my reputation and possibly my life just to endure your insults. Let me go. It is obvious we have nothing further to say to each other."

"I wouldn't say it's so obvious, Miss Wellington. I generally demand a good deal more explanation than that when someone knocks me in the stomach. But if you're going to insist upon behaving as a hysterical female, I can see where it might be useless to continue our discussion."

"What discussion?" she cried in frustration. "I'm the one who discovered the illegal brandy. I'm the one who came up with the names. And so far, I'm the only one who has come up with any ideas as to how to catch them. All you have done is snipe at me with masculine bigotry. I hit you in the stomach, Mr. Hampton, because that's what a man would have done in my place."

She wriggled desperately to the end of the blanket, trying to escape his unrelenting hold and the dark mask of anger upon his countenance. She had reacted instinctively and with anger, not with any smidgen of common sense at all. Any fool could see he was twice her size and capable of great harm. Even another man would have thought twice before doing what she had.

To her surprise, he regarded her with a calm lift of his brow and dropped her arm. "I see. Instead of calling me out, you prefer fisticuffs. You are a most unusual woman, Miss Wellington. I'm not certain how to proceed."

"You may proceed by getting on your horse and riding out of here, Mr. Hampton. I no longer require your assistance."

"If that harebrained scheme of yours is how you intend to catch a wily band of smugglers, Miss Wellington, you need my assistance more than you can imagine. If this is any example of how you generally conduct your business, it is a wonder your father did not marry you off long ago to some brute of a husband who would beat some sense into you."

Evelyn's muffled scream of outrage gave fair warning this time, and Alex caught her by the waist and flung her back against the blanket before she could launch another attack. She was up in a flash, but he caught her shoulders and held her down again.

Instead of giving her the tongue-lashing she deserved, he found himself staring into furious violet eyes that seemed to beckon at the same time they hurled daggers. He could see tempting rose-colored lips begin to form words he didn't wish to hear, and reacting naturally to the feel of a soft, supple body in his hands, Alex leaned over and swallowed her accusations with his lips.

Instantaneous lightning bolted through them, the heat melding their mouths closer and the shock wiping out all thought but the physical sensation of their bodies lying together in the warmth of a summer day.

A bee buzzed lazily somewhere overhead as Evelyn found her lips going soft and pliant beneath his kiss. Alex's hands were large and heavy where they held her pinned against the blanket, but they were gentle. She became aware of his greater weight pressing against her upper body as his kiss deepened. The heat and hardness of his chest against her breasts as his lips played along hers were far from unpleasant. She did not seem able to escape the insistent pressure upon her mouth that bruised and produced joy at the same time. A mindless lassitude hitherto unexperienced overtook her, but when her lips finally parted fully to his demands, she discovered the forbidden pleasure of his tongue, and she panicked.

Evelyn clamped her teeth closed and beat at Alex's powerful arms with her fists and writhed furiously beneath him in an attempt to cast him aside. He moved his exploratory kisses to the side of her mouth and along her cheek, but she continued to fight, tossing her head back and forth so he could not find her mouth and tempt her anymore with his touch.

Finally Alex pushed himself up and stared down into her terrified face with a mixture of anger and puzzlement. "You do not like that manner of kissing? Or did I mistakenly eat garlic for lunch?" This last he asked with a wry expression as she again tried to free herself from his hold.

"Of all the arrogant, presumptuous, dunderheaded, mindless jackasses of men I have ever had the misfortune to meet . . . Let me go!"

It was a severe temptation not to comply. She had returned his kiss with an innocent passion Alex had seldom experienced and wished to know more of. Even now he could see her breasts rising against the confinement of the modest cotton, and he knew he had only to touch the erect tip pushing against the thin material to persuade her back into his arms. Her face was flushed with pleasure and beautiful with her desire. But he was no longer sixteen and didn't need to exhaust his lust with every female that came along. He sat up and began to brush himself off.

"My mistake. I rather thought you enjoyed it too."

Before she could deliver a scathing reply or scramble down the haystack and away from him, the barn door creaked and a sliver of light pierced the gloom.

"Miss Wellington? Is that you? I can explain about the hay—" The man entering stopped abruptly as he regarded the two disheveled young people rapidly sliding from the stack. He gave Hampton's tall frame a sideways look, then, staring at the floor more than at his tenant, he finished hastily, "I'll be removing the hay shortly if you have need of the storage. Good day, Miss Wellington. Sir."

The color had drained from Evelyn's face by the time the man left and Alex returned his startled gaze from the door to her. Her eyes were huge wafers beneath sable lashes, and his lungs took a sharp intake of breath at how fragile she suddenly seemed. He had thought her as strong as he, he realized suddenly. That was an entirely idiotic notion, considering the differences between their ages, sex, and experience.

"I am sorry. Is he likely to carry tales?"

Evelyn squeezed her eyes closed and tried to control her furious embarrassment. "I don't know. I don't know him that well." She shook her head, took a deep breath, and replied more certainly than she felt, "It doesn't matter. I am twenty-one and responsible only for myself."

Alex heard this with a hint of disbelief and gave her a skeptical look. Any young lady of his acquaintance caught in such a compromising manner would be screaming marriage, particularly since he had initiated the action. He found it hard to believe that she was the type of woman who had no reputation left to damage. Her pompous uncle would have packed her off to China if that were so. More likely her schemes had come to fruition faster than she expected, and she knew better than to press the point.

Deciding he had only himself to blame for falling into such an obvious trap, Alex shrugged off the incident. He wasn't the type to cry marriage either. Perhaps she had learned her lesson. "Very commendatory of you, my dear, but perhaps I ought to take you home now before anyone else steps in."

"Yes, go on. I'll walk. Perhaps you might just tell me your suggestion to our problem sometime at the office. Or give me a letter. I don't care. Go away."

Amused by her sudden abstraction in comparison with her normally clipped, precise thinking, Alex shook his head. "I'll admit readily to being a cad, but I do try to keep up gentlemanly appearances. You will ride with me, and to hell with your neighbors. Now, come on."

Evelyn jerked her elbow from his grasp and glared at him with exasperation. "Haven't you pushed me around and caused enough trouble for one day? I am accustomed to walking. It is not that far. I don't need your charity or your company."

"What you need is a little more respect and a little less tongue, but I won't hold my breath. You will either ride out of here under your own volition or I will pack you out of here over my saddle. If that doesn't convince you, think of your mother. How will she feel if the gossip reaches her and she hasn't even met me?"

She had tried not to think about that. She really didn't want to think about any of this just yet. And she certainly didn't want to share a horse with this villain. But she did not even have to look him in the face to know that grim determination was setting his jaw now. Shuddering, she marched out into the sunlight as if to her own hanging.

Alex threw her up on the swaybacked nag that it had been his misfortune to rent, then quickly joined her before she had a chance to change her mind. Her hair beneath the silly hat was all tousled, and he plucked a straw from it. Mischievously, unable to resist the temptation of her slender curves in his arms, he nibbled lightly at her ear. "You look like you've been rolling in the hay, Miss Wellington."

"Stop it. Just stop it, or I will get down. I will never

be so glad to see a man leave this town as I will you. When do you sail?"

Her words were low and choked, and he guessed he had touched the impervious Miss Wellington a little more than he had expected. He had ever been prone to overindulgence. One of these days he was going to pay for it.

Taking up the reins, he held her waist with one arm and sent the nag into a jarring walk with the other. "The *Minerva* sails when I tell it to. That won't be until I find out who dares to use me as a pawn in his rotten game. So you might as well get used to my irritating company. Your office is my best source of information."

She muttered something that sounded like a particularly pithy curse and remained silent the rest of the way into town. By the time they reached the house on Treamount that she said was hers, Alex could appreciate her penchant for walking. If he were to stay here much longer, he would have to buy a horse.

He helped her down and politely took her elbow to guide her toward the house. The modest brick structure sat practically on the street, with only a small picket fence and a trim of flowers to call a yard. By the standards of the neighboring houses, it had a look of comfortable means about it, although it was not as pretentious as her uncle's three-story contemporary structure. This house did not sport the fashionable balance of an equal number and size of windows on either side of the door, but seemed to have been expanded at some time, making one side longer than the other. The front steps led directly into the front room, he discovered as Evelyn stiffly brought him inside.

"Is that you, Evelyn? Could you come here, please? Jacob seems to have been fighting again." The voice held a mixture of concern and resignation.

Evelyn sighed and discarded her hat. "If you will have a seat, Mr. Hampton, I will see what Jacob has broken this time, and my mother will be right out to meet you."

Instead of obeying, Alex followed on her heels. At her questioning look, he shrugged. "I daresay I have rather more experience in dealing with the results of fisticuffs than you do, Miss Wellington. I might as well take a look at the boy and make myself useful."

She gave him a shrewd look that said she saw through that ploy, but she held her tongue. Her mother wasn't the type to be impressed by a man's pretense at helpfulness.

Mrs. Wellington looked up in surprise as her daughter entered the spacious kitchen with a strange man trailing behind her. A small, plump woman who preferred the comfort and security of her home to the outside world, she still had a keen eye for people. Evelyn never trailed strange men into the house, particularly men of this caliber. A closer look as introductions were made revealed an aura of uneasiness or tension between the two that made her glance a second time at their rumpled clothes. There was definitely more here than Evelyn would tell her.

Jacob looked up defiantly through the swelling of his eye, setting his jaw at the sight of the elegant Englishman. "Billy started it," he informed anyone who cared to listen.

"Looks like Billy ended it too." Alex bent over to inspect the gash above the rapidly blackening eye. "I don't think it will need stitches, just some ice for the swelling. I've suffered enough of the same to know the treatment. The bully I used to fight always aimed for the head first. How did Billy go about it?"

Evelyn watched in amazement as Hampton carelessly straddled a slat-back kitchen chair and seemed ready to listen with absorption to the tale of a small boy's street fight. He had removed his hat in the front room, and now she could see a small sprinkling of straw dust in his ebony hair. A heavy, coarse strand was attempting to pull loose from its binding, and she fought a writhing embarrassment remembering how it had got that way.

"Well, he said something nasty first, so I hit him in the stomach. That's when he popped me one in the eye and ran." Jacob waited suspiciously for the Englishman's verdict on this conduct.

"What did he say that was so bad that you had to hit him, Jacob?" Unconcerned by the methods of the fight, Evelyn sought the cause.

Jacob squared his shoulders and drew up his ruffled dignity to meet his sister's eye. "He said Uncle George was a no-good bloody Tory who ought to go back to England where he belonged."

Alex caught the look on Evelyn's face and stored it away for future reflection. He had considered the colonists to be English subjects and more or less looked on the colonies as part of England. Jacob's words delineated a difference he hadn't recognized. He knew the colonists tended to be more of the Whig persuasion than the landed upper classes, but the conflict seemed to lie deeper than that. No eleven-year-old boys in England came to cuffs over their fathers' politics. What was going on over here that caused this seething rebellion that cropped up in the oddest ways?

"Uncle George is a Tory," Mrs. Wellington replied calmly, applying a chip of ice a maid had retrieved from the ice cellar. "A Tory is a man who supports the king. There is nothing wrong with that."

Alex felt the exchange of looks between the family over his head and knew he was being excluded from something that the locals didn't wish him to know. This grew more interesting all the time, but now was not the time to probe into their political beliefs. He gave the boy an unsympathetic look.

"If you're going to lead with a blow to the stomach, then you have to follow up with another to the chin or you're going to get beat." He threw Evelyn a mocking look to see if she registered this information. Her return glare assured him she would remember the advice. "Or if you do happen to let your opponent get off a blow to the head, you must block him, like this." He raised his arm in an example of blocking a blow with the length of one muscular arm while bringing up the other hand in a fist.

Jacob's eager look and his mother's frown brought Hampton up from his chair. Sketching a slight bow, he apologized. "I beg your pardon, Mrs. Wellington. The house is no place to teach boxing. You will forgive me?"

Pepper-and-salt hair pinned and capped into the tight coif of an earlier time, Amanda Wellington wiped her hands on her apron and regarded the tall gentleman with approval. "Take him behind the house and teach him your tricks, Mr. Hampton. Evelyn and I will have dinner ready shortly. You must stay and have a bite."

"That is kind of you, ma'am, but I could not impose—"

"Nonsense. I always cook too much anymore. There is plenty, and I pride myself that you will appreciate the fare more than a tavern's. Go on with you. Jacob will never forgive me, elsewise."

To Evelyn's astonishment, Alex nodded his acceptance of this arrangement and gestured for Jacob to follow him without a second glance. Never had it occurred to her that the arrogant Englishman would lower himself to their simple company. What was he up to now?

4

The irate message from Evelyn's uncle followed Alex from the tavern where he was staying to the *Minerva*, where he had decided to entrust the ex-smuggler captain with his problem. Hampton scowled as he read the angry slashes of ink on the expensive vellum when it finally caught up to him. Folding it, he shoved it in his pocket, and lowering his chair to all four legs, scraped it back.

"I don't think the brandy's getting into England by legal channels. I've written a letter to Cranville and Maclean to try to trace it on their end. When I go through Wellington's files I'll have a better idea of what else they need to trace. This is the end I'm concerned about. Whoever's doing this knows that as an English merchant I'm much less likely to be searched than a colonial, but I cannot see that the profits can be large by the time they pay my fees."

Ruggles walked with his employer up onto the deck. The heat had broken slightly this day, but the stench of raw fish and sewage still permeated the harbor air. To him, it was a natural smell, and he lifted his head appreciatively to the breeze off the water. There were few ships in the harbor, many fewer than this time last year. With the war over and speculation ended, trade had dropped off drastically. The latest tariffs had apparently been the straw that broke the back of many a shipping firm. The normal clatter and hammer of shipbuilding was ominously quiet this year. He pulled a pipe out of his capacious pocket and sought to light it.

"You think someone's using us to cover a larger operation," he finished Hampton's thoughts for him.

Thinking of the message in his pocket and the warehouse stocked with goods from nearly every country in the world, Alex nodded grimly. "As I understand it, the Maclean simply dealt with people he knew, unloading in secluded coves, avoiding customs, and leaving the problem of storage to his buyers. It's a good thing he got out of it when he did. Tightening the Navigation Acts makes that a risky business if you're caught without the proper papers now. So instead, we're getting the goods through customs for the villains, getting them proper papers that, with a little forgery, a switching of crates, or whatever, they can use to move anything they might be storing. A really large operation would need a warehouse and easy access to both legal and illegal shipping. It's more complicated than before, but still profitable."

Ruggles nodded. "You saw that grand house on the hill? That's Thomas Hancock's. You want to see what kind of profits a little evasion of the laws can net, you take a good look at that place. These Yankees ain't dumb. You'd be better off turning the whole thing over to the court and getting out of here. It ain't none of your affair."

Alex's mouth set in a tight line. The vision of violet eyes made him flinch inwardly. If he could believe Evelyn's complicity in this operation, he would find it easy to sail away without a second thought. Until he had met his cousin Alyson, he had been incapable of believing innocence in a woman; he would have been certain that Evelyn was involved. His doubts now made it difficult to act with his usual rashness. Maybe he was growing old.

He stared out over the water to the clutter of houses and shops along the harbor before climbing into the boat that would take him back to the wharf. If Evelyn were truly innocent, she was in way over her head. She was a fighter, but she had little chance of winning on her own. He'd run away from fights before; he wasn't the heroic type. But he was easily bored, and this promised to be an entertaining puzzle to pass the time. With the tantalizing prospect of a grateful female wrapped in his arms as the prize, the challenge could be rewarding.

Remembering the enchanting innocence of passionate kisses, Alex stepped down into the boat. Even if Evelyn were guilty as hell, he'd enjoy tasting that heady wine again. Bent on self-destruction, he signaled the sailors to begin rowing. He had a damn good notion why George Upton was summoning him. He'd best have all his defenses ready.

Alex's defenses didn't last much longer than a single sight of Evelyn's tear-ravaged face as she sat in one corner of Upton's ostentatious library. Somehow, someone had turned that striking beauty into washed-out shadows and hollow angles, and he felt rage building in him before anyone said a word.

His dark gaze turned coldly on the bewigged and garishly garbed gentleman behind the desk. "There is some explanation for this?" Alex threw the folded vellum on the desk.

If he thought to intimidate Upton, he failed. The man didn't even look at the scrap, but returned his gaze boldly. "Were you any gentleman at all, you would have been here without my summoning you. I demand to know your intentions toward my niece."

Evelyn's wickedly husky voice lost none of its seductiveness even through tears and anger. "Please ignore him, Mr. Hampton. He has no right to do any of this. He is related to me only by marriage. We neither of us owe him any explanation."

Alex turned to eye her skeptically. "Then why are you here?"

"Because she knows what's good for her, by Jove!" The man at the desk brought his fist down with a force that sent his quill flying. "Evelyn, leave the room. I will deal with Mr. Hampton."

"I will leave with Mr. Hampton and not a moment sooner."

Her belligerent tone answered Alex's question. She had stayed to protect him! He would have found the thought greatly amusing had the situation been less grim. Realizing their escapade in the barn had been uncovered, Alex prepared himself for a long siege. Without permission, he appropriated what looked to be a comfortable leather chair, sat down, and propped his shoes on the edge of the desk.

"So it seems we are both at your disposal, Mr. Upton. What can I do for you?"

His insolence raised Upton's temperature another degree, and his face began to take on a purple hue beneath the perspiration on his brow. "Your arrogance in this matter does not help your cause, Hampton. Perhaps you can get away with it at home, but not here. Wellington is a respected name in Boston, and I intend for it to remain that way. Rumors of your dalliance with my niece will be quickly halted upon announcement of your engagement. As a gentleman, you must recognize there is no suitable alternative."

Evelyn watched in terror as Hampton's broad shoulders shrugged beneath the rough weave of his coat. He was unpredictable, and she could not presume to guess his answer. She just prayed it would be sensible. Judging by the calm look on his dark countenance, he wasn't exceedingly concerned by her uncle's unreasonable hysterics.

"I don't remember introducing myself as a gentleman, Mr. Upton. On the contrary, I have made no pretense at being any other than what I am. Had you made any inquiries at all, you would have been well apprised of that fact. I have no intention of marrying your niece over the exchange of one or two kisses. Are there any other questions?"

Evelyn sucked in a breath of relief that he was at least supporting her in this, humiliating as it might be. She was curious to know what made him believe he would not be regarded as a gentleman in these provincial quarters, but that was inconsequential to the matter at hand. Uncle George's furious explosion burned her ears.

"You have ruined my niece, sir! Were I a younger man, I would call you out for that. As it is, gout prevents me from giving you the thrashing you deserve. Perhaps you think I am powerless in this matter. I can assure you I am not." Thoughts of just how much power he held over the insolent young pup calmed him to a degree, and he regarded Hampton's chiseled visage almost with benevolence. "Let us be reasonable about this. Evelyn is of excellent and well-respected family here and in England. You may know of the Adrian Wellingtons in

Somerset, an old family, high in the king's favor. She will bring you no shame. Her father left her a rich dowry. She is no pauper. The sale of the warehouse will more than double that amount. You have chosen well, and the advantage is all yours."

Evelyn clenched her fingers around the handkerchief in her hand. Uncle George was selling not only her but also her brother's livelihood! She had always known him to be a fool, but she had not fathomed the depths of his treachery. She could not imagine why her gentle Aunt Matilda had married him, and she would not complain if Hampton ran him through with a sword right now. Unfortunately, she realized Hampton never wore a sword, and she wondered again about his claim of not being a gentleman. Surely he wouldn't accept the offer!

It was impossible to gauge Alex's thoughts by his expression. She had never seen him smile, but she was aware he possessed a humor of sorts. Surely a man who owned a ship like the *Minerva* would not consider her dowry a plum. She could see only the profile of his face, framed by the thick coarseness of his black hair. The muscle over his cheekbone had tightened in a definitely angry line, but his words were as cool as she could desire.

"You mistake me, Mr. Upton. Miss Wellington's very respectable family would scream in horror should they hear of her betrothal to me. I cannot imagine you would wish to sell your lovely niece to a rake and a bankrupt. Let us forget this conversation ever came about. I will apologize for being the cause of any rumors, I promise to treat your niece with all due respect in the short time I remain here, and I'm certain Miss Wellington's name and behavior are so far above reproach that no one will lend credence to any further tales."

Evelyn would have smiled had she not been so fascinated by these revelations. Bankrupt? Even she found that hard to believe. How could he expect her uncle to believe that? But he was being more than reasonable, and for that she was grateful. That she also felt vaguely insulted at being cast off so assiduously was irrelevant.

She felt Hampton's appraising glance on her and met his gaze, feeling a jolt of something unfamiliar as his long-lashed eyes seemed to darken at the sight of her.

The cynicism in his look as it raked over her shook Evelyn more than her uncle's threats. Surely he did not think she was responsible for this imbroglio! Of all the conceited, arrogant . . . Of course, he did!

Rising hastily before her uncle replied, she straightened her skirts and started toward the door. "I told you that, Uncle George, but you wouldn't listen to me. You are not being quite rational about this. Will Black saw nothing but what was in his own dirty mind. Now, if you will excuse me, I've been humiliated enough for one day. Mr. Hampton, are you ready to leave? I'll accompany you and extend my apologies for this scene."

Knowing full well the man behind the desk hadn't had his say yet, Alex rose and scraped a brief bow, admiring her grace under fire. He could do worse than a dragon like this. She could do better. He offered his arm.

"I sincerely apologize for the trouble I've caused you, Miss Wellington," he said humbly as her slender hand came to rest in the crook of his elbow. Then, taking the crumpled handkerchief from her hand, he wiped her tear-streaked face with a proprietary air, ruining his polite apology with his usual carelessness. "I've always wanted to do that."

She slapped his hand away at the same time her uncle came to his feet. "I'm not through with you yet, you damnable cur! Evelyn, go on, and I will take care of this."

She turned and eyed her furious relative with curiosity. "I really cannot understand what you are about, Uncle George. Mr. Hampton has been more than patient, and I've already explained everything thrice over. There is nothing more to be said."

"There is this to be said." He pointed an accusing finger at the imposing young man, looking at him as if he were a bug in his soup. "You and the *Minerva* will not leave port until my niece is safely wedded. I have had a report that you are carrying illegal brandy. The ship will be impounded and you will be jailed until the matter is settled."

Alex heard Evelyn's startled gasp at his side but did not dare turn his gaze from the wily devil behind the desk. With practiced arrogance he answered coolly, "I need only write Cranville to have the matter settled well above your head. I'd rather spend three months in jail than a lifetime in the prison of marriage."

He could have left it at that. Upton was turning purple again, and although Alex could sense Evelyn's tension, she made no protest. But even if she said nothing, they both knew that the mention of the brandy spelled trouble for both of them. Before Upton could burst a blood vessel, Alex casually continued, "But perhaps if you would give me some time to discuss this with Miss Wellington, we can come to a more amicable conclusion."

"Evelyn has naught to do with this. This is a matter between the two of us. Let her go on, and we will come to terms." Regaining control of himself, Upton directed a commanding look to his niece. Unfortunately, she did not obey as readily as his wife and daughter. She continued staring at him with incredulous blue eyes.

"On the contrary, Mr. Upton, marriage has everything to do with Evelyn and nothing to do with you. If you will leave us, please, we have a few matters to discuss."

Patting a handkerchief to his moist brow and adjusting his sliding wig, Upton came out from behind his desk grumbling. "This is unheard-of. I ought to have you thrown in jail immediately. Evelyn, if you give me any trouble over this, I'll take a switch to you. You will accept his proposal, and that's an end to it."

He waddled out, shutting the door hard in irritation.

Alex caught Evelyn by the waist before she could flee to the other side of the room. He needed to be reminded that they were in this together. Her startled look at his action reminded him of more interesting things, like the decided kissability of that full mouth now frowning at him expectantly.

"Your face is going to freeze like that," he scolded, before bending to sample the wine he had decided worth fighting for.

Evelyn tried to shove away, but Alex's arm held her firmly, even more intimately than the day before. His other hand came up to rest at the back of her head, holding her still while his lips deliberately wreaked their havoc. Evelyn had to stifle a gasp at how swiftly the heated sensations of his touch rendered her helpless. She wanted his kiss, wanted more of what he had taught her yesterday, but she could not afford to succumb to this seduction. Before her hands could rise to cling to his broad shoulders, to taste the texture of his thick dark hair, she turned her head away and pushed against his chest.

"Mr. Hampton, this is serious. Can you think of nothing but your own pleasure?"

"Give me some credit, Miss Wellington." Alex amused himself by tracing the delicate outer shell of her ear with his fingers. "I am thinking of your pleasure too. I would hate to see you leg-shackled for life if you could not abide my touch. I am a man who enjoys the physical pleasures in life, Miss Wellington. I just wish to assure myself that you do not find me repulsive."

His words sent a shiver down her spine, and Evelyn looked up abruptly, catching what amazingly appeared to be amusement in the dark gleam of his eyes. She shoved from his grasp and, surprisingly, he released her. Hands on hips, she glared at him.

"I'm glad you're so nonchalant about this. I trust that means you have some solution to our predicament?"

The color was back in her cheeks, and she looked more herself now. Glancing down at the enticing swell of her breasts beneath the respectable black-and-brown plaid of her bodice and imagining the length of lovely leg hidden beneath her skirts, Alex wondered if he were making a mistake in avoiding marriage. He could see coming home to the likes of that for many nights to come, if only she would hold her tongue. Regretting that impossibility, he returned his gaze to her furious eyes.

"You have considered the danger you are in if your uncle truly knows of the smuggling?"

Evelyn swallowed her sharp remarks and stared at him. "You say that as if he might be involved. That is ridiculous. He's a loyal officer of his majesty, sworn to uphold the law, and proud of his position. He's simply making trouble. It's not unusual."

She said it bravely enough, but Alex heard the hint of doubt in her voice. "Methinks the lady doth protest too much," he answered cynically. "You had better consider the possibility before we make any hasty decisions."

"What is there to decide? Marriage is impossible, you know that. Why can't you just board the *Minerva* and sail away? He cannot stop you."

She was getting even with him for his earlier remarks, and Alex had to admit that the rejection stung. She acted as if he were the last man on earth she would consider. A little deceit on her part would have been less hazardous to his masculinity.

Reserving these thoughts for himself, Alex implacably led Evelyn toward the only solution. "I cannot sail for the same reason you did not leave the room. We are in this together. It is imperative to both of our livelihoods that we find the smugglers, and I'll be virtually useless if I'm in prison or on my way to England."

Evelyn watched him warily. "I'm not certain marriage is any solution. For all I know of you, you may already be married."

His thin lips curled upward slightly at one corner. "You can be assured that I never considered that respectable estate. Perhaps when I write to my family of our proposed betrothal I should ask them to reply with a character reference. It should be very amusing to hear their opinion of me."

"Proposed betrothal? I will do what is necessary to keep you from jail, but be assured I will not consider so much as a proposal, and certainly not a betrothal."

"You have such a soothing way with words, Miss Wellington. Or shall I call you Evelyn, under the circumstances? If you are any more agreeable, I will be tempted to leave you with your uncle's wrath and do as you suggest and sail away."

"I cannot see any other solution," she replied irritably, stalking to the far end of the room to glare out the window.

"It's quite simple, Miss Wellington. Unless you harbor a *tendre* for someone who will be quite heartbroken at your abrupt change of heart, we agree to this marriage your uncle is so eager to carry out. Have you any idea exactly *why* he is so eager to see us wedded?"

Evelyn paled at Hampton's calm proposal. How could he take something as important as marriage and treat it so lightly? She had heard that many things were different in England, but surely even there marriage must be considered a sacrament. They had known each other all of three days. It was patently ridiculous even to consider it.

She turned and eyed his rakishly handsome form with disfavor. "I daresay he hopes you will haul me off to England where I won't embarrass him anymore. When my father was alive, he could say nothing, but ever since my father died, he has been trying to run my life. I won't have it, Mr. Hampton. I won't marry just to make him happy."

"I should hope not," Alex agreed, sitting on the edge of the desk and crossing his arms over his chest. Her hair shone with glints of red and gold in the sunlight, a most attractive shade, he decided. But the sun at her back cast her face in shadow and he could not read her expression. He couldn't tell if she had considered what would happen to her warehouse if she married and left for England. He had a very good suspicion of what George Upton planned for it. "We will only agree to the marriage," he explained soothingly. "We need not go through with it. A long betrothal is called for under the circumstances, would you not agree? And when we have our villains behind bars, we will have a violent disagreement—not at all out of character, considering our propensity for argument—and you will throw me out on my ear. I shall sail away, never to be seen again. Will that work?"

Evelyn considered it. She disliked being dishonest, but she could tell the deceit didn't bother him at all. She also disliked the idea of being constantly thrown in his company, which this specious engagement would entail, but it would also make it easier for them to work together. Had he finally realized he would need her help in this matter and planned it that way?

She looked up to where he sat carelessly swinging his leg from the edge of the desk. He didn't seem concerned one way or another about her decision. His striking looks made it difficult to think this out logically. She could not imagine why a man like Alexander Hampton would even consider pretending to be betrothed to someone like her. He hadn't insulted her once this day, unless she counted his refusal to marry her. That could scarcely count, since he really knew very little of her. He might be in for a bit of a surprise before this was all over. Then again, so might she.

Returning to the Persian carpet in front of the desk, Evelyn tilted her head and regarded him quizzically. He was really too rude-looking to be called handsome in the conventional sense. He certainly didn't have a pleasant demeanor. He never smiled. His mouth was more likely to be turned up in a sneer than in humor. Those blasted eyes always hinted of mockery, even now when he sat calmly under her perusal. She would like to shake his self-assurance just a little, but he was far more likely to shake hers.

"Tell me, Mr. Hampton, just exactly what is a rake?"

That twisted his mouth quickly enough. He met her gaze with equanimity. "A rake is a man who over-indulges in all the vices. The name is Alexander, Miss Wellington, or Alex, if you prefer."

"*All* the vices? That must be time-consuming, and very expensive. Are you truly a rake?"

Alex sighed in exasperation, uncrossed his arms, and stood up, towering over Evelyn by nearly a head and dwarfing her slenderness with his greater breadth, a physical intimidation that worked well on most people. "Be assured, Miss Wellington, I am not known for my temperance. A long betrothal to me could very well ruin your reputation, should mine become known. That will give us greater incentive to finish the job quickly."

Evelyn tilted her head back to meet his dark gaze with a frown. "Do the vices a rake indulges in include lying and stealing, Mr. Hampton?"

"No, and not murder either, although I'm willing to make exceptions. Are you going through with this or do you wish to see me languishing in jail?"

His impatience oddly pleased her, and she smiled. "As amusing as it might be to see you behind bars, I can see it might be preferable to keep you from corrupting our criminal elements. Generally, they overindulge in only one vice at a time."

She was laughing at him! He had terrorized most of the women in London and nearly half the men, and this little chit of a female thought him a laughing matter!

Alex raised one eyebrow in his loftiest manner. "Does that mean we are betrothed, Miss Wellington?"

"Oh, certainly. Why not? I have never been betrothed to a rake and a bankrupt before. I am certain my reputation can only be enhanced when I display my excellent taste in choosing you. Shall I have to see you very often when we are officially affianced?"

Alex eyed her slender neck with a view to breaking it, but decided it had much more interesting purposes. His fingers closed about her nape and she started, but he made no attempt to release her. "Every night, my dear, until I teach you respect. Don't you think that's fair?"

His mouth closed over hers, and Evelyn shut her eyes and gave herself up to the kiss. It was a reckless, mad thing to do, but she wanted it, and it seemed only fitting to seal this insane betrothal with an equally insane kiss. Besides, she doubted that she could deny him if she tried.

His lips were strong across hers, knowledgeable and demanding. He knew what he wanted, and as his dark head dipped to extend his claim, Evelyn grabbed his shoulder to balance herself, succumbing rapidly to the tempest he aroused in her. She was almost relieved when the furious knock came at the door.

Upton threw open the door without waiting for a reply. He caught them with their heads together, one black and beribboned, the other chestnut-hued and pinned softly. The sight made him catch his breath, and he expelled it in a loud cough. Only then did they part, a secretive smile on their lips as they gazed into each other's eyes. He didn't like it. He didn't like it at all. But obviously he had them where he wanted them.

He heard gasps behind him, and turning, found wife and daughter staring in shock at the sight of Evelyn wrapped in the stranger's embrace.

"That's not fair! You wouldn't even let me go down to the wharf to see him, and you leave *her* alone in there with him all she likes! You don't want me to even have a chance." Petulantly Frances glared at her father and the couple in the library, then fled before their surprise.

Evelyn could hear what very much sounded like a chuckle in her ear, but when she looked up to Hampton with suspicion, he was as solemn as ever. A slow flush colored her cheeks as she felt her aunt's shocked stare and realized the dratted man had not yet released her. As if he were divining her thoughts, his fingers closed tighter around her waist, keeping her close to his side.

"Evelyn has done me the honor of accepting my proposal. There is only one obstacle, and that is a mere formality. Since I am his heir, I must notify my cousin, the Earl of Cranville, and receive his approval before taking any vows. Not to do so would offend him, and he is quite capable of disinheriting me altogether and leaving me with nothing but his title. A man of your consequence can understand my position, Upton, can't you?" The mockery in his voice dared an officer of the crown to challenge him.

The strangled noise from the woman at his side provided as much amusement as Alex could desire without watching Upton turning purple again. He glanced down into a lovely oval face livid with fury. No Tory here, he wagered, and for the first time in their acquaintance, he grinned.

And Evelyn could do nothing. An earl! A damned arrogant bloody earl! Lud, but she'd be drummed off the streets of Boston when they heard this. Heir to an earldom. Maybe he was lying. He had said his vices didn't include lying, but a liar could say that with impunity. He certainly didn't look as if he had noble blood. Evelyn met Hampton's grin with a glare.

Her uncle looked thunderstruck. Rather than relieve his shock, Evelyn smiled up at her "fiancé" with the sweetest, most insipid expression she could muster. "The Earl of Cranville? Does that mean you are heir to an earldom, dearest Alexander? I have so wished to be a countess."

They said revenge was sweet, and she seemed to be savoring it with unholy glee. Alex's grin soured at her simpering expression. He knew she was only getting even with him for surprising her, but he had rather envisioned a different reaction to his surprise. Instead of being delighted with the prospect of a title, she buried a knife in him and twisted it viciously as she displayed her scorn by acting the part of her cousin Frances, behaving just as her uncle expected. She did it too damned well.

"Quite right, my dear. Someday you shall be a countess." Hiding his grimace, Alex turned to watch her uncle revising his opinions and experiencing regret that he hadn't shut his daughter in a barn with the perverted heir. Such a charming family. He glanced over Upton's head to the nervously hovering woman behind. She, at least, had a look of concern on her face as she watched Evelyn's unusual performance. Alex spoke to her more than to the others. "The time it takes for my cousin's approval to reach us should be sufficient for us to become better acquainted, don't you agree? We needn't make the betrothal official until then, if you prefer."

Evelyn's aunt looked anxiously to Upton. "This is rather hasty, isn't it, George? I do believe the young man is correct."

Obviously George wished to disagree, but the promise of an earldom in the family was too much temptation to bear. He nodded reluctantly. "We will make no formal announcement, just let it be known that the marriage has my approval. That should be sufficient for now." He gave Hampton a warning frown. "Your ship will still not be allowed to sail with you on it."

Alex chucked his simmering fiancée under the chin. "I wouldn't think of going anywhere without my own dear Evelyn."

5

August 1765

Wearing an extravagantly expensive silk habit of an unusual silver gray, an embroidered vest of black on black, and a powdered cadogan wig tied with a black satin solitaire and pinned in front with a diamond, Alexander Hampton appeared every inch the noble dandy he purported to be. Evelyn wished she could jerk his snowy cravat, kick his elegant silk stockings, and send him crashing down the majestic staircase they had just ascended.

In these weeks of being feted by the elite of Boston, as was befitting the fiancée to an heir to an earldom, she had grown weary of pressing and cleaning her only two decent ball gowns, of talking of the delights of the "home country" with women who hadn't seen England in years, and of being looked upon with suspicion by people she had once considered her friends. The tasks of managing her family's business all day and dancing all night had drained her energy and left her nerves on the breaking point. Again she glanced at her partner with venom as he graciously greeted their host. She was quite convinced he was more liar than heir.

Not even glancing at his companion, Hampton led her into the ballroom. Keeping his voice low, he steered her toward the refreshment table. "People will not think all is well between us if you continue glowering at me like that, Miss Wellington. We are making too much progress for me to spend the next months cooling my heels in your estimable jail."

"I am beginning to think that is where you belong.

When do you start borrowing money from these wealthy fools for a 'worthy investment' or just to 'tide you over' until your quarterly allowance? They're eating out of your hand right now. Do they need to lick your boots first before you allow them to hand over their money?"

Alex lifted one dark eyebrow as his gaze finally turned to regard her with amusement. "My, my, have we a little cynic here? I am impressed with your astuteness, my dear. At one time I would have done just that. Perhaps I'm just keeping in practice to guard against recurrences. Would you begrudge me my fun?"

"Yes, I would. Why should you be having fun when I am not? The last of those blasted crates went out today, and I can't see that you have done anything at all to trace them."

"You weren't meant to see anything at all. That is the whole point of the exercise. Have a little more trust, my dear. I really didn't have to stay to carry out this charade, you know."

That was what made Evelyn grind her teeth together and endure this torment. If she knew nothing else about him at all, she knew he was quite capable of rowing out to the *Minerva* one night and sailing away and never looking back. That he did not leave forced her to believe he really was trying to find the men who had threatened his ship with their illegal goods. That was a good selfish motive, and one she could believe of him.

"I beg your pardon, my lord," she replied sarcastically. "I shall take my humble self to some corner while you parade around the room looking for smugglers. My feet hurt."

Alex handed her a lemonade, and nodding acknowledgments to greetings from those around him, steered her toward a silver damask settee. "We only just arrived. How could your feet hurt? And I am not a lord, just cousin to one. You need to learn the proper etiquette."

Wearily Evelyn sank down upon the cushion. The ice-blue silk of her favorite gown billowed out around her, but she failed to appreciate its elegance any longer. "I have been on my feet all day trying to find places to store that latest shipload. The warehouse is full to bulging. No one has the money to come claim his stock. And I don't want to know the proper etiquette. I have no earthly use for it."

Hampton sipped his punch and eyed her with disfavor. "A refusal to learn is a sure sign of a closed mind. And why must you personally oversee the damned warehouse? It is not very becoming in a lady. You have hired help."

"So do you. Why don't you send *them* to find your smugglers? There's no more narrow mind than a prejudiced one, Mr. Hampton. If idleness characterizes a lady, I shall never be one."

Usually their arguments stirred a fire in her, but tonight she was overweary and depressed. What she needed was a glass of warm milk and her bed, not this overbearing man and his ill-mannered arguments.

In these last weeks Alex had treated her circumspectly, seeing her only in the company of others. If they whispered together, none could complain. They were treated with the condescension awarded new lovers and idiots. They had no need to meet any more privately than that, and Evelyn had easily avoided the temptation of his destructive kisses. Unfortunately, the more she avoided them, the more she thought about them. And the more she thought about Alex's kisses, the further her thoughts strayed, wondering where those kisses would lead. Despite her exhaustion, her sleep was not restful.

Hampton, too, seemed to be under some strain, but she could not imagine what it might be. He idled the day away in taverns and in the company of his new friends, then spent the evenings escorting her from drawing room to drawing room. They had even attended a rout at the governor's mansion and a musicale at the lieutenant governor's. Such a life could scarcely be considered a strain, but there were taut lines at the sides of his mouth that hadn't been there before, and the mocking gleam of his dark eyes had lost some of its glitter. At times it was almost thoughtful. Evelyn shivered at what his thoughts might be.

He was staring at her that way now, not taking her up in badinage as usual, but apparently considering her description of a lady.

"That's only fitting, I suppose. I never felt called upon

to be named a gentleman. Why should I expect you to behave as a lady? I have never been fond of the company of idle twits anyway. But there is something to be said about occasional idleness. I will take you home early, and you will sleep in late in the morning. That's an order."

Evelyn stared at him as if he had taken leave of his senses, but in the way of all good parties, another couple arrived and interrupted their tête-à-tête. Before long Hampton was caught up in an irate discussion over the use of a generalized writ of assistance to search the house of one of the merchants the night before, and she was left discussing the latest coiffures from England with her aunt.

Thomas Henderson arrived to politely exchange greetings, and finding Evelyn without male company, offered to escort her to the dance floor.

Too tired even to feel animosity toward the handsome lawyer, Evelyn declined. "It has been much too long a day to play the butterfly all night, Mr. Henderson. Perhaps you could just escort me over to my cousin Frances. I haven't said a word to her all evening."

Bowing politely, he took her hand as she rose, and placed it on his arm as they made their way around the perimeter of the room to the corner where Frances was holding court. She had come into favor with some of the Harvard men when they learned of her impending connections, and she was wielding her charm as briskly as her fan.

"Your cousin is an enchanting child, Miss Wellington. I daresay she will soon be following you into matrimony."

The panniers of her skirt kept her escort at a distance, and Evelyn was untroubled by the familiarity of the gaze he bestowed upon her. She had known Henderson since she was a child and was well aware he looked at all women like that. He wasn't so tall as Alex, but taller than average, and his ascetically narrow face and pale good looks were attractive to most women. She supposed, like Alex, he just liked to keep in practice. She had never given him any reason for amorous displays.

"One certainly hopes so," she replied with a cynicism that would make her fiancé proud. Frances was still sulk-

sulking over Evelyn's "capture" of the most eligible man in town.

"Have your plans progressed any further in disposing of your father's interests in the warehouse? I'm sure once you are in England with your husband, we will seem very far away here."

Evelyn sent him a wary gaze. "I have made no plans to dispose of anything, Mr. Henderson. The trust only provides that my share in the warehouse goes to Alex as dowry when we marry. You forget, I have a younger brother who will one day wish to claim his share."

"I drew up your father's will, Miss Wellington. He leaves you sole executor of his estate. If it should become advisable to sell his interest, you have the power to do so. It might be more beneficial to invest it elsewhere. As a friend of the family, I only wish to make you aware of that."

"I thank you for your concern, sir." Curtly dismissing the topic of her only livelihood, Evelyn turned her attention to greeting the other young people around Frances.

From across the room, Alex watched as the lawyer stayed at Evelyn's side, then persuaded her onto the dance floor. Henderson was agreeable enough and had put himself forward a time or two to help in his inquiries, but he could not like the way the man looked at Evelyn. The color she wore tonight did not suit her, and she looked particularly fragile with the hint of dark circles beneath her eyes. Henderson shouldn't be looking at her as if she were a slab of meat to be gobbled up.

Shouldering his way through the throng, Alex reached Evelyn's side just as the music ended. She glanced up at him in surprise and, he almost imagined, relief.

Taking her hand in his, he nodded affably at the lawyer. "Thank you for taking care of my fiancée while I neglected her. She is very patient with my foibles."

"It is always a pleasure to have Miss Wellington's company. I'm willing to be of assistance anytime." Politely Henderson bowed over Evelyn's hand and departed.

Henderson, too, sported one of the same fashionable wigs as Alex, and Evelyn stared after the satin bow in his queue with displeasure. "He has always found me too argumentative before."

Hampton stifled a grin at her frown and started for the doors open to the terrace. "There are times when you would do better to keep your tongue still, but on the whole, I prefer your waspish tongue to simpering silence."

He seemed unusually amiable tonight, and Evelyn shot him a suspicious glance. "Your praise overwhelms me, sir," she answered dryly. "Why are we going out here? Are you taking me home?"

"I have said farewell to our hostess for you. I thought you might enjoy a little fresh air before we find the carriage."

Her uncle's grandiose carriage was another sore point between them, but Evelyn kept silent on the matter this time. Her feet hurt too much to object to the ride for the short distance home. She drank in the heady scent of the herb garden near her feet, and bent to pick a sprig of thyme.

"Sometimes you are almost considerate, Mr. Hampton. It is a terrifying thought." Crushing the tender leaves between her fingers, she absorbed the pungent scent before tucking the aromatic bouquet into his buttonhole.

Alex halted and swung her around, his hands firmly circling her waist as he stared down into her pale face. "Sometimes I even terrify myself, Miss Wellington. Like now, when I wish to scold you for working too hard. I know it's none of my business, but there's no need to worry yourself ill. I really can handle the matter of the smugglers without more than occasional information from you. You needn't stay awake nights worrying over it."

If he only knew what she stayed awake nights worrying over, he'd really have reason to laugh. Nervous at this unexpected proximity, Evelyn tried to step away from his hold. "You fail to understand the seriousness of the situation, Mr. Hampton. Please let me go," she added when he refused to release her.

"I understand a good deal more than you give me credit for, but as long as your uncle is the customs officer, you need not worry over being found out. Wellington Storage will be the last place to be searched."

"That's what's so unfair," she whispered, looking away to the overhanging branches of an apple tree. "They're using me, and I am losing my friends because of it." Catching herself, she turned back to meet his puzzled look. "Let's go. I am tired."

He was missing something here, but Alex wasn't certain what. The look on her face clouded his thinking: both wistful and slightly rebellious. He knew that feeling too well himself. He didn't know why someone surrounded by loving family and friends would feel it, but he could sympathize. He could do more than that.

Cupping her hollowed cheek in the palm of his hand, Alex succumbed to the temptation of those lips he had mentally forbidden himself.

Evelyn made a brief struggle, but she really was too tired to fight, and she wanted this meeting of their mouths too much to protest. Telling herself she needed just a little reassurance to lift her depression, she slanted her lips against his and braced her hand against his broad chest.

His touch was gentle at first, just feathery kisses to the edge of her mouth as if unsure of the welcome he would find there. Evelyn felt her heart race faster when her palm came to rest above the thudding of Alex's heart, and his kiss suddenly became more daring. The magic hadn't receded but had escalated over these last weeks, becoming more intense than she remembered. As she mindlessly returned his passion, he caught her up in his arms, and the only thing keeping them from coming closer was the pressure of her hands upon his chest.

As she felt his kiss become more demanding, deepening to that madness she had almost succumbed to in the barn, Evelyn breathlessly turned her head away, though she made no attempt to leave his arms. She could feel his strength in the masculine body embracing her, in the hands caressing her back, and knew the danger of this proximity. She rested her heated cheek against his shoulder as Alex pressed kisses against her hair.

"Do not do this to me, Alex, I beg of you. It is not seemly." Her voice sounded strange even to herself. She was reluctant to say the words. A strange humming sensation had entered her veins, a vibration that required his touch in places she did not even name to herself. No one had ever touched her like that before, and this was the last man on earth she desired to do so.

"Seemly. That's a fine word." Alex stood still, holding her until both their pulses slowed their racing. "You are right. This is not seemly. We should be in the privacy of our chambers with only a bed to see us." He felt her jolt of irritation and smiled grimly to himself. That should be sufficient to restore them to their usual footing and put an end to temptation.

Evelyn shoved from his embrace, and lifting her skirts, started down the path to the street. Alex quickly caught up with her, taking her arm through his.

"You're an unmitigated bastard," she hissed, trying to jerk her hand away.

"I wouldn't be the earl's heir if I were that, now, would I?" The carriage was easily located, and he helped her in, signaling to the coachman to pull out.

"I doubt that you are any such thing. While the House of Lords may be filled with dunderheads, I doubt that they are all degenerates like you."

Alex sat back against the cushion across from her and chuckled. "Then let me not introduce you to the vices of the lords in the Hellfire Club and their peculiar associates, my dear, if you think my natural suggestion is degeneracy. The shock would be too great for your feeble heart."

"Feeble! I can assure you there is nothing feeble about me. I'm just being sensible, and I suggest you be the same. Your 'natural suggestion' can only lead to one conclusion, and I have no desire whatsoever to be shackled to a rake or an earl's heir or whatever you are. You'd be wise to remember we are a trifle more moral here than in London."

"Is that so? Then the custom of bundling over here is only a rumor? And I suppose when betrothed couples like your friends Sally and Henry tell their parents they are spending the night with friends, they really and truly are with friends and not with each other? And of course that buxom barmaid down at the Goose serves only drinks. Morality abounds, I can tell."

Staring out the window, Evelyn didn't deign to give

him a reply. All his charges were true, but she couldn't make him see the difference. Bundling happened in the country only when the couples already had an understanding but little time together because of the miles between their houses. And if Sally and Henry spent the night together with the same friend, it was only a few weeks until their marriage and to be expected after waiting years to have the money to set up housekeeping. The barmaid—well, the barmaid might be immoral, but she did provide a service of sorts. It simply wasn't the same as what Hampton was suggesting.

The carriage halted and they climbed out. To Evelyn's surprise, Alex sent it on without him. She jerked her hand away and started for the door. He grabbed her waist and forcibly steered her toward the alley leading to the kitchen gardens.

"What do you think you are doing?"

"It's difficult to tell. When I'm around you, I become quite irrational. I had some notion of speaking with you in private." The irritation in his voice was obvious.

Evelyn hurried to keep up with his long strides. On a garden bench beneath another apple tree, she took a seat and refused to go farther. Her mother was within screaming distance of this spot. "So, talk."

Alex knew better than to sit beside her. Glaring down at the crystal blue splash of color in the darkness, he reined in his lust again and set his mind on business. "I have traced two of the four companies who received the shipments of brandy. I have men working on discovering their owners, but we know where the goods are. Another of the companies should be discovered after today's shipment is followed. Unfortunately, the fourth, the Stockton Company, had a driver who eluded my men. He disappeared in the woods near Sudbury. Unless we can find some other means of tracing them, they will escape our net."

In the window above the apple tree, hidden by its branches, Jacob Wellington leaned out to catch the low murmur of voices below. He could see the giant shadow of Mr. Hampton and recognized the glints of blue from his sister's gown. They always got quiet when he was near, so he knew they discussed something they thought unsuitable for childish ears. Somehow, he would like to make them see that he was old enough to help. Ever since the Sons of Liberty committees had started meeting together in the tavern, he had been attending on his own. That meant the patriots trusted him. Why couldn't Hampton and his sister?

He frowned as he caught the words "smugglers" and "Stockton." It took more phrases than that and a brief argument when they both raised their voices for Jacob to realize they were conspiring to catch smugglers. He knew smuggling was illegal and that the redcoats would come and tear a man's house and shop apart looking for illegal goods, but he also knew that almost every man with a ship indulged in it. He was familiar with the Stockton Company too. His uncle had taken him there to help load some crates last autumn. Jacob knew his loyalties belonged with Evelyn, but he couldn't help worrying that maybe she was mixed up in something she shouldn't be involved with. She'd been awfully unhappy these last few weeks since the Englishman had come into their lives.

He watched as Evelyn came out from beneath the tree and ignored Hampton's outstretched hand as she climbed the steps into the kitchen. He liked Mr. Hampton, even though the man strove to look bored whenever he taught him the tricks with strings or listened to his news about the fight he'd won with Billy. He listened, and that was more than most of Evelyn's friends would do. And if Evelyn was going to marry him, he was practically family and had to be trusted, despite what was being whispered at the patriot meetings. Evelyn would never turn her back on friends and become a Tory.

He'd have to go to Sudbury and prove it for himself.

6

Evelyn's frantic message reached Hampton at the unmentionable hour of eight in the morning after a night of drowning his misery in a bottle of rum in the company of Jack Ruggles. As the boy at the door waited patiently for some reply, Alex staggered to the dormer window of his tavern room to read the letter. Garbed only in hastily donned breeches, sporting a day's beard, with thick dark hair tousled and untied and falling to broad bare shoulders, he was a formidable sight, and the messenger was right to remain safely in the doorway.

It took a moment before Evelyn's frantic phrases could penetrate the thick fog in Alex's mind. When they finally did, he crumpled the letter and sagged briefly against the low ceiling, his head upon his arm as he tried to concentrate. Why would the boy go riding off at midnight to Sudbury? Where in hell was Sudbury?

Realizing the messenger was waiting patiently, Alex reached in his pocket and flung him a coin. "Tell Miss Wellington I'll be right there. And tell the stable to saddle my horse."

Thank the devil he'd purchased a decent mount last week. He had a grave suspicion Sudbury was not in the immediate vicinity. Jacob had seemed like a sensible lad. Why the deuce would he ride out in the middle of the night, leaving only a note to tell of his destination?

As Alex hastily jerked on yesterday's shirt and pulled on the first stockings to come to hand, memories of last night's argument with Evelyn vaguely came to mind. The memory of how she had felt in his arms came much more vividly, and he groaned as his loins instantly responded.

There weren't enough barmaids in all of Boston to satisfy his craving for the termagant. Even the demon rum didn't help.

Jerking on his boots, Alex tried to remember the words of their argument. They had made no mention of Sudbury—of that he was certain. He'd never heard of the place. They'd fought over the best way to find the Stockton Company or whether they should just leave that up to the courts. Could Jacob have overheard that argument? He tried to place the position of the boy's room in his mind. His own access to the upper regions of the Wellingtons' house was minimal.

He stomped out of the inn without shaving or locating a pressed cravat. The August heat was sufficient to ignore the formality of coat or vest. He had combed his hair back with his fingers and wrapped a ribbon in it to keep it from his face, but he probably looked like hell. He might as well look like he felt. If the brat had left at midnight, he was over eight hours gone. He could be anywhere.

Evelyn opened the door at his rap and stared at his apparition in a kind of horror that left her shaken as her gaze glanced over Hampton's half-dressed state. Wearing the respectability of his elegantly tailored clothes, he had at least given the impression of a gentleman. Like this, he appeared more the murderous pirate. As she gestured for him to enter, she could not keep her gaze from straying to the coarse ebony curls appearing above the loose neckline of Alex's shirt. They made her remember all too clearly how her hands had rested there the night before. But then he had been decently garbed in linen and satin. Now she was forced to recognize the physical nature of the man beneath the clothes. The knowledge created an odd knocking in her insides and did not clear her frantic thinking.

"What is this nonsense about Jacob running off to Sudbury? What is in Sudbury?"

Hampton practically filled the formal front room. His great size dwarfed the delicate Queen Anne sofa and chairs and threatened the existence of a corner cabinet filled with porcelain figurines. Evelyn sent his polished riding boots a nervous glance, but he managed his size gracefully, avoiding the curved legs of the cabinet.

"I don't know. He's never done this before. Mama has gone over to Uncle George's to see if he can help, but he's no great horseman. The carriage will take hours on those rutted roads."

"Jacob rode? On what?"

"They said at the livery he took the gray a little after midnight." She didn't mention that he had used a secret patriot password to take the horse. Hampton wasn't likely to understand that in a thousand years. They didn't have that much time.

"What makes you think the boy is in any danger? It sounds as if he knows what he's doing to me."

Evelyn stared at her clasped hands and not Hampton's broad silhouette against the morning sun through the paned glass. "He was still awake when I came in last night. I heard him moving about. Alex, I think he overheard us. I think he might be looking for the smugglers in Sudbury. And if Uncle George does have any connection . . . I tried to stop Mama from telling him, but what could I say?"

Her plaintive cry brought a string of curses. Alex shoved a loosened lock of hair back from his forehead and glared at Evelyn's pale face in the sunlight. She was all violet eyes and smudged lashes this morning. Even her lovely hair was still caught in the single braid she must wear to bed. Wisps curled about her face, caught in the sunlight, and he touched them wonderingly with his fingers. She had called him by his given name. He was making major progress. She didn't move beneath his touch, and Alex sighed in surrender.

"Give me the directions to Sudbury. I'll find the young scamp and give him the dressing-down he deserves."

He displayed no doubt of his ability to find Jacob, and Evelyn finally took a deep breath of relief. "I could go with you. I don't know the road well, but—"

Alex interrupted with an abrupt gesture. "I can go faster by myself. If he is in any danger, I don't wish to worry about another hostage. You stay here in case he does get back or if there are any messages."

Such as ransom notes or reports of dead bodies; Evelyn read that thought in his black eyes. She paled even further. "Let me call on some friends to help. You cannot go alone. I know we make deliveries to the inn at Sudbury. It must be twenty miles or more."

"Good, then if I'm not back within three hours, send your most trusted friends, ones you can be certain have naught to do with this." Alex caught her chin in his hand and pressed a kiss to her brow. "Do not look so, love. Jacob is probably sound asleep in a hayloft somewhere. I'm not one inclined to risk my precious hide by attacking a band of dangerous thieves. Quit fretting and be patient. I'll be right back."

The look of relief on her face was so obvious that he felt a great scoundrel, but he left her with the lie. Twenty miles could be covered three times over in eight hours, even with the livery's worst nags. The boy had better be sound asleep somewhere. Alex owned only one pistol, and that was aboard the *Minerva*.

Riding out of town, Alex sought someone who might give him directions. His customary ill luck held off this time. Before he could reach the guarded brick gate to the town, he found a rustic walking down Orange Street, a long-barreled rifle and a powder horn slung over his shoulder. Within a matter of minutes Alex possessed both weapon and directions, and the farmer sported enough coins to buy the best rifle in town, with enough left for a ribbon for his wife. He shook his head and went off whistling at the extravagance of the mad English.

The dust flew beneath the horse's hooves as Hampton left the town's cobblestones behind. In fits of restless energy he had ridden out this way before, but never with any destination in mind. It was time he began learning the lay of the land.

Over the first miles he cursed himself for never having joined the army or learned anything constructive that would aid him in a situation like this. He knew how to wield a sword, but only in play. He was an excellent marksman, but he had aimed a weapon only against game birds and the occasional fox. Despite his protestations to the contrary, he had led the life of an idle gentleman for too many years. Now that he had discovered he enjoyed using his hands and wit to earn his way, he had little time to practice weaponry. He still led a gentleman's life. The most dangerous ruffians he had encountered lately were drunken sailors in the back alleys of the ports he frequented. His size alone was sufficient to end those encounters.

The next miles Alex spent contemplating just what kind of situation he might find when he reached Sudbury. It was doubtful that he would be recognized, but he could scarcely walk into a roadside tavern and ask if anyone had seen an eleven-year-old boy, particularly if it were a smuggler's nest.

Alex's numerous failures haunted his thoughts, but not more so than Evelyn's lovely face lighting up when she thought her brother safe because he said so. That had been a fool thing to do. He should have warned her of the improbability of finding a needle in a haystack. She was as cynical as he. Why had she believed his nonsense? They both had moths in their upper stories.

Cursing his untimely gallantry, Hampton drove his mount harder. He had despised all women as fools for as long as he could remember. Why was he suddenly concerned about one sharp-tongued colonial and how she felt? He wanted to bed her. There was no doubt about that. Who wouldn't? But he had never been overly concerned about the feelings of the women he bedded. When he was in funds, they looked at him with favor. When he was not, they scarcely disguised their disgust of him. Some gave him pleasure, and vice versa. Some did not. That was all there was to the process. He'd better solve this smuggling problem before he lost track of the way of the world. Before long he would even begin imagining she felt something for him beyond the lust they shared.

That steadied him. Passionate women were just as susceptible to nest-building as other women. Evelyn was just too inexperienced to recognize the symptoms. She was too intelligent to see him as a husband, but she hadn't learned to control her passions as he had. He would have to do better in the future. She need not develop wrong notions about his behavior. He'd find her brother and leave her be. Whether or not she was a virgin held no sway over him. He'd take her to his bed if he thought he could have her without consequences, but she had warned him fairly enough about that. So he'd better keep the hell away from her from now on.

Those reflections brought Alex to the clearing with the substantial establishment the farmer had assured him would be the Wayside Inn. The lack of originality in the name matched the inn's appearance. It was a roadside tavern and nothing more. He looked around for some sign that would indicate the direction of the town or the Stockton Company. Presumably that would be the direction Jacob would have taken.

Seeing nothing that so much as represented human habitation besides the inn, he cautiously dismounted by the stable. Jacob's horse hadn't returned to the livery. It had to be somewhere.

Tying his horse to the hitching post, Alex glanced inside the dim outbuilding. Business apparently wasn't booming. He could see only two moth-eaten nags in the place, and one looked distinctly familiar. Glancing toward the windows of the inn and seeing no one, he slipped into the cool darkness of the stable to verify his suspicion.

The mottled gray was unmistakable. The livery had only one mean animal of that description. Luck was with him. Jacob had come here. Remembering his words to Evelyn, Alex hastily climbed into the hayloft to see if the boy were there.

That was too easy. No sign of Jacob or the usual vagrants who paid a penny for a night's lodging. The morning was growing too late for anyone to be abed. Dropping down, Alex started for the inn. He had no idea how one went about searching for a boy without raising suspicions, but he knew people fairly well. He would judge his actions based on the kind of people he found inside.

That decision lasted only long enough to discover there were no people inside, or at least none to be seen. Hoping Jacob would hear him and give some sign of his whereabouts, Alex raised his voice in bellows that should have shaken the rafters had they not been three-foot timbers. "Halloo-oo! Is anybody here? Where the deuce is everybody? I'm a starving man!"

If Jacob were anywhere within hearing, he certainly couldn't have missed that. Alex prayed the lad wasn't too terrified to recognize his voice.

A worn middle-aged woman in unpressed cap and spattered apron appeared from behind the bar in the tavern. The room had only one window, and at this time of day, no lamps were lit. The smoke-blackened timbers made a dim background for the plank trestle tables, and Alex scarcely noticed her until she spoke up.

"Is there something you be wanting?" She spoke without inflection, but the lack of polite address hinted at insult.

Alex chose caution as he regarded her lined and weary face. "I'm starving, madam. There's too long a ride to Boston to wait. Have you a bite to eat?"

She gave him a suspicious glance reserved for strangers. There was that in the way he moved and spoke that did not reconcile easily with the way he looked. Still, there were oddities enough about these days, and if he had the coins to pay, she wouldn't begrudge the time. She gave his soft linen shirt and the ancient rifle and powder horn a second glance, then shrugged.

"There be a rasher of bacon and an egg or two, I wager."

"I could eat half the hog and as many eggs as the hens can lay," Alex boasted with a swagger toward the tavern door. "Cook up whatever you can find while I make use of your facilities. It's been a long night."

As in any other inn, the hall would eventually lead out back to the privy and possibly a public washbowl. But there were rooms to either side that he could check while the woman was busy in the kitchen. Watching her amble off and checking the stair to the rooms above and finding no one in sight, Alex started with the first door on the left. The private dining room was unlocked and empty. He found a larder and a closet with no visible means of hiding even the smallest of boys. He didn't dare search the kitchen yet. It would be more likely the boy would be kept upstairs if he were there at all. But before risking that, he would check the outside buildings.

It was after Alex checked the toolshed and the firewood bin that his gaze came to rest on the trapdoor to the cellars beneath the inn. The cellar! If Jacob had some notion of proving that this inn kept illegal brandy, he would check the cellar first. Glancing around to be certain he remained undiscovered, he strode across the dirt yard to the trapdoor.

A bolt held it in place, but no key. Sliding the pin from the bolt and carrying it with him, Alex swung the door open. He had no lamp to search the dark that met him and no time to look for one. Hoping for the best, he stepped down the crude stone steps into the darkness.

He halted at the foot until his eyes adjusted. A muffled cry caught his attention, and before he could move two steps forward, a small figure flung himself out of the black and hurled himself into Alex's arms.

Before he could even verify that the boy was unhurt, a shadow crossed the opening above. Thinking quickly, Alex grasped the back of the boy's shirt and shook him. "You little fool! What have I told you about running away like that! When I get you home I'm going to thrash you within an inch of your life, just see that I don't! I don't know what the deuce—"

A voice from above interrupted. "There some trouble, mister?"

Alex glanced upward as if in surprise. "You the owner of this place?"

"And if I am?" The man stood with arms akimbo in the cellar entrance. Little of his features could be seen against the bright light of the sky behind him.

"If you are, I'm much obliged to you for keeping this rascal under lock and key." Alex shoved Jacob toward the stairs. "Get up there, boy. Your mama's worried sick."

Jacob didn't have to be told twice. Terrified, he scrambled away from the huge Englishman toward the safety of daylight, even if it meant scampering between the legs of the man who had imprisoned him. The man stepped out of his way to let him by, and following more nimbly than his size should have permitted, Alex emerged in time to catch Jacob's shirt by the neck again.

He faced the wiry, unkempt inn owner with a shrug of

his shoulders. "The lad's willful and knows when he's going to get beaten, so he runs away. I'm obliged to you for teaching him a lesson. His mama is poorly, and she's almighty shaken by his contrariness."

The innkeeper squinted at the stranger's dark, chiseled features beneath a day's growth of beard and found it safer not to argue. Shoving his hands in his pockets and glaring at the pale-faced boy in the man's grasp, he spat a wad of tobacco into the yard. "Found him down in my cellars last night and thought he was a thief. That his horse I found in the woods?"

"He stole it from the livery. Always does. Like I said, he's lazy and willful. If you don't mind, your woman is cooking up some breakfast inside and I'm starved, came away without a bite to eat. I'll pay you for your troubles. The lad will work it out in wages later." Alex was already edging his prisoner toward the inn. If he had to make a break for it, he wanted to be as close to his horse as possible.

The mention of money seemed to remove any further suspicion. The man shrugged and began to amble off. "Thrash him for me when he gets home. Women are too soft on them."

Alex released a ragged sigh as the man disappeared around the corner. Not daring to look the terrified Jacob in the face just yet, he pointed at the washbowl. "Scrub. We're not going anywhere until I eat."

As it turned out, Jacob ate half the huge meal the woman laid out for them. The mug of ale Alex had ordered sat virtually untouched as he watched with amazement as the boy put away what must surely have been his weight in food. When he wiped the plate clean with a crust of bread and polished his mouth with his napkin, Alex asked dryly, "Would you care for more?"

Jacob grinned and stifled a burp. "No, thank you. That'll hold me."

Alex rose and laid the coins for the fare on the table. "I'm going to recommend that thrashing when we get back. I'll personally administer it, if necessary."

The smile left Jacob's face and he watched Alex warily as they left the inn for the stable. "I was just trying to help. The crates are down there. I saw them."

Alex threw the boy up on his miserable nag and climbed onto his own horse, waiting until they were clear of the stable before replying. "Would it have helped if you got your fool head shot off? As it is, if the man has any brains at all, he'll move the crates tonight. We have to work together, not all go our separate ways, if we wish to accomplish anything."

"That's what they said at the meeting the other night," Jacob informed him gloomily, "but I don't see nobody getting much done."

"What meeting?" Alex stared at him after this odd reply.

Realizing he'd said too much, Jacob shook his head. "I'm sorry. Is Mama truly scared? I thought I'd be back before she got up."

"Your whole family is scared, including your sister. I ought to thrash you just for that. From now on, if you've got any bright ideas, take them to me or Evelyn before you act."

Jacob yawned hugely and nodded. "I knew you were a right one, Mr. Hampton. I told them so, but nobody would believe me. You ain't no Tory, are you? The smugglers are. I'll make them understand so they won't be mad at Evelyn anymore."

He was rambling, half-asleep and still in shock. Alex didn't know how much sense to make of his words. Since most of the colonists were Whigs, he could almost wager the smugglers were too, but what politics had to do with anything eluded him. "Tory" seemed to be an epithet with more meaning than he applied to it. And who was this "they" who were angry at Evelyn? Was there some other reason besides overwork that was causing the sleepless shadows under her eyes?

Vowing to find out more, Alex almost missed Jacob's nodding forward over his saddle. Just in time, he grabbed the boy's shirt before he could slide off. Too sleepy to protest, Jacob obligingly snuggled down into Alex's arms as he was lifted to the other horse. Bemused by finding himself a cradle for a young lad, Alex gingerly made him comfortable in the saddle, and leading the livery nag, started the long ride home. His friends in London were never going to believe this.

* * *

Evelyn flew out the door as Alex arrived with Jacob safely tucked in his arms. Her mother was close on her heels, and both women managed the tricky task of grasping the sleepy boy as Alex lowered him. Mrs. Wellington led Jacob away, scolding softly while examining him for injuries at the same time. Evelyn stayed behind.

When Alex made no effort to climb down from his horse, she laid a hand on the bridle and glanced up at him. "Won't you come in? I'll have Molly bring you some tea and breakfast. You must be starved."

He studied her proud face carefully. There was a suspicion of moisture in the corner of her eyes, and for the first time he could remember, she was speaking to him softly, without the harsh hints of anger that so frequently came between them. He didn't need that. He had no desire to be wept over by an emotional woman. He shook his head curtly.

"We ate. He'll tell you about it when he wakes up. I better go make myself respectable." Alex was suddenly conscious of his crude appearance in Evelyn's eyes. He was badly in need of a bath, and his face felt like a porcupine must look.

"I don't think that's possible. Presentable, yes. Respectable, never. Come down or my mother will never forgive you for making her appear ungrateful. She'll remember you're here in a moment."

That sounded more like the Evelyn he knew. Swinging down, Alex landed in front of her, a dangerous glitter in his eyes. "Do you wish to show me your gratitude too?"

"I would if I thought there were any way to do it and still keep my respectability. As it is, you will have to be satisfied with this." Resting her hands on his chest, Evelyn stood on her toes and lightly kissed his bristly cheek. He smelled of horse sweat and ale, but she didn't mind. The masculine scents went straight to her head, and when he caught her hands and held them against his shirt, she was grateful for his steadiness.

"Did you think doing that in public would keep it respectable?"

The dark glimmer of his eyes held her enthralled. Not a hint of a smile cracked his hard features, but she heard his pleasure in the low rumble of his voice. With a wide grin, she gave him back his own. "No, I figured your stink would accomplish that. I'll get no closer."

He growled and she shrieked in mock terror, and when Amanda Wellington came down the stairs a minute later, she was nearly bowled over as the two charged through the front room like a couple of yearlings.

Shaking her head at the madness of young lovers, she followed in their path, beaming an indulgent smile. Evelyn had certainly done herself proud, finding a young man like Alexander Hampton. There had been times when Amanda had worried about their precipitateness and wondered at the anger between them, but she should have known she had no cause for concern. Evelyn had a good head on her shoulders and her father's passion for life. Judging by what Amanda had seen of young Hampton, they were well suited.

Within a year, she could very well be a grandmother.

7

Unable to breach the Sons of Liberty meetings now that they had moved to all-male taverns, Evelyn found herself as much in the dark as the rest of the populace on the morning of the fourteenth of August. When the effigies appeared in the massive spreading branches of the elm just off Newbury, word spread quickly. Evelyn joined the crowd emptying the town to stare at this declaration of rebellion.

An effigy labeled Andrew Oliver, the appointed stamp-tax collector and one of her uncle's closest cronies, hung beside a boot stuffed with a devil. The poor pun on the hated Lord Bute was crude and harmless enough, but the other made her stomach twist with worry.

She wished she knew more about what was going on. Surely the patriots did not mean to actually hang Oliver? It looked like a threat, but surely they would not resort to murder. And if they did, would they stop at Oliver? There were too many hated names on people's tongues these days, her uncle's among them. The threat of violence smoked the air they breathed.

As she hurried away from the mob and toward the warehouse, she met Alex coming toward her. He caught her arm and hauled her around.

"What is going on here? The whole damned town's on holiday."

How could she explain? He knew nothing of the patriots, cared less about their problems. Wordlessly, she turned and led him toward the Liberty Tree.

Alex stared in amazement at the throng gathering beneath the spreading branches. These weren't the riotous noisemakers who occasionally tore up the streets of London, but a holiday crowd of respectable people. True, there were those who were drinking, and small boys pitching stones at the dummies, and angry voices lifted in argument, but for the most part the crowd merely seemed triumphant to have their opinions displayed.

Recognizing a friend of the governor's, Alex caught his sleeve and inquired, "Why is nothing being done to disperse this mob? Isn't it potentially dangerous?"

The man shrugged. "Aye, it is, and the governor sent the sheriff to stop it. See that man over there?" He pointed to a man lingering against a fence on the outskirts of the mob. "That's the sheriff. I'm sure he'd appreciate any suggestions on how to make them all go home."

At that moment Alex experienced the same dread Evelyn had felt earlier. His gaze scanned the growing mob of thousands and returned to the single man standing alone on the outskirts. The sheriff had a few deputies to help him uphold the law, but what could those few men do against a mob of this size? Even if the lawman's sympathies weren't with the crowd, which Alex very much doubted. The mob was lawful now, but what would happen when night came and the drunken elements grew more boisterous?

Alex caught Evelyn's arm and hurriedly steered her toward the relative peace of a side street. "I assume Oliver has been informed and is taking the proper precautions?"

"He would be a fool if he hasn't. Did you see the big man back there, the one wearing the blue-and-gold uniform and carrying a cane?"

"The one passing the bottle? I saw him. Rough-looking brute."

"That's Ebenezer McIntosh, leader of the South End mob. If that gang breaks loose tonight, Mr. Oliver had best be safely out of the county."

Alex glanced down at Evelyn's grim face, realized there was more to this story than the peaceful holiday mob under their "Liberty Tree," and hurried their steps back toward the house. "What the deuce is the South

End mob and how much do you know of what's going on out here?"

"If you've never seen our Pope's Day riots, I cannot explain the South End mob to you. If what I think comes true, you'll see it for yourself tonight, but instead of a wagonload of dummies, I suspect they'll find other targets for their violence. I cannot tell you more than that, Mr. Hampton. Just stay off the streets tonight. You will not be among their favorite people."

Alex remembered her words later that night as he watched the glare of torches from his inn window as the new customs office was demolished stick by stick. The next morning he came down to the tavern to hear of the mob's procession through the State House with Oliver's effigy in a coffin and the riot at Oliver's house that resulted in the lieutenant governor being stoned as he tried to stop them. He heard rumors that the royal governor had already fled to the island fort in the harbor, and wandering out to the streets, he arrived in time to watch Oliver offer his resignation from the position of stamp tax collector to the mob after the night of violence.

Shaking his head, Alex advanced determinedly on the warehouse owned by the stubborn female with whom he had somehow become enmeshed. Thinking of the thick lengths of glorious hair in which he longed to bury his fingers, the long slender limbs that yielded to him so eagerly when he held her, and the delightful taste of her kisses, he could easily soften and excuse her from all doubts. But remembering her sharp tongue, quick wit, and the accuracy of her predictions, he felt his temper rise. This was one lying female who wouldn't deceive him.

Evelyn looked up in surprise as Alex entered. She already knew him well enough to recognize the dangerous flash of those dark eyes behind the ridiculously long lashes, and she hurriedly wiped her ink-stained hands on her apron as he leaned over the counter. She felt his insulting gaze as it swept over her simple brown cotton dress and returned to the length of ribbon she had used to loop her hair out of her face. She fought the urge to raise her hand to see if the ribbon was still in place.

"To what do I owe this honor, Mr. Hampton?" she inquired quietly, refusing to retreat before his dark look.

"The name is Alex, and I believe I have every right to ask my fiancée to have lunch with me. Close up this place for an hour. It's time to eat."

"I have an apple and some cheese in my desk, Mr. Hampton. There is too much to be done to dally over lovers' luncheons."

Evelyn glanced nervously to the empty warehouse behind her as the dark gleam in Alex's eyes grew brighter and he started around the counter toward her. Jacob and Benjamin had gone home, leaving her to mind the office while they ate. It seemed Hampton was already apprised of the fact that she was all alone here.

"I had thought to be polite and take you to a public place, but if you insist on being alone, I will be happy to oblige. The flour sacks in back should make a comfortable resting place, don't you agree?"

With one powerful arm Alex caught Evelyn by the waist and lifted her against him before she could make any decision to escape. Spreading tantalizing kisses along her jaw and down the side of her neck, Alex taunted her with her helplessness. She balanced her hands against his chest and kept her face buried against his wide shoulder, fighting the urges that just his touch generated. She loved the smell of him, the faint scent of shaving soap, the masculine musk of his skin, the trace of wine on his breath as he nuzzled at her ear. The coat beneath her fingers had a rough texture, but she need only slide her fingers beneath to encounter the cool silk and linen of his vest and shirt. She could feel his heart pounding beneath the powerful breadth of his chest where he held her, and that more than anything else warned he was human and not the monster he purported to be.

"Alex, don't," she whispered. "You have no right."

Feeling her slender warmth pressed against him, he could have argued that point. The way she fitted so neatly into his arms, felt so right against him, and stirred longings he had once thought buried told him he had every right to hold her. She belonged in his arms, but that courted madness.

Setting her firmly in front of him but not releasing her

waist, Alex studied her flushed and nervous face. "You grant me that right every time you look at me like that, but one of us has to be sensible. Take off your apron, and I'll help you lock up."

Mentally berating herself for feeling disappointed that he gave up so easily, Evelyn did as told. Perhaps he had come to tell her he had caught the conspirators and was returning home. She ought to feel relieved at the thought. Oddly enough, she didn't.

The tavern kitchen had packed them a basket, and they spread the contents out on the stone bench in the enclosed yard of the old church. Anyone could walk by, so they were in public, but no one did, and that left them private beneath the overhanging branches of trees and shrubs.

"What did you wish to speak to me about? Have you found the smugglers?" Evelyn spread the napkin he provided over her skirt and broke off a corner of the tremendous sandwich of crusty bread, beef, cheese, and ripe tomatoes he offered her.

"I don't know the owners of the companies yet. Apparently they are registered elsewhere or not at all. I have men searching records in New York and Philadelphia, but it will be a week or two more before they can report to me. The court cannot very well convict a piece of paper. We need the men behind the paper. Can I not just want to see you without having some reason?"

Evelyn sipped the warm ale Alex offered and eyed his dark face dubiously. "No. If nothing else, you are bored and have found no one else to seduce. Since I cannot believe that even you practice seduction in the middle of the day, I surmise you have something else in mind."

"Have I?" One dark brow lifted as he drank of his ale and studied her high-boned countenance. There was passion in the fullness of those lips, and he would dearly like to see warm invitation in those violet eyes. The skeptical look he encountered there instead warned this was not the usual light-headed female to be fooled and played with. "I have no aversion to making love in daylight. If you show any inclination to be seduced, I'll oblige without any qualms whatsoever."

Evelyn bit viciously into her sandwich and glared at

him, not deigning to make any reply. He wanted something. She didn't intend to make it easy for him.

Alex shrugged. "It would be a pleasant way to spend the afternoon, but if you're not interested, we can move on to other things. Such as how you knew that peaceful mob would attack Oliver's house last night. Why didn't they just indulge in the usual brawling and stone-throwing?"

"Anyone with an ounce of common sense could have figured that out. Of what interest is it to you?" Puzzled by this choice of subjects, Evelyn ate more slowly and watched his face for clues.

"No self-respecting mob parades in such orderly fashion as they did through the State House last night without some preparation. Someone planned that demonstration. I think it got out of hand later, but perhaps that was their intent. And I think you know more about it than you're telling. Are we going to be subject to more of these demonstrations or were they satisfied with Oliver's resignation?"

Evelyn gave a casual shrug. "They'll not be satisfied until the Stamp Act is repealed, if that's what you're asking. You can go back and tell your noble cousin to come out against it or the safety of the crown's officials here will be in jeopardy until they do. Is that what you want to hear?"

"What I want to hear is the truth. I have a lot of time and money invested in this shipping venture. If it's going to become dangerous for my ships and men to enter this port, I'll have to order them elsewhere."

"Good. I would suggest you keep them from all other American ports, also. This outrage isn't localized. Question your men when they come back from New York and Philadelphia. Why should you take away our profits? Go back to England and leave us alone and we will be fine without you."

Alex looked momentarily scandalized, and she felt a brief triumph at his reaction. Then his face grew harsh, and a cold wind blew through her heart.

"You are talking anarchy and rebellion. The colonies would not exist without England. I hope you're not involved in this. Reports will already be going back to

London. If the riots continue, troops will be called out, and the leaders will be imprisoned. I'd hate to be the one responsible for seeing you behind bars."

Evelyn gave him a bleak look and pushed aside the rest of her food. "Are you a spy, then? You needn't worry about me. I've been an outcast since our names were linked, and rightly so, it appears. I didn't think it of you."

Alex took a long pull of ale and thoughtfully contemplated Evelyn's averted face. Somehow, he had disappointed her. Why should that hurt as much as an abscessed tooth? "I am no spy, but you cannot believe that I will go back to my cousin and not report what is happening here. And your Lieutenant Governor Hutchinson has already asked for my aid. He seems to think you might be able to tell me more than you have. From what have you been outcast because of me, Evelyn?"

"Never mind. In a few weeks you will have your reports and be gone. I can survive another few weeks." She folded her napkin and placed it in the basket, then stood up. "Thank you for the luncheon. I must get back to work now."

Alex rose but did not try to stay her. There were no words he could use; she had said them all. In a few weeks he would be gone, and none of this would be any of his concern. Still, he regretted not seeing a smile on her lips and invitation in her eyes as he had that day he returned with Jacob. He had rebuffed her then, and she had wisely retreated. Now he was sorry there could not be more trust between them.

"I believe we have an invitation to attend some function at your uncle's tonight. Shall I come by at the usual time?"

She wanted to beg off. She wanted never to see him again. Life would be much simpler if she could just go back to the way she had been before Alex strode off that wretched ship and into her life. The sooner she could return to that sanity, the better off she would be. But her uncle would not accept her refusal, especially after last night. He would want full attendance and all the pomp he could muster to prove he was unaffected by the night's activities.

She nodded acquiescence and walked off, leaving Alex to repack the hamper by himself. She had needed this reminder of their political differences. She had been in danger of once more losing herself in the dark need of his eyes. Lud, but what a fool she was to think she was the one he needed.

8

Only a week and a half later Evelyn was again doubting her sensibility. Alex had been more solicitous than he had ever been before. She mistrusted this new, more attentive Alex, but she could not help enjoying his ability to cajole her into a better mood or lend his sympathetic ear when she chose to speak. Instead of constantly barraging her with suggestive words, seductive touches, and taunting looks, he behaved the part of the gentleman. His choices of subjects to converse upon heightened her suspicions, but she could not help hoping to convert him to her beliefs.

Jacob continued slipping away at night and coming back with the exciting news of what the Sons of Liberty planned next, but none of the plans seemed definitive or even practical. Evelyn carefully kept any mention of this organization from Alex, but she did her best to repeat their arguments to him. Perhaps Parliament would listen if one of their own would speak in the colonists' defense.

On the night of the twenty-sixth of August, they had no engagements, and Evelyn sighed with relief as she walked home in the sultry heat. She would go home and soak in cool water and put on her thinnest shift and curl up in the east window with a book in hopes of a breeze. She needed a break from the routine of heavy gowns and hoops and crowds of sweating people in smelly wigs in stifling rooms. Even the memory of last night's heated discussion with Alex in the garden did not appeal. Her heart had not been in the argument but on his lips so close to hers. It was insufferable to think she was being reduced to a mindless rag by a man who would undoubtedly turn her in for treason if he thought she deserved it.

Not that anything they were contemplating could be considered treasonous, she told herself sharply. They supported the king; it was Parliament that was being unreasonable. If they had adequate representation in Parliament as Alex suggested, perhaps then things would return to normal. There would be no need for protests or acts of defiance to make themselves heard. That's all anyone wanted.

But when Evelyn reached the State House on King Street and saw the stacks of firewood and old trash systematically being gathered by bands of small boys and other less-than-respectable characters, she began to feel doubt. People like that didn't act together on impulse. Someone had ordered this, and she could imagine who. The problem was defining their intention. Surely they didn't mean to set fire to the State House?

She hurried home just in time to catch Jacob before he slipped out the back gate. Grasping him by the collar, Evelyn refused to acknowledge his irate struggles. "What do you know of the bonfire on King Street?"

"Bonfire? It's not dark yet! They can't have started the bonfire."

That answered any questions about the extent of her brother's involvement, and Evelyn gave a ragged sigh. "What are they planning to do, Jacob? If they let McIntosh's gang run wild again, it could be disastrous. What is the bonfire for?"

"They're just going to protest a bit and then maybe march by Judge Story's house. It's the Admiralty Court that's causing half our problems, ain't it, Evelyn? We'll let him know he can't go searching our houses whenever he pleases. Has Alex found those smugglers yet?"

"The smugglers are breaking the law, Jacob, and marching on William Story won't stop him from sending them to jail. If the mob is going to be out tonight, you'd better stay home. They can get ugly when they're drinking. You don't want Mama to worry, do you?"

"I'm just going down to help for a while. I'll be back by dark, don't worry. I gave my word I'd be there. You wouldn't want me to break my word, would you?"

No, Evelyn couldn't ask him to do that any more than she could let the matter go unattended. The last riot had created another whole set of tensions, and there were those in the community who had vowed to take arms against the rioters if they struck again. Caught as she was in the middle, she could feel the division cracking open and slowly shattering life as she knew it. She had no desire to take up sides between her uncle and his family and her friends.

In a few hurried words to her mother, Evelyn explained what was happening and ran upstairs to change her clothes. So much for a cooling bath and relaxing evening, she thought grimly as she pulled on the old pair of breeches and shirt she used at the warehouse. Rather than wear the heavy coat, she found a leather jerkin of her father's and hoped it would serve as sufficient disguise in the darkness. Tucking her hair into an old hat, she waited impatiently for dusk to grow to night.

The anonymity of mobs made it singularly easy to blend in with the crowd as dark fell and the bonfire was lit. Evelyn recognized a few faces in the glow of the flames, but mostly they were the ruffians who roared and thundered through the streets on one day a year and disappeared into the back alleys on the rest, not the respectable merchants she knew. She didn't like the feel of this eerie scene at all.

The cacophony of conch shells, whistles, and drums silenced when McIntosh rose to make his drunken speech against tyranny. The words sounded vaguely familiar and not at all what the man would have said for himself, and Evelyn suspected the manipulative hand of Sam Adams behind it.

When the local "tyrants" were mentioned, however, she gasped at the names on this list of targets and slipped away, praying Jacob had the sense to do the same. Before long, the speeches would become hotter and heavier. It didn't take much imagination to know what would follow next. Her uncle had to be warned.

The Upton house wasn't far away. Unconscious of her less-than-feminine attire, Evelyn hurried down back alleys to warn her mother's family of the night's events.

Judge Story might not be the only one to receive unwelcome visitors this night.

The house was well lit but the insolent maid tried to make Evelyn stand on the doorstep while she went in search of her employer. Evelyn ignored the command to wait and walked in, calling to her aunt from the front hall. She became briefly conscious of how she must look when her cousin Frances appeared on the stairs in a gown of fragile blue, but she pushed aside the feeling as both her aunt and uncle arrived from different directions.

"Evelyn, what the deuce are you about like that? By Jove—"

She interrupted before her uncle's tirade could continue. "There's a mob at the State House, and they're working up to another riot. You and Judge Story are on their list tonight. There doesn't seem to be anybody in control and they're getting ugly already." She turned to her aunt's frightened face. "Aunt Matilda, why don't you and Frances get together a few things and come back to the house with me? You don't want to be here when they arrive."

"They wouldn't dare come here! The governor will call out the militia! You are just courting trouble, Evelyn. Why your father didn't—"

"The governor is hiding on Castle Island, Uncle George, too afraid of the mob to show his face. If you will excuse me. . . ." Impatiently Evelyn hurried after her aunt. There wasn't time to listen to her uncle's speechifying.

As it was, there wasn't time for anything. The sounds of whistles and drums and the voices of hundreds grew louder even as they packed the more precious ornaments and valuables in satchels. Matilda glanced out the upstairs window and paled with fright.

"They're here! What are we going to do now? My word, they've got torches! There must be thousands. Evelyn, we can't go out there. Just look at them!"

Her frightened voice drew Evelyn to the window. Below, the narrow street thronged with the eerie aspects of dark and pale faces in the flare of torchlight. Their voices carried but the words did not, and Evelyn was grateful for that. Her aunt would faint should she hear the obscenities and threats Evelyn had heard earlier that evening.

As a stone crashed through a lower window and the mob began pressing against the picket fence, Evelyn flew to the windows in the back bedroom. Already men were filtering between the houses and down alleys to reach the vulnerable kitchen entrance. Not carried away yet by the power of the mob, they milled harmlessly, swigging from jugs, shouting curses, and greeting each other as if this were a social occasion. There would be no easy escape here.

From this height, she could see the lights of the wharf and harbor, and her heart made a sudden leap of hope. She feared it would be dangerous to smuggle her aunt and cousin out of here on her own, but with a little protection . . .

Not daring to think too closely on the matter, she turned back to her aunt. "Put on old clothes and shoes you can run in. I'll be back in a few minutes."

Before her aunt's wails of protest could be heard below, Evelyn ran down the back stairs and slipped out the French side doors. Coming through the hedge, she avoided the attention of the mob. In jerkin and breeches, she blended in with the crowd, and she silently escaped down a side street without notice.

The night was ominously humid and hot, and the cries of the mob as it made its way through the town carried on the still air. Doors were bolted and lights doused in all the respectable homes as they prepared themselves as they usually did for a Pope's Day riot. In the morning, they would come out to survey the damage and all would go on as it had before. They just hadn't realized yet that these riots were not the same as the holiday.

Evelyn drew a deep breath of air thickened with smoke and hastened toward the wharf. The cobblestones beneath her shoes made it dangerous to run, but she could not help fear from increasing her pace as a particularly loud cry from the mob erupted behind her.

The revelry in the tavern had not been diminished by the scenes taking place within the town. Out here on the wharf the town seemed far distant. The gulls crying overhead and the water lapping at the pilings and the ever-present stench of fish created another world. Catching her breath, Evelyn stared at the lights of the inn and prayed.

Not daring to hesitate further lest she cry craven, she entered the front door and sought the owner. He recognized her and gave her working clothes an odd look, but gave the directions she sought with a knowing smile.

Refusing to contemplate the meaning of that smile, Evelyn took the stairs two at a time. Alex had to be there. He was the only one she knew who had a crew of men at his command who could be relied upon to support an officer of the court on a night like this. Her patriot friends apparently supported this outrage, or at least had made no attempt to stop it. She understood their position, but that did not prevent her bitter rage of helplessness.

Finishing the mug of rum, Alex set it aside to admire the buxom beauty gracing his bed. The maid had been more than accommodating these last weeks, and she had grown overconfident in her role. He had come in to find her already half-undressed and lolling upon his pillows. At the time, he could think of no reason to throw her out.

Joining her now on the bed, Alex found himself less than ecstatic about the pleasures of the flesh she offered. The doxy apparently hadn't bathed since the last time he'd had her, or the first time, more likely. Alex tried to conquer the protest of his nose as he reached to further untie the stay laces that kept her overflowing breasts pushed temptingly upward. She giggled drunkenly as she spilled into his hands, and he began to knead the flabby flesh.

He'd once thought her bounteous breasts a pleasant temptation that made it easy to cast aside his distaste for her crudities, but he could no longer manufacture any desire to sample her wares. Instead, he let his thoughts turn to a slender beauty whose slim curves and delicate scents enticed his imagination, and he found it easy to recover desire. Wondering how it would feel to hold Evelyn's firm and supple figure against him without clothes, he felt a surge of pure lust that brought more ecstatic giggles from the whore beneath him as she rubbed her hips to his.

The sound of a knock at the door interrupted his pleasant reverie. Cursing, Alex ignored it in favor of removing the last of the laces, revealing all of his bedmate's plentiful curves. She was already working at the buttons of his breeches, and he surged impatiently against her hands, eager for the release from the hampering pressure of tight cloth.

The knock interrupted again, more frantic this time, and biting back a stream of invectives, Alex groaned and returned his boots to the floor. Standing, he made a futile attempt to restore his buttons as he stumbled toward the door. His only thought was that there must be some trouble with the ship.

When he threw open the door to find Evelyn standing there, her eyes wide with fright and growing shock as she saw the naked woman sprawling across his bed, Alex was tempted to slam it shut again. Cynically, he left it open, leaning against the frame as he made a show of refastening his open shirt. "To what do I owe this honor?" he inquired, mimicking her haughty words of a few weeks ago.

Evelyn tried not to look at the huge breasts of the woman nonchalantly pulling up the covers in the bed behind him. But the only other sight to focus on was the breadth of Alex's chest before her. She could scarcely keep her fascinated gaze from the whorls of dark hair spiraling across the muscular ridges revealed by the open shirt. It took an act of tremendous will to raise her gaze to the sardonic gleam of his damned eyes.

Disgust and anger rose up in her as she realized this same man who had kissed and held her came here at night to lie with a tart like that. She could not let her emotions drive out her purpose here, but she could not control the quiver of fury in her voice either. "I thought to seek your help, but I can see you are otherwise occupied."

Frustrated at her inability to speak her thoughts, Evelyn turned away, but Alex's mocking baritone called her back.

"I'm in no hurry, my dear. Why don't you come back

and join us? If you're willing to try bundling, I'll even throw Tess out."

Fury brought tears to her eyes, and clenching her fists at the sound of the irate wail behind him, Evelyn swung back to confront him. "I wouldn't bed or wed you if you were the last man on earth. I came here to ask your help and warn you that the mob is out again, but I can see you care only for your own selfish pursuits. The mob is probably too drunk to figure out how to reach the *Minerva* anyway."

Hard fingers caught Evelyn's shoulders and jerked her back before she could make her escape. Alex scowled as she averted her face and refused to meet his eyes.

"You have no right to come here and condemn me for what I do in the privacy of my rooms. You're not my wife. I never had any intention of tying myself to a woman's mewling whims, for just that reason. I don't need a horde of whining brats to prove I'm a man, and that's the only reason I can see for marrying. I'm a free man and mean to stay that way. Now, get off your damned high pedestal and tell me what you came here for."

Shaken to the core by his harsh words but refusing to reveal it, Evelyn continued staring at the wall as Alex's fingers dug into her shoulders. Her breath came in short spurts at this unreasonable proximity to his overwhelming size, and she fought back the tears streaming down her face.

"The mob is rioting again. They surrounded my aunt's house before I could get her away. They've broken up in groups. There's one gone to Judge Story's. They're threatening to come burn all the English ships in the harbor. They were smashing in the fence at my uncle's when I left."

At his curse, she tried to get away, but Alex's grip didn't loosen as he tried to absorb her words. No longer caring what he thought, Evelyn brought her heel down on his instep. "Go bed your doxy. I'll take care of it myself."

Alex caught her up short, jerking on her shirt collar and glaring down into her face. The hatred in her eyes caught him by surprise, and he responded with the venom that he kept for the rest of the world. "Don't look at me like I've just committed adultery. You can't control my life. We're nothing to each other. Do you understand that?"

The words pierced her like bullets, but Evelyn vented her rage without acknowledging the pain. "I understand you're a bloody bounder just like you always said. Now, let me go." She swung her foot at his shin, and he had to loosen his hold to dodge the blow. She flew from his grasp and down the stairs before Alex had time to do more than yell her name.

Not until Evelyn was out of sight did Alex realize what he had done. Leaning his head against his arm where it rested on the doorframe, he cursed himself for three sorts of fool. He had thrown accusations at her that rightly belonged to another, and so had destroyed the very small hand of trust she had offered to him. He deserved her curses. His rashness had destroyed more than one relationship before. It seemed he was doing his best to end another.

Giving no thought to the woman in his bed, Alex turned and threw open a dresser drawer, pulled out his pistol, checked the load, and thrust it in the pocket of the coat he quickly donned. Grabbing the sword gathering dust beneath the bed, he buckled that on too. Rescuing fair maidens wasn't in his line of work, but he rather fancied the dragon.

Clattering down the steps, he called to one of his crew in the tavern, gave a terse message, then turned to step out into the night. The smell of smoke had even begun to reach the wharf.

9

Evelyn stifled a sob of fury as she ran down the alley behind the Upton house. She could hear the yells and cries of the mob in front, heard the smashing of glass as the threats increased, and shuddered as she nearly ran into a burly trio uprooting a fence post.

They let her pass and she slid through the shrubbery to enter the way she had left. Her uncle was a fool to linger longer. There would be no protecting his precious possessions if he insisted on staying put and antagonizing a mob. She could hear his voice in the front room throwing curses back at the vandals. They wanted his head, but they would be satisfied with whatever they could lay hands on. She couldn't tell her uncle which was more valuable, his life or his library. She ran on up the stairs to where her aunt was waiting.

Frances' idea of old clothes was a sprigged muslin she had worn last season. Evelyn sighed at the vivid white and multitude of petticoats. She would stand out like a lighthouse on a stormy night.

Turning, she found Jacob helping their aunt shove jewels and coins into the overburdened satchel. He raised a frightened face at her exclamation.

"They've found Story's wine cellar." The words spilled out quickly at the welcome sight of his sister. "They're too drunk to follow orders. They're tearing up the judge's study now, looking for I don't know what. They weren't supposed to harm anyone, Evelyn, I swear."

"We'll not take any chances. We'll try the side door. They haven't noticed it yet. They're probably looking for the wine cellar here too. Come on, Aunt Matilda, we'll get you to Mama. They won't bother us there."

Jacob stood and shifted from foot to foot uneasily. "Uh, Evelyn, that might not be so good. They're watching to catch Uncle George, and they've got our house posted. They'll come there next if we get away."

Frances began to wail hysterically, and Matilda sat down abruptly, her terrified eyes searching the room as the sounds of violence outside erupted in a wild cry of triumph. The cellar door leading to the wine must have been discovered.

As the sounds of George Upton screaming obscenities at the intruders carried upward, Matilda shook her head and covered her eyes. "I want to go home. I don't know why I ever came here. They're all savages. All of them."

Evelyn was quite convinced she classified her husband in the same category, and she was inclined to agree in that particular case. Grabbing the heavy satchel of valuables that had been packed, she moved toward the hall. "We'll go somewhere. We've got to get out of here."

They hurried in single file down the back stairs. No one sent a second glance back to the man berating the mob from the library. He had taken no thought to their care, and they gave him none now. Matilda silently slid a hand over the mahogany breakfront, her pride and joy, as if saying good-bye. The fragile china inside gleamed with the loving care she had given it. Evelyn dropped the satchel and hastily opened the silverware drawer, pulling out the utensils she knew her aunt had brought with her from England. She dropped them in Jacob's pockets until they were filled to overflowing, then wrapped the remainder in her jerkin and carried it as a bundle in her other hand as she picked up the satchel again.

They crept out the side door while whoops of triumph echoed in the back and angry shouts erupted with another crash in front. The humid air seemed to carry the tension in waves through the night, and Evelyn nearly jumped from her skin as two men rounded the corner of the house, almost bumping into her.

Without the jerkin, her disguise was well nigh useless. The two rogues stared at Evelyn in confusion for a moment before discovering Frances in her white dress behind her. Their gazes quickly took in Matilda and Jacob and finally came back to the satchel in Evelyn's hands. Drunken laughter escaped them as they realized what they had discovered and reached for the valuables.

"Leave us be. If your cause is liberty and justice, you have no reason to harm women and children. Go back to your toys. We'll not take them from you." Evelyn glared at the bottle in one man's hand and attempted to push toward the opening in the hedge she had used before.

"Not so fast, wiseacre." The ruffian caught her arm and she could smell the fumes of alcohol on his breath. "The others can cry for liberty and what-have-you, but I got better things in mind. Give over the satchel, lady."

His fingers hurt her arm, and she wanted to weep at being treated thus twice in one night. It was too much to be ignored by the men she had called friends, cursed by a man she called her fiancé, threatened by hooligans, and forced to slink through the streets of her home. This wasn't the political justice she sought, but a band of thieves out for what they could get. Mentally calling Sam Adams and his concerned committee every vile name she had ever heard, Evelyn swung her foot hard, connecting squarely with the man's shin.

He screamed a curse and raised his arm to give her the blow she deserved. Before she could dodge, a rough hand grasped her attacker's elbow and bent it backward. The painful crack that ensued made Evelyn wince and brought screams and whimpers of pain.

"That's the last time you'll lift a hand to a woman, my friend," the warm voice murmured beneath the shouts around them, ripe with mockery and something else, something infinitely more dangerous.

Alex. Evelyn closed her eyes with a shudder. She heard the thieves scurrying off into the night and opened her eyes in time to see the silver gleam of his sword being returned to its scabbard. She stared at the weapon in growing horror, but her cousin and aunt held no such qualms. They hurried to grab his arms and cover him with welcome. Evelyn caught the dark gleam of his eyes as he glanced over their heads to her, but she couldn't respond. She felt frozen to the spot, weighed down by the enormity of his appearance and her memory of how she had seen him last.

"I have men waiting in the street. Come, I have to get my ship out of here. Are you ready?" Alex grabbed the satchel from Evelyn's hand, carefully avoiding touching her as he led the way through the break in the shrubbery.

He was moving the *Minerva* out. She didn't like the sound of that, but she hurried to keep up. She felt more than saw the shapes of men keeping pace with them as they hurried down the street. Torches flickered everywhere, and the cries of angry, drunken men filled the air. None came out to stop the mob. It would be madness to do so. Evelyn took another fearful breath and followed the broad shoulders of the man in front of her. She had lost all direction this night. She needed time to think.

When it became apparent that Alex and her Aunt Matilda had come to some agreement involving rowing out to the ship, Evelyn retreated. If they were planning to escape to England, she wanted no part of their plans. She handed over the jerkin full of silver to Alex but did not join in this leave-taking. When Alex reached for her next, she shook off his hand.

"I'll not go with you. Take care of Aunt Matilda. I have other things to do." She turned and started down the wharf.

Alex grabbed her shoulder and spun her around. "My men have orders to sail at the first sign of trouble. Your aunt has already agreed to go with the ship. I'll go back for your uncle. I don't want to have to track you down too. This whole damn town's gone mad. The ship is the safest place to be."

"Not if it's going to England." Not flinching from his furious dark glare, Evelyn stood up to him and waited for him to release her. "This is my home. I'm staying. Jacob's already gone back to warn Uncle George, so you may go with Aunt Matilda now. Get on your ship and sail away. We'll be fine." The flames from the bonfire at the State House streaked the sky behind her, putting the lie to her words.

Alex's hand slid from Evelyn's slender shoulder. The

night would only get worse instead of better. The situation was deteriorating rapidly in the hands of the drunken mob, and he couldn't risk leaving his ship in port any longer. There would be martial law or anarchy by morning. It was imperative that he leave, but he didn't want to leave Evelyn behind, roaming the streets in that revealing costume. He wanted her safe, where he could find her.

Instead, she stood there staring up into his face, her violet eyes quietly saying good-bye against the backdrop of a town gone mad. Then she turned and walked away, slipping into the darkness as if she were no more than a shade or a memory.

Alex let her go. He had no other choice. She didn't belong to him any more than he belonged to her. He had a ship already stocked and ready to sail, and long overdue. He owed it to his partners to see that it returned safely. He couldn't risk letting it wait to be destroyed by these madmen.

Turning on his heel, Alex shouted to the men on the dinghy, "Tell Ruggles to sail at the first sign of trouble. I'll find my way out later."

With a curse to himself, he strode toward Upton's. He didn't owe the bastard a thing, but he couldn't send the man's family off to England without at least warning him.

The worst of the damage had already been done by the time Alex arrived. The magnificent library had been shredded to papers drifting up and down the street. The china crackled under Alex's feet as he walked through the hollow house searching for any sign of the inhabitants.

He found Upton standing in his front room, still shaking his fist at the now invisible intruders. When Alex entered, he turned on him.

"You! Where were you when I needed you? Go back and tell his majesty the travesty that has been wrought this day! I demand justice be done."

Alex found a still-intact decanter of claret and poured himself a glass. "Go tell him yourself. Your wife and daughter are on the *Minerva* waiting to sail. The mob's moved on to Hutchinson's, from all reports. There will be a boat waiting to row you out at the wharf. That's the best I can do for you." He waited with interest to see the man's reaction.

Upton began to turn purple, as if all the bile he had accumulated this night had built up to cut off his breathing. He spluttered and squirmed and finally protested, "I'm not leaving! I have a job to do. I'll not let the bloody bastards drive me away. That's what they want, you know. They'd drive us all out so they could take over. I'll not go, I tell you!"

Alex had to admire the man in a certain odd way. Upton wasn't a complete fool, nor did he lack courage. He was just too much of a jackass to know how to make the best of his more admirable qualities. Alex swirled the claret in his glass and contemplated how he had succeeded in making the best of his own worst qualities, and he gave the older man a wry toast.

"Suit yourself. I'll send you the bill for your family's fare. I don't suppose you happen to know where I could find your niece and nephew, do you?"

Upton just glared at him and turned to scream for the servants. Alex shrugged, set down his glass, and departed by the gaping hole that had once been the front door. He could follow the trail of broken bottles and locate the mob. He could hear the weird echo of their voices from a distance, but his interest didn't lie with them. He wasn't sure what he sought out of this night, but he knew where his duty lay next.

He made his way to the modest house on Treamount. The entire street was dark and quiet, and he had an odd premonition that he wouldn't find what he sought there. Still, he needed to speak with the lady of the house.

Amanda answered the door, her face pale with worry, her hands wrapped in frustration in the wrinkled folds of her apron. At sight of Alex, she gave a cry of relief.

"Tell me where they are! I have been in torment not knowing whether to go look or stay here in case they needed me. Bless you for coming, Mr. Hampton."

He felt a cad for coming without answers to her questions. He had no hat to remove, and he stood awkwardly on the step, searching for lost words. "Alex, ma'am, the name's Alex. Jacob and Miss Wellington were with me when we put your sister and Miss Upton on the *Minerva*.

I thought perhaps they came back here for you. I've ordered the ship to sail if there's any increase in the violence. I thought you might want to go with it. Mr. Upton is staying here. He can ship your possessions later, if you wish."

She stared at him with round eyes and for the first time he realized they were the same shade of violet blue as Evelyn's. He felt as if Evelyn had impaled him with one of those outraged glances of hers. Here he was trying to do the decent thing for a change, and all these Wellington women could do was treat him like some kind of lower form of reptile. Be damned to the lot of them!

"Leave Boston? Don't be ridiculous. Give me time to find my shawl. If they were down at the wharf with you, then they must have stayed to protect the warehouse. I should have known."

Alex couldn't very well walk off and leave her. He tried to persuade her she was safer here, but she was more stubborn than Evelyn at her worst. Sighing, he restricted his pace to that of his companion as they hurried down the dark street toward the harbor.

"I don't think this is a wise idea, Mrs. Wellington. The worst of the mob is in this direction. I was willing to risk it if you wished to sail with your sister, but I cannot believe it is the safe thing to do just to check on your children. Why don't I take you to Mr. Upton while I go down to the warehouse?"

"Nonsense." She stepped briskly alongside him. "George and I have never got along. I wish to see Matilda off, if that is possible. You are very generous to see to her safety. She has never liked it here. I should never have asked her to come. She and Frances will be much better off with our family in England."

Alex was beginning to feel as if whatever good deeds he had performed tonight were merely parts of a grand plan created by the intrepid Wellington ladies. How convenient that he had a ship ready and waiting to sail for the unhappy Mrs. Upton and her daughter. What other plans did they have in store for him tonight? Had they orchestrated the riots too?

The smell of smoke began to permeate the air as they came closer to the town center, and Alex deftly led his companion down an alley, away from the drunken revelry at the State House. The Hutchinson house was farther into town. Since there were few signs of the mob here, he trusted that palatial mansion was now bearing the brunt of the night's horrors. Perhaps they were safe in returning to the wharf.

That notion was soon dispelled as he heard a sudden roar of voices farther down the road. Mrs. Wellington grasped his arm nervously, and Alex's hand instinctively reached for his sword. This was madness. He should have climbed in the boat with the Uptons and left this chaos behind. They were the only ones who had shown any sense this night.

Refusing to be weighed down by the burden of the woman on his arm if he had to face a mob, Alex abruptly drew her toward the tavern on the corner. Bewildered, Amanda followed.

Alex quickly located his landlord, and releasing Mrs. Wellington's arm, gave a curt command. "Keep her safe until I get back."

Without listening to any protest, he strode quickly out in the direction of the riot on the wharf.

Evelyn shoved another crate to the barricade she and Jacob had built in front of the door and stopped to wipe the perspiration from her brow. Her younger brother peered out of the tiny office window anxiously, keeping his head down as another object bounced off the outer wall.

"It ain't supposed to be like this," he whispered in protest, defending the cause that had set this mob in motion. "They weren't supposed to come down here at all."

"That would be McIntosh's idea." Wearily Evelyn sat on a crate and contemplated their next move. All the doors were barricaded, but she had no way of protecting the windows. The sounds of splintering glass in the warehouse brought her back to her feet. "Papa fired Eb's son last year for drunkenness. This is his opportunity to get even."

She wished for a weapon, any weapon, but she had none. Most of the windows were too small to make access easy, but a determined man of the right stature could do it. She didn't know what she would do if one tried.

With all the doors and windows blocked, the building was airless, and the day's heat had no chance of escape. Evelyn moved without her usual quickness of motion, a singular lethargy taking root in her limbs as she sought the crowbar they kept for opening crates. Her heart wasn't in any of this. She was on the wrong side of the wall. The mob wasn't supposed to turn on her. She was one of them.

It didn't help that she kept remembering Alex standing on the wharf, his broad shoulders outlined against the sky as she turned away from him. Now she would never know the magic of standing in his arms again, feel the excitement of his lips on hers one more time. She had known he would be leaving soon. She just hadn't expected it to be so abruptly.

As she found the crowbar, she forced herself to remember the lewd female in his bed, and anger wiped out all traces of any other sentiment. She should be glad to be rid of a villain like that. There wasn't an honorable bone in his body. She didn't even know why he had followed her to her uncle's. There had to be some purely selfish motive in it somewhere.

She heard the mob's roar of triumph at the same time that she heard the hollow thuds of footsteps upstairs. Lud, but she had not worried about the second floor!

Crying to Jacob, she ran to shove the closest barrels and crates across the door to the stairs. There was little she could do to save the stock on the upper floor. She would have to settle for protecting this one.

She wanted to cry and scream and berate the mob for their drunken madness, but unlike her uncle, she knew the stupidity of loosing her tongue on the mindless. The only thing they would understand now was a cannonball.

"They're throwing bolts of cloth out the windows!" Jacob raced back to help her, his wiry frame jerking the heavy crates on top of each other as Evelyn shoved them toward him.

"That ought to bore them soon enough. They can't

drink cotton." Furiously Evelyn kicked another crate across the floor in his direction.

The triumphant yells suddenly turned angry. Worried, she climbed up on a barrel to see out the nearest window. "They're fighting over the ladder! Someone must have called out the militia! I see swords. Lud, Jacob, there will be bloodshed over this. You said they promised no one would be hurt. Asses! What did they think to accomplish with violence?"

The peaceful demonstrations she had wholeheartedly supported before when they were discussed had turned into something much more dangerous than anyone had ever anticipated. From this angle, she couldn't see much of the fight, but the temper of the mob had changed. Drunken revelry had become ugly curses. She didn't like the sounds of it at all.

The ladder went crashing into the mob, leaving some besotted fool stranded on the window ledge, from the sounds of it. Jacob ran from window to window, trying to get a better view of the brawl but not succeeding.

Perhaps it wasn't a sword she had seen, but an ax. She heard the unmistakable crunch of metal against wood. Mentally she tried to remember what was in the crates directly in front of the doors. Axes were more lethal than swords against her defenses.

To her surprise, a man on horseback appeared on the outskirts of the fray. He was shouting something and pointing in the direction of the north part of town. His shouts diverted the attention of the men on the edges of the crowd. The man on horseback disappeared from her field of view, and Evelyn ran to the other side of the warehouse, trying to find him again. There had been something distinctly familiar about that silhouette.

"They're still fighting over the ladder!" Jacob screamed, hopping down from his sentry post. "I want to go out there, Evelyn. I can get out the window. Give me a crowbar!"

"Jacob, you can't go out there! You'll be hurt."

Jacob ignored her and grabbed a bar from the toolbox and scrambled up a stack of crates to a broken window. Before Evelyn could say anything more, he was over the ledge.

That left her little choice. With a sigh of resignation she brushed the glass from the ledge and swung her legs over. No one even noticed her. There was a long drop to the street, and she wished she had chosen the front window, which was at least almost at eye level.

The mob seemed to be gaining momentum in the direction the horseman had led them. She heard shouts of "Hutchinson!" and "Militia!" as they hurried back toward town and away from the wharf. Still, there were the diehards fighting over the ladder, professional thieves, more than likely. A night like this must be heaven for criminals.

Raw curses reached her ears, and steeling herself, Evelyn leapt from the ledge, crowbar in hand. She couldn't let anything happen to Jacob. She felt guilty enough for letting him get embroiled in this. Perhaps she should have packed him in the dinghy with Aunt Matilda.

Too late now. The man suspended in the window was growing belligerent and screaming vile threats to the brawlers below. She couldn't figure out who had taken the initiative in defending what was, after all, only a warehouse. As she approached, she watched one bully lift a barrel stave over his head, prepared to crack it down over the head of the man demolishing the ladder. Without a second thought, she swung the crowbar at the back of the bully's legs.

He screamed in agony and crumpled to the ground. The ax-wielder glanced around in surprise, caught the flash of Evelyn's white shirt in the darkness, and grinned through the soot on his face. "Thanks, mate." He saluted her and returned to wrecking the ladder.

It made no sense at all. She didn't recognize the man, but in this light she would have had difficulty recognizing her mother. A fistfight a few yards away ended in one contestant sprawling along the street. A small figure immediately leapt out of the darkness, crashing headfirst into the soft belly of the victor. Jacob! The man went down with a thud, and Evelyn hurried to make certain he stayed down.

Gradually the combatants were disappearing from the scene. Several bodies lay scattered along the walk, but from the fumes rising from some of them, drunkenness had as much to do with their unconscious state as anything. The ax-wielder had disappeared, leaving the ladder in splinters. Evelyn swung around, looking for someone else to fight, but the night had grown quiet. Even the man on the ledge had given up screaming and retreated to the interior. She would have to send someone up there to have him arrested.

She exchanged glances with a weary Jacob, then looked up at the sound of a distinctly familiar voice coming toward them. "Thank goodness! You're all right. Now, where's Alex? I have a thing or two to say to that man."

Evelyn stared in astonishment as her mother hurried toward them, her petticoats whispering against the stones. Her mother never came down here anymore. And Alex? Had she lost her mind?

"Alex left with Aunt Matilda, Mama." She glanced toward the harbor where the *Minerva* had been anchored. The ship's lights had disappeared when the first of the mob poured onto the wharf bearing torches. Alex was gone. "I'll tell you about it when we get home."

Exhausted, Evelyn wiped her grimy face with her sleeve. She would have to send Jacob home with her mother, then go find someone to get the thief out of the warehouse before he could do any more damage. She scarcely registered her mother's words until they were out.

"He can't be. He's here somewhere. I saw him ride this way, and that's his horse over by Dennison's. I hope he hasn't been hurt."

Evelyn didn't try to identify the myriad emotions washing over her. Feeling a sudden weight lifting from her shoulders, she sent Jacob in one direction and she hastened in another. A man the size of Alex couldn't disappear easily.

She found him lying deathly still in the alley beside the warehouse. Crying out to the others, Evelyn dropped to her knees and searched for some sign of life.

She had never caressed him so intimately before. His flesh was warm to the touch as her fingers skimmed over the rough stubble of his beard, finding the pressure point beneath his ear. The throb of life she found there brought a tight knot to her insides. As other figures ran up to help, her hand slid through his thick dark hair, finding the stickiness of blood along his scalp. With a groan, she cursed and scarcely noticed the men scurrying to act upon her mother's orders.

"Find a wagon! We'll need to take him back to the house. Jacob, go find the doctor. Quickly!"

In her mind, Evelyn protested. He couldn't still be here. He should be on the *Minerva*, sailing out of her life. Alexander Hampton belonged in the fashionable glitter of London, not in this filthy back alley of Boston.

When the wagon arrived, she silently clambered up while the men lifted Alex's heavy body into the bed. She crossed her legs and pillowed his injured head on her lap as they jolted away. Her fingers wound through his hair, and she held herself still, as still as the man sprawled across her lap, the man who shouldn't be here.

10

"Bloody, thrice-damned idiot!" Alex grabbed his aching head and sank back upon the pillow, squeezing his eyes closed against the throbbing pain. "Damnation!" he muttered under his breath as he tried to turn his head and grope for the bottle that surely must be on the table beside him.

He hadn't drunk enough to wake with a head like this in years. He remembered all too clearly the morning he had woken to remember hiring a band of thieves to kidnap his cousin Alyson, one of the low points of his life, admittedly, although his intentions toward the heiress had been honorable. Damn, but he hadn't drunk that much since.

He squeezed his eyes tighter, trying to remember the train of events that had set off this spree. He always remembered the night before. It was the only thing that had kept him from going off the deep end years ago. The headache was degrading enough. Remembering the embarrassing atrocities committed in the name of drink was enough to make anyone swear off.

Oddly, he had no recollection of how he had got this way. That was a bad sign. The pain throbbed a little worse, and Alex felt the return of the niggling fears that haunted his nights. The guilt of thirty years of sins made the future mighty grim in the dead of night.

"Are you awake yet or do you always grimace in your sleep?"

Bigad, that seductive voice was unforgettable. Alex groaned again, remembering Evelyn's shocked face in the door of his room. Devil take it, surely he hadn't dragged her in. How else could he wake to the sound of her voice at his side? The thought of the hell to pay had he done the unpardonable caused Alex to reach tentatively over the smooth linen sheets in search of her.

His hand fell off the edge of the bed. That shocked him into opening his eyes again. He stared up into concerned violet eyes, and his breath caught in his lungs as his gaze eagerly drank in the creamy satin loveliness of her delicately sculptured features. Accented in vivid blue with hints of rose, and framed in rich, lustrous chestnut, her face alone eased his pain. He quickly ascertained that she was fully dressed and didn't appear ravaged in any way, and he let out his breath again.

Evelyn gave him a puzzled look and set the tray down on the table beside the bed. "I've brought you some apple juice. I wasn't sure if you would be ready to eat yet."

Alex covered his eyes with his hand and felt the coarseness of a day's worth of whiskers on his cheeks. "I don't suppose it's fermented?" he muttered with little hope.

"Not yet. It's too early in the season." She poured the juice and stood uncertainly at his bedside. He dwarfed the narrow bed, and she tried not to contemplate what lay beneath the thin sheet covering him. The doctor had sent her out of the room when he examined his patient. When she had come back, Alex's head had been swathed in white and his shoulders bare. She tried not to look too closely at the powerful curve of those shoulders now, nor at the dark whorls of hair peeking out from above the edge of the sheet.

"The doctor said we must keep waking you every few hours. I'm sorry if it hurts your head. He left some powder for the pain. Shall I mix it in the juice for you?"

Doctor. Alex moved his hand higher, finding the bandage held to his forehead by strips of cloth. Things were getting clearer by the minute, if not any better. "What the hell happened?"

Gingerly Evelyn lowered herself to the edge of his covers. She refused to be frightened by his size or proximity. He could scarcely do her any harm when he hadn't even the strength to keep his eyes open. "From what I've been able to determine, you and some friends of yours attacked a mob. It wasn't particularly sensible, but I thank you for it. They would have carried off half my warehouse if you hadn't arrived when you did."

He remembered now, and he groaned. The *Minerva* had sailed without him. More fool he. The soft scent of some summery fragrance enveloped him as Evelyn nervously rearranged his covers, and he felt the familiar stirring in his loins that had got him into more trouble in his lifetime than he dared admit.

Alex caught her arm and held it still as he tried opening his eyes again. She looked vaguely troubled, but his thoughts couldn't focus on anything but the incredible discovery that they were alone and he was decidedly naked beneath this sheet. If his head didn't hurt so damned much, he'd take advantage of the situation, but he didn't think she would willingly undress and accommodate him so he didn't have to move his head. Rather than endure the pain from two locations, he chose to get rid of the source of one.

"Well, if you have come to reward me for my bravery, you'll have to find a better time or bring me a keg of rum. My head hurts like hell."

"I wouldn't want to spoil your reputation by commending you," she replied tartly. "I just thought I'd keep you from dying on our hands and having to dispose of the body. The juice is on the table should you wish it. I'll be going now."

Evelyn tried to shake off his imprisoning hand, but Alex was beginning to get a grasp of the situation now, and he held her back. He wondered if she always looked this good in the early morning or if he were receiving special treatment. Deciding the latter was unlikely, he tried to imagine how she would look with that roll of lovely hair loose and tousled and tumbling about her shoulders. That thought did not diminish the growing ache in his loins.

"Where are we?" he demanded. They certainly weren't in his sparsely furnished room over the tavern, or in his well-appointed cabin on the *Minerva*.

"My mother had you brought to our house so we could look after you until you're well. Are you well yet, Mr. Hampton?"

The note of irritation almost made him smile. Almost. His testy Evelyn wasn't out to win any awards for congeniality, but she couldn't disguise the expression of concern in her eyes, nor her nervousness as his fingers began to make circling motions on her wrist. He hadn't had anyone look at him like that since he was a lad in leading strings. He rather liked the feeling, actually. Closing his eyes, he kept her fragile wrist firmly caught in the circle of his hand.

"Not yet, Miss Wellington. I think it may well be a long time before I recover. I don't suppose you sing lullabies, do you?"

She had to stifle a laugh at his outrageousness. She didn't understand why he did most of the things he did, but she knew a play for sympathy when she heard one. Daringly she pressed a kiss against his bristly cheek and whispered next to his ear, "If you don't recover soon, I'll have to marry you just to protect my reputation. I wish you speedy recovery, Mr. Hampton."

She freed herself from his loosened fingers and made a strategic retreat, leaving Alex to contemplate the soft scent of violets she left behind.

After that early-morning visit, Evelyn went down to the wharf to start the task of cleaning up the debris from the prior night, leaving her mother to tend to Alex. Troops of militia patrolled the streets, and faces wore grim expressions as the extent of the damage was surveyed. Evelyn contemplated seeing how her uncle fared, but didn't have the heart for it.

Everyone was eager to gossip, and before she reached the wharf she had a good grasp of the extent of the destruction. After emptying the wine cellars at her uncle's and the judge's, the mob had congregated at Lieutenant Governor Hutchinson's. They had torn his exquisite home to the ground, complete to the manuscript he had been working on. The house where she and Alex had danced not many nights before no longer existed.

Shuddering at the thought of what might have happened had Alex not drawn off the small mob at the warehouse, Evelyn set to work with a will. There was no sign of the *Minerva* in the harbor. Evidently it did not mean to return for Alex. She wondered at the implications of that, but until he was in some condition to speak sensibly, she would not know.

The entire day had a lingering unreality to it. Her aunt and cousin were on the way to England. The man who should have gone was still here, in their guest room. After a night of rioting, the town seemed subdued, and the troops patrolling the streets added a tinge of uneasiness. Home was no longer home anymore, but a battlefield, with people she loved taking opposite sides.

Unable to deal successfully with this mixture of emotions, Evelyn concentrated on work and hurried home at the end of the day with a deliberately blank mind. She bathed and ate and, unable to relax, offered to sit up with their patient when her mother began to yawn.

Amanda looked doubtful at the suggestion, but sensing her daughter's restless irritation, she nodded. "He has slept most of the day. I just changed the bandage. If you would look in on him occasionally to see that he doesn't run a fever, it should be all right. I left some food warming in case he wakes. You might see to the fire."

Doing as told, Evelyn then curled up with a book and a candle in her bedroom chair. Leaving her door slightly ajar, she could hear any noises from the bedroom down the hall. Jacob's room was just across the hall from the guest room, but Jacob slept like one of the dead. He would be virtually useless should Alex wake and call out.

Not that she expected Alex to do anything so sensible as calling out should he need food or water or medicine. She rather expected he would wake as he had that morning, cursing. She wondered if that were his normal way of waking. She hoped he lived alone, if so.

He really should have looked more ill and helpless than he did after the blow he had received. Instead, he had looked startlingly strong and healthy. And grubby. She smiled to herself, remembering how his usually neatly tied hair curled about his face from beneath the bandage, adding to the piratical image of his unshaven heavy black whiskers. The noble dandy would have a proper fit if he could see himself now.

Deciding she'd better check to see if he were still

breathing, she laid her book aside and quietly slipped down the hall.

She found Alex lying with hands behind head, staring at the limited view of the sky from the window beside his bed. When she entered, he turned his head to watch her, but he didn't smile or greet her in any way. Worried, Evelyn daringly came forward to lay the back of her hand against his cheek to test for fever.

"I'm fine. My head still hurts, but it's not likely to rot off anytime soon. I thought everyone was asleep."

He didn't catch her hand or make the usual insinuating suggestions or even look at her boldly. Really worried now, Evelyn clasped her hands in the folds of her gown and stared hesitantly down at the exceedingly masculine face on the pillow. When he had his hair tied in a satin bow and wore lace at his throat, he looked the part of English dandy well enough. Like this, bare-chested and with his jaw unshaven, she couldn't place him in that slot. He was a man, pure and simple, and she felt a strange nervousness at the thought.

"Only good people sleep, I guess." She made a nervous gesture that he did not see, since he wasn't looking at her. "Would you like something to eat? Mama says you haven't eaten all day."

That caught his interest, and he turned to look at her at last. "I'm starved, but I don't want to cause anyone any trouble. If there's some bread or cheese lying about . . ."

Evelyn shook her head and stared at him with incredulity. "You really are ill, aren't you? Perhaps I should call the doctor. It might not be wise to feed you too much if you're starting a fever."

Alex searched her face in the candlelight, testing her words. Realizing it was sarcasm and not feigned sympathy, he began to grin, and the grin widened appreciatively when Evelyn did not move. "Would you feel better if I cursed and demanded my supper and threatened to get up and get it if you didn't go to fetch it right now?"

Mesmerized by the sight of that charming grin he so seldom used, Evelyn answered with the first thought in her head. "I'd think you fully recovered and tell you to get it yourself, which would be a dreadful mistake." Her gaze swept knowingly over his sheet-covered nudity and back to his dark eyes. "Obviously you are not yourself yet, so I will go fetch for you. This time."

She heard his chuckle as she swept out of the room, and she blushed at her own wayward behavior. What was it about Alexander Hampton that made her act like a wanton in his presence? She was a modest person, accustomed to working with men, not flirting with them. Somehow Alex brought out a side of her that she hadn't known existed. It was a pleasurable, exciting feeling, but exceedingly dangerous to her well-being.

When she returned with the tray, she found Alex sitting on the side of the bed. He had somehow contrived to get to the wardrobe where her mother had ordered his clothing transferred. He now wore breeches and a maroon dressing robe that did not significantly disguise the breadth of his chest or the dark hair there. She avoided looking at him as she set the tray down on the table.

"That smells delicious. Don't tell me I'm not limited to rations of bread and water." He didn't attempt to rise as she entered, but held himself steady with one hand propped on the bed behind him.

"Not in my mother's house. She is thrilled to death to have another man to dote on, although I believe last night she might have hit you over the head if someone else hadn't beaten her to it." Evelyn handed Alex a napkin and hovered uncertainly. Propriety called for her to leave immediately, but she found it difficult to do. She wanted to stay and talk with him, hear his view of the past night's events. And she was not at all certain he was well enough to sit up and eat that entire meal without help.

Alex solved the problem by waiting politely for her to sit down before he touched the food. When she finally alighted on the edge of a wooden chair near the table, he reached for the mug on the tray and drank deeply, then spluttered and set it aside.

He gave her an accusing glare. "Milk? Apple juice this morning and milk tonight? Are you trying to poison me?"

Evelyn smiled in relief at this return of his normal ill

humor. "On the contrary, the doctor says it will wash the poisons from your body. As long as your head continues to hurt and you need the powders, he advises against alcohol. So you will have to heal rapidly."

He gave her cheerful expression a murderous glare. "Your mother wants to dote on me when she doesn't want to beat me over the head, and you're doing your best to get rid of me. Are things always so agreeable around this house?"

"We get along." She waited patiently for him to begin eating. It didn't seem fair to keep him talking when he must be starving, but it was a trifle awkward sitting silent while she sat in a nearly naked man's bedroom watching him eat.

When it became apparent he was more interested in the food than in her, she started to rise. "I'll leave you to your meal, then. Good night."

Alex scowled and motioned for her to sit down. "Not so fast. I'm still waiting to hear why your mother wanted to beat me over the head but changed her mind. There are a few other questions I have in mind also, but first things first." He leaned back on his hand again, studying her as he sipped gingerly at the milk.

Evelyn debated the wisdom of remaining, but he seemed weak enough not to be dangerous. She could tell from the small frown above his eyes that his head still hurt, and he was still unsteady enough to have to balance himself. She stayed seated.

"You didn't really think she would be pleased to idle away in your room while a mob threatened her children, did you? You could have given her a weapon or two and she would have been right at your side, probably preventing that nasty blow you took."

He lifted his brows in mild astonishment. "Are all females over here so intrepid? My mother would have fainted and had to be carried away before we even made it to the wharf." He didn't mention the fact that it was doubtful if his mother would have left the house to inquire after him in the first place. She would certainly have never left herself open to such a melee.

"This isn't London. We do things for ourselves here. We don't have footmen to send out to see what's happening. As it was, Mama recognized several of the men in the tavern and made them come with her, but you seemed to have done well on your own. I thought your men sailed with the *Minerva*. Whom did you have helping you?" Evelyn couldn't help asking; her curiosity had been held in check too long.

Alex shrugged. "There are a few local men on my payroll. I don't know the area well enough to make all inquiries on my own. They've been helpful." He calmly bit into a roll, leaving Evelyn to stare at him in wonder.

She was inclined to think of him as an indolent nobleman because he dressed and acted that part when they attended the necessary public functions together. But she had to remember that only a shrewd businessman could operate a firm as large as Cranville Enterprises, and a businessman would have all possibilities covered. That he had hired ruffians on his payroll was credible.

"Why didn't you go with the *Minerva*?" she finally blurted out.

Finishing the last of the food on his plate, Alex wiped his mouth and leaned back against the pillows propped at the head of the bed. His gaze wandered back to the window. "That was what I was asking myself when you came in."

So much for any romantic theories she might have secretly harbored deep in the hidden recesses of her heart. Alex wasn't a man prone to the subtleties of seduction, she suspected. He took what he wanted without any pretense. His bluntness came as no real surprise. She began to believe he would not lie to her. She wasn't sure if she wouldn't have preferred just a little lie in this instance.

Evelyn stood and picked up the tray. "Surely there will be another ship arriving soon. This way you will have time to turn your information over to the Admiralty Court. Have you found out the names of the men yet?"

Alex turned and lifted his eyes to the fair shadow of her face in the semidarkness. He could not read her expression, but there was an undercurrent of something in her voice that called to him. He resisted the pull, not believing the imaginings of his addled mind.

"No, they're more clever than I expected. The companies appear to be registered in England. I'll need the information I requested from my partners before I can confirm my suspicions."

He sounded tired, and Evelyn regretted her earlier sarcasm. "I'm sorry I ever suspected you of smuggling. We'll do our best to make you comfortable until a ship arrives." She backed against the door, pushing it open so she could leave with her hands full of tray and utensils. His hollow reply stopped her in the doorway.

"It will have to be a Cranville vessel, my dear. The *Minerva* sailed with the last of my funds."

Was that a hint of challenge in his voice, or just his usual sarcasm? Evelyn hurried out without inquiring further.

11

"What are you doing in here?" Evelyn hastily tucked the rest of her shirt into her breeches as she swung around to find Alex leaning against the doorjamb. The doctor had examined his wound earlier and announced it healing nicely, but Alex still wore a small bandage wrapped above his eye.

"I'm tired of playing the part of invalid. Have all evening activities come to a crashing halt since the riots, that you must occupy your time working at night?" He gave her boy's clothing a disparaging look.

"You would certainly look dashing with that bandage dancing through a ballroom and fainting at the first reel," she said loftily, annoyed with herself for not having closed the door tightly. "You don't have to worry about it, though. Since the governor is still in hiding and Hutchinson's house has been demolished and my uncle has quit entertaining, there is little in the way of society these days. The militia patroling the streets might have something to do with the lack of interest in frivolity."

Alex ignored the sharpness of her words in favor of the information offered. This last week imprisoned in the upper-story rooms of the Wellington household had left him sadly without contacts to the outer world. Jacob and Evelyn weren't always the most communicative of souls.

"I thought you said they caught McIntosh. Surely they're not afraid of more riots with the ringleader behind bars."

Evelyn reached for her jerkin while covertly studying Alex's sculptured features. He hadn't precisely been a model patient this past week, but he had been rather more subdued than she had expected. She suspected his graciousness was for her mother's benefit. He seemed a bit in awe of her. He reserved his boredom and irritation for Evelyn.

It suddenly occurred to her that she had the means to keep Alex royally entertained until one of his ships arrived to rescue him. He obviously had a penchant for getting himself embroiled in trouble, and she knew the best troublemakers in town. The question was, did she dare introduce him to the radical ideas they espoused?

Carefully she watched his expression as she reported, "McIntosh was released days ago."

Alex straightened and stared at her as if she were crazed. "You're joking. Jacob said he was the one who led the mob from the State House to the judge's and then to Hutchinson's. There can't be two men out there who look like that."

Evelyn shrugged. "Do you want to be the man responsible for holding someone who can control a mob?"

"How can he control anything from behind bars?" Alex's astonishment turned to suspicion as he finally detected the wary look in her eyes. "There's something you're not telling me. There has been all along. Where are you going, dressed in that costume?"

He had helped her and her family when he didn't have to. He had endured her uncle's insults, protected her with his name, and rescued Jacob from thieves—all greatly against his will, she suspected. Still, she didn't think Alex capable of spying. He was an Englishman with no notion of what it was like to be a colonist. Maybe it was about time he learned.

"To meet some friends. Would you like to come?"

Alex read the challenge in her eyes well enough. She was about to get him into something particularly unpleasant. But he couldn't resist the opportunity to get out of the house any more than he could resist the temptation of her slender curves in breeches. He replied with his usual rashness. "Do I need to wear a costume?"

Evelyn grinned, a laughing, dancing curve of her lips that illuminated the hollows of her cheeks and made her eyes shine like summer. Alex had all he could do to keep from sweeping her into his arms and laughing with her.

Only the knowledge that such an action would immediately wipe the smile from her face checked his impulse.

"I think the pirate look will suffice." She sobered somewhat as she asked, "Are you certain you are well enough? I don't want you stumbling down the stairs and breaking your leg. I don't think I could bear your temper for as long as it takes a leg to heal."

"If I break my leg, I will arrange for it to be elsewhere so I needn't endure the temptation of your charming insults." Alex hooked his arm over Evelyn's shoulder and made a great display of limping along beside her as they turned toward the stairs.

"You're an insufferable cad," she said coolly as he caught the banister but continued to rest his arm on her shoulders.

"I'll pay you back in kisses later," he whispered wickedly in her ear as they descended.

From below, Amanda Wellington watched in horror as her breeches-clad daughter swung her fist at their injured guest's stomach. Only his howl of laughter prevented her interfering. The young certainly had strange ways of courting, she decided as she turned back toward the kitchen. In her day, they would have dressed in their best finery and fluttered fans and made elegant legs while exchanging extravagant flattery. How odd that things could change so much in the space of a few decades. Or perhaps it was this new country.

Alex frowned. Evelyn evidently intended to lead him into a dockside tavern. He caught her arm and held her back. "Have you taken leave of your senses? You can't go in there. Even in that garb, no one is going to mistake you for a man."

Evelyn lifted a corner of her mouth in a smirk as she met his dark gaze. "Oh? Am I not tall enough? I haven't got your shoulders, I admit, but I think I make a passable boy."

"Even a blind man could see you are no boy. You curve in all the wrong places and smell of violets. And if this is your way of seeking flattery, I'm too out of patience to offer more."

From Alex, that was exceptional flattery, and Evelyn

grinned a little more at drawing that much from him. She curved in all the wrong places. Lud, but he'd have her head spinning with such sweet phrases! "I thank you for your gracious compliments, sir, but I can assure you I will be perfectly safe in here. Skirts are a little obvious, and they're rather nervous about having females around as it is. So I sit quietly in the corner and blend into the woodwork. You'll see."

"Dammit all, Evelyn, I didn't bring sword and pistol to protect your virtue in a place like this. I won't see. The jest is over. Let's go back."

She neatly sidestepped his grasping hand, opened the tavern door, and walked in. He could stay behind if he liked, but this was the first time the committee had agreed she could sit in on their meeting. She had ripped Sam Adams up one side and down the other for McIntosh's behavior with his personal vendetta. He owed her this.

Of course, this was only an informal gathering. She wouldn't have dared to bring Alex to one of their closed meetings. Here, he could just see her as meeting with friends, as she had said. He could make what he would of the discussion.

Pilgrim greeted her with a jovial grin and a few of the other, younger men lifted their mugs in recognition as Evelyn took a bench by the fireplace near the table where they were seated. Their grins disappeared as the broad frame of the Englishman appeared behind her. In the dim light of smoking oil lamps and candles, the table of patriots watched this heir to an earldom with suspicion.

"Miss Wellington, you did not tell us you were bringing a visitor." Sam Adams sat back in his chair and pulled on his pipe, his hand trembling with the palsy that sometimes afflicted him.

"Is this not an open discussion? Don't you think it's time that some of your complaints be heard by someone who might be in a position to do something about them?"

Alex glared from the slender figure by the hearth to the gray-haired, ill-dressed man at the table. He had known the little brat was going to get him into trouble. He still wasn't certain of the cause, but he could smell the source a mile away. He waited for the older man to speak as he closed his hands over the back of a vacant chair.

"Not a blamed Tory, Miss Wellington! That's the trouble with females, they don't think with their heads. You don't understand politics." He turned his gaze on the intruder. "Mr. Hampton, I apologize for the lady's mistake. You will not find our company very congenial."

The old man knew his name. That was interesting. Judging by the tense faces around the table, the others allowed this man to sit in judgment. Alex wasn't fond of dictators, and he suspected Evelyn had her reasons for bringing him where he was clearly unwanted. He swung the chair around and sat down.

"On the contrary, I am eager to meet friends of my fiancée's, particularly if they can tell me why her establishment was attacked the other night." That was a wild guess, but the guilt registering on several faces told him he'd struck a point. He waved his hand to the barmaid for a mug.

"It won't happen again, I assure you, Mr. Hampton. The Wellingtons are a respected family in this community. An error was made, as occasionally happens due to the human element."

Alex glanced to Evelyn to see if she caught that revelation. The old man was insinuating the riots could be controlled. She didn't seem to be surprised. He took a sip of his ale while he formulated a reply.

"Dealing with mobs involves more human element than is safe around women and children. Mrs. Upton and her daughter were set upon by thieves. Isn't there a more orderly manner of accomplishing your objectives?"

Adams sat back and let one of the younger men plunge into the much-debated subject. "We have tried proper channels, Mr. Hampton. Has Evelyn told you nothing? The representatives of all the colonies have sent formal letters of protest. Our own royally appointed governor and lieutenant governor have objected. No one listens. If polite argument won't work, what else is there? Parliament must be made to see that the entire populace objects to these chains around our necks. We will not accept tyranny!"

Evelyn watched as fascination warred with cynical amusement on the face of her "fiancé" as the discussion grew more heated. She didn't know what kind of life Alex led in England, but she doubted that it included radical political discussions. He had too active a mind not to be caught up in the possibilities being suggested here tonight. He would have laughed had she suggested them. The knowledge that these men sitting at this table could control a mob hooked him much more firmly than she could have on her own.

By the time they left the tavern, Alex was furious, but it was a fury gained of fomenting ideas. When they reached the street, he gripped her upper arm with a painful grasp.

"What are you doing involved with men like that?"

It was useless to try to jerk free from that powerful hold, so Evelyn simply kept on walking, forcing him to keep up with her or rip her arm off. "What do you mean, 'men like that'? They're friends of my father's, friends of mine. They are respectable, intelligent people. Have you friends who are any better?"

Since he had cut himself off from his drinking, gambling, whoring acquaintances some years ago when he went into trade, Alex could not respond adequately. He still found it hard to deal with the idea of a lady in breeches. To think of her in terms of friend to radical Whigs was almost beyond his capacity. For the better part of his adult life he'd had only one use for women, and the word "friend" did not apply to it.

"They might have been your father's drinking buddies, but they are no friends to you if they entangle you in their seditious activities. You would do well to stay away from them."

Evelyn turned in fury at the patronizing tone of Alex's voice. Why had she ever thought to find understanding in a dunderheaded Tory? "Then perhaps you would do well to stay away from me. I am not a child or a fool. I am as capable of reasoning as you are. More so, obviously. You have no right to dictate to me."

Angry women, Alex understood. Generally, it was just simpler to walk out on them, but he had no desire to leave this one alone. Knowing what he had in mind would make her even more furious, he couldn't resist the temptation of flashing eyes and taut curves tensed for battle. The fight he had in mind had naught to do with words.

Alex's arm whipped around Evelyn's waist and lifted her into the darkness of a nearby alley, where his lips bent to silence their argument in the best manner known to him.

Evelyn instinctively pounded on Alex's rock-hard chest with both fists as his mouth closed over hers, but she couldn't summon the strength to turn her head away from his seeking lips. His hands left her waist and captured her fists, holding them to the heated strength of his chest while his lips closed over hers. When she refused to succumb to his pressure, he teased light kisses along her mouth until she was leaning into him, seeking more. This time when he asked for entrance, she gave it. The torment of his touch left no strength of her own; she felt the excitement race clear to her toes, draining away all protest.

The touch of Alex's tongue shook Evelyn's very foundations, and from the sudden tension in the muscles beneath her hands, it did not leave Alex unaffected either. His arms returned to her back, pulling her closer, fitting her against him as their kisses deepened and strained for some closer joining. The sheer impossibility of what their bodies wanted brought tears to Evelyn's eyes. When they began to course down her cheeks, Alex discovered them with wonder, kissing away their saltiness, releasing her mouth while still holding her close.

"Don't cry, little tyrant. I didn't mean to hurt you."

There was almost remorse in his voice, and instead of pulling away, Evelyn rested her head on his broad shoulder, clinging to this moment of closeness. Alex held her lightly, rubbing his hand up and down her back, and she wished they could stand this way for eternity. She discovered a most terrible need to be held this way, to feel the support of someone as strong as she, and she could not immediately summon the necessary anger to break the hold.

Alex felt the satin-soft brush of her hair against his cheek and marveled at the sensation. He had never held a woman in innocence, with only just the need to comfort her. He had time to absorb the tiny sensations, the sweetness of her breath, the silkiness of her cheek. The lust was still there, but muted somehow by the discovery of her tears. She fitted so perfectly into his arms, curving into him in all the right places despite his height, that he was reluctant to end his hold without fully exploring this novelty. He pressed a kiss above her ear and allowed his hand to slide to the tempting curve of her rounded bottom.

"We have a problem here, my darling." The drawl in his voice was mocking, but the mockery was for himself. When she tried to push away, he gentled her with soft strokes. "Don't be angry again. I'm trying to learn. It just takes some getting used to."

Evelyn turned to stare up at him in wonder, wishing there was light to better see his face. The blur in the darkness revealed only a slight twist to the lips that had so recently destroyed her. She spread her palms flat against the linen on Alex's chest and tilted her head back to observe him better. "I'm angry with myself," she whispered. "We had better go home now."

She made no move to leave his arms, and Alex didn't know whether to be relieved or annoyed. She made it impossible for him to think. His only impulse was to hold her and never let go. "That's an excellent idea. Do you remember how to get there?"

Evelyn laughed softly, feeling joy rippling through her that he was as lost as she in this new discovery. It didn't seem possible. It was totally insane. In the morning they would wake and come to their senses. Right now, she didn't want it to end. "Home is somewhere out there on the other side of the moon. Perhaps if we tried walking, we might find it."

"I fear not, but I'm willing to try if you'll stay by my side. I don't want to go alone." Alex wrapped his hand firmly around one of hers and held her gaze, willing her to understand what he could not fathom himself. All his life he'd been empty inside. Now suddenly, strangely, he'd begun to feel again.

She touched his bandage with her free hand and smiled

softly. "I think the blow affected your brains, sir. You had best not be left unattended."

With a wry smile he made a leg and gestured with his hand to the street. "Shall we go, then, my lady?"

Keeping her hand securely in the embrace of his, Evelyn followed him back to the cobblestone street. This feeling was too new and too fragile for words.

"I have a mad cousin by the name of Alyson who believes the moon drives us to strange notions. Moon dreams, she calls them. Do you think she may be right?"

"Almost certainly. Daylight ought to be a cure. Shall we write to your cousin and ask?"

"The reply is not likely to be sensible, and I have a feeling sensibility is required here." Alex squinted upward and found the sliver of moon overhead. That particle of light couldn't be sufficient to drive men mad. Rationality was already returning.

Evelyn felt it too, and she sighed. "Is your cousin truly mad? It might be the better way to be."

"On the whole, I daresay you're right. Alyson is utterly content in her own little world. She lives on the outer borders of nowhere in the heathen hills of the Highlands with an equally mad Scot and two holy terrors and an assortment of ferocious characters who would make Blackbeard shiver. And she loves it. In her case, madness is a definite benefit."

Evelyn couldn't wipe the smile from her face. He spoke nonsense just to keep from thinking of the impossibilities, but she couldn't help enjoying it. For just this one perfect moment, they were in harmony. She would enjoy it while it lasted. "I wish I could meet her. Perhaps her happiness could be contagious."

The mood slithered away faster than Alex could grasp it. Ugly reality had a way of rearing its head too often for him to indulge in flights of fantasy. He shook his head and felt the dull ache return. "Not for us. We've been inoculated with common sense. Alyson's husband once said Alyson would go happily to meet her death. The two of us would fight death every inch of the way. There have to be people like us to protect the Alysons of the world."

Death wasn't the only thing they would fight. Evelyn

understood the import of his words. Their argument of earlier would be only one of many. They were too different, too far apart in their thinking to ever get along with even a modicum of agreement. Their kisses were only a mad flight into fantasy. She knew that; she just had a hard time accepting it.

"Shall I disagree with you and give us something new to argue about?" She lifted her eyes to meet his and caught his rueful grin.

"It's a topic I'm willing to argue but not eager to win. I've never kissed a lady in breeches before. Do you think we might try it just one more time before the moon goes down?"

They had wandered to the enveloping shadows of the grove of elms and the Liberty Tree. The first leaves were just turning yellow, but the shadows were deep and welcoming. Without a word, Evelyn turned and came into his arms and surrendered her sanity for the sake of a dream. Rebellious dreams, perhaps, but joyous ones.

Alex's lips were both gentle and hungry as they touched hers. There had to be a time and place for the two of them. Evelyn wrapped her arms around his strong neck and felt herself caught up in his embrace. If only now could be the time. She parted her lips and twined her fingers in his dark hair. Now. She needed him now.

She closed her eyes and drank deeply of the strong wine of his caress as the moon spread its silver tentacles along the canopy of trees.

12

Evelyn dug her fingers into her hair and stared blankly at the ledger page as she had for hours. Her brain had ceased to function, but still she sat there contemplating figures that could have been hieroglyphics for all she cared. The fight with Alex this morning before she left had unnerved her more than she had thought humanly possible.

What did she care if he went bankrupt moving into a tavern where he couldn't pay the fare? Let him starve on pride if he liked. He would hurt her mother's feelings tremendously if he moved out, but no more than they both would when Amanda discovered their deception. Her mother already thought of the Englishman as her son-in-law. The pain would be mortifying when she discovered they had no intention of marrying. How had she got herself caught in such a coil?

Her stomach contracted in knots as she thought of the night before. That was the reason Alex was moving out, she knew. It was impossible to live in the same house and remember those kisses and not reach out for more. She groaned inwardly and covered her eyes with her hand. How had she let him go so far? Her flesh burned with the memory of his touch, betraying her anger. She could feel the tips of her breasts rubbing against the fabric of her cotton chemise, aching for the brush of his hand. The coil in her stomach burned hotter, spreading its wickedness through her midsection. Alex had known he was doing this to her, the dirty, rotten seducer. She ought to be glad he was gone.

She slammed the ledger closed and looked for some

physical activity that would drive out these demons he had implanted in her blood. No man had ever made her feel this way. No man ever would again. She had to find something to do.

The tramp of soldiers coming down the street momentarily distracted her. The militia had little or no formal training except what some of them had learned in the war against the French and Indians. They seldom patrolled in anything resembling an orderly manner. This steady rhythm indicated trained troops. She had thought the main body of redcoats out on the island fort with the governor. What occasion had brought them to town?

Before her thoughts had firmly reached "general warrant" to wonder what poor soul's house was to be ransacked now, the office door burst open and she was staring into the cold eyes of a British officer.

"Miss Evelyn Wellington?" he demanded without inflection, already reaching into his pocket for the piece of paper that gave him freedom to search as he willed.

Evelyn stared in horror as the paper appeared. She had never found any way of disposing of those last two crates of brandy. Surely they would never find it on that high shelf in crates of porcelain. She nodded slowly.

"The whole town is beginning to talk! I say we cry the banns now. You cannot continue living in the same house with my niece without declaring your intentions. In three more weeks, you may have heard from Cranville and the wedding can be held immediately." George Upton paced the parlor furiously. The library had been closed and boarded up since the night of the riots.

Alex leaned against the mantel with a bored air, but his eyes narrowed shrewdly at the older man's continued nervous pacing. "I have already informed Mrs. Wellington of my intention to move out now that I have recovered my health. Unfortunately, there is the small matter of paying my way, since your wife and daughter sailed with my purse. If you could advance me their fares, I'll remove myself immediately from your niece's home."

"That won't do . . . that won't do at all! I must think of Evelyn's welfare. She is headstrong and does not realize the damage she has caused her family by consorting with radicals and garbing herself like a man. Now this! No, it won't do at all. The two of you were seen last night coming out of that tavern together. The banns must be cried immediately." Upton stopped his pacing long enough to face the idle young fop with his dandified clothes and walking stick. His glare was meant to force the issue.

Upton found it returned with an even more intimidating black stare. Alex lifted his shoulders from the mantel and stood up to his full, broad-shouldered height. "In all due respect, I think not, sir. I will be at the King's Arms; you may send your fare there. Evelyn plans to be involved in auctioning off some unpaid consignments these next weeks. I thought I would lend my hand. If you are concerned about what people may say, we would be glad of your help."

Alex stalked past the livid figure of Evelyn's uncle and out the door. Had he turned, he would have seen Upton turning pale and reaching for quill and ink with shaking hand. Unfortunately, he was too upset with himself and this new turn of events to care what the old rogue was about. If Upton were involved with the smuggling and the warehouse, as he suspected, this small warning should return his senses. Didn't the man realize the harm he could do his family by playing in the same dangerous circles as smugglers and thieves? He had no patience with fools like that.

Still ranting and raving to himself about a man who would endanger the ones closest to him for the sake of money, Alex progressed toward the tavern he had chosen for his newest abode. He wouldn't go back to the one in sight of Evelyn's warehouse. He would be at the window every day looking for some sight of her. And then he would be straining his brain to find some way to invite her to his rooms. He knew himself too well, and he was beginning to know Evelyn even better. Her kisses meant one thing and his meant another. They never shared a common ground.

He didn't want to hurt her, but that was all he would accomplish if he lingered where he could see her every day. She didn't even bolt her doors. The thought of that open invitation just down the hall had driven him to madness for what little night remained after he had brought her home. She wouldn't have stopped him if he had come to her during the night. They had both been so caught up in their lust that sense would not have returned until too late. He had to take precautions against that happening again. He had a good deal more experience than she. It was his duty to be the responsible one, particularly since she would think their lovemaking meant marriage and he had no intention of binding himself to anyone. Resolutely he continued on to the King's Arms.

Alex returned to the Wellington home at noon to collect his clothing. Amanda Wellington fluttered and protested, but it was as much for her sake as her daughter's that he had to move out. He liked the woman too well to hurt her by dishonoring her daughter, and he felt shame at the deceit he had forced on them both. It had been his idea to carry out this mock betrothal, and even to himself he had to admit that his intentions at the time had not been precisely honorable. It had been an easy solution to her uncle's protests, but he could have let the old carrion try to put him in jail. Instead, he had opted for the pleasure of being thrown in the constant company of the very tempting and very passionate Miss Wellington. Damned if he didn't get into more trouble when he let his loins do the thinking.

He had accepted Amanda's peace offering of tea when Jacob came crashing through the front door screaming at the top of his lungs. Alex could make no sense of his words, but he rose hastily at the noise. The woman's face paling across from him made his heart skitter and jump. He grabbed Jacob by the collar as he came flying through the kitchen door.

"Speak slowly and stop screaming, lad. You're scaring your mother." To Alex's surprise, Jacob threw himself wildly into his arms.

"They took Evelyn! The redcoats came, and they tore up the warehouse, and they took Evelyn! You've got to get her! Hurry, please, before they take her away. They'll hang her like they hanged Tommy Jones." He grabbed Alex's hands and pulled with the strength of terror, nearly unbalancing the much larger man.

Amanda rose shakily, bracing her hands against the

table. "Quiet down now, Jacob, you're talking nonsense. Tommy Jones was a dangerous smuggler who outran the law once too many times. Evelyn never smuggled anything."

Jacob threw Alex an anguished look. "You know. They found the brandy and all sorts of things. They knew just where to look. There was Madeira and coffee and I don't know what all hidden in some of those kegs. Evelyn didn't put them there. I know she didn't."

Alex felt the emptiness return, the blank fury with which he had faced the world for so long. Evelyn might have done it, for all he knew. She might have used him as women so often tried. She could be guilty as hell. He didn't care. He just didn't intend to let her rot in a common jail cell with thieves and other fiends while her damned uncle continued to roam the streets.

Without a word, he walked through the house to the street. The man he had hired to wheel his trunk back to the inn watched in astonishment as Alex strode off without a word of instruction, swinging his fancy walking stick as if he meant to whip anyone in his way. Jacob tore after him, his small legs doing twice the work to match Alex's long strides.

At South Church, Alex met Sam Adams hurrying from the State House. The thunderous fury on Alex's face brought the older man to a halt even before Alex had time to block his path. His gray head tipped back in surprise as he heard Alex's words and searched his face for expression.

"If you're going to put your damned mob to good use, you'd better call them together tonight if I don't get Miss Wellington out of whatever hellhole they've put her in. If you're going to protest, protest something practical, like imprisoning innocent citizens."

Adams shook himself off and dusted his already dirty coat as if Alex had physically assaulted him. Then in cold tones he addressed the younger man. "That is exactly what we have been protesting, but we do it for the sake of all the people, not just one. We'll be at Faneuil Hall tonight. If you're ready to see reason, you're welcome to join us."

Alex wasn't in any humor to argue the fine points of

democracy. Tucking away the name of the meeting place in case of need, he hurried on to the British garrison nearest the warehouse. He had no high opinion of mankind in general, whether they wore red coats or called themselves Whigs or Tories. He just prayed Evelyn had fallen into the hands of someone who had at least made some pretense of being a gentleman. He didn't want to think about what could happen to a woman in the hands of a randy brigade of soldiers.

His curt questions and authoritative mien brought him to the office of the battery commander. The man behind the desk ignored him as Alex entered, but he couldn't ignore the violent rap of the fashionable cane as Alex whipped it across the wood beside him.

Looking up and finding himself addressing a fashionable London macaroni with a look of livid fury on his noble face, the officer reluctantly rose to his feet in case some gesture of respect was called for.

"Where is Miss Wellington?" Alex had learned the trick of physical intimidation long ago, but he had found it unnecessary with a certain level of thinking. As the next Earl of Cranville, he held considerable sway over the opinions of that kind of mentality, and he could read the signs of reluctant respect in this one's eyes even before he identified himself. Alex swung his walking stick back to his side and frowned imperiously. "Don't just stand there, man. When your superiors find you have taken an innocent female into custody, they will have your commission."

"Miss Wellington is under arrest. She cannot be released without the authority of the judge."

"She will be released, and this minute, or you will find yourself before a judge. I came here on behalf of the Earl of Cranville to investigate the reported atrocities of his majesty's finest against loyal colonists. I did not believe the charges until now. You are holding an innocent woman, Captain. If you don't release her, I'll have you charged with complicity and bring the judge down here to order your arrest. I wish to see Miss Wellington immediately."

The officer had identified him by now, and his Adam's apple bobbed nervously as he glanced from the earl's heir to a door leading into the back of the building. "She is being kept comfortably, sir. I have no power to release her. She will come before the judge in the morning to decide whether there is sufficient evidence to warrant a trial. If she is innocent, she will be released then."

Alex's lips tightened. "You misunderstand me, Captain. The lady will be released now or you will come before the judge in the morning. Is my meaning clear now?"

Confusion warred with fear on the soldier's face. He was accustomed to taking orders from superior officers, and an heir to an earldom was certainly more superior than any officer. Yet he had made the arrest and knew the lady's guilt. Reason and justice demanded she be held. Fear for his lucrative commission and his freedom cried that she be released.

"Perhaps bond can be arranged," he equivocated. "Let me send a messenger to my officer to set an amount. The lady will still have to come before the judge in the morning."

Alex's only wish at the moment was to get Evelyn out of that cell. If anyone were going to hang her, it would be him. Reaching for the quill and ink on the man's desk, he gestured impatiently. "Give me some paper, Captain. I'll give you my note for a thousand pounds. That should be sufficient to cover all charges the lady could possibly be held on."

A note hadn't precisely been what had been on his mind, but to reject Hampton's signature would be an insult requiring satisfaction. The officer hastily provided the paper requested.

Five minutes later a subdued Evelyn was led into the office. She had worn one of her drab gowns to the warehouse that day, and her hair was simply tied in a loop at her nape. None of the fire and passion of which she was capable seemed apparent as she stepped into the military office. Even when she discovered Alex standing there in all his finery, her eyes remained blank and full of pain.

This was no smuggler, but a beaten woman. He had let her down by not finding the smugglers before they endangered her. Alex gritted his teeth to keep from saying something rash to the damned puppy waiting for praise for his quick action.

Nodding curtly at the officer, Alex held out his arm for Evelyn to take. "I will see that you are not mentioned unfavorably in my report, Captain. Your superior officer will bear the consequences of this outrage."

He caught Evelyn's hand against his arm and stiffly led her out, fighting his fury. He had her back. Now what could he do?

Jacob let out a whoop of joy and ran to embrace his sister. She gave him a faint smile, touched his hair, but gave no answers to his eager questions.

Worried, Alex set the lad to a task to occupy his high spirits. "Go send for your uncle's carriage, Jacob. Evelyn and I will wait for you over on those benches." He indicated a place near a closed shop where the building's shade cast the street in shadow.

The boy ran eagerly to do as told, and Alex settled them out of sight of passersby. Evelyn offered no argument to his decision to use the closed carriage to transport her back across town.

"Jacob said they found other contraband besides the brandy. Did you know it was there?" That was a fool question even in his own ears, but he had to bring up the topic somehow.

"And if I did?" She gave him a bitter smile, the first sign of spirit she had shown since her release.

"Dammit, Evelyn, you scared hell out of me! Don't look at me as if I'm judge and jury. Are you all right? They didn't hurt you, did they?"

"Just my pride." Sighing, she stared down at her hands. Alex in his elegant silk coat and expensive lace was a man beyond her world. She didn't even know what he was doing here. Surely a few stolen kisses didn't obligate him to bribe government officials.

"That makes two of us, then. I didn't think your uncle would let your precious reputation be touched. I thought you would be safe. So much for my understanding of the criminal mind." Alex wanted to hold her, but he kept his distance. She was still in a state of shock, and he still had enough scruples not to take advantage of the situation.

Evelyn sent him a curious look. "Are you saying my uncle was involved in my arrest or that he did not involve himself when he should have?"

"I am saying nothing. I have no proof. I do not trust or like the man, and we argued rather fiercely this morning. I feel as if my words triggered some reaction. I told him you intended to auction off your unpaid consignments. I had hoped if he were involved that would serve as warning that the game was up. It looks to me as if he chose to call my bluff."

"Oh, lud." Evelyn grimaced and stared out at the empty street. "If he is truly involved, Aunt Matilda will die of the shame. And Frances will never make the respectable match she has her heart set on. They have no funds of their own, only Uncle George's. My mother's family is puffed with pride but has little wealth. It would break my mother's heart to think she encouraged her sister to come here, only to sink her beyond reproach."

"I'd rather see him behind bars than you." Alex scornfully dismissed this conception of family pride. His family had been splintered for generations. He saw little reason for Evelyn's to stick together over such an issue.

"I'd rather see neither of us there. You cannot imagine the humiliation, Alex. I'm not sure I can ever hold my head up again. What happens if the judge finds me guilty tomorrow?"

That was a point he didn't want to consider too closely just yet. If he had a ship in port, he would just put her on it and sail away. Cut off from family and funds as he was, his only influence was himself. He was not at all certain that his influence was the kind a respectable woman needed.

The carriage arrived before Alex had time to answer. He handed Evelyn in, gave Jacob, beside the driver, a nod of approval, and climbed in to join her.

"I'll go talk to your lawyer this afternoon. Then perhaps I can track this judge down. I'll find out what I can. Don't worry about it until you have to. There has to be some kind of trial before they can sentence you. We have time." Alex reached to take her hand, feeling safe to do so in the privacy of the coach. The interior was too small for little more.

"You shouldn't have to do this. It really is not your concern, Alex. I appreciate your thoughtfulness, but perhaps I ought to be the one to look after myself. You don't have to keep up appearances for my sake."

Alex angrily withdrew his hand and looked as if he would slap her. Evelyn sat back in astonishment at this reaction to what she had meant to be a release from their deception. He had the perfect excuse to end their mock betrothal now. She had not expected him to find the thought offensive.

"You really do believe me a cad, don't you, Miss Wellington?"

They were back to formal titles again. Evelyn hid her dismay as she stared at her hands. "No. I only believe you have been caught up in something that you would not normally be involved in because of me. I don't wish to be the cause of trouble for you."

"I am perfectly capable of finding my own trouble. You need not protect me. Few others care to curry my acquaintance for other than selfish reasons. I thought we had a better understanding than that. If I am wrong, I will remove myself from your acquaintance at once."

He spoke curtly and with every appearance of arrogance, but Evelyn heard the hurt and wondered at it. A man like Alexander Hampton should have an enormous circle of friends and family. Why, then, did he sound so lonely?

"I did not want to cause you any scandal that would put you in trouble with your cousin," she replied quietly. "I would do the same for any friend."

He unbent slightly and favored her with a grimace that would have to pass for a smile. "Then allow me to do as I see fit. Go in, comfort your mother, take a bath and do whatever ladies do to relax, and let me play the part of anxious fiancé. I have a little more experience in avoiding jails than you do."

When the carriage came to a halt, Alex assisted Evelyn out and led her into the arms of her mother. No further mention was made of his moving out as he took his leave of the tearful women.

That night, after Alex returned to dine and inform them of the progress of his day's activities, Evelyn watched from her bedroom window as he departed on still another errand. He had discarded his walking stick and elegant silk coat in favor of broadcloth, and he walked away from the house with purposeful strides.

Why had he made inquiries into the activities at Faneuil Hall?

13

Mid-September 1765

Evelyn glanced up from her ledgers as Alex entered the tiny office. She wore a creased and dusty apron over an indigo gown of light wool, and her hair had tumbled down in glinting strands of reddish-brown over one ear. She rubbed at a smudge of dirt she felt on her forehead, missing the one across her cheek. When he cracked a small grin, she gave him a look of irritation. He was a picture of immaculate finery, as usual.

"If you just came to laugh at those of us who must work for a living, you may leave right now. I'm in no humor to endure your jests." In truth, that odd little lopsided smile made her heart lurch with longing. He so seldom smiled that her fingers ached to trace the wonder of it.

In the past few weeks Alex had been all that was proper, a fact she greeted with mixed emotions. The strain of preparing for the trial had left her nerves ragged and her emotions teetering on the brink of chaos. She longed for the comfort of his arms but knew she had no right to ask it of him. The situation was too volatile for common sense. She would only harm herself, and him, to indulge in the needs of the flesh. Still, she reveled in these small moments when he looked upon her with what almost appeared to be fondness.

"I only came to admire your loveliness, little tyrant. Would you deny me that pleasure?" Alex came around the counter and smoothed the straying strands of silken hair behind her ear; then, licking his finger, he scrubbed the smudge from her cheek. "It's rather like discovering the beauty of a Greek ruin after the dirt is scrubbed off."

His touch released something light in her that she had not felt in weeks, and Evelyn laughed at his nonsense. "Greek ruin? Thank you, my beloved. Your flattery always leaves me speechless."

Alex's grin grew a little wider as he leaned back on one elbow against her high desk and admired her laughter. "Obviously I don't flatter you enough, then. I've come to walk you home. Those books will still be there in the morning."

The laughter fled and she turned on her high stool to stare at the neat lines of inked figures. "The auction is in the morning. I need to know exactly how many blocks must be sold off to meet those debts most pressing. There are some who have come to me and begged that theirs not be sold. They are trying to raise the funds to pay me."

"Then let them pay you by the morrow or do not worry about them," Alex responded coldly, lifting her from the stool. "You must learn to be businesslike about this. You have enough problems of your own without taking on those of others."

Evelyn stepped from the tingling sensation of his hands but took his arm and allowed herself to be led from the office. What he said was essentially true, but she had no real desire to be ruthless. On her own, she would never be any great success as a businesswoman, but she had Jacob to think of also. For his sake, she must learn to be more practical.

"Thomas has not found any new way of presenting my case?" She knew Alex had been at the lawyer's office. He always dressed more carefully when he had a problem to confront. She straightened a bit of lace at his throat that had become dislodged when he lifted her down.

Alex's expression was grim as he helped her lock the door. "We simply don't have enough evidence to make it convincing. I've had the court send men to search the warehouses the brandy was taken to, but they came back empty-handed. I still have no names to charge the crime to. I have ridden out with the men to help in the search and question the owners of those storage places, but they are uncommunicative and unhelpful. Without evidence against them, there is nothing further I can do. I will testify on your behalf. We will present the invoices ordering the goods that the contraband came in and show that it's the same four companies who made all the orders, but none of that is sufficient to prove your innocence. I've done you no favor by playing the part of fiancé all these weeks. My testimony would be more effective were I impartial."

Evelyn's fingers closed more tightly around his arm. "Nothing you could have done would have freed me from this coil. I've rather enjoyed being courted by a notorious rake, although you really have not kept up your role very well lately."

There was small humor behind the curve of his mouth. "My dangerous pursuits of late have been of a more subtle kind. Were I in London, I would be looked upon with horror."

"What are they discussing now?" She did not need explanation of his pursuits or to clarify their identity. Alex's attendance at the Sons of Liberty meetings had been something of a sore point between them. She had been forbidden to attend any but the open meetings and Alex had frowned on those. He, on the other hand, was welcomed by some of the more enlightened members who sought the influence he might wield on return to England.

"They are continuing with their plans for a congress of all the colonies to band together against the Stamp Act, although it seems a trifle late to me. They should have done that when the act was first proposed."

"Better late than never," Evelyn intoned gloomily. She had lost concern for these political arenas in the face of her more personal loss. Any actions taken now would be too late for her, any way she looked at it.

Alex glanced down at Evelyn with concern. She had become more withdrawn these last weeks since the judge had declared there was sufficient evidence to support a trial. The bond he had offered kept her out of jail as much as her name and sex, but the moment of decision was close at hand. Henderson had told him the possible penalties if she were found guilty. None of them were pleasant.

He looked back at the harbor, where the only vessels in evidence were a navy frigate, a few fishing boats, and some American traders. He had wild thoughts of abducting her and carrying her off to safety, but Evelyn wouldn't think much of his notions of safety. He didn't think much of them either. They included insane fantasies of Evelyn alone with him in a ship's cabin with only a bed for furniture. Damn, but it seemed he behaved like a lustful schoolboy whenever she was around.

Alex turned his gaze back to the proud tilt of Evelyn's head at his shoulder. She walked with the straight stance and hauteur of a duchess now, but he had seen her smile and greet one of the chimney sweeps roaming the street in the same manner as she would himself or the governor. She was an amazing contradiction in so many ways that he could no longer think of her with any certainty at all. It had been much easier to think of her in the same terms as other women—as deceitful, manipulating liars. But he had not yet caught her in a lie, and he failed to see how risking the humiliation of a trial was manipulating anyone.

"Evelyn, have you considered what you will do if the judge finds you guilty?" They had avoided the topic long enough. The trial was two days away. He could not wait any longer.

"You mean *when* he finds me guilty?" Evelyn couldn't keep the bitterness from her voice. "Thomas says I will most likely be made to pay a fine. The proceeds from the auction might help, but I'd rather they went to the men I owe and who need the money as much as I. In any case, it is not likely to be sufficient. That is as far as I get in my thinking."

The next step was not paying the fine and going to jail. Alex couldn't blame her for not wanting to think of that. Troubled by conflicting emotions, he tightened his grip on her arm and offered the only solution she might possibly accept. "Henderson says it is possible that they may give you time to get the money to pay the penalty. I am expecting another ship in a few weeks. When the contents are sold, I should have sufficient funds to advance you a loan. Then, when I hear from my cousin with the names of the smugglers, I will be able to present that as evidence to have your case appealed. It will be time-consuming. I wish I could think of something that would end this nonsense now, but short of hanging the judge, I've failed to come to another solution."

Evelyn strode silently beside him, contemplating his offer, increasing Alex's anxiety with every step. This was worse than chasing Alyson across the Atlantic and back. At least then he had been able to take some action in the matter. In this, his hands were tied. He could do nothing but wait for the legal process to settle the problem, and he felt guilty as hell that she would be the one to suffer. He'd seldom been inclined to bouts of guilt after gambling his allowance away or being caught with another man's wife or meeting one mistress while walking with another. He had found such diversions momentarily amusing, but he'd been guilty as sin then. Now, when he had no responsibility whatsoever for this woman's plight, he felt guilt. He definitely possessed a perverted conscience, Alex decided grimly as he awaited Evelyn's reply.

"I thank you for the offer, Alex. I will consider it as one made by a friend and consult with my mother and Jacob about it. Unfortunately, my family is still under the impression that we are to wed and do not consider the matter very serious. I think it is time I enlighten them to the truth."

That thought jarred Alex from complacency, and he glanced down at her with a surge of dismay. "Don't be too hasty in that, Evelyn. We still have your uncle to deal with, and he could make things very unpleasant for you if he chose." He didn't understand his reaction to ending their mock betrothal, but he could think of all sorts of rationalizations. He had grown to enjoy the comfort and companionship of the Wellington home, for instance. He would have to move out and endure the scorn of Amanda Wellington for his deception. He didn't like the idea of that one bit. The artificial distance it would create between himself and Evelyn surely played only a small part in his reaction.

A small frown developed between Evelyn's eyes as she

considered this additional problem. "I just wish I understood why Uncle George has not supported me in this. Surely he must know I wouldn't willingly engage in smuggling."

Alex had his own theory on that matter, but he wouldn't raise her ire by attacking her family. He made soothing noises and changed the subject until they were home. He wanted to protect her, but he found it exceedingly difficult to do without destroying the remainder of her family. Deciding he had built his own hell, he kept silent.

The day of the trial it rained. Evelyn made small platitudes about being grateful that it had waited until after the auction, but she looked relieved when Alex arrived in the carriage he had commandeered from her uncle.

She held her head up and refused to resort to tears as she got down from the carriage and entered the building where the trial was to be held. Her family stood at her side, Alex was behind her, but it wasn't enough. She felt icily alone as she joined Thomas Henderson on the planks in front of the wooden podium.

The verdict was a foregone conclusion. Evelyn listened to Alex's impassioned testimony on her behalf as if it were a speech made by an orator at Faneuil Hall, having no connection to her at all. She did not know whether the judge realized the men filling the benches of the courtroom and the upper gallery were in all probability the same ones responsible for breaking into his home during the riots, but she couldn't find any strength within herself to care. The judge didn't seem in the least intimidated by his audience when all the evidence was presented and he found Evelyn guilty without benefit of jury as suited the charges on which she had been tried.

She sat still as stone as the court named a fine worth more than the value of her family's warehouse and all its contents. Anger simmered through the courtroom and emerged in shouts of "Outrage!" and obscenities as to the origins of the judge's antecedents. The mob had intimidated the governor into leaving town and Oliver into resigning his post as stamp collector, but the judge obviously considered himself safe. Evelyn scarcely heard as he entered into complex negotiations with Thomas and

Alex over the time needed to gather the sum. She couldn't sell the warehouse. She would have to go to jail.

Somehow she made it home that evening and retired to her room without speaking more than two syllables to anyone. She heard Alex go out. She heard her uncle arrive and begin shouting, most likely with frustration, when he found only her implacable mother available to bully. She heard Alex return at a late hour and hesitate outside her door. She wasn't certain whether she wanted him to enter or not. She didn't think it would be possible to ever sleep again. If she could just get some rest, she might think of some way out of this predicament. As it was, her brain had ceased functioning.

Like an automaton, Evelyn rose and went to the warehouse the next day. On the way, she heard the judge had been hanged in effigy last night and demonstrators had surrounded his home and harassed him with shouts and stones, but that didn't make her feel any better. She felt the presence of the militia and the British troops like an invasion of privacy as they passed her in the streets. In six weeks, the Stamp Act would go into effect, and she dreaded the conflict that was building. Her case was just a pebble in a riverbed.

When she returned home that night, she heard Alex and her uncle arguing furiously in the front room, but she didn't have the courage to join them. Somehow she must make her family understand that she and Alex had never meant to marry, but it seemed such a niggling point in the face of the much larger problem looming over her that she concentrated on the more important and ignored the other.

There really was nothing Alex could do now. The judge had given her six weeks to find the funds. Whichever way she turned she would lose either the warehouse, their livelihood, Jacob's future, or her freedom. Even if Alex's ship should arrive, it might not be in time to save her. She wasn't at all certain she could accept Alex's generous offer in any case. She suspected he owned neither ship nor contents. Whatever his relationship with the powerful earl, it could not be enhanced by selling what was not his. It in all probability did not bother Alex, but it did not sit well with her.

Her thoughts constantly turned to flight, but that would leave her mother and Jacob in Uncle George's unforgiving hands. If she could sell the warehouse and its contents and add the proceeds to the amount gained in the auction, she might come close to the fine needed to keep her from jail. Their other debts wouldn't be paid; they would be bankrupt and without a means to make a living, but she would be free to look for work.

That thought did not lighten Evelyn's mood. She doubted that there was a man in Boston willing to hire her as more than tavern maid or housekeeper. Her father had needed her help and accepted the practicality of her working by his side until Jacob was old enough to learn the business. No other man had that incentive.

She should have married. That was the only respectable occupation for a woman. Then she would have a husband to protect her and her family. Not that any of the men who had offered would be of much use in this situation.

Despising her weakness, Evelyn avoided Alex. He had told her in no uncertain terms of his opinion of marriage. She could not look for help from that quarter, and she would not let him think she expected it. After all, he was little more than a stranger who had somehow become entrapped in her life one day and would soon fight his way free. She couldn't blame him if he decided to take one of the traders out to the nearest port that harbored one of his ships. As it was, without funds, he was stranded here. She owed him for that and more. She could not saddle him with any further responsibility, no matter how she longed to turn to him for comfort.

Irritated by Evelyn's refusal to give him so much as the time of day, and frustrated by his helplessness, Alex threw himself into the volatile politics of Boston as a solace. He met the wealthy John Hancock and contemplated seeking his help for Evelyn's future, but he disliked the man's ineffectual weakness and hypochondria and didn't further the acquaintance. He listened to impassioned speeches and conceded the colonists had some reason for complaint, but they were better off making their speeches to Parliament and not to each other. They argued so bitterly over ways and means that Alex felt it unlikely they would ever accomplish anything, but he was willing to do his share when the time came simply because it offered action to alleviate his restlessness.

In the back rooms, out of the public speechifying, Alex found more concrete issues discussed. As much as he disliked the crotchety Sam Adams, he had to admire his thinking. The man knew how to get things done. If all the colonies could be made to defy the Stamp Act, as he claimed, there would be very little Parliament could do short of war to enforce it. Alex prayed sensible heads would prevail in England if it should ever come to that stage.

Each night he returned late to the Wellington home and hesitated outside Evelyn's bedroom door. He wanted to discuss what he had heard with her, to bring the issues into perspective with her commonsensical views, but she no longer seemed interested in what he had to say. In any case, he would lose all interest in talk once he was in her bedroom. He hadn't been with a woman since the night of the riot, and his physical needs were unaccustomed to being neglected.

He knew she was awake. He could see the candlelight beneath her door and hear the pages of her book turning. He could stand there forever and imagine how she would look in a thin muslin nightdress with her hair tumbling down about her shoulders and breasts. The picture of a virgin queen, he grimaced to himself. Not for the likes of him. That thought drove him down the hall to his own room.

Alex wasn't there when George Upton finally caught Evelyn alone at the warehouse. She watched his approach without emotion. Now that she had made a decision of sorts, she had to cling to it and forget all the violent emotions that protested the unfairness of life. Her uncle couldn't stir her one way or the other.

He tried to look concerned. He tried to look sympathetic, but she saw only triumph in his eyes as he spoke. They had never got along. She had been a thorn in his side ever since he married her aunt, although she didn't know why. She held nothing against her uncle but the fact that he was obnoxious and arrogant. As a child, she hadn't even felt that. Gradually his words began to pierce the fog of her brain.

"I have found a few friends of mine who are willing to buy the warehouse at what I consider a very fair price. It's not sufficient to pay the fine, of course, but I might possibly have enough to lend you whatever difference you might need. Your fiancé can pay me back when you are married."

Her uncle made it so easy to say that Evelyn almost smiled. She didn't, however. It would only have angered him more. Instead, she broke the news with no emotion at all. "There will be no marriage, Uncle George. I'd rather go to jail than sell my family to the damned British courts. Your offer is appreciated, but tell your friends I will not sell."

It was almost worth going to jail to see the stunned look on her uncle's face. It quickly turned purple, and his usual blustering tirade fell out. "Not marry! You will disgrace your family and your father's name! You must be mad! I have offered you the easiest possible solution. You need only sail away with your new husband to leave all this shame behind. What on earth possesses you, child? I am only trying to look out for your best interests."

Perhaps he was, but he didn't know she had no husband to go to, and Alex wasn't any solution at all. Even if he offered, she couldn't marry him. Jail was a simpler solution than wife of an English earl. Evelyn didn't even attempt to explain that to her uncle, and he left in a huff.

When, a week after the trial, Alex received a message from a small boy while he sat at a tavern discussing plans for the upcoming congress, he couldn't help but consider it doubtfully. He asked the boy to repeat it, and wondered that Evelyn wouldn't have written such an urgent request instead of sending a verbal one. It had been so long since he had made other than polite conversation with her that he couldn't be certain of her mood, however.

Cursing her daring to continue their investigation without him, he gave the boy one of his small store of coins and excused himself from his companions. The damn proud fool wouldn't have requested his aid unless it were truly serious.

A trifle shaken at the import of that thought, Alex hurried toward the livery housing his horse. How in hell had she got to Sudbury, and what was she doing there? It didn't make sense, and he didn't like things that didn't make sense.

Alex rode by the warehouse and stopped at Evelyn's home to verify she was in neither place. He could think of no good reasons for her to be in Sudbury, only bad ones. That she was free to send a message could be considered reason not to fear, but his bones told him otherwise. Something was wrong.

Adding pistol and rifle to his saddle, Alex sent his horse into a gallop out of the city. This was an action he knew how to take, no matter how much he disliked it. While he lived, no man other than himself would lay a hand on Evelyn Wellington.

14

Having worked himself into an overwrought state bordering on the maniacal by the time he reached the Wayside Inn, Alex felt a certain letdown when he discovered no more than an old swaybacked horse in the inn yard. If Evelyn were being held captive by unknown and dangerous rogues, they certainly had a sorry taste for mounts.

Feeling a trifle foolish trailing into the sleepy inn with pistol and rifle in hand, he tucked the pistol out of sight in his trouser band and prayed nothing would disturb it into exploding while in such a position. He rather treasured that part of him that would be removed by such an untimely incident.

Shouldering his rifle, Alex sauntered into the tavern. He heard no screams or moans, but he did not trust the peace any more than he trusted the inn's owner. Jacob's experience here made him wary, and when the same laconic fellow appeared as before, Alex's grip tightened on the rifle.

To his surprise, the narrow-faced proprietor nodded in recognition and gestured toward the stairs. "Hampton? The lady's waiting for you upstairs. Room on the right."

He didn't like the sound of this at all, but the man made no attempt to take his weapons, and feeling a bit of a fool, Alex took the worn pine stairs two at a time. What in hell would Evelyn be doing in this out-of-the-way hole alone, and waiting for him? Nothing that he could think of would induce the prim-and-proper Miss Wellington to such compromising circumstances.

He knocked cautiously at the right-hand door. Despite the inn's weathered appearance, the door seemed sturdy and Alex doubted his ability to break it in with anything less than an ax. The low ceiling brought his head uncomfortably close to the rafters, and when, miraculously, he heard Evelyn's voice on the other side of the door, he had to duck to enter the low door frame.

She stood in the center of the loft, wearing a wine wool riding habit and soft wool cloak, nervously clasping her hands in front of her as she stared with wide, frightened eyes at his approach. Her expression nearly made him forget the wide bed situated not feet from where she stood.

"Thank goodness! Your message nearly frightened me to death! What is it, Alex? Have you discovered something? I've been so worried waiting here alone. I thought something had happened to you."

Shocked at finding her here like this, alone and unharmed, it took Alex a minute to grasp the content of her words. When he did, he stared at her in befuddlement. "My message? You're the one who sent the message. You damned near took a year off my life, thinking you were in the hands of brigands or worse. Whatever made you choose this deuced place? I don't trust the proprietor any further than I can throw him."

"I didn't send any message." Bewildered, Evelyn scanned Alex's dark face, trying to determine his seriousness. Surely he had not schemed to bring her here. It made no sense to do so. The boy had been quite specific in his message. She had prayed all the way out here that he had discovered something that would redeem her innocence. Disappointment warred with confusion. "Are you telling me you found nothing new? That we were both brought out here for naught?"

A forbidding frown had already begun on Alex's face. At her words, he grabbed her arm and headed for the door. "Let's get out of here. It's almost dark already. I don't like this one bit."

They clattered down the stairs to find no one at the bottom. Not stopping to inquire why, Alex hurried Evelyn out the front door and into the inn yard. They would be lucky to make it back to Boston by dark. Thoughts of ambush pried at his fears. Or worse yet, something was happening back in town that they could have prevented. There was no time to lose.

Not finding his horse at the post where he had left it in his hurry to reach Evelyn, Alex started for the stable. Evelyn scampered beside him, silent as always when she was worried. She had a damn sharp tongue when she wanted, but she knew when to hold it. Alex gave her credit for that.

When they reached the twilight gloom of the shed that passed for a stable, Alex could scarcely credit the sight that met his eyes. It was empty. That wasn't possible. They were twenty miles from nowhere, and not a horse in sight.

He turned a suspicious gaze to Evelyn. "Did you order the horses stabled?"

She shook her head, staring at the empty shed with quiet resignation. "I didn't expect to linger. I rode one of the horses from the livery and left it outside. No horse thief in his right mind would steal that creature."

Keeping his curses to himself, Alex dragged her back toward the inn again. "There has to be an explanation for this. Let's see if I can't get to the bottom of it."

Evelyn allowed herself to feel a glitter of hope. Alex was twice the size of the innkeeper. She didn't think he would use his guns, but she felt certain he would have few scruples over using his greater size to threaten the man. Surely the man wouldn't dare steal their horses and keep them hidden while Alex was around.

Alex's roar as they entered the inn echoed strangely empty. Shouldn't a place like this have customers by now? No one sat at the tavern tables or waited behind the bar. Evelyn felt a twinge of prescience as the back door opened and a stout, weary old woman entered.

"You want summat?" She wiped her hands disdainfully on her dirty apron as she stared at them.

"We want our horses. Where is your husband?" Irritated that he had no one to throttle, Alex waited impatiently for a reply.

The woman gave him a look of scorn. "Ain't got no husband. Mr. Stockton took the wagon to town for supplies and won't be back until morning. I don't know nothin' about no horses."

Alex's patience was growing thinner as the room grew darker. "Our horses are gone. We need to get back to town. Don't you have any other patrons? We need some means of travel."

She turned her scornful stare to look the lady in fancy riding habit up and down. "Everybody knows we're closed Monday nights when Mr. Stockton goes to town. He just said to fix you and your fancy lady some supper when you're ready. You ready?"

Evelyn could feel herself turning crimson under the woman's crude stare. She caught Alex's arm, wishing she could urge him to leave this place at once, but his rigid stance warned of an anger too great to listen.

"Later." With that one word, Alex turned on his heel and stalked outside again. Evelyn ran to keep up with him.

"Alex! What are we going to do?" It was already too dark to see the yard clearly. She stumbled over a tree stump as she tried to follow Alex's shadow.

"Listen for horses. Scream for help. Hell, I don't know. Have you some suggestion?"

"We could walk," she offered tentatively. "Perhaps we'd meet someone on the road."

"Probably. Thieves and cutthroats are fond of traveling by night. Can't think of anyone else who would."

"We can't stay here," Evelyn protested hoarsely.

Alex turned and stared down at the soft white glow of her face in the dark. A sardonic quirk twisted his lips, but she could scarcely be expected to see it. His mind had rapidly discounted many notions already. Another one was rising to fill his mind, one that made sense to him and was more in character with women as he knew them than with the paragon of virtue she purported to be. "Why not, Miss Wellington? It is safer than being set upon by cutthroats. Our friendly innkeeper will be back with his wagon in the morning to rescue us. It sounds like the thing to do to me."

"Alex, we can't!" Evelyn couldn't believe he was so thick-headed. "My family will be worried sick. And if we're gone all night together . . . It won't do. We'll have to walk."

Alex turned back toward the inn. "When neither of us

returns, your mother will know we're together and be quite content with this turn of events. I imagine she and your uncle were beginning to grow a little worried about our dilatory courtship. This should quite effectively put an end to their concerns."

"Alex, have you gone mad?" Evelyn reluctantly hurried after him. The whole world as she knew it was rapidly turning upside down.

"Oh, no, my dear. On the contrary, I am beginning to return to my senses. You're a very clever wench, you know. You should be quite proud of yourself. Come, abominable as she looks, our hostess is quite a formidable cook. We might as well make ourselves comfortable; we have a long night ahead."

Evelyn tried to puzzle out his meaning. His words had an ominous ring to them, but they were quite pleasantly said. He should be furious, but he didn't seem to be, not any longer, leastways. She caught at his arm as he yelled for the cook. "Alex, have you thought of something? If so, please tell me. You're terrifying me."

He looked down at her with that sardonic venom she remembered from their first meeting. "Aye, I've thought of something, and strange as it might seem, I'm not totally averse to it. If a man has to be leg-shackled, it might as well be to a woman as sensible and independent as he, who won't weep buckets when he indulges himself in recreational pastimes or takes it into mind to do a little traveling on his own. On the whole, I approve of your ingenious plan, although I fear you may not be quite as pleased as I."

The cook entered and Alex signaled to her. "We'll take our supper upstairs as soon as practicable. The night will be too short as it is." At the cook's curt nod, he caught Evelyn's wrist and pulled her in the direction of the stairs.

She was staring at him in horror, not believing her ears. He seemed perfectly rational, but his words were madness. The black glitter of his eyes warned that he did not take her reluctance readily. But if she understood anything he said at all, she was better off staying in the tavern. Evelyn dug her heels in and refused to budge.

"I don't know what mad bee you have in your bonnet,

Alex Hampton, but I'll eat down here, thank you. This whole situation is unseemly enough without adding to the disgrace."

Alex lifted one black eyebrow in a villainous manner that must have taken hours of practice to perfect. "Unseemly? You threw that word at me once before, and I told you my idea of 'seemly.' Now it appears we have little choice in the matter. Will you come quietly or shall I throw you over my shoulder?"

"I'll not come quietly, I warn you of that right now. Hadn't we ought to sit down and talk this over? I am certain there must be some way out of this." Evelyn nervously tried to twist from his unrelenting grasp, stepping backward away from him as she did so.

"We'll talk upstairs. I do not like leaving my weapons behind to free my hands to grasp you properly, and I have no intention of waving a gun in your face like a proper brigand. So come along quietly and we'll talk upstairs. I daresay this is a den of thieves and it would not be any safer for you to stay below than to go with me."

Evelyn suspected he had the right of it there. She glanced nervously around, not liking the heavy shadows or the stale smells of smoke and ale, remembering with creeping flesh the look the proprietor had given her earlier. For some odd reason, she had always felt safe with Alex. She gave him a surreptitious look, not liking the impatient menace in his expression. Her gaze fell to the pistol in his trouser band, barely concealed by his unbuttoned coat and vest. It was too intimately situated for her to reach out and grasp.

Instead, she held out her hand and politely requested it. "I'll go with you if you give me the pistol."

A gleam of something closely resembling humor leapt to Alex's eye but disappeared just as quickly. His hand closed around the pistol butt. "Do you know how to handle one of these? I'd not like to see you shoot your toe off through ignorance."

"I'm no marksman, but I know the basics. It's not my toe that will be endangered."

With a formal bow he presented the pistol. "Now, upstairs with you. I have large plans for this evening."

There was that note in his voice again. Clutching the pistol in her hand, Evelyn glanced helplessly up the shabby stairs. The idea of spending the entire night in the same room with Alex left little to the imagination. He had been too surprised and angry for her to believe he had planned it this way, and he was probably right that they had little choice but to stay. That didn't mean they had to engage in anything improper while they were here. Remembering the door on the left side of the loft and that the woman had said there were no other guests, Evelyn put her foot on the stairs with a little more confidence.

Alex stayed close behind her, and she was very aware of his larger form in this proximity, but he did nothing to stop her when she reached for the door to the other room. She rattled the latch and found it locked.

"I daresay that's part of his storage. As uninhabited as this place seems to be, he wouldn't need more accommodation than the one room. The bed could easily hold three and the floor would take a dozen pallets. We're lucky to have it all to ourselves."

Evelyn sent him a sharp look, but Alex's expression was bland as he opened the bedroom door for her.

Nervously she took in her surroundings more carefully than the first time. Alex struck a flint to the lamp on the table, and the room came flickering into view. The round table and two chairs were a nicety that Evelyn didn't have enough experience to appreciate. She noted the cracked pitcher and bowl on the washstand but turned her attention to Alex as he threw back the worn quilt on the bed. The clean sheets beneath apparently met with his approval, and her anxiety escalated as he swung around and came back to her.

"We'll be here all night, so you might as well make yourself comfortable. As lovely as that habit is, it must be a trifle warm. Let me help you with the jacket."

His fingers were assuredly unfastening the buttons before Evelyn could protest. The brush of his hand against her breast as his fingers slid beneath the fastenings left her breathless, but he gave her no time to resist. He slid the coat from her shoulders with astonishing speed, leaving Evelyn to wonder if she would find herself completely unclothed before she had time to say a word.

To her relief, Alex turned his attention to his own coat, shaking it off and hanging it over the other chair. His billowy shirtsleeves gave his masculine physique freedom of movement, and Evelyn couldn't help but watch with fascination as he lifted his wide chin to unfasten his lace jabot. His dark eyes caught hers and held her intently. She wished desperately that he would leave the shirt fastened. She remembered all too well her reaction to his open shirt on the night of the riot.

Since he wasn't obedient to her silent wishes, Evelyn turned her back on him to casually observe the uncovered floor of this barren half of the room where men presumably spread their pallets. She didn't hear Alex's footsteps behind her until it was too late. One heavy arm slid around her waist while the other deprived her of the pistol, laying it on the table behind them.

His voice was a warm murmur against her hair. "It's too late for shyness, Miss Wellington. We both know what will come of this night. We might as well begin enjoying it now. Pretend it is our wedding night, if you like. It is just as good as taking you to a room at the King's Arms or spending it on one of those narrow beds at your mother's. Or don't ladies think of marriage beds when they trap men into taking vows?"

His broad hand splaying across the thin linen covering her ribs was comforting and almost welcome. His words brought Evelyn's head up with a snap. When she tried to pull away, the comforting arm became a band of steel.

"You are mad! Let go of me this instant! I no more want marriage than you do. I'll not be forced any further, Alex. I don't think I can bear it."

She sounded faintly hysterical, and Alex relented enough to turn her where he could kiss her lovely mouth. Her eyes flashed deep purple fires, but he only admired the display as he lowered his lips to hers. "I'll not force you, little tyrant," he murmured against her mouth, tasting the sweetness of her breath. "I'll never force you. There's no need to. See?"

His mouth fastened gently to hers, seeking response as he plied her with soft kisses, touching her lightly with his tongue. Evelyn tried to ward him off, but he had fed her dangerous addiction to his caresses too well. He made no aggressive moves but held her carefully until she had to bring her hands to his chest to keep her balance. The heat of his skin beneath the fine cambric effectively melded her in place, and her head slanted slightly to better receive his kisses.

She shuddered as his tongue sought and found the slight opening between her lips, and then she closed her eyes and allowed the searing invasion to fuel her senses. She was aware that his breath quickened as well as her own. His heart took on a faster pace beneath her hands as he drew her closer, and his kiss became more demanding than gentle as she pressed into him.

Alex's muffled groan as he ran his hand into her hair brought Evelyn back to her senses, what few of them remained. She wanted the comfort of his embrace much more than she had ever dreamed possible, but not at the cost of all her principles. She turned her head away from the drug of his mouth but could not yet summon the strength to push from his hold. His kisses strayed across her hair as she leaned into him.

"Alex, this is impossible. We would do better walking back to town than remaining here."

His hand ran up her spine, pressing her closer into the curve of his body as his other hand sought the pins securing the heavy masses of her hair. "The result would be the same, my dear. You're quite properly ruined in the eyes of the world whether you spend the night in my bed or on the road. Let's not fight it anymore."

A knock on the door warned that supper had arrived. Alex cursed as Evelyn hastily pushed away and began to arrange her hair. Standing behind a chair to disguise his arousal, he ordered the woman to enter.

He despised the cook's sly looks as she took in Evelyn's disheveled shirt and hair, but he reminded himself that Evelyn was the one who had brought this embarrassment down on their heads. He was fully aware her situation was quite hopeless and marriage to him would be her best solution. He had just not thought her capable of this level of deceit. He sent the cook away as soon as the table was laid and crossed the room to bar the door after her.

When Alex swung around again, Evelyn was looking at him as if he were the devil himself. Vowing she wouldn't leave this room until she wasn't a virgin any longer, he pulled out a chair and gestured for her to sit. Seduction worked much better on a full stomach.

With the safety of an entire table between them, Evelyn elected to sit. She had sat across from Alex at a dinner table many times, but never quite like this. Wearing no coat and with his shirt unfastened, he lost some of the facade of civilization that had held him aloof. If she lifted her eyes, she became aware of the stubbornly square chin and jaw accented by the heavy black frame of his hair and the dangerous flash of his eyes as they caught her regard. Lowering her eyes again, she was forced to observe the immense capability of wide, strong hands as they manipulated his fork and knife. She knew what those hands could do to her, and her stomach shriveled up in horrified anticipation.

"You're not eating," he commented quietly.

"I'm not hungry." She pushed away her plate and clasped her hands nervously in her lap, not looking at him.

"If you don't eat, I'll assume you're eager to share my bed, and I will gladly oblige." Alex calmly sliced off a piece of beef and put it in his mouth, watching her carefully.

Evelyn paled and sent a nervous glance to the large bed with the covers thrown back invitingly. She reached for her glass of water and sipped at it hastily.

"I would have suggested wine as the better choice, but I doubted that our hostess had anything potable to offer. There's a pitcher of ale. Have some. It will relax you."

"I don't want to be relaxed." Evelyn cut sharply into her meat. "And I don't intend to share a bed with you. The world can believe as it wishes. I don't know what's the matter with you tonight. You behave as if it's my fault that we were tricked out here and our horses stolen. You would do better to apply your thoughts to who would do that and why."

"I have a very good idea who would do that and why.

I apologize for not considering this solution to your dilemma earlier, but I have a rather narrow-minded aversion to marriage that generally keeps my thoughts from straying in that direction. Now that the choice has been made for me, I can see that you are quite right. We shall suit nicely as soon as I rid you of a few missish inhibitions."

Evelyn's stomach contracted painfully and she forced her gaze up to meet his. "I don't know why I stand accused of this atrocity. What have I ever done to make you believe this of me?"

Wearily Alex dismissed the subjcct with a wave of his hand. "It's no matter. I daresay you have done us both a favor. My family has been anxiously trying to marry me off for years. They will gladly lend their influence to catch the real perpetrators and clear your name. In the meantime, you can return to England with me. The court won't be able to reach you there, and even if it does, my family will see the fine paid before letting you go to jail. The solution is quite ingenious and requires only a certain delicacy of timing. We can cry the banns when we return, and pray one of my cousin's ships arrives before you have to go to jail. With any luck, we will be married between the two."

Evelyn forced herself to continue eating just to keep him talking and delay the fight to come. "There is only one problem, my friend. I refuse to marry you."

A pained smile twisted Alex's lips. "Just once, I would like to hear a woman say yes to my proposal. This continual rejection is damaging to a man's pride. Come now, you are only playing with your food. Share my ale and be sensible."

She sipped gingerly at the warm drink while keeping a wary eye on him. She could not imagine any woman rejecting his suit. Perhaps he was not precisely the suave, debonair type that need only smile to twist a woman's entrails, but she preferred his square-jawed masculine features. True, there was a hard look about his eyes that could make a woman shiver with fear whenever he was angry, yet now the hardness seemed turned only on himself. She felt no danger, though the evidence of his greater strength was displayed in the breadth of his shoulders and chest as he sat relaxed with one arm over the chair back. No, he was certain to attract his fair share of women, particularly with title and wealth at his fingertips.

"I am being sensible. I don't belong in England. You do. Tell me about the other women who rejected your proposals. I am certain they did not reject *you.*"

Those black eyes gave her an odd look, but since she was making an attempt to eat, Alex played along with her choice of conversation. "I was only sixteen when the first woman rejected me. I find it difficult to discriminate between rejections of my person and my proposals. Perhaps you could enlighten me on the difference?"

Evelyn sipped at her ale and tried to ascertain how much of his speech was glib words and how much an honest reaction. She had not known Alex to dissemble before. She felt there was a hard kernel of truth to his casual questions.

"If you were a colonist, if you were not heir to an earldom, if you were an honest workingman, I would be a fool to reject your proposal. But I cannot live in England away from my family and friends, and I cannot live the idle life of a countess. It is the outcome of our marriage that I object to, not you."

A small smile began to twist Alex's lips to match the gleam in his eye as he leaned forward. "So, if I were to stay here and tell my cousin to find another heir, you would consent to marry me?"

She had trapped herself with that one. Giving up any pretense of eating, Evelyn tried to honestly determine the answer. Her physical reaction to the idea of spending the rest of her nights in his bed screamed "Yes, yes!" but lust had little to do with logic. Would he make a good husband and good father? She looked up to the eager gleam in his eye and her heart lurched.

"I've never thought of you in that way before. It's very hard to think of you as a man who comes home to his tiny house after a hard day's work, hugs his children, and kisses his wife. You told me you never wanted marriage and children. I would have to turn my thinking around to give you an answer."

"So would I, I fear." Alex sat back again and studied her slightly bewildered expression. "I'm not that man and never will be. You made no mention of love. Shouldn't that be a deciding factor?"

Evelyn met his gaze squarely. "If a man and a woman like and respect each other, love will grow with time. I think friendship and respect should be the deciding factor."

Interest flared briefly in his eyes before he quenched it for his usual bland expression. "That's a fascinating theory. How do we know if we're friends?"

She had thought they were, but he was putting the lie to her beliefs. A friend wouldn't force her to do something against her will. "What does it matter? This does not solve the problem of why we are here or how we are to get home."

Alex rose from the table and held out his hand to her. "I'm no longer interested in hows and whys. It is very possible that I could spend the entire evening conversing with you, but we have a lifetime for that, and I have more urgent matters on my mind. Don't be shy, little tyrant. You are too intelligent and sensible to fight the inevitable."

She remained seated. "You are not the inevitable. Weren't you the one who once said he'd rather spend a few months in jail than a lifetime in marriage?"

Alex gave a wry quirk to his mouth as he leaned over to lift her from her chair. "The consequences of my hasty tongue often haunt me. And a man can deal with a life behind bars easier than a woman. You're not going to jail. You're going with me." As he succeeded in bringing Evelyn to her feet, he wrapped his arms around her and stared down into her face. "I'll show you that it won't be an entirely unpleasant fate."

When he bent to start his kisses once again, Evelyn knew the desperation of her plight. She turned her head away and pushed futilely against his chest. "This is humiliating, Alex. Haven't I endured enough humiliation these last weeks?"

Irritated, Alex dropped his hold and glared at her. "Now I am humiliating. Are there any further insults you wish to hurl at me before I take you to bed?" He caught her chin and forced her to look up at him. "I am taking you to bed, Evelyn. There's nothing you can do or say to change that. I've done my best to play the part of gentleman for two months now. You've driven me insane with your kisses, but I've respected your wishes. Tonight that's all changed. Tonight we'll see where those kisses lead."

His fingers brushed her cheek, and she felt the wanting build inside her. He did not even need to kiss her to stir these mad desires. She wanted to be in his arms, feel his caresses, and discover where they led, just as he promised. Suddenly it did seem quite inevitable. Captivated by the almost tender look on his face, Evelyn licked her lips nervously and heard her voice crack as she spoke.

"Alex, I'm terrified. I have no experience at this sort of thing. You said to look upon it as our wedding night, but I do not even have a gown, much less a trousseau. Isn't the groom supposed to leave his bride alone to prepare? There are certain necessary . . ." She waved her hand awkwardly, seeking the polite word. ". . . functions," she added lamely, "or do they not matter when we . . . ?" She gave up in disgust. "I need to wash, at least."

Amusement played along his lips as Alex watched her evident distress. "I apologize, my love. I'm new at this business of seducing virgins. We'll have to learn together." He slid his hand along her cheek and buried his fingers lightly in her hair. "I tend to be impatient and hasty. You will need to slow me down when I go too fast for you. I'll send that hideous old woman up to clear the table and bring you some warm water. That will give you some privacy. Don't look at me like that, Evelyn. I do think of you as my wife."

He bent and placed a chaste kiss upon her nose, and before Evelyn could believe it was true, he was gone from the room.

She hadn't realized how much she felt his proximity until the room was empty. She stared at the shadowy four walls in bewilderment, wondering where this aching emptiness had come from. She felt certain it hadn't been there when she arrived earlier in the afternoon. Or had it? There had been fear and hope then, but hadn't she carried an eagerness that had more to do with Alex than the news she hoped to hear? What was happening to her?

The old woman came to carry away the tray, jarring Evelyn back to reality. Alex wasn't going to take no for an answer. He had warned her that he wasn't a gentleman, and now she knew what he meant. She had a choice now of running away into the darkness of those unknown woods outside or staying here to be ruined. The gun wasn't an alternative. He knew she wouldn't use it on him.

Perfunctorily performing the necessary ablutions when warm water was brought, Evelyn wrestled with the problem. This night in all probability would ruin her just as he said. Selling all her possessions or going to jail would equally diminish her hopes to none. She was fighting Alex merely on principle, not because she wanted to fight him. Lud, but she didn't want to fight his kisses at all.

So where would principles get her? She started nervously as the door swung open quietly behind her. Principles. She had to remember principles. She swung around to meet the man barring the doorway, and all thoughts fled. Principles didn't exist in his world.

15

He smelled of soap and his hair was still damp where he had slicked it back out of his face. He must have borrowed a razor to shave, and the evidence of that thoughtfulness reduced her flagging will to jelly.

Alex was trying to please her. Evelyn stared at him in something bordering on astonishment. The selfish, arrogant man she knew would never have thought of pleasing anyone but himself. His actions here tonight were proof positive of that. But why else would he go to the trouble of shaving and trying to make himself presentable when there was no one about to impress but her?

He quietly closed and barred the door behind his back, never taking his eyes from her. Evelyn was conscious of the water droplets still clinging to the hollow of her throat where she had not yet dried herself. She had opened her shirt to wash more thoroughly and had not yet fastened it again. Her fingers nervously plucked at the edges of the linen, pulling it together as his gaze dipped to the swell of her breasts beneath the lacy chemise. She felt a flush of heat as he strode forward.

"I'll buy you nightrails dripping in lace just for the sheer pleasure of removing them." Alex's fingers trembled slightly as he loosed her grip on the shirt and began to tug it gently from her skirt.

"Alex, please," she whispered, but her fingers were curling in the soft folds of his shirt and not fighting to hold hers. A fierce rush of pleasure spread through her middle as his broad hands circled her chemise-clad ribs and rose slowly to just below the curve of her breasts.

The intimate touch left her shaken. She could not look him in the face. Neither could she pull away.

"Did I ever mention how very lovely you are?"

His breath was warm as he bent to kiss her hair. His hands stayed where they were, as if afraid to move. Evelyn felt the need for them to rise higher, to caress the growing ache of her breasts, but she wanted to linger and learn more of this man too. Even after all these weeks, he was an enigma. He could have taken her at any time. He didn't need to be gentle. He had admitted he was an impatient man. Why was he trying to be patient now?

"You don't need to speak words you don't mean," she murmured sadly. "We both know you would have sailed away with the first ship that came for you. Let's at least try to be honest."

Alex smiled and moved his hands from the temptation of her breasts to release the ribbons of her hair, carelessly dropping them on the floor. Evelyn dared to breathe and look up at him again, and the sight of his warm smile drove her newly released breath from her lungs. He looked nearly angelic when he smiled like that. Why had she thought his would be a devilish grin?

He pressed a kiss to her brow when he realized she was watching him. "Honesty is not one of my better qualities, I admit, but I'll not lie to you about this. I only lie when I need to, and I don't really need to with you, do I?"

Evelyn's fingers gradually relaxed their tense grip enough to enjoy the sensation of Alex's muscular chest moving beneath her fingers. He pulled her hair down about her shoulders, gently releasing it from her collar as he gazed down into her face, waiting for her reply.

"No, there's no need to lie," she admitted. He didn't need to murmur pretty compliments and words of love for her sake. She was about to give herself without any promises at all.

"So believe me when I tell you that you are lovely, that I have wanted to twine your hair in my hands since the day I met you. It's like thick, rich silk. I've never felt anything like it." His kiss strayed to her ear this time, sending a shiver up her spine. "I want to feel the rest of you, Evelyn. Will you let me?"

She had little choice, but the truth of the matter was that she wouldn't stop him if she had one. The loosened shirt fell easily from her shoulders, dropping to the floor with a twist of Alex's fingers. She continued to scan his face as his gaze absorbed the way her chemise clung to her breasts, leaving her throat and much of her shoulders bare. She had worn one with only simple capped sleeves beneath the riding habit. She wished for one with oceans of lace to make her feel more feminine right now. She was painfully aware that she did not have the full, curved figure men preferred. Yet Alex's expression displayed no displeasure at the sight revealed, and she felt a deep desire to please him when he looked upon her.

"This is what you would come home to if you so foolishly married me." She couldn't hold the words back. No matter how much she wanted the touch of Alex's hands, she did not want to be taken like any doxy off the street, to be used for a moment's pleasure and forgotten later. If she had only this one chance at knowing happiness, she wanted it to be complete, knowing he wanted her as much as she wanted him.

Alex chuckled and slid his hands to the fastenings at her waist. "You'll not scare me off like that, little tyrant. I've been around enough to know what I want. Did you think I would get myself embroiled so thoroughly in your affairs for any other reason? I'll admit, marriage wasn't what I had in mind, but your company has been worth the wait. We'll suit, even if we do have our differences of opinion."

Those differences made Evelyn close her eyes now as he slid the skirt over her hips into a puddle on the floor. They would never suit in any way but this. She felt embarrassment flood through her as Alex's hands moved caressingly down her hips to cup her buttocks, shaping her chemise to the flesh beneath. When he pulled her close, fitting her against him so she could no longer deny the maleness of him, her eyes flew wide with fright.

"You have nothing to fear, love. All good things come with time." He soothed her with words as he took the kiss he had been denying her as well as himself.

Evelyn's hands fled to Alex's shoulders at the fiery impact of his lips. No gentle teasing was necessary now. The need between them was strong and immediate, and she parted her lips and clung to him desperately as his tongue moved into her, staking a claim of possession she hadn't felt before. Everywhere he touched her there was fire, and she flung herself wildly into the flames, meeting it gladly with her mouth, seizing more as she pressed closer into his embrace.

Alex lifted her to sit on the edge of the bed, and she protested blindly when the fire moved from her lips to lick harmlessly at her ear. Then Alex straightened to lift her legs and remove her half-boots, sliding strong hands up her calves to remove garters and stockings, and the fire found new fuel. When his fingers slid further to caress the sensitive flesh of her inner thigh, Evelyn gave a strangled cry and opened her eyes to stare at him wildly.

Boldly Alex stood with one knee between her legs, his dark gaze challenging her as he reached to remove his own shirt. In fascination she watched as the material fell away to reveal the amazing ripple of muscle and sinew as he threw the shirt aside. Tentatively she reached to touch what she had denied existed before. Clothing gone, he was just a man. Titles and wealth had no meaning.

Alex caught her hand, pressing it to his lips and kissing the fingers before returning it to press her palm against his chest. Holding her gaze, he moved her hand downward, letting her explore the feel of him, the soft mat of hair disguising the hard ripple of tissue, the taut band of muscle over his waist, slowly guiding her toward the buttons of his breeches. She flushed scarlet when she encountered the smooth doeskin cloth, but obediently she helped unfasten him as he had her. He rescued her trembling fingers before they came too close to the core of his need.

At her questioning look, he sat down beside her. Pulling his hand through long silky strands, he pressed a brief kiss to her swollen lips. "I want to pleasure you first, but I fear I will burst with wanting you if we go too quickly."

Evelyn smoothed her hands over his bent back as he leaned over to pull off his boots. If she were his wife, they would do this every night, and she would grow accustomed to the sight of those broad shoulders, the texture of his smooth skin beneath her fingers. As she imagined how he would feel when he bent over her in these next minutes, Evelyn's face flushed with heat again. She would know his flesh very intimately then.

He didn't give her time to grow terrified of the enormity of that next step. Throwing his last boot to the floor, Alex turned and took her in his arms and greedily captured her mouth in a long kiss.

Before Evelyn knew how they came there, she was lying across the sheets with Alex half on top of her, and the flames had become an inferno from which escape had become impossible. His hand boldly captured her breast, pushing it up to fill his palm and caressing it until she was swollen with a need she did not understand until he pushed the chemise aside and took her in his mouth. She cried out with the bliss of this excruciating pleasure, felt the need spread in undulating waves to the place between her thighs, and knew she was lost.

Eagerly she helped him remove the last of her garments, grateful she had worn no corset to hinder their pleasure. She lifted her shoulders from the pillows so he could push the untied chemise off and down her arms. Keeping her trapped with the garment half on and half off, Alex feasted on the delicate fruits of her breasts until her cries of pleasure made him impatient for more.

His broad hands slid upward over her thighs, pulling the chemise with them. As Evelyn struggled to free her arms, Alex found the part of her that burned the most, and she whimpered slightly and fell back against the pillows, flooded with shame as he caressed her there. The shame became something else, something powerful and intense as he stroked and played, then came up beside her to breathe kisses across her skin.

"I want you, little tyrant. I want you here." His finger probed the tender flesh, making her writhe with the need to take him in further. "Do you understand what I will do to you?"

Alex's words were low and sensuous, and Evelyn had difficulty recognizing them as a question. She didn't understand precisely what he would do to her, but she was beginning to understand it better every minute. "I don't know," she murmured huskily, moving her head as his lips sucked gently at the base of her throat. "Will you show me?"

The words were rhetorical. She knew he would. But she sensed his need to be asked. He had been right. He didn't need to force her. She gave herself up willingly to this exquisite torment.

His finger thrust deeper, and she turned her face to bury it against his shoulder. Flames of embarrassment and desire swept over her skin until she was completely ablaze, and she felt no relief when he removed his hand to caress her breast.

"I'll show you, love," he whispered near her ear. "But I cannot give it back once I take it from you. There will be no other after me. I'm going to claim you as mine. Your children will be my children. Don't think it will ever be otherwise."

In this instant his words made sense. She desperately wanted his children. His promises inflamed her desire to new heights, and her hips rose to seek his, not knowing what they sought but knowing the motion instinctively. Alex's hand returned to assuage her need, but it wasn't enough. Evelyn bit her lip to keep from crying out her frustration. Alex moved slightly away from her then, and his kisses stopped momentarily. Not even realizing she had closed her eyes, she opened them again.

In the lamplight his skin gleamed a golden bronze. She watched in fascination as Alex unfastened the remaining buttons of his breeches. He bent to unfasten the buttons at his knee before removing the last garment between them. It seemed to take an interminable time, but through eyes glazed with desire, Evelyn thought his motions to be perfection. She would never grow tired of watching the play of muscles across his broad back or admiring the way they narrowed to lean and very masculine hips. When he raised himself to finally pull the garment off, Evelyn couldn't close her eyes any longer.

He was more magnificent than she had imagined, and more terrifying. As Alex threw the breeches aside and turned back to her, she had a fleeting look at a black pelt of hair narrowing to a jutting staff, and long muscular legs that swiftly moved to cover hers.

Then she gave herself up to the terrifying pleasure of his heaviness weighing against her in odd places, the sensation of his muscular legs caressing hers, and the fires of his kiss as he returned to her.

"You feel so good, my love, I want to touch you all over." And he did, caressing her in places she turned pale to think about, stroking the fire into spreading everywhere his fingers touched.

It took no daring to wrap her arms around Alex's neck or spread her legs at a pressure from his. It came naturally and without thought, just as she absorbed the pleasure of his touch. As he bent to suckle at her breast again, she muffled a faint cry and buried her hands in his thick hair, holding him there. When his hand returned to explore the moist place between her thighs, she rose eagerly to meet him, and Alex groaned.

Lifting his head to look into Evelyn's desire-flushed face, he felt an instant's panic at the protective tenderness rushing through him. It had never been like this before. He had a healthy appetite and enjoyed giving pleasure to his women, although their pleasure had never been his major concern. But he didn't want to fail this one. He wanted her to feel what he was feeling, to want him as much as he wanted her, want it enough to ask for more.

Seducing virgins was more complicated than he had imagined. He didn't want to hurt her. She was looking at him so trustingly, expectantly, not having any understanding of what came next. He was pounding with his need to plunge into her and take what he wanted, to have her at last. But he had to pave the way for a lifetime of pleasure. The responsibility was more enormous than he cared to contemplate.

He brushed her cheek with his kisses, found her mouth, and drank deeply of her passion, using his tongue to show her the intimacy to come. She welcomed him eagerly, with no sign of fear. There was nothing for it but he must breach the last remaining barrier that severed their freedom and joined them irrevocably forever.

"I don't want to hurt you, little tyrant, but sometimes it does. Make me stop if I go too fast."

Her hands slid across his chest and encircled his neck, and that sultry, husky voice of hers responded with a sensuousness that shivered down his spine. "I can do anything you can do," she promised with a wicked smile that relieved all fears. This was Evelyn, not some weeping, vaporish miss. And she was his.

Evelyn felt the brush of hardness where Alex's hand had been just moments before. Then he was cupping her buttocks, lifting and spreading her legs to receive him, and the pressure grew. Where just his fingers had entered her and left her aching, now a thickness probed and pushed. She closed her eyes tightly, fighting back the panic. Alex's words whispered along her skin, soothing her, reminding her it was he and not some invisible monster forcing her. Forcing her. He must not think he forced her. She had told him she could do this, and she would.

She relaxed, letting his murmurs wash around her, and the flames danced again. She moved tentatively against him and felt the pleasure of his moan as he moved inside her. There were pain and pressure, but also an escalating excitement as her body realized this was what she needed to fill the emptiness.

Alex moved slowly in and out, preparing her until she writhed with the need for more. Then, with eyes open, needing to know all of her, he made the final plunge.

Evelyn jerked in his hands, then quivered at the sensation of having him full inside of her. He stopped, giving her time to adjust, and she opened her eyes to find him watching her. In that moment he revealed more of himself than she had ever seen, and her heart twisted from her chest and leapt to join his. There was vulnerability in his eyes and tenderness in the curve of his mouth as he watched for her reaction. She wanted to love him, to hold him, to tell him everything would be all right. All she could do was hold out her arms and bring him down for her kiss. Her body would have to say what her words could not.

The quivering grew into eagerness to move against him. Her hips rose slightly, bringing him deeper, and

Alex's sudden thrust warned that his patience had come to an end. Evelyn bit back a cry of alarm as he withdrew and thrust again, but then there was no need to fear. He carried her with him, making her feel his need, teaching her the rhythm of his pleasure until it became hers too.

She could not have known it would be like this or she never would have allowed it. He not only possessed her, they possessed each other, responding equally until their movements became one and the pleasure rose to an exquisite torment that could not last without destroying them both. Alex smothered her groans with his as he made the final lunge and the explosion came, quaking their bodies and melding them with the heat of volcanic lava, sending his seed searing through her center.

They rested quietly then, not moving. Alex's heavy weight pushed Evelyn into the mattress, but she wanted it that way. She wrapped her arms around his neck, loving the warmth and smoothness of his broad shoulders beneath her fingertips. There was pain where they joined, but she didn't want him to leave ever again.

It couldn't last, of course. Alex finally stirred himself, rolling gently to one side so as not to crush her. Evelyn felt the cool air rush between them, and she turned to follow, staying close within the circle of his arms, very aware of their nakedness but not frightened by it. Alex holding her like this was the most natural thing in the world. She could not imagine how she had ever felt otherwise.

She looked up to see him watching her warily, and a sleepy smile crossed her face. She touched a finger to his newly shaved jaw and smoothed straying strands of hair behind his ear. "Did I go too fast for you?" she asked wickedly.

Alex grinned then, a heart-stopping grin that tickled Evelyn to her toes and made her want to kiss him until he took her again. Why couldn't he look like that more often? In wonder she curled closer against his chest as his words rumbled into her ear.

"You can go as fast as you like with me, my dear. I'll keep up somehow." Alex smoothed his hand down her back, bringing her closer and fitting her more intimately into the curve of his body. He could feel his body responding to her already, but he was aware of her difficulty earlier and knew he'd caused her pain. Her tightness had been pure rapture for him, but he would give her time to recover. He kissed the top of her head as she snuggled against his shoulder, and pulled the quilt higher around her. "We have the rest of our lives to learn different paces. I'm in no hurry."

He drove the first crack into Evelyn's comfort. She wanted to sleep. Her whole body felt relaxed and blissful and she wanted time to absorb the myriad sensations to which he had introduced her. She could still feel the heated moisture of him between her thighs. She was insane to let his words disturb her. But she couldn't let them go unanswered.

"I'll still not marry you, Alex," she murmured cruelly against his shoulder.

His hand stopped its gentle stroking to grip her shoulder and push her back against the pillow where he could see her face. "You have no choice. I told you that. You could be carrying my child already. I'll not lose this one too."

It was evidence of the extent of his desperation that he let this slip out, and Alex regretted the words as soon as he had said them. She had torn aside all his emotional barriers and left him more vulnerable than he had been in years. In that moment he hated her for it, and the scowl between his eyes grew menacing.

Evelyn ignored the scowl, seeing only the pain she had caused. It did not make sense with the man she knew, and hesitantly she sought understanding. "You had a child?"

His intrepid Evelyn always succeeded in entering where angels feared to tread. All thoughts of sleep fled as Alex threw himself back against the pillow, fighting long-denied memories. But he needed them if he were to make her see. He must put that long-ago pain to use to protect his future happiness, and hers. Struggling for the right words, Alex tried to put himself back in time.

It had been the spring of his sixteenth year. He had outgrown his tutor, but the man had no other position to go to and did not reveal his uselessness. Alex wanted to go to Oxford, but his mother would use the same excuses and fainting spells to keep him tied to the house that she had used when he had wanted to go off to school with the other boys. He was restless, with no outlet for his energy.

He had been aware for some time that Sir Hugh had been calling more frequently than usual, but the man was soft and old and of no interest to an impulsive, headstrong sixteen-year-old. So when one day Alex's mother called for him while Sir Hugh was with her, he had thought nothing of it. She liked to parade him before her friends. All his clothes were tailor-made in the latest fashions to suit her taste, and she would have the vapors should he ever appear with a tie or a button out of place. Since she was the only family he knew, Alex tried to please her, but the task had grown more irritating with the years.

When his mother announced that Sir Hugh had asked her to marry him, she might as well have announced that the moon was made of blancmange for all the sixteen-year-old Alex believed her. For most of his life she had been telling him how wicked his father was and that she would never allow another man into her home again. He had taken it for granted that he would be the only man in her life. They had had a number of disagreements lately. Probably he shouldn't have taken his new mount out galloping at midnight. And perhaps he shouldn't have joined the footman in tippling in the wine cellar the week before. But he was bored, and he had to do something. Surely she wouldn't marry fat old Sir Hugh just because he was sowing a few wild oats.

But as their words and promises washed over him, Alex saw the way the old man was looking at his petite blond mother, and he wanted to smash his fist into the randy old goat's face. When they waited for his approval, he gave a curt "Fine. Why not?" and walked out.

He hadn't believed she would do it, but within the month they were married and on their wedding trip and planning to return to the baronet's hideous modern mansion. Alex had never felt so alone in his life. His tutor was there, and a houseful of servants. He was waited on hand and foot, but he was alone.

Until the day he found sweet Bess. She was a plump

armful, all sunshine smiles and golden curls. They were much of an age, but she had more experience than he, and he had considerably more wit than she. It didn't matter when they discovered the pleasures of their youthful bodies in the summer heat of the hayloft. The scent of new-mown grass still filled his nostrils as he remembered it.

She was lovely, and they learned their pleasures together. Without a hint of shame, she described how her father used her when he felt the need. She assured him she had felt no pleasure until Alex came along. Jealous, Alex had ordered her to start spending her nights at the house instead of going home to the village. He wasn't certain she obeyed. The servants' rooms were in the attic, and he didn't have the courage to run the gauntlet of footmen and maids to find her bed. He just felt confident that she was happy to be safe with him, and thought no more about it.

By the time his mother moved in with Sir Hugh, Alex had decided to remain where he was. She took the news with surprising equanimity, only looking mildly faint and asking her new husband to help her back to the carriage. This rejection no longer held any surprise for him. Alex watched her go with the first layer of callousness he had learned to don.

By the end of summer, Bess was swelling with his child. They admired the hard curve of her belly with equal pride and no shame at all. The child was something they had done together, a symbol of their independence. Alex asked her to marry him, but she put him off with giggles and pulled him down into the hay. Her swelling breasts were a temptation he could not resist, and he let her lead the way. He just knew she was his. The child growing between them was proof of that.

The day that he couldn't find her anywhere put an end to that fantasy. Fearing her father had come for her, Alex had ridden into the village in a frenzy of worry. The man showed no fear of him when he arrived. He looked at Alex slyly, spat in the dirt, and announced his Bess was happily wedded to the father of her child.

Alex went a little crazy after that. He had just turned seventeen. He owned nothing of his own. His mother's estate now belonged to Sir Hugh. He lived on their charity. He was helpless to fight this crime in any way but rage.

He finally located Bess one lovely September day when the air was crisp and cool and the sun shone so painfully he had to pull his hat over his eyes. He had been drinking with the footman again, but the alcohol had not alleviated the pain. When he rode up to the solid brick farmhouse and stared out at the well-built barn and acres of field around it, he knew what Bess had done, but he refused to admit it. He dismounted and sought her out to prove it to himself.

She was six months pregnant by then and more beautiful than ever. She met him with the same eager kisses as before, let him touch her belly and breasts, but laughed when he offered to take her away.

"Why should I go?" she had asked cheerfully, gesturing toward the comfortable rocking chair beside the warm fire in this jewel of a farmhouse. "Can you give me all of this?"

He had given her love and his child, but he could give her nothing else, and she knew it. He protested. He threatened to tell her husband. He raged and pleaded, but she couldn't be stirred. Her husband had married fully believing he was the only one and that the child was his. He'd had no children by his first wife, and he dearly wanted this one. It could be his. It might be. Who knew?

The full extent of her betrayal came to Alex slowly, in bits and pieces over a matter of weeks. By then he'd persuaded Sir Hugh to send him to Oxford. He wasn't home when Bess had the child. He never really went home again.

His drinking and his womanizing got him sent down so many times Alex lost count, and finally he just forgot to go back. The quarterly allowance from his stepfather was sufficient to find him a small suite of rooms in London. It didn't pay for his expensive habits, but he was aware by now that he was the only heir to the elderly Earl of Cranville. His creditors were willing to wait.

Alex fell silent, not certain how much of his thoughts he had spoken out loud. Apparently it was sufficient to put Evelyn to sleep. She said nothing when he didn't go on. He didn't tell her how his disillusionment had led him to one deceitful whore after another. He always felt a certain satisfaction when he found them out, and he never had any objection to sharing the beds of wives of other men. If they didn't cheat with him, they would cheat with others, he had rationalized. It had become a way of living, and he had seen nothing wrong with it. Not until he had Evelyn in his arms and knew he couldn't share her did he have a better understanding of the harm he had done.

He didn't want to think about that right now. He needed her again, and he turned on his side to wake her. To his surprise, her eyes were open, and she was staring at him with torment darkening their depths to almost purple.

"I'll love you, Alex, but will you ever be able to love me back?"

16

Stunned, Alex stared unbelieving into Evelyn's wide eyes. His recital hadn't caused tears of pity or angry denunciations for his wasted years as he had expected. He could tell her much worse if he chose, but he suspected she already knew that he wasn't exactly a temperate man. And still she made this impossible declaration.

"I didn't ask you to love me." Irritated but not knowing why, Alex returned to his own pillow. The damned woman made a habit of getting under his skin. He didn't know how long it would take to develop a tolerance for that.

Evelyn lay silent, unable to think of a witty reply to offset that hurtful remark. He had opened his soul to her, and she had accepted it. Why couldn't he accept her? Stupid question. He had just told her why. Perhaps she hadn't quite accepted everything he had said yet. He hated and distrusted all women. Yet there had to be some feelings for her, or he would never have offered marriage.

It didn't matter. Everything he had said just made it that much clearer that she couldn't marry him. He would never love or trust her; the wounds he had taken were apparently mortal ones. And she couldn't go to another country and face the hostility of a new life without at least the slender support of her husband's love and trust. It was quite impossible.

"I'll do as I please," she finally answered stiffly. Seeing no point in continuing to lie naked in his bed, Evelyn started to rise to look for her clothes.

Alex caught her arm. "Where do you think you're going?"

"To hell, evidently. I want to get dressed." She tried to jerk away, but he rose on one elbow and pulled her back. She found herself glaring up into his darkened face.

"The night has just begun. There is no reason to go until dawn. I don't think you found what we did together terribly unpleasant."

Alex's fingers were pressuring her back into the pillows. She had no defense against his greater strength. She could use words to wound him, but that might only make him angrier and more hurtful. Besides, she didn't want to cause him pain as those other women had. She didn't want to give him reason to lump her with all the rest. What difference it would make in the end was beyond Evelyn's ability to comprehend, but some things had to be taken on instinct.

His kiss was angry, and his grip on her shoulders was painful, but she wouldn't let him force her. He had enough guilt on his conscience. She didn't need to add to it. Quite shamelessly she wanted him to love her again, but not this way, not with anger.

Evelyn caught her hands in the raw thickness of Alex's hair and arched against him invitingly with her body while her lips parted and caressed and drew him in. Alex uttered a low groan, and the rigid anger drained out of him as he eagerly sought the solace she offered.

He lost himself in her caresses, determinedly forgetting old memories now that they were said. He wanted to wipe the slate clean and start afresh, and Evelyn offered him that chance. She had a worldly cynicism to match his own sometimes, but in this she was as innocent as the wind. He felt new again just in touching her, in receiving the pleasures of her untutored kisses. She gave without reservation, without wanting anything from him but the magic they somehow created together.

His need for her was almost frightening. Alex knew the savage hunger of lust well enough, but not like this. It wasn't just lust beckoning now. He had satisfied his physical hungers the first time. He took her now for reasons beyond his knowledge, obeying a deep craving to conquer and possess and make this woman his alone. He had enough experience to know that they were not likely to create a child in one night, but the desire to fill her with his child was part of his urgency.

When Alex drove into her, Evelyn cried out, but it sounded like a cry of triumph more than pain. He knew he was being hasty but he couldn't stop now. She was still so narrow that he knew he must cause her pain, but she took his breath away when her passion closed around him and drew him deeper. Lost beyond thought, Alex followed her responses until the world went away and there were only the two of them, and they became one.

Evelyn clung to the strong arms on either side of her, gasping for breath as the final aftershocks rolled over her. Alex didn't leave her, but remained in the position of triumphant conqueror. She could feel his shuddering breaths as well as her own. The pain he had caused was as nothing to the pleasure, and she feared she would be his captive forever because of it. She would never be able to share this with anyone else, and a tiny tear crawled down her cheek as she recovered her senses.

Alex finally moved to take her in his arms, lying on his back and pulling her half on top of him so she couldn't get away. Evelyn kissed the salty perspiration beading on his chest and knew she loved him. It was a hopeless feeling. On top of everything else, she didn't need to fall in love with a hard-hearted bastard like Alex, but there wasn't much she could do about it now.

As he lay silently stroking her hair, Evelyn whispered against his skin, "Do you know for certain the child is yours? Have you ever seen him?"

Alex flinched but didn't hesitate in his answer. "The child was a girl. She's a little older than Jacob now. She had no brothers or sisters. And no, I have never seen her."

She heard the anguish and knew he was still fighting old hurts. If he saw the child, the visible proof that she was his, he would not be able to leave her where she was. It was better not to know, not to think about it. Sighing, Evelyn brushed kisses across his muscular shoulder. His physical strength was no protection against emotional wounds.

Since words only caused disagreement, they said nothing further. Alex continued to hold her even after he knew she slept. They might have many more nights to come, but he wanted to hold this one as long as he could. He wanted to remember innocence and trust and hang on to them through whatever came their way next. He wanted to believe in her.

Evelyn woke at dawn to the cry of a jay outside their window. At the same moment, she realized she was trapped against the warm nakedness of Alex's chest, with his heavy legs entwined with hers. His arm was thrown over her as if to prevent escape while they lay face-to-face. Or more like face-to-shoulder, Evelyn decided as her eyes opened to meet the formidable solidity she rested against. He must be terribly uncomfortable lying like that.

Tentatively she moved her legs away from his. The cold rushed up her thighs, and she regretted the move immediately. She hurt where they had joined together last night, but even the hurt stirred longings she must get used to ignoring.

She wasn't certain she could so easily escape Alex's imprisoning arm. She touched her fingers to the welcome warmth of his chest and found it difficult to pull away. Some change in his breathing made her look up to his face. Beautifully lashed dark eyes greeted her without expression.

"Good morning," she said softly, fighting the flood of embarrassment she suddenly felt at waking naked in a man's bed. She was all too aware of her body and of his to be comfortable.

He said nothing, but pressed a kiss against her brow and drew her closer against him. Evelyn went willingly, loving the sensation of being held. The gray dawn gradually grew brighter with streaks of rose tinting their skin as they lay together. If they were married, they could have this every day. Why couldn't everything be simple?

"We have to go home. Mama will be terrified," she finally summoned the courage to say.

"I was just thinking it might be simpler if we never went back, but I suppose running away doesn't solve problems." Alex released her, gently pushing her back against the pillows so he could see her one more time.

Violet eyes watched him warily as he cupped and stroked her tender breasts, then drew his hand lightly down her side, over the curve of narrow waist and hip, to come to rest at the juncture of her thighs. He wanted her again, but he could wait until it would be good for her. "Are you very sore?"

His tender words caught Evelyn by surprise. She had thought he was building up to another argument. Perhaps he was no more desirous of the fight to come than she. She smiled a trifle nervously as he continued to hold his hand there. "I think I'll live. I won't promise I'll be able to walk twenty miles, though."

"We have a better chance of finding someone to give us a ride during the day, but I suppose we had better get started if we're to get anywhere." Alex withdrew his hand and reached over the side of the bed where he had flung his breeches, turning his back on her tempting loveliness. "You had better dress quickly. I can't promise how long I can remain noble."

She was reluctant to leave the warm covers and man beside her for the chilly room, but she had to learn to do without him. Bracing herself, she slid to the floor to begin searching for her scattered clothing.

Wearing only his tight breeches, Alex joined her. Evelyn had to keep her eyes from straying to that part of him that she had never dreamed existed until last night. She had known baby boys were different from baby girls. It had never occurred to her that the difference would grow so marked with time. The bulge behind his breeches warned she had better dress quickly.

She quickly pulled on her chemise and tied the ribbons high to avoid Alex's lecherous gaze. She refused his offer to help with her stockings and pointed out the fact that he would do better to don his own.

Alex chuckled and pulled her toward him for a brief kiss. "I knew I liked women with spirit, but you are very much in danger of becoming a shrew, little tyrant. Somehow we'll have to learn to soften each other's edges."

"I don't think there's been a grindstone made that could soften yours, sir. I'm neither shrew nor tyrant, just practical." In a huff, Evelyn jerked on her shirt and grabbed for her skirt before he could make further invasions upon her person. The wool was sadly crumpled, but she pulled it on without further thought.

Alex caught the thick length of her hair and pulled it from her shirt collar. It fell nearly to her waist and shimmered with almost a reddish hue in this light. "One of us must needs be practical, I suppose. Still, I can think of a thousand things I'd rather do than leave this room right now."

"A thousand? In this room?" She raised a skeptical brow as she buttoned her shirt.

His grin was the devilish one she had expected the night before. His appraising gaze as it swept over her told her what he meant before his words did. "At least a thousand. Do you think there is only one way of making love? Remind me sometime to teach you more."

Flushed at the thought of ever finding herself in bed with him again, Evelyn turned away. She must not let him think in those terms again or she really would end up carrying his child. As she fastened her skirt, her fingers nervously brushed the place between her hips where a child would grow. Surely he had not already planted his child in her. She tried to think of how long it had taken friends of hers to get pregnant after marriage, but the thoughts weren't reassuring. Susan had had her babe only six months after she was wedded, and Mary's had come nine months to the day. How long had they been indulging in these sinful pleasures before they were actually married? She couldn't say.

Refusing to contemplate the possibility that one night of pleasure could lead to a lifetime of misery, Evelyn hastily finished dressing and tried to tie her hair into something approaching respectability.

Alex came up behind her and prevented her from doing more than tying it back from her face. He wrapped the silky length about his hand and kissed her lightly, doing no more than teasing her lips. "I like seeing you with your hair down. That first day I saw you, I wanted to jerk the ribbon from your hair and see how it would look spread upon a pillow. Now that I know what it looks like, I don't think I'll ever get enough of it."

His seductive words sent more shivers through Evelyn

than his touch. She had to remind herself that he was well-practiced in saying these things to women. Mindlessly she returned his kiss, but somewhere inside of her, she practiced restraint.

When they went downstairs they found the old woman waiting to tell them their horses had miraculously returned during the night. Instead of being amazed and delighted at this news, Alex looked decidedly grim. Evelyn sent him an anxious glance, wondering if he still blamed her, but he gave no hint as to his thoughts as he ordered their breakfast.

Afterward they rode in relative silence, each wrapped in his or her own thoughts. It was the beginning of October and the maple leaves had reached the height of their brilliant color, but what had occurred between them the night before was more overwhelming than this stunning autumn day. With every jolting stride of the livery nag Evelyn was reminded of what she had done, and her gaze strayed more than once to Alex's masculine frame riding straight and tall slightly ahead of her. She wasn't quite convinced it was all real. In this new light he appeared quite revoltingly handsome and very much the noble lord. Had she really lain naked beneath him not more than a few hours ago? The thought made her feel incredibly vulnerable.

She couldn't really believe she had refused his offer of marriage either, but watching his aristocratic stance gave her courage. She couldn't destroy his life by involving it with hers. He didn't love her, so she would hurt only his pride with her continued refusal. She loved him too much to make him miserable for the rest of his life. She couldn't be a countess or go to London, and that was obviously what he needed and where he belonged. After a few years in prison, she would forget all about him and go on with her life when she got out. Jacob and her mother would have the warehouse, and she could visit New York or Philadelphia and start over. It would work. It would have to.

They had little to say as they stopped outside her mother's house. Alex climbed down first and caught Evelyn's waist to help her. He flicked a finger over her pale cheek as she faced him.

"Courage, little tyrant. I'm used to taking the full force of the blow. Just having you beside me will make it easier."

He took her arm and turned toward the house before he could see her astonishment. She had thought he was still angry and blaming her for what had happened. What had brought about this sudden change to tenderness? Tenderness! From Alex! She sent him a surreptitious look to see if he were the same man who had stood in his tavern room with his doxy behind him hurling insults at her. Which Alex was he now?

At Alex's call as they entered, the front room burst into life. Amanda Wellington flew in with reddened eyes and sodden handkerchief. Jacob raced down the stairs with suspiciously moist lashes as he leapt toward Alex. And even George Upton appeared from the study where he had apparently made his vigil.

"You're safe! Oh, thank God, you're safe! You have no idea . . ." Amanda's voice trailed off as she hugged her daughter.

Upton's words, in contrast, were less than cheerful. "At least you had the sense not to elope, but you could have left some lie to placate Amanda until you returned. You both ought to be ashamed of yourselves. Hampton, I trusted you to act with a little more responsibility than this."

Evelyn disentangled herself from her mother and squeezed Alex's hand, but he spoke before she could silence her uncle's obnoxious tirade.

"My apologies to all of you. There was a slight accident that forced us to stay longer than we planned, and we couldn't make it back before dark." He made a gallant bow in the direction of Mrs. Wellington. "You are already aware of my feelings toward your daughter. Under the circumstances, I think it is time to cry the banns."

Amanda burst into more tears and George looked placated. Only Evelyn appeared shocked, then grim.

"I told you, Alex, I will not marry you or anyone else. Now, if you will excuse me . . ." She made an abrupt curtsy and started up the stairs.

Below her, she could hear Alex reassuring her family.

Let them go on with all the plans they wanted. They could not force her to say the vows.

By the time Evelyn reached her room, her head was pounding dreadfully, and she flung herself upon the bed for a long cry. Why did everything that felt so right have to be so wrong?

The first banns were cried that Sunday. Evelyn found herself flocked with eager well-wishers after church, most of them female and most of them casting jealous eyes at Alex at her side. Evelyn had little to say and walked away as soon as was possible. She had begged and pleaded with him to be reasonable, but Alex had remained unmoved. There was no point in arguing with Uncle George. Already he was smugly accepting congratulations on his future nephew-in-law. This was what he had wanted all along. There would be no changing his mind.

Evelyn considered appealing to her mother, but she had no arguments that her mother would understand. Amanda was already contemplating returning to England to visit her family and wondering if she ought to place Jacob in school there. She would be free to return anytime she wanted, but Evelyn would not. Marriage was for life. If Alex returned to his tomcat ways, she could do nothing but sit in some empty house in a strange country and contemplate killing him or herself. It wouldn't serve. She knew deep down in her heart that this marriage was wrong. But she could not tell her mother why.

Alex was the only one who understood, but he refused to hear reason. She told him he would have to drag her tied and bound to the altar and hold a burning brand to her back before she would agree to the vows. He only replied that he would wait until she was in prison for a week and then ask her again. He suspected that might be a little more persuasive than a brand. She railed and ranted, but he remained unmoved.

Evelyn continued to refuse to sell the warehouse. Her uncle obviously thought it wisest to wait until she was married, when he could consult Alex on the matter. If they married the same day the final bann was cried, nearly a week would remain before the fine had to be paid. She had no intention of marrying that day or any other. She was of age and there was nothing that could be done about it. She would go to jail and Alex would have to return to England where he belonged.

That thought terrified her, but not as much as the alternative of being Alex's wife and living in England. She might imagine herself in love with him because he was so terribly masculine and physically attractive and willing to listen to her on most subjects, but she was smart enough to know love didn't guarantee happiness. If Alex loved her, she might consider things in a different light, but as it was, she knew she had little chance of softening his heart.

Alex once again offered to remove himself to an inn to avoid the appearance of any further impropriety, but Amanda refused to hear of it. Evelyn suspected her mother rather enjoyed having a man to cook for and flirt with again, and Alex obviously soaked up the attention with great pleasure. From what she had heard of his mother, Evelyn couldn't deny him this small recompense. It just made things doubly difficult for her to come down each morning to the sight of Alex eating breakfast with her family, sharing in the family discussions as if he were already one of them. His smile for her was always welcoming, but she still felt the wariness behind his dark eyes. There was still too much disagreement between them to be easy in their meeting.

Sometimes Alex ate dinner with them and sometimes he was off about the town with his new acquaintances. Evelyn found it fascinating that he could share dinner with the acting governor at his mansion in the country one night, and attend a meeting of patriots in a tavern the next. She didn't know how he could keep from betraying one faction to the other or how either faction could trust him, but Alex seemed to keep it all straight.

Frequently when he came home from these meetings to find Evelyn still up, he would sprawl on the sofa in the front room and tell her all that had occurred, embellishing the tale with his opinions along the way. Those times were the easiest because they could argue on equal, impersonal levels, exchanging ideas instead of violent emotions. The conversation might get animated and loud, but constrained by their surroundings, they were limited to exchanging words.

Evelyn listened eagerly to the reports of what they planned for what they now called the "Stamp Act Congress," but she could see little hope for the immediate future. The act would go into effect in less than three weeks, and this congress of colonial representatives was just beginning to gather. The tension in town had become unbearable, with militia in the streets to quell the crowds and the governor still hiding in the harbor. Everywhere Evelyn went, voices were raised in argument, and the few British soldiers stationed at the batteries suffered insults or worse if they entered town. The men going to the congress might declare themselves free, but there was a long distance between talk and action.

When their arguments died down in the wee hours of the morning, Amanda would discreetly intrude to suggest that Evelyn ought to retire. Under the circumstances, there could be no touching or kissing, and Evelyn was relieved of the effort needed to fight her desire. She knew, had Alex made any attempt at all, she would not have resisted his touch. She lay in bed at night wishing he would appear to drive away the frustrating needs that left her sleepless and miserable. But he kept a circumspect distance between them, only stealing an occasional chaste kiss when they were left momentarily alone. Even that left her longing for more.

When Alex didn't return at a reasonable hour on the night before the second bann was to be read, Evelyn retired to her bed in the fruitless hope of getting some sleep. A week and a half wasn't enough time to forget their lovemaking, she decided. She just needed more time to make the memories go away. Then she wouldn't relive every moment of that night over and over until her skin was flushed with heat and her fingers wandered to the place between her thighs where he had claimed her. Once she was behind the cold, hard bars of prison, surely these feelings would go away.

She was still awake when she heard the sound of unsteady feet coming down the street. Her room overlooked the front door, and she rose to watch as the feet seemed to turn in the direction of the house.

It didn't surprise her to see Alex staggering toward the door, but his less-than-orderly appearance gave her cause for concern. The fringed black cocked hat he had worn when he left was no longer in evidence. The sleeve of his good navy broadcloth coat appeared to be pulled from its seams. The ribbon of his queue was half-untied and his hair in danger of becoming fully unbound. The rip in his expensive silk stockings added the final touch to his bedraggled appearance.

Evelyn meant to turn away in disgust and return to bed, when the man below suddenly moaned and bent over the frostbitten flower garden by the door. Without a second thought, she fled from her room and down the stairs. Whatever had occurred this night, Alex had been hurt by it. She could not leave him injured by the doorstep.

Garbed only in a frail flannel nightrail, she hastily threw open the front door. Alex was still bent over the ground, half-kneeling as he vomited the contents of his stomach into the dirt. Evelyn quickly knelt beside him, searching his coat pockets for the large handkerchief she knew he kept there. Finding it, she helped him dry his mouth when he finished, then lent her shoulder to bring him to his feet.

Without exchanging a word, they made their way to the kitchen, where the fire had been banked several hours before. Alex lowered himself into a chair while Evelyn stirred the fire and pumped some fresh water for him to wash in. Unsympathetically she gave it to him cold, deciding he needed the sting to freshen him. He made no protest, but cleaned himself while she brewed a pot of coffee over the newly kindled fire. When he was done washing, Evelyn brought the lamp to the table to better examine the extent of his injuries.

The wound he had sustained in August was nearly healed and undamaged by whatever altercation he had entered this night. There was a slight puffiness about one eye and a cut on his chin that had already stopped bleeding. He closed his eyes as her fingers gently searched for other damage.

"I'll be fine, Evelyn," Alex said unsteadily, reaching to remove her hand. Just clasping her fingers between his jarred him as if he had been hit by lightning. He quickly released her hand and let her move away.

She returned to the fire to remove the coffee. Nervously avoiding his gaze, she busied herself seeking cup and saucer, sugar and cream, and setting them on the table, carefully keeping to the far side.

"Is brawling in taverns one of your vices too?" she inquired softly, not accusingly.

Alex gratefully took the cup and warmed his hands around it. "I've done it before," he agreed curtly. "I try not to make a habit of it."

"Wise man." This time the sarcasm was more evident. Pouring herself a cup of the strong brew, Evelyn sat opposite him. She was shameless in her desire to be with him, even when he was drunk and battered and in a foul mood. "I suppose there was a good reason for this particular fracas."

Alex shrugged and sipped at the coffee, allowing his gaze to linger on the soft lights flickering through her hair from the fire behind her. She wore it loose and flowing, and he followed its path over the creamy cloth covering her breasts. He could see her nipples pressing against the soft material. He wagered she wasn't aware of how provocative that was to a man in need, and he had no intention of telling her.

"At the time, I thought there was. Liquor gives a man a new perspective on things." Actually, he had punched a lout for saying the same things about Evelyn aloud that he himself had thought a few months ago. He had never been as much of one for defending a lady's honor as for taking it, but he had learned tonight how it felt to be on the other side of the fight. He didn't want other men speculating about what Evelyn was like in bed. He didn't even want them looking on her in lust if he could help it. He was glad he had been close enough to hear that particular remark. There would be a couple of soldiers reporting in sick in the morning, but his stomach still heaved at the thought of what would happen should she insist on going through with this farce of refusing him in favor of a jail guarded by those same soldiers.

"I can imagine." Evelyn watched Alex warily when he did not reveal the topic for battle. "If you think you will be all right, I'd better go to bed now. I don't want to wake Mama."

"I'll bank the fire in a minute. Go on up." Alex tried not to look as she rose and her slender curves were outlined in the fire's light, but the temptation was great and he wasn't feeling particularly strong. He admired the sway of her hips as she left the room, and groaned silently to himself, remembering how they had risen so eagerly to accept him, and how soft she had felt beneath him.

Sometime later Evelyn heard the sound of Alex's tread on the stairs. Evidently he had removed his shoes so as not to disturb the household. She pulled the covers up and stared at the door as she followed his progress down the hall.

It didn't surprise her at all when the door opened to reveal Alex standing there.

17

He had removed his ruined coat and waistcoat, holding them in his hand as he propped his shoulder against the doorjamb and let his gaze sweep over the narrow bed and its occupant. He appeared more tired than drunk, and rather than issue an immediate protest, Evelyn raised herself on one elbow and returned his gaze.

"May I come in?" He had tried his damnedest to play the part of gentleman these last weeks, but the worry and frustration over her refusal had finally worn down what very little restraint he possessed. Drinking to assuage his fears had not been a particularly intelligent thing to do, Alex concluded as he watched the blanket slip away from Evelyn's shoulders to fall to her waist. The gentleman was gone. In his place was a man who desperately needed what she had to offer and feared he could not have it.

He was already moving toward her before Evelyn had time to answer yes or no. The door behind him closed softly. She sat up, still not knowing whether to refuse him. "You can't come in here," she whispered, as much to herself as to him.

"You shouldn't leave your door unlocked." Carefully Alex sat down on the narrow edge of the bed beside her. His hand moved of its own accord to stroke her hair. "I need you, Evelyn. Don't make me go."

She almost thought she imagined the words as he leaned forward, cupping her head to keep her from retreating from his kiss. The whisper was so soft it was more like a growl from his throat as he brushed his lips across her cheek before settling on her mouth. But she did not need imagination to feel the need in his kiss. It was as intense and desperate as her own.

"Alex, we can't, not here." She barely caught her breath long enough to gasp the words. Alex's hand had already slid to her breast, and the other seemed to have the fabric of her gown well in control and above her knee. Her body had no desire whatsoever to deny him, but her mind still clung to the reality of the situation.

"Let me show you." Alex captured her protesting lips again as he lowered her to the bed, holding her tightly against him until they lay side by side on the narrow mattress. He breathed a sigh of pure joy as he lifted her hair from between them and spilled it down her back, sensing her acceptance in the way she let him take the lead. Someday she would be brave enough to come to him, but not just yet. Alex understood that and was relieved that she allowed this much liberty. His desire for her was overwhelming. He didn't think he could be a gentleman had she refused him. His palm stroked the side of her breast to the valley of Evelyn's waist, then pulled her hips lightly toward his. "I just want a little, love, just enough to hold me until I can have you every night."

Lud, but the words were seductive! Every night like this. Imagination could run rampant with such bliss, so Evelyn banished the thought from her mind. She couldn't banish what he was doing to her, however. Alex's very masculine body in her childish bed was an incongruity she was not prepared for. The heat of him enveloped her. The gentle caresses of his hand recalled previous passion, and the coffee taste of his mouth sent shivers of hunger through her. With the wall at her back and Alex in front, there was no escape even if she so desired. And once she felt the urgency of his need, her desire was for anything but leaving him.

Awkwardly her hands slid over his shirt to locate the buttons of his breeches as he had showed her once before. He uttered a muffled groan against her ear as her fingers rubbed against him, and when she hurriedly tried to remove her hand, he caught it there, pressing her fingers against his burning flesh.

"It's all right for you to touch me, just as I like to

touch you. But I'm like to burst from the need of you, love." Alex's voice was almost rueful as he traced his kisses over her delicate jaw to her throat.

Evelyn tentatively explored the place where he held her. The knowledge that she had the power to make him as crazy as he made her thrilled her, but she was still uncertain of her abilities. Alex's breath blew across her skin as he unfastened her gown and trailed his kisses downward to the aching peaks of her breasts. In a dreamy lethargy from which there was no release, she offered herself to him and felt the blood in her veins turn to molten lava as he took her in his mouth.

Slowly their clothes became disarranged enough to feel flesh against flesh and to escalate the urgency to a burning need. Evelyn bit her lip as she felt his hardness slide between her thighs as she lay on her side facing him. Here was the brand he would use on her that would take away her freedom, but at this moment she had no desire for liberty. When he lifted her knee to give him entrance, she arched her hips to ease his way.

He took her swiftly, with all the need she had felt in him when he first appeared at her door, and Evelyn followed him without hesitation, taking him deeper, reveling in the strength of him as he drove her to boundaries previously unreached. She had never known it could be like this, like a tumultuous storm swirling them away until one mighty blast dissolved the world and the storm and they floated weightlessly in each other's arms.

Foolishly Evelyn felt the tears of joy rolling down her cheeks as her body achieved release in his. She had wanted this so much, she could not be angry that he had broken her family's trust to come to her. She bent her head beneath Alex's chin and felt him moving gently against her, rubbing lightly at the soreness until she glowed with desire again. His breathing was labored as he finally extricated himself and smoothed her gown back over her legs.

"Now there are only nine hundred and ninety-eight more ways to teach you." His breath teased along her ear as he clasped her hands against his chest.

"That's not possible," she argued despite herself. "I cannot possibly think of more than four or five."

"And I doubt that more than ten or twelve are physically practicable, but I'm willing to try them all and invent some new ones if you are willing. Hold me just a little while, and then I'll behave and return to my room." He released her hands to pull her close and sleepily trace a pattern of kisses across her cheek.

"Alex, we cannot do this again," she admonished, not as severely as she ought when it felt so good to be in his embrace with her head resting against his broad shoulder. "What if there were a child?"

"I hope there is," he informed her firmly. "I fully intend to watch you grow big and round with my child. I want it more than anything else I can think of at the moment."

Evelyn lifted her head to gaze at him with curiosity. "What of your precious freedom? Imagining catching me in such a state is one thing, but what happens when I produce that mewling, whining brat you so despise?"

"That's what nursemaids are for. When he reaches the age of reason, I'll take him with me to learn those things he needs to know to survive in this world. I won't neglect our children. You need not worry over that."

He had ignored her question of freedom and deftly avoided all the important issues involved in the raising of children. One did not just shove an infant in an oven until it was properly done. She wanted her children to grow strong and free and independent, to know the value of hard work and the pride of love and friendship. She didn't want the jealousy brought about by title and entailment. Why should one son be given a fortune while the other was forced to work or marry well for his living? She had no use for the system that had left Alex to idle away his youth in hopes of inheritance. She shook her head against his chest, but she was too weary to dispute the argument now.

"I'll not worry, because there'll be no children. Go to your bed, Alex. We are being foolish even to consider such things."

The sadness in her voice took away the sting of her dismissal. Alex kissed her brow, then found the trace of tears at the corners of her eyes. Her words had torn a gaping hole in his side, but he wouldn't reveal the hurt.

"This is one argument I'm going to win, Evelyn. I'll probably be a rotten husband and an even worse father, but even that is preferable to rotting in prison or starving. You're going with me, Evelyn, whether you like it or not."

Alex pulled the covers snugly to her chin to keep out the cold caused by his departing. He left a lingering kiss on her lips to soften his words, but Evelyn felt the fierceness of them just the same. He was not a man accustomed to taking no for an answer. The battle ahead loomed terrifyingly real, more so for the fear that she had a good chance of losing. He had everything and everyone on his side. Even her own body betrayed her. How could she fight for an ideal in the face of such weapons?

She watched as Alex slipped from the room wearing only breeches and a partially open shirt, the rest of his clothing in his hands. Anyone seeing him leave would know precisely what they had been doing. She buried her face in the pillow and drank in the musky scent of him there, and with the imprint of Alex's caresses lingering on her skin, she slowly drifted into sleep.

The second announcement of their impending marriage was made in church the next day. Evelyn held a trifle unsteadily to Alex's arm as they stepped out into the October sunshine. The memory of the prior night was still strong in her mind, and she was surprised that no one saw her disgrace. Was she the only one who noticed how Alex's hand lingered proprietarily at her waist, how his eyes lit with deep fires when they turned to her? She felt trapped and helpless in the ring of fire that consumed them. The touch of his hand created a longing for more. She waited for his kiss, physically absorbed the deep rumble of his voice as he spoke to the others around them, and couldn't part from his side without great effort.

Alex seemed as aware as she of these physical bonds that held them captive. She sensed it in the wry way he kissed her hand when she came down that morning, his mocking words as he wrapped her in her cloak, and the way he jested at himself when he refused to leave her side at the invitation of his friends. He was as bewildered as she by this turn of events, but determined to make the best of it.

"I will be quite domesticated by next week," he whispered close to her ear as they moved toward the street and away from the assembly of churchgoers. "How much longer will it take for you to catch up with me?"

"If last night was an example of your domesticity, I am far ahead of you, sir. At least I stay at home at night and avoid tavern brawls."

He winced. "Well, perhaps I shall never quite be a domestic fowl, then, but I cannot imagine you fluttering happily about a chicken coop either. Still, I understand even certain wild birds mate for life. Is my plumage grand enough?"

Since he was as elegantly garbed as ever in a coat of rich brown velvet, brocade vest of gold, fawn breeches, and immaculate lace, she could certainly not fault his plumage, and Evelyn laughed at his nonsense. "Your plumage suits me very well. And how does the cock select his mate? Her plumage is rather drab, I believe."

Today she wore a gown of modest gray adorned only by the delicacy of the lace at her throat and wrist. Alex surveyed the costume with an air of authority. "The cock sees further than the plumage, I believe. A most perceptive bird, although the shape the plumage covers does create a certain susceptibility to make decisions on the basis of less intellectual qualities."

Their laughter was interrupted by a shout from down the street. Someone answered the call with a query, and in a matter of minutes a number of men were striding purposefully in the direction of the harbor.

Wearing a worried expression, Evelyn started to follow. Alex quickly halted her, recommending her to the company of her mother nearby. She sent him a look of irritation. "If there is something happening at the wharf, I would know of it."

"In a few weeks you will be in jail if you have your way. Get used to having someone else deal with the warehouse. I suspect it's in no danger. Go with your mother and I'll be right back."

Evelyn held his arm. "What is it, then? You know something."

"They have been waiting for a ship from England bearing the stamps. I suspect one has been sighted." Alex did not mention that he hoped it was one of his that he had expected this last week and more. It was overdue, and there had been time enough aplenty for his cousin to have received his letter and found the answers to his queries. He didn't wish to get Evelyn's hopes up if he were wrong.

Evelyn let him go and watched as he strode rapidly away. Alex's was an imposing figure of authority not easily ignored even when he dressed the part of dandy and spoke with the accents of the despised aristocracy. He had proved easily adaptable to the capricious elements of her world. If the stamps were on that ship, Alex was better capable of dealing with the angry mob that would ensue than she.

Feeling oddly unnerved by that knowledge, Evelyn reluctantly followed her mother home to prepare the Sunday repast. She had no fondness for cooking as her mother had, but the events of these last weeks had disturbed her state of mind to the point that the simple task of creating a meal suited her mood. She took some satisfaction in the fact that one dish was goose pie.

Jacob came scampering in less than an hour later, bouncing with news. Evelyn raised a skeptical brow as she pinched the last of a pie crust and waited for him to blurt it out. From his excitement, it was evident that the news could not be entirely bad.

"There's an English ship in the harbor! They're trying to keep it from docking, just like we planned, but Alex says it's one of his. They're arguing something fierce, and Alex is swearing he'll take a sword to any man daring to keep him from his own ship. I think the ship has cannon! I saw them rolling one out on deck."

The words poured out in an unleashed torrent and Evelyn could not get a word in until he gasped for air. Hastily she inquired, "The name of the ship, Jacob?"

"The *Neptune*. I'm going back to see what happens." He swung around to fly back out, but his sister's words caught him in mid-step.

"Not without me, you aren't." Taking off her apron and dropping it on a kitchen chair, Evelyn grabbed for a cloak by the kitchen door. "Mama, you might want to make a few more pies. That is one of Alex's ships. After this ordeal, he might wish to invite his officers to a meal. I'll be back as quickly as I can." She kissed her flustered mother on the cheek and took to the street with Jacob.

The scene at the wharf was the chaos she expected. Every available fishing boat was in the process of being manned to form a feeble flotilla to keep the towering *Neptune* from the wharf. Alex had mounted a barrel to shout reason at the men gathered at his feet. Although some seemed to listen, many more preferred action. The hated stamps would not be allowed if there were any earthly way to prevent it. Tarring and feathering of interfering Englishmen seemed high upon the list.

Evelyn found Sam Adams stroking his chin on the outskirts of the crowd and tugged at his coat for attention. "Wouldn't it be more sensible to let the *Neptune* dock and then go aboard and seize the stamps if they are there? You cannot reasonably expect to keep a ship that size from landing where it will."

"You're quite probably right, Miss Wellington, but if your forceful young man cannot convince the crowd of that, I can assure you that my chances are slim. I take it that actually is one of his fleet?"

"With a name like *Neptune*, can you doubt it? All the Cranville vessels have classical names. His cousin apparently has a sense of humor as well as an education."

"Well, the god of the sea will have to spew forth his trident to attempt landing in this mob. I don't envy your fiancé."

Evelyn contemplated pushing her way through the crowd, when she noted Alex had evidently given up on reasoning. He leapt from his barrel and minutes later she discovered him in a small dinghy, garbed in his best Sunday suit, rowing toward the immense brigantine floating in the harbor.

Alex's abrupt change from speech to action caught the crowd by surprise, and they watched in puzzlement as the English dandy rowed with expert skill, expensive lace flapping in the cool October breeze as he maneuvered near the rope ladder thrown over the ship's side. Evelyn had to hide a sardonic grin at the crusty comments around her as Alex swiftly climbed the ladder to join the ship's crew, shaking hands with the waiting officers in a manner that left it evident that his hands went undamaged by the coarse ropes. Her fishermen friends couldn't quite find it conceivable that a man in velvets and lace could do physical labor, but she knew Alex's strength and had never doubted his ability. His willingness might occasionally be called into question, but not his competence.

The crowd watched for further enlightenment, but to their disappointment, Alex and his officers disappeared down the companionway. The brigantine made no further attempt to land, and the flotilla of fishing boats bobbed idly without direction. If Alex had accomplished nothing else, he had caught their attention.

Obviously pressing his advantage, Alex appeared several minutes later, making a show of handing a letter to a crewman. The sailor nodded and swiftly clambered down to the dinghy. The crowd waited in anticipation.

The young sailor docked the boat at the wharf and nervously climbed the stairs toward the threatening mob. He cast a quick glance around and looked relieved when his gaze found whatever he sought. Skirting the crowd, he came to a halt before the only lady in sight.

Evelyn took the letter in mild astonishment, but Alex's quick black scrawl spoke loudly enough.

"I told the lad to deliver this to the aggravating female in dowdy plumage," he had written. "As long as you must disobey orders, at least make yourself useful. Persuade some of your more persuasive friends to join me. If there are stamps aboard, I will gladly hand them over and pretend they've been delivered honestly."

Evelyn could tell by the tone of the letter that the stamps were not there, but the crowd would never believe his word. Without comment, she handed the missive to Adams. She wondered how Alex had seen her in this mob, and she threw a speculative glance toward the ship while her companion perused the letter.

She heard Adams chuckle and turned to catch him watching her for some sign of indignation at the letter's contents. When she displayed nothing more than impatience, he nodded agreement. "Your gentleman has a head on his shoulders, and I trust his heart is in the right place. Will you join us?"

"Tell the conceited beast that I have gone home to finish cooking the meal he had better arrive in time to eat. If he isn't hanged before then, he may invite his officers to join us."

She spun around and walked off. The men near them had missed little of this scene. Adams would have no difficulty finding volunteers to join in the ship's search. She had every confidence that the whole farce would be at an end by dinnertime. She reserved her irritation for the man who dared speak of her in such terms and order her about as if she were already his wife. He would soon discover that she was a more formidable adversary than he expected.

18

The ship's captain tactfully bowed out of his cabin, leaving the owners of the vessel to their awkward meeting. Not having expected his cousin's arrival, Alex was slightly taken aback at being confronted with the earl. Quickly recovering himself, he strode forward to shake the older man's hand.

"Your letters intrigued more than informed. I rather expected to be returning with your body and a weeping female heavy with child. Are you leading that mob out there or running from it?" The earl's dry tone conveyed his opinion of his heir's frequent impetuous escapades. The two were much alike in too many ways to make their relationship smooth, but in the five years of their acquaintance, a mutual respect had developed between them.

Alex didn't look amused. He had enough problems at hand without worrying about how the earl could complicate things. "I'm fighting it at the moment. I just sent a note with one of the sailors to ask that a few friends of mine be brought aboard shortly to establish the fact that we're not the enemy. I don't know how closely you've paid attention to what's going on over here, but we almost have a small rebellion on our hands. Before company arrives, tell me, did you find the answers I needed?"

The earl went to the desk and withdrew a stiff brown packet of papers. "They're all here. You're sitting on a veritable nest of vipers."

"Is Upton one of them?" That was his greatest concern of the moment, an insurmountable complication if his guess were correct.

"George Upton?" The earl withdrew the topmost paper and nodded. "He heads the list."

Alex groaned and took the paper. Upton and Evelyn's lawyer and a few more of her uncle's cronies graced the page. He swore long and vividly as he returned the packet.

"There are no females on it." Cranville watched his cousin carefully at this outburst. "Your lady friend isn't involved."

"I didn't think she was, but they've arranged for her to be arrested anyway. It's a long story and time is short. Say nothing of the contents of that package to anybody. They are all friends and relatives of the lady concerned. I'm not certain how to deal with that information without destroying a number of innocent people."

Alex paced the polished teak floor wishing he were anyplace but here. To free Evelyn, he would have to accuse Upton. She wouldn't be any more pleased at destroying her aunt and cousin than she would be about her mother and brother. To protect the Wellingtons' interest in the warehouse, she could go to jail. There wasn't anything she could do to save her aunt and cousin. They would be ruined, financially and socially, on two continents.

The sound of approaching footsteps warned that his company had arrived. Excusing himself, Alex hurried from the cabin before he was forced to introduce the Earl of Cranville to these Whig rebels. Damn, but he could foresee only more complications than solutions ahead. He was but one man. He would have to take them one at a time.

In any event, Alex was forced to introduce his noble cousin before the patriots could be convinced they were hiding nothing that might hold the stamps. There were no royal dispatches, no parliamentary packets, nothing but one earl who watched the proceedings with mild amusement. These Sons of Liberty showed little awe of his lofty personage but greeted him with respect, accepting the fact that he had arrived to attend his heir's wedding. Cranville sent Alex a surprised look at that assumption, but he didn't deny it.

When the flotilla of boats cleared the area of the wharf

so the *Neptune* could dock, and the patriots had left the two men alone again, Cranville waited a trifle impatiently for his heir's explanation.

All he got for his trouble was Alex's restless pacing as he waited for the ship to position itself so he could disembark.

"You might give me some clue as to what to expect when I go ashore," he finally prompted him. "Or am I to remain in hiding and not be introduced to your fiancée?"

"That would suit me, had I a choice," Alex responded gruffly, staring out over the wharf of now familiar buildings. "But I cannot keep the news of your arrival from her now that it's out. She's expecting me to arrive with guests. You should make an unpleasant surprise for her."

Rather than becoming irritated with his younger cousin's outrageous attitude, Cranville chuckled. He was beginning to understand that Alex's relationship with this unknown female was a tenuous one and that he greatly feared any disturbance of its current state. Wondering what kind of female would put his jaded heir on tenterhooks, Cranville pressed for enlightenment.

"You made light of the forced betrothal. Do not tell me you have truly been trapped into marriage with one of these impudent Yankees?"

Alex grimaced and continued to stare out over the city. Smoke rose from hundreds of chimneys, smudging the colors of the setting sun. The odors of whale oil and fish around the wharf had become familiar to him now, and he scarcely noticed them except at times like these, when forced to look at this place from the eyes of a stranger. Cranville would see a quaint village with ill-mannered, argumentative inhabitants. The earl was certainly no stranger to colonial towns, but the gracious plantations of Barbados had no relation to these harsher, more democratic environs. For all that, he found himself wanting his cousin to like these people as he did, and he braced himself for the interview to come.

"I have trapped myself," he answered reluctantly. "The final bann will be read next week. The wedding will need to take place immediately so I can get her out of here. The Admiralty apparently intends to make an example of her. The timing is poor, to say the least. If they try imprisoning her on the same day they begin enforcing the Stamp Act, that mob you saw out there today is quite likely to start a rebellion that will spread like wildfire throughout the colonies. See that peaceful village?" Alex gestured toward the panorama of Boston. "It's a veritable powder keg. I intend to get Evelyn and the *Neptune* out of here before it explodes."

"You are marrying to protect the crown's interests? How noble of you."

Alex didn't miss the sarcasm. "You will see her in a few minutes. I'll not influence your opinion. Come, they're ready to lower the plank."

Evelyn had taken time to change into a fresh gown for dinner, but when Alex returned with an earl in tow, she could have kicked him for not sending a warning. She had not even worn a dinner gown, but had garbed modestly in a high-necked indigo velvet so as not to appear too ostentatious to sailors long from home. Luckily she had warned Molly, the maid, to use the best plate and silver so Alex would not be shamed by their hospitality, but even their best wasn't good enough for an earl. They should have sent to Uncle George's for his silver service and porcelain.

Sending Alex a glaring look as the earl bent over her mother's hand, Evelyn quickly recovered her composure as she was introduced. Cranville's weathered face showed lines about his eyes, and his hair was now more silver than gold, but he was a young-looking man still, slender and athletically graceful. Evelyn wanted to like him at once, but she forced herself to reserve judgment. This man could help her or hurt her. She would bide her time.

During the meal they indulged in the pleasant pastime of learning all that was new in London and comparing family and acquaintance. The earl believed he might have been in school with Mrs. Wellington's elder brother, and of course he knew Adrian Wellington, who held a very prominent position in the Commons now. Amanda knew little of the earl's world, but she believed her grandmother was related to his mother's sister through marriage, although she was unclear as to the ties. The two older people had such a merry time comparing anecdotes that they failed to notice the general silence among their youngers.

Evelyn and Alex made polite comments as required but otherwise kept their thoughts to themselves. Alex warily regarded Evelyn's silence as either disapproval or the opportunity to scheme some new and disastrous plot against him, or more likely both. He had more than a week to keep her in line, and they had yet to even set a date. He couldn't believe she would truly choose prison over marriage to him, but remembering words hastily said in anger, he had to admit she had a right to reservations.

After dinner, the men lingered over their port while the ladies helped Molly clear away the dishes. Jacob disappeared about his own business, as was his wont, leaving Alex to hold his own against the earl.

"She seems a quiet, modest sort, not at all your type, I must say," Cranville mused once the women had retired to the kitchen.

Alex made an inelegant sound and sipped his drink. "You have not met the real Evelyn yet. I don't think she was even with us tonight. I suspect she was plotting some hair-raising plan to indict the entire Admiralty Court and me with it on charges ranging from abduction to . . ." He pondered a moment. "What crime begins with Z? Surely there must be one. Whatever it is, she'll think of it. She is my counterpart in everything, and therein lies the rub."

"By Jove, the thought makes the mind curdle." The earl shivered as he considered a female Alex. "You need a steadying influence, someone who can keep the title from being disgraced too thoroughly. Since I cannot rely on you to keep the family name unscathed, you must choose a wife to bear the torch. A woman who has already been found guilty of smuggling and is evidently involved in worse is not the choice I would make. Perhaps I should speak to the young lady alone. I have some experience in these matters."

Alex leaned over the table and pierced his relative with a fierce gaze. "You do not understand, Everett. I *want* to marry her. I'm not leaving here without her."

Satisfied but not willing to show it, Cranville merely

touched his napkin to his lips. "I would speak with her just the same. I believe I saw a study down the hall. Send her to me in there."

Alex cursed, threw down his napkin, and glared at the earl's back as he departed. He liked and admired the older man, but at times Everett could be damned arrogant and opinionated.

Evelyn entered the small, stuffy room with some trepidation. Her father had never got around to having enough shelves built to house his rampant collection of books and papers. Pamphlets and newspapers spilled from every available surface, held only by the teetering mountains of books stacked on top of them. Many of the volumes were still open to the pages he had last read, and Evelyn herself was guilty of leaving several of them about. She had always meant to return the room to order, but she hadn't been able to part with these reminders quite yet. Her hand brushed reverently against a volume of Shakespeare of which her father had been particularly fond. She drew strength from feeling her father's closeness as she faced the most honorable Earl of Cranville.

He turned from unabashedly perusing an old copy of the *Boston Gazette* lying across a corner of the desk. He indicated the editor's rather vehement diatribe against Parliament as he gestured for Evelyn to take a chair. "Are all your newspapers over here quite so openly seditious?"

Evelyn removed a precious copy of Johnson's *Dictionary*, two old ledgers, and a pamphlet by James Otis and stacked them on the floor before sitting down. Twining her fingers together, she tried to reply sensibly, although her knees were quaking. "Sedition incites the overthrow of government. Ben Edes asks that our government's constitution be upheld instead of ignored. Can that be a crime?"

"Wilkes went to the Tower for it. This constitution he rants about is a rather nebulous document, is it not?"

"We have centuries of law to support the rights of British citizens. Was the Magna Charta nebulous?"

"Seditious, certainly, but not nebulous. I have not come to argue politics or law. I only wish to know you better. Apparently much has happened since those first letters I received from Alex. They were sufficient to drag me from my home to save his thick hide from whatever trouble he had invoked now, but it seems you are the one in trouble, not he. I believe your uncle accused my heir of smuggling contraband. What has happened to those charges?"

Evelyn spread her hands in an unconsciously appealing gesture. "My uncle was satisfied once Alex declared his intentions toward me. He would never have actually charged him with anything. He just has a bad temper and speaks out of turn. There was no need for Alex to offer for me." She hesitated, gauging the earl's reaction before saying more. He seemed a reasonable man, and he would not have come all this way if he were not concerned for Alex. Gambling on this little bit of knowledge, she continued, "I would ask your aid in this matter, if I could."

The earl looked up with interest. He had settled himself in the desk chair and now drew the remains of an old quill between his fingers as he studied the young woman before him. The lamplight did her little justice. He could tell she was quite lovely, but the shadows hid the roses in her cheeks and made dark pools of her eyes. He rather expected she had a keen mind and was about to sharpen it on him. He nodded. "I am at your service, Miss Wellington."

His quiet confidence restored hers, and she formed her words with care. "I would like you to tell Alex you would have to disinherit him if he insists on marrying me. He places much store in you and in his work and is not likely to give them up just to satisfy his sense of honor. You must see that this marriage is quite unsuitable for both of us, and it could only do him harm to persist in it."

Cranville waited for further explanations but she evidently thought she had made the case clear. Like Alex, she was not given to revealing her feelings easily. He smoothed the feather between his fingers as he contemplated the possible reasons for her suggestion. "You would cry off because you feel your reputation would harm his?" he asked quizzically. Although he had used this same argument with Alex earlier, he could not quite believe the woman meant it.

She heard his disbelief and gave him a wry look. "I am not so besotted as to think Alex possesses a sterling reputation with his peers or that it is his sense of honor entirely that compels him to marry me. I just know that I cannot be the lady he deserves to have at his side, and in time he will learn to resent me for holding him back from those places where such a lady would be welcome. I am accustomed to life here and cannot change my ways to suit your London ways. The only harm done will be to Alex's pride, and that will not be so damaging as a lifetime of marriage with a woman he feels obligated to wed."

She phrased her words carefully, but Cranville thought he read a little more between the lines than was spoken. Alex's pride was an intangible property that had seldom propelled him in any sensible direction. His obstinacy was another matter entirely. Raising his eyebrows and keeping these thoughts to himself, he answered cautiously. "You are aware that Alex expected to inherit my father's title and wealth upon his death five years ago? My untimely return from Barbados cost him a great deal. To deny him his expectations again is a cruel thing to do."

Evelyn had known nothing of the sort, but the knowledge only reinforced her beliefs. Alex would not sacrifice fortune and title for lust and honor. "I have no desire to deny him his expectations. I wish Alex's happiness as much as you do. Forcing him to make this choice will make it clear to him that I am just a passing fancy. You need not fear you will lose your heir."

Deciding this ought to make quite an entertaining confrontation, the earl nodded cautiously. "Very well, Miss Wellington, if that is the way you feel, I shall give it a try. I only wish my heir happiness, as you say. If you think he will truly be unhappy with this marriage, then I shall do what I can to prevent it."

Feeling her heart turn to lead as she sealed her fate, Evelyn merely nodded her gratitude and prepared to rise. To her surprise, the earl waved her back to her seat.

"I would have this done at once. I'll call Alex in here now."

Evelyn kept her head bowed when Alex entered. She could feel his gaze sweep directly to her, but she could not meet his eyes. She loved him too much to wish to see him harmed, and she knew what they were about to do would cause him some anguish. But not as much as a forced lifetime together. He did not love her and would soon forget her. Much better that way than the stormy life they would lead when his lust wore off and his infidelities began. He would resent his loss of freedom and regret marrying a Yankee Puritan who insisted on upholding their vows. Their differences were irreconcilable. She could spend an entire day enumerating them. The passion they shared would not weigh heavily enough against such a list.

Alex turned his suspicious gaze from Evelyn's bent head to his cousin. "Why do I get the feeling you are not about to give me your blessing?"

Cranville twisted the feather as he leaned back in his chair to stare up at the young man towering over him. "Probably because you are already aware that I am right. This marriage is not suitable for a future Earl of Cranville. If you persist in it, then I have the power to disinherit you of all but the title and the estate in Cornwall. You already know how worthless an empty title can be. I could have the family tree searched to see if there is not another cousin equally deserving of even that. I'm sorry, but since Miss Wellington agrees with me, I feel no harm will be done if the betrothal is broken now."

At the mention of Evelyn's name, Alex's head jerked and swiveled to her unusually docile demeanor. His rage simmered, but he had it well under control. Taking the few strides needed to cross the room to her side, he gripped her shoulder in a gesture of protection and faced his elder.

"I am sorry you feel that way, sir, but you make my decision easier," he answered steadily, without hesitation. "I have known that Evelyn is reluctant to leave home and family for a strange land and new life. Now I do not have to ask that of her. You can have your title and estate. I will stay here."

Evelyn's head shot up to reveal eyes filled with amazement, dismay, and relief. Alex studied that expression carefully, making certain that it was truly relief he saw in the curve of her lips and the sparkle returning to her eye. He held her chin upward with his finger and bent to seal his words with a kiss.

His announcement left Evelyn breathless. Despite his cynical attitude, she had always sensed that Alex enjoyed his position and power. She also knew he was very good at what he did and his talents would be wasted in so small a world as this. As much as she longed for the promise of his words, she could not let him ruin his life for her. She shook her head free from his caress.

"You can't do that, Alex. I won't let you. How do you think I'd feel knowing I'd robbed you of your life?"

Alex's dark gaze continued to rest thoughtfully on her face, and his hand refused to surrender possession. Before he could reply, his cousin intruded.

"If he is willing to sacrifice his life for you, Miss Wellington, perhaps you could see your way clear to do the same. I'm not comfortable with sacrifices of any sort, but I'm willing to rescind my decree if you are willing to bend a little in yours."

Alex sent the earl an enigmatic glance at this gracious retreat, but his concentration was on the Lucretia Borgia at his side. She had a wicked mind, but this was one battle he meant to win.

"I have no intention of changing my mind, Evelyn. You can fling all the obstacles you can find in my way, but you'll not stop me. If your objection is to England, then we'll stay here. If your objection is to London, we'll stay in Cornwall. If your objection is to titles, you have little to worry about. Everett's good for another hundred years, as you can easily see. Name me some others, tyrant."

Alex hovered over her so close that she could not think. Evelyn rose hastily, tearing from his grip to stand by the mantel and stare at the miniatures of her family in the frame resting there. Joy warred with disbelief at his words. He had said he would never marry. He had sworn never to curtail his freedom for wife and children. Yet here he was offering to give up everything for her.

Why? Why would Alex do that? She could not believe he felt honor-bound to keep his promises in the face of everything that had been thrown at him this day. He was a man of enough experience to find other outlets for his lust. So why did he insist on going through with this marriage?

"You leave me little choice," she murmured to the mantel. "I cannot ask you to leave your family when I know my own will eagerly accompany me. I cannot ask you to give up all you possess for what little I will have left. I'd be a fool to refuse you, and I am no fool. I just cannot believe this is what you want or what is right for you."

"Dammit, Evelyn! Let me decide what I want! Don't you think I have the wit to know what is right for me?"

His anger she understood better than his earlier acquiescence. She spun around to face him. "You are the one who swore not two months ago that you would never wed! How am I to know if you will not change your mind again two months hence?"

"Two months ago I was trying to keep you at your damn distance! I failed at that but I will not fail at this. Did you think I would blithely sail away and never worry whether you paid your fine or went to prison or carried my child? The choice was made long since."

"Alex!" Evelyn glared at him in horror at the lengths to which his anger carried him. She could not look at the earl as he rose from the desk.

"Child? If there is any question of a child, then this argument is ended right now. Set the date and settle your differences later." The earl's tone was harsh as he, too, glared at Alex.

"One week from today," Alex announced firmly, not turning from Evelyn.

His jaw was set with grim purpose, and Evelyn felt a faint tremor of real fear, fear of her own raw emotions. She really was going to marry him. She couldn't quite believe it, but looking at Alex now, with his muscles pulled taut over his jaw and his familiar dark eyes glaring arrows at her, she knew she could not say him nay. She had thought he would be more relieved than hurt when offered an excuse to cry off. She had been wrong.

Still, she wouldn't give in easily. He couldn't order her life about as if he owned her. She might as well make that clear right now. "You will have to bind me hand and foot and drag me screaming down the aisle," she warned.

A gleam leapt to Alex's eyes. "I believe last week it also required a branding iron. Perhaps by next week you will be so submissive I need only drag you by the hair."

"You will be lucky if you have any hair left should you try such a thing! If we are to marry, you might as well learn that I am not accustomed to being given orders."

"If we are to marry, you might as well learn that I am accustomed to beating disobedient little chits!"

The earl watched with considerable bemusement as they ranted and railed, but only recently having married for the second time, he was no stranger to the undercurrent flowing beneath the words. The looks this pair sent each other would be sufficient to sizzle a man to bacon should he be foolhardy enough to come between them. Discreetly he inched his way from the room.

In the hall he was met by Evelyn's anxious mother, who twisted her hands nervously at the sound of upraised voices beyond the door. She sent a glance his way, and Cranville shook his head in confusion.

"How have you kept your sanity with the two of them about? I thought when I first met Alex that I had never met a more arrogant, opinionated person in all my life. I fear he has met his match in your daughter's stubbornness."

Hearing the voices on the other side of the door subside to giggles and chuckles, Amanda managed a smile. "As long as you do not oppose the match, they will take care of each other. Our only difficulty now will be keeping them apart until they are wedded." She nodded toward the door, from which now came only an ominous silence.

Cranville lifted his brow as he caught her meaning and remembered his heir's words of earlier. He wouldn't give a ha'pence for their chances of keeping those two apart. A smile widened his mouth as he offered the widow his arm. "There are wedding plans to be made, madam, and I fear we are the only ones to make them. Shall we begin?"

19

The small Wellington front parlor was filled to overflowing with females garbed in their best petticoats and ribbons, giggling and gossiping and lending their words of wisdom to the bride-to-be. The men had migrated to the newly cleaned study to sip their port and argue over politics, with an occasional spicy jest for the groom. For this last gathering before the nuptials, only the bride's closest friends had been invited, and there was a surprising lack of powdered hair and wigs, perfumes, and silk.

Alex looked relaxed as he leaned his long frame against the bookshelves and sipped his wine, but he kept his conversation to a minimum as he nervously listened to the ladies laughing in the next room. This last week of tension had been pure hell. He was still uncertain that Evelyn meant to go through with the ceremony and not disappear in a puff of smoke or a rain of cannonballs.

As the sound of a spinet tinkled from the front room, Alex had his reason to leave. When he excused himself and bowed politely to the male company, they smiled knowingly, but several of the younger men followed him not long after. Music was made for dancing and there was a room full of attractive ladies waiting to be chosen.

Alex found his lady escaping through the kitchen. Evelyn glanced up in surprise as he caught her elbow, but she didn't seem displeased at his presence. She smiled and set aside her teacup.

"I thought if I heard one more smirking reference to our wedding night, I would have to inform the company that I was already acquainted with my wifely duties and enjoyed them very well. I fear I have not been blushing properly, for some of the ladies are beginning to look at me quite peculiarly."

Relief swept through Alex as he finally allowed himself to believe she really meant to go through with the wedding. Giddiness made his head unnaturally light, not the small amount of port he had consumed. With a growing smile he steered her toward the kitchen door. "Shall I restore your blushes for you? I rather enjoy them, you know."

The late-October night was frosty, but they both wore warm velvets and wools and carried the heat from the house with them. The sounds of the spinet had been joined by a fiddle. There would be enough room in the front parlor for a small reel. Soon they would be missed, but not just yet. Alex swept Evelyn into his arms and carried her through the steps of the dance in a jig of sheer jubilation, swinging her in strong arms until her laugh broke in crystalline notes through the night air.

He felt so good against her, so strong and tall and masculine. The large hand at her waist left her more breathless than the impromptu dance, and the deep laughter rumbling from his chest as her hair tumbled to her shoulders made her as giddy as he. This was their last day of freedom. Tomorrow they would be wedded for eternity. Their exhilaration was needed to keep fears at bay.

She was soft and sweet in his arms, a swaying reed that filled Alex's senses with a seductive music all her own. It was difficult to wipe the smile from his face as he gazed down into amazingly liquid violet eyes and drew his hand through the silkiness of disheveled chestnut tresses.

He'd known many women before: sophisticated ones with arched eyebrows and sultry kisses, petite blonds with sulky lips, mischievous gamines looking for trouble, but they had all represented a few hours' pleasure and no more. This one was not only different from every woman he'd ever known but also completely his. It seemed incredible to believe that he could find a woman as lovely and intelligent as this one and that she would agree to marry him, even knowing of his dubious past. He didn't deserve this reward for bad behavior, and he greatly feared she would be taken from him, but for now he would enjoy the promise while he could.

When the reel ended, Alex pulled Evelyn into his arms to seek the kiss she had been avoiding all week. He knew Cranville's aristocratic presence made her nervous, but he would no longer be denied that which he needed so badly. He gave a soft growl of pleasure as she melted against him and returned his kiss with a matching passion.

Her lips burned against his flesh as he lifted her closer. The heavy honey of her breath engulfed Alex, and her vulnerable slenderness cradled in his arms made him ache with need. Gently nipping at the corners of her mouth, he retreated slightly, still keeping her warm in his embrace.

"I'm trying to do the honorable thing by waiting for our wedding night, but you are making this damnably difficult for me."

His lips were still leaving fiery trails across her skin, and her breasts were crushed against the hardness of his chest as he spoke. Evelyn could scarcely gain her breath to answer. She wanted his hands to move higher, to take the aching swell of her breasts and not stop until they both had what they desired. Dizzy with desire, she threaded her hands through the thick hair at Alex's nape and tried to be sensible.

"They will be looking for us. We have to go in. It's only one more night." One more night! Evelyn couldn't help a shudder of hunger sweeping through her as she imagined an entire night in his bed. To be able to wake with Alex's dark head at her side was all the future she craved right now. She slanted her mouth across his and drew him closer.

Alex cursed the glare of light from the house and contemplated drawing her to the garden bench, where he could easily imagine a third method of making love to teach her. Gently riding his hands up the sides of her breasts, he tried to resist temptation. It was not something he wished to make a habit of, but for one night and for Evelyn's sake, he would try it.

"I shall imagine you sleeping in our bed tonight and

not be able to sleep a wink." He pressed a kiss to Evelyn's temple.

She blushed at the thought of the big double bed he'd had delivered to her room for just these few nights remaining here. Her mother and Jacob had accepted the invitations of friends to stay with them while the household was being prepared for closing for an extended period of time. The earl was staying at her uncle's home. They would have the house to themselves on the morrow.

"It will seem very strange sleeping in such a bed by myself. You shouldn't have gone to such expense for so short a time. Other arrangements could have been made."

Alex had seen the pleased look on Evelyn's face when the bed had been delivered and he had announced his plans for it. He ignored her polite protests now. "It will not be wasted. The bed goes with us. Our marriage bed will be the same one our children are delivered in. You need only decide whether you wish that to be Cornwall or London. Both places are filled with ancient furniture that has been used by my ancestors for centuries. I mean no disrespect, but I wish to have something of my own in those halls. A Yankee bed is perfect."

Evelyn laughed and leaned her head against his shoulder. Moments like these were too few and too far apart not to take the maximum benefit now. Alex would not be an easy man to live with, and their relationship was destined to be a stormy one, but moments like these would keep her happy. She loved this impossible man, and perhaps someday she would hope he would love her. She would teach him love.

"I trust a Yankee bed and a Yankee wife will be sufficient. I do not want you seeking out Cornwall beds and London beds and women for them." She had never said such to him before, and she regretted saying it now. She could feel his muscles tense beneath her hands. She prayed he would not start an argument now, on this last night before their wedding.

"I make you no promises," Alex warned carefully. "I would like to start anew with you. I want us to be able to trust one another. I would be less than honest if I made promises I'm not certain I can keep."

Tears wet Evelyn's lashes as she buried her face against his shoulder. Alex's arms held her tightly and there were no other arms she wished to do so. Why couldn't he feel the same? It was unfair, but she was growing calloused against injustice. She would fight to keep him by her side. There had to be ways to do it. Surely she had some advantage if she were the only one he chose for wife.

"I don't take vows lightly, Alex," she murmured softly, keeping the tears from her voice. "But we can live one day at a time. I'll have you to myself all the way to England. Mayhap by then you will be prepared to admit defeat."

Alex smiled softly against her bent head and crushed her close in relief. "If anyone can make an honorable man of me, it is you, my dear." He broke the moment with a leer that could be heard even in his voice. "Do you have any idea what I can do with you while you're trapped for six weeks in a cabin with me?"

Evelyn blushed heatedly and shoved away just as voices began calling their names from inside the house. "I don't even want to think about it."

"Ummm, but like me, that's all you can think about, isn't it?" Alex laughed as she lifted her skirts and flew toward the door. He would have to cool off before he could follow her, and that might not be anytime soon. The image of Evelyn's lithe curves sprawled across that big bed upstairs filled his thoughts.

The earl found him some minutes later leaning against a tree and staring at an upstairs window. Cranville hid his grin, remembering the sad state of disarray the fiancée had been in when she had run up the back stairs. The Hampton name might be carried on yet, for what it was worth.

"Upton's been questioning me about your plans for the warehouse, Alex." The earl brought his heir down to earth abruptly. "It seems your bride has complete control over a very expensive and important property. The community will be harmed if it is left to stand idle. As a concerned citizen, he would like to know your intentions."

Alex shrugged. "As his friend the lawyer will tell him,

her father left that investment very neatly tied up in trust. I cannot touch it and would not if my life depended on it. I have suggested leaving a man I know in charge, however. Upton won't like that answer, so I suggest you delay giving it to him."

The earl gave him a shrewd look. "Are you going to tell Evelyn that her uncle is responsible for the smuggling?"

Alex grimaced and returned to staring at the upper-story windows. "Do you have any idea what her reaction would be if I told her?"

"She would deny it?" Cranville suggested, disbelieving it. The girl showed too much sense.

"She would be forced to make a decision. To protect her family and Upton's family from ruin, she could tell me to keep my knowledge quiet. Or she could get furiously angry, take the charges and her uncle to court, rip open the town with the scandal, call the crown down upon her head, and clear her name. Which do you think she will do?"

The earl grunted sardonically. "I see what you mean. Better keep it quiet for now. We'll get her out of here and safe first, then decide how best to handle it. I'll see about getting the charges quietly dropped when we reach London."

Alex gave him a crooked grin. "I always knew you were an intelligent man."

They returned to the house in mutual agreement. Trouble had its own way of appearing; there was no sense in seeking it.

Evelyn nervously smoothed the lovely deep blue silk of her *robe a la française* for the thousandth time. The pagoda sleeves held back with bows revealed yards of creamy lace to match the ivory satin of her underskirt. Panniers held the skirt and robe in gracious drapes at her side, revealing tiny blue slippers when she walked. For this formal ceremony, her mother had insisted she powder her hair, and it was now dressed neatly against her head and adorned with only small gold pins. Catching a glimpse of herself in the hall mirror, she wasn't at all certain that she was the same person she had thought she was.

She wished she hadn't agreed to so hasty a wedding. There ought to be more time to think these things out. Within the space of a week she would be a married woman on her way to England with a man who had just walked into her life a few short months ago. Everything that was familiar to her would be lost. It was an unnerving thought even if Alex were the kind and considerate gentleman she had vaguely imagined one day marrying. The fact that he was moody and intemperate and didn't love her made her question her sanity in going through with this.

Of course, the alternative was being marched ignominiously to some filthy prison for an unknown number of years. Until she paid the fine or fled, that possibility continued to threaten her. Alex had promised she wouldn't have to sell the warehouse, but every time she saw a soldier she feared he had come for her. There was still nearly a week left before she need pay the fine. Surely the *Neptune* would be ready to sail before then.

The only knowledge that she held easy on her mind was the fact that Alex needed her as much as she needed him. She didn't think his kisses lied. She had never felt this kind of physical attraction for any other man before, and the rightness of Alex's embrace convinced her more than anything else that this marriage would work. Perhaps it was different for men, but Alex's words and actions belied that thought. She knew he felt the same as she. That had to be enough, for now.

The Upton carriage came to carry them to the church. With tears in their eyes, Amanda and her daughter embraced; then, erasing all trace of that brief weakness with a handkerchief, they carefully maneuvered their full skirts into the narrow coach. Jacob had wisely chosen to find other means of transportation.

The afternoon was fading fast as the carriage arrived at the church. Rain clouds hung on the horizon and the air was cooling rapidly. The few people remaining outside to await their arrival quickly helped them from the carriage and hurried them into the church. There was little time left to think.

The minutes flew even faster once they were inside the vestibule. A signal started the music. Her uncle appeared to escort her. Her mother disappeared down the aisle. And then it was Evelyn's turn.

Her fingers shook as she took her uncle's arm and made the first few tentative steps toward her future. When she reached the center aisle, her gaze found Alex standing tall at the far end beside his cousin, and her gaze focused steadily on him. For the sake of convention, he wore his powdered wig with the black satin bow in back, but it only served to emphasize his dark features. His black silk coat was cut away at the front to reveal an elegant silver-gray vest and breeches. The severity of the cut of these clothes was matched by the small amount of lace at throat and wrist. Never had he looked more handsome, and Evelyn clung to the intensity of his dark gaze as he followed her progress toward him.

She needed the strength of his hand in hers when she reached the altar, and she waited impatiently as the minister slowly intoned the words that released her from her uncle's possession into Alex's. When he finally stood by her side, she felt comforted. His fingers were strong and sure as they wrapped around hers.

Words went spinning past her ears until she realized Alex was looking down at her with a look she knew well. As the minister asked her to "love, honor, and obey," his dark eyes gleamed appreciatively, and Evelyn had a sudden urge to ask if she might not reword that vow. Alex looked as if he half-expected it, but she surprised even herself by obediently answering, "I will."

Alex's reply echoed firmly through the hall with no hint of hesitancy. He had the ring ready when Evelyn removed her glove, and the band slid smoothly on her finger. Ignoring the minister's phrases, Alex lifted her hand to his lips and pressed a kiss where this symbol of his possession came to rest. The heat of his hand and his bold gaze prevented hearing anything else but Alex's words as he took her as his wife.

The music told Evelyn when the ceremony ended, but Alex's arms as he claimed his kiss made the finality certain. It was no modest peck, but a full measure of his desire, leaving Evelyn oblivious of the gasps and titters of half the town. She was his, and he would let the whole world know it.

As Alex finally released Evelyn to face the crowd, her face was flushed and her hair already slightly disarranged. Her smile lit the room, however, and the groom's proud gaze as he took his bride on his arm made every romantic heart weep with joy.

Only Evelyn heard Alex's whisper as they neared the vestibule. "Is it time for bed yet?"

Biting back a laugh, she trod on his foot as hard as she could, and he had to hide his wince as the first of their guests came to greet them.

The church bell made its solemn intonations overhead as the earl came to claim the bride's kiss, and Amanda happily bussed her son-in-law's cheek. Hesitant to step out into the chilly wind, the crowd lingered in and around the vestibule, exchanging greetings and laughter and tears.

Pilgrim Adams came to steal a kiss and doff his hat under Alex's glare. Thomas Henderson ignored the glare and boldly captured Evelyn's lips as he wished them happy. Evelyn knew Alex was in a hurry to leave for the party his cousin had arranged for them at the Uptons', but she could not ignore these friends she would leave behind.

Bells were still ringing as they made their way from the church, and Evelyn puzzled briefly over the fact that there seemed to be more than one of them. She didn't have time to ponder this curiosity as Alex handed her into the carriage and climbed up beside her. Like royalty, the bride and groom were escorted through the streets.

However briefly, they were alone together, and Alex quickly reached to take his wife's hand. "How do you feel?"

In the semidarkness her eyes were wide and nearly round as they searched the shadows for his face. "Nervous. Terrified. And you?"

"Witless," he agreed, stroking her hand. "But it's done and I have no desire to turn back. I've never much cared for other people's opinions, but I find myself striving for your approval. Do you think that might go away in a few months?"

His question sounded almost hopeful, and Evelyn laughed. Alex never did what was expected, and as much as it might infuriate her at times, she loved him for it. She couldn't feel free if he doted on her all the time, and she wouldn't feel appreciated if he did not occasionally let her know how he felt. He had found a happy medium between the two that left her relaxed and content in his company. Except when he was kissing her, which he evidently meant to do as he leaned forward with that laughing look that meant danger.

Fearing she would be truly tumbled before they reached her uncle's, Evelyn forestalled him with a gloved hand to his chest and her head tilted to catch the sounds from outside. "The bells are *still* ringing," she said with puzzlement.

Halting his forward movement, Alex peered between the carriage curtains to look outside. The growing darkness prevented seeing far, but the men in the crowd seemed to be peeling away at a mysterious rate, and he cursed.

Evelyn caught his hand as he dropped the curtain. "What is it? Is something wrong?"

"That's the signal that an English ship has arrived. This time, it could very likely hold the stamps."

Evelyn turned her fingers into her palms and prayed. Rumors had been flying for weeks. The governor remained protected on his island fort surrounded by troops. Rumor had placed the stamps there days ago, but no one had the facts. Whoever held the hated things was in certain danger. Boston had been filling with angry farmers and unemployed laborers for days. Such a mob wouldn't be satisfied until the stamps were destroyed, and this time violence looked likely. The British troops wouldn't look the other way or disappear into the streets as the local militia was apt to do when the mob struck. They would fight if attacked.

"It can't come to weapons, Alex. Surely it cannot. We would only lose against trained and armed forces. The stamps can't matter as long as there is no one to distribute them."

Alex wished he could reassure her. As the day the act was to be enforced came closer, tension had heightened and tempers flared. There were those who talked of war. Alex was inclined to agree with Evelyn, but reason did not always win when emotion came into play. The tax had become a symbol beyond its original meaning. It represented tyranny in the minds of these men. He foresaw no simple solution.

"There will always be someone like your uncle willing to seek influence and wealth by pleasing the crown and taking the distribution position. If the stamps have arrived, they will be used. Your friends are well aware of that."

"My friends? Are they not yours too? You must persuade them from this folly, Alex. They will not heed me, but they will heed you. Can you not keep them from using violence?"

Alex shoved his hand beneath the irritation of his wig. This was to be his wedding night. The last thing in the world he wanted to do was go talk a hotheaded mob out of the violence they were bent on. Let one of these infernal Yankee politicians use his smooth tongue for that. He wanted champagne and his wife, not necessarily in that order. He turned his gaze back to Evelyn's pleading, adoring look and cursed viciously to himself. It was easier being a villain than a hero.

"Let me find out what is happening first before deserting our guests." Alex was rewarded by a smile replacing the anxiety on her face. Being a hero was going to be a damned sight harder than he had imagined, but he had a definite aversion to losing Evelyn's misplaced confidence in him. Maybe that would go away in a few months too, but definitely not on their wedding night. He squeezed her fingers reassuringly, as if he knew precisely what to do and everything was in control.

The Upton house had undergone extensive repair since the night of the riot, but the library remained closed off. The guests circulated through the wide hall and spacious parlor and through the connecting doors to the formal dining room that had been thrown open to allow a full circle of movement.

Evelyn found herself carried off with one eddy of the

crowd while Alex was carried off in another. For a time she could see him towering over a circle of men in the far corner. He occasionally glanced up to find her, lifting his champagne glass with a wink or giving her a smile of promise, but it seemed no easy task to cross this room of well-wishers to stand at his side. The next time she looked, the circle of men had dispersed and Alex was gone.

Surely he would have come to her if he meant to leave the party. He had to be here somewhere. Discreetly Evelyn started working her way through the parlor, greeting old friends, exchanging laughter, until she reached the dining room. The earl had spared no expense in supplying the wedding feast. The table was piled high with delicacies from the sea, but it was also harvesttime, and the number of vegetable dishes exceeded the imagination. Even the lowly pumpkin had been converted to spicy tarts, and the pastry table alone was enough to make one's mouth water. The crowd in here was so dense Evelyn could scarcely make her way through it, but unless Alex were seated, he was not here. No tall shoulders loomed above this crowd.

The hall was less populated but contained no trace of Alex either. Feeling a nagging disappointment that he had not thought enough of her to warn her of his departure, she started down the hall to the parlor again.

The sound of voices coming from the closed library caught her attention. Uncertainly she pushed the door, and it gave easily. The room was unlit, but the voices were clear.

"I still think you ought to leave the contents of that packet here with someone in authority. Surely there must be someone you can trust with that information. It is like walking around with a cannon shell in your pocket. You're a married man now, Alex, you cannot continue inviting trouble."

"There is no trouble if we're the only two who know of it. I'd rather be responsible for keeping explosive material safe than leaving it in the hands of someone who might use it for other purposes." As if a sixth sense warned him, Alex looked up to catch the gleam of ivory in the doorway. "Come in, my dear. You have found us. Are you ready to leave?"

Evelyn heard the suggestive note in his question but dismissed his attempt at diversion with her irritable steps as she joined him. "What explosive material are you carrying? If I am to be blown sky-high with you, I should have the right to know."

Alex stroked her nose with his finger. "Calm down, little tyrant. We are only speaking figuratively. I was about to come looking for you. It seems a ship has landed on Castle Island. I'm going to have to leave and I might be a little late getting back."

That was a dismaying thought, but she had already expected that. Evelyn shook off his pacifying finger and held on to her annoyance. He had been discussing something with the earl that only the two of them knew about. What dangerous material could they possess? A sudden suspicion came to mind, and she stared up at the blur of Alex's face in the darkness. "You have the information on the smugglers, don't you?" She turned to the silent earl. "You found out their names. Who are they? Why has no one given them to the court?"

Alex caught her by the waist and pulled her against him. "Leave this to us, Evelyn. My first concern is for your safety. Now, give me a kiss and go back to your party. No one's going to be hurt, I promise."

His mouth closed over hers, silencing her protests, but, suddenly frightened, Evelyn held out against the seductive taste of Alex's lips. She bit him and kicked his shin and eluded his grasp when he was forced to drop her. "You can't do this, Alex Hampton. I have a right to know. I'm the one suffering for their crimes. Tell me who they are!"

Ignoring her tantrum, the pain in his bruised lip turning his mood to foul, Alex stalked toward the exit. "I'll do what the damned hell I please! I'll see you later."

He was too furious to see the scurry of motion outside the partially open door as he approached. When he strode out, he looked neither to right nor left and so missed the portly figure of George Upton hurriedly returning to the dining room.

The knowledge that his wedding night would most

likely be spent in a smoke-filled tavern with a group of surly men kept him from paying attention to anything at all but the ache in his loins produced by the feel of a certain slender witch in his arms and the haunting scent of violets Alex carried with him even as he stepped into the brisk October night.

20

The carriage took her home, alone. Amanda offered to accompany her, but Evelyn refused. She didn't know when Alex would return, but she preferred not to have anyone witness the scene when he did. The ache in her heart nearly matched her anger, and she wasn't certain which one would win by the time he returned.

He knew the smugglers! All this time, and he had not given any hint of his knowledge. Blast the man, did he think her a fool? Admittedly, her mind had not been on the smugglers for some weeks past, but that was no reason to hide the truth. If he had turned that information over to the court, she could be free today, without the hideous threat of fine or jail hanging over her.

That thought hit her with the force of a punch to the jaw as she climbed the stairs to her lonely bedroom. Alex had the evidence that could make her free. Did he hold it so he could force her to leave with him?

Sitting down abruptly on the expensive bed he had bought for this night, Evelyn shook her head and tried to clear her thoughts. He had said they would be married whether she willed or not. He had let the banns be cried despite her protests, knowing he held the key to her future. He had known she had no choice but jail or him. Why? Why would he do such a thing?

It made no sense. She had no wealth, no power, no name. The fear that she might carry his child was a specious one. He had only to wait a few weeks to know if his fears were confirmed. Besides, he had bedded other women without such concerns. He could have bastards scattered all over creation by now. Why would he force her into this marriage by withholding the information that would make her free?

She paced the room, unwilling to undress and wait patiently for him to appear. How could she be wife to a man who would treat her that way?

The dreadful feeling that she had made some terrible mistake overwhelmed her, suffocating her with fear. She refused to believe Alex's name was somehow on that list, or her own. He must be protecting someone, somehow. But whom? And why?

The questions would drive her to madness. She could not lie here all night and quietly go insane. She wasn't some passive, helpless female he could order about. He might as well learn that right now. Maybe he would realize his mistake and turn the information over to the court so he could be free of her.

Fingers working rapidly at the lovely wedding gown she had once hoped Alex would divest her of, Evelyn shoved aside all such thoughts and pulled the gown off. Sumptuous folds of silk and satin crumpled to the floor, held up only by the panniers she had hastily untied and let fall with them. Stepping out of the horrendous puddle of fabric, she jerked open the bottom drawer of the armoire and pulled out the breeches she had vowed never to wear again. It had been a stupid, romantic notion that she could please her husband by always appearing as a lady. He probably wouldn't even notice the difference.

Within the half-hour Evelyn was slipping along silent, dark streets in the direction of Castle Island. If everyone had gone on boats to intercept the English ship, she would be out of luck, but she didn't think they would risk such a foolhardy attempt without a great deal of discussion. The island couldn't be seen from land, but she knew the closest wharf, and the closest tavern to that wharf. She wagered that was where she would find the plotters.

She disliked entering taverns where she was not known. She lingered in the shadows outside, waiting to see or hear someone she knew before entering. The angry sound of voices from the tap room did nothing to reassure her. It was difficult to distinguish voices through thick log-and-clapboard walls. It could be a sailors' quarrel for all she knew. Pulling her hat further over her eyes, she shrugged back her shoulders and pushed open the door.

She found no sign of Alex, but she immediately recognized the inhabitants of the largest table by the fire. Slipping into a darkened booth nearby, she ordered an ale and sipped at it as she listened to their argument.

She was disappointed that they made no mention of Alex. Surely this was where he had come to put an end to the foolish notion that they could storm the castle in pursuit of the stamps. But it seemed they had heard no words of caution. All their plans involved the number of men who would volunteer and the quantity and quality of arms that could be found. An angry dispute broke out over a general question of converting the militia to their own use as an army against the British troops, and Evelyn's fingers bit into her palms with frustration. They were talking war. This could not be.

Realizing it was pointless to interrupt an argument over the extent of hostilities when no one considered peaceful solutions, Evelyn quietly paid her fare and slipped out into the street again. She had accomplished nothing but wasting away the hours of her wedding night. What if Alex had returned to find her gone?

Hurrying back toward the house, she debated the question. If Alex were not here dissuading these fools from their course, where was he? Did he deceive her in this too? How could she return obediently to the bed of a man she knew nothing about, who kept secrets and manipulated her to his own uses? Her mind rebelled at the thought, but her body remembered all too well the desires he had taught her. She had awaited this night with an eagerness bordering on the demented. Even now, when she was furious with him, her body craved the pressure of his hands, the heat of his kiss, and the demanding thrill of his possession. She knew she would seek explanations rather than refuse him outright. She wanted desperately to believe, so desperately that she rushed home to his bed without any other thought.

He wasn't there. She knew it as soon as she saw the single candlestick burning on the newel post where she had left it. Taking the ring of the holder with her finger,

Evelyn slowly returned upstairs. Let him find his way in darkness.

She debated sleeping in some other room, but the beds had been stripped of linens and the feather mattresses taken out and beaten in preparation for storage. The house rang strangely hollow as she walked through it. Carpets had been cleaned and stored with cedar shavings to keep out insects, and there was little left to muffle the sound of footsteps. Within a week this would no longer be her home. She felt a stranger here already.

If she could only persuade Alex to give up the evidence on the smugglers, she could stay. What dangerous game did he play that he would withhold such information? How could she go away to another world with a man she could not trust? She didn't even know where he was now.

All the uncertainties of these past months came rushing back to fill her with gloom. As she removed her jacket in the silence of her empty room, she turned to bolt her bedroom door. She needed time to think.

Unaware that he had a second rebellion on his hands, Alex sipped silently at his Madeira and listened to the arguments of the well-dressed gentlemen around the acting governor's table. Hutchinson would have to give in under the pressure, but he wasn't at all certain that the same could be said of the man on the island fortified by troops. Some way would have to be found to persuade the governor to release those stamps from the island before all hell broke loose.

At the thought of being caught in some petty colonial war over a box of tax stamps, Alex grimaced to himself. He would much rather be in the warm arms of his new bride, although he half-suspected she would brain him with the chamber pot before he reached that happy state. But the way things looked, they were all in danger until this matter was settled, and he saw no opportunity of joining her anytime soon. He had a plan that might involve a minimum of bloodshed if the earl could be persuaded to it. It just awaited the proper moment to be introduced.

Glancing at the rising sun outside the window, Alex eased himself back in the chair. So much for wedding nights. He adjusted his position and turned his thoughts away from hot kisses. It would be hours before Cranville could even be approached if his plan were approved. And it would be hours before it could be carried out. Perhaps he could sneak back to the house for just a little while. A quick tumble in daylight wasn't quite as satisfactory as a full night of seduction, but he was willing to take any crumb offered. That one brief coupling more than a week ago couldn't satisfy a hunger as enormous as his.

Unable to sleep in more than fits and starts, Evelyn finally gave up trying by midmorning. There were no bells, no people rushing through the streets, no gunfire. If the stamps had arrived, there was no visible sign that anything had been done about it.

Not willing to sit idle and wonder where Alex was, and unable to face her mother when she arrived to finish packing, Evelyn dressed and hurried on to the warehouse. She didn't know what she would do with herself when she left her home behind, but she had plenty to do while she was here. The paperwork had been sadly neglected this past week.

The man that Alex had recommended was already at work when she arrived. He greeted her with a cautious nod and set aside his pen when she entered.

Unaccustomed to seeing anyone but herself or her father with the books, Evelyn nervously fussed with removing her gloves and cloak. The weather was growing steadily worse and she sent an anxious glance to the ships in the harbor. Most of them would be leaving for warmer ports shortly, if they had not already left. The *Neptune* was the only one of any size remaining.

"I did not expect to see thee here today, Miss Wellington . . . Mrs. Hampton. Is there aught I can do for thee?"

He spoke like the Quaker he was. She could understand why Alex trusted the man, but she could not help the vague uneasiness eating at her nerves with just the sound of her new name. The warehouse had been her family's livelihood for years. While they lived with Alex, they would not need the income to live on and could very well afford to pay this man, but if the economy grew worse and her mother and Jacob desired to return here, there would not be enough cash to support this man and her family. They would have to rely on Alex for their livelihood.

She didn't like the thought of that. Firmly hanging her outer garments on the cloaktree by the door, she came around the counter to join her new manager. "I have neglected my work this past week, Mr. Johnson. Perhaps I could take a look at the correspondence and our ledgers and see where we stand?"

He quietly brought all she required and retired to the warehouse to begin the inventory that Alex had requested he take. It was none of his business that the owner wished to spend the first day of her marriage poring over dusty ledgers.

Evelyn worked longer than she expected, calculating profits for the next year based on the diminishing income of these past months. It did not look promising, but with careful management the warehouse would survive. How long would it take before things changed for the better? Survival did not include sufficient income to support her family and a manager too.

Reminded by Mr. Johnson that it had grown dark, Evelyn reluctantly donned her cloak and allowed herself to be escorted back to Treamount. She was mildly surprised that Alex hadn't come down to the warehouse looking for her.

There were lights in the windows and she unconsciously increased her pace.

The delicious aroma of clam chowder greeted her as she entered the house. Mr. Johnson politely declined her invitation and went on his way, leaving Evelyn to seek the source of the smells by herself. She had nibbled at an apple and some toast for breakfast and completely ignored lunch. She was thoroughly starved by now.

The familiar sight of her mother bending over the fire sent both warmth and worry through her. She should have been the one here preparing the meal for her husband. She glanced around and found only Molly kneading some bread and Jacob licking a cake bowl, just as it used to be before Alex came into her life. Where was Alex?

They all glanced up as she entered and didn't seem surprised that she had spent the day after her wedding elsewhere. She was handed a stack of plates and silverware and ordered to set the table.

Counting the dishes and finding only enough for themselves, she hesitated. "Has Alex sent word when he will be home? And Lord Cranville, should we not have asked him to join us?"

That caused her mother to turn and look at her in surprise. "Did he not tell you? Well, I suppose he thought I would get the message to you. I just assumed when you weren't here . . ." She didn't continue that thought but went on to the next. "Alex and the earl have gone out to Castle Island to talk with Governor Barnard. They didn't say, but I believe they are trying to persuade the governor to place the stamps in the earl's custody. I find it hard to believe that a man as loyal to the crown as Lord Cranville would undertake such a dubious task, but Alex can be rather persuasive, I suppose." She sent Evelyn a look that said just how persuasive the gentleman could be if he could talk her daughter into doing what she shouldn't.

Evelyn hid her blush by turning her back and heading for the dining room. "The earl spent many years in Barbados," she threw over her shoulder as she left. "I wouldn't put too much reliance on his loyalty to anyone, just like Alex."

That seemed to be the most reasonable solution to all her questions. Both men were shrewd businessmen looking to protect their interests in whatever way they could. She wasn't certain where she fitted into their plans or if she did fit into them, but the likelihood of ever prying anything out of Alex was small. Telling her something of his past was an anomaly he would not repeat anytime soon. Their discussions seldom centered on feelings or beliefs or ephemeral topics like that. The only plan for the future she could get out of him was the desire to have their children born in the bed upstairs.

Slamming the dishes onto the table, Evelyn cursed her stupidity in marrying a man who didn't love her. He had no intention of changing his way of life for her. That much was obvious. But she had to throw away everything she knew and loved for him. It wasn't fair.

His continued absence did not lessen her sense of injustice. When her family left her alone later that evening in expectation of Alex's imminent arrival, she contemplated barring the door again. Only the thought that he would simply return to the doxy at the tavern made her hesitate. She was the one who would suffer. Not he.

Damn! Evelyn slammed the bolt open and stared at the huge empty bed with tears in her eyes. Why had she ever been fool enough to believe that her love alone would make this marriage work?

Alex stifled a yawn as the earl and the governor delved into the diplomatic intricacies of releasing the stamps from the protection of the fort. With night, the drafty building had become chillingly cold, but the two statesmen had usurped the best places near the fire. They didn't even need him except as a buffer when the negotiations grew hostile. No sleep last night, little enough the night before, and it appeared he would be here for the night again at the pace the present proceedings were progressing. Damn, but what he wouldn't give just for the luxury of sprawling across a feather mattress with Evelyn in his arms.

The thought of Evelyn brought a black frown to Alex's brow. After stopping at Upton's to wake the earl, he had gone back to the Wellingtons' to explain to Evelyn why he would be delayed. He had hoped to find her alone, but he would have settled for some tea and a kiss and a moment's conversation with her if she had not been. Instead, he had found the house hauntingly empty.

He had known where she was, but he had no desire to track her down at the warehouse in view of the entire world on the day after their wedding. He had tried to be reasonable the night before when he had sent a messenger with his apologies to explain he wouldn't be home. When the lad had returned to say no one had answered, he had thought of any number of reasons why Evelyn hadn't been there waiting for him. She could have fallen asleep and not heard the knock. She could have grown lonely or frightened and gone to her uncle's or to her mother for company. There could have been any number of reasons she had not answered that knock, but he knew there was only one. She had waited until he had turned his back and then run off to join her rebellious friends as usual.

Alex took another long drink of the hot rum in his cup and felt the heat seep through his cold bones. Why had he thought that, once married, Evelyn would settle down to a wifely existence like every other woman in the world? He must have been temporarily insane to believe his name and his financial support would relieve her of the need to run a business and play at politics. Supporting her family was only an excuse to be a meddlesome tyrant.

Well, that would all end when he put her on the ship for England. She would have no choice but to settle down and play wife and, eventually, mother. Why, then, did he feel distinctly uneasy when he tried to fit Evelyn into that picture?

21

Evelyn was frantic when still another night passed without word from Alex. She dressed hastily the next morning and hurried to her uncle's, only to discover from a maid that the earl had spent the night away too.

Before she could escape, her uncle caught up with her. With a gesture toward the breakfast room, he indicated that she join him. Reluctantly Evelyn followed in his footsteps. She was in no hurry to endure a conversation with Uncle George, but she could think of no way of politely refusing him.

"I've been meaning to have a talk with your husband, but he seems to be a busy man these days. Do you have word yet when the ship sails?"

That seemed an innocent-enough question and Evelyn settled her skirts over the chair offered and accepted some tea. "By the end of the week, I am told. They are still in the process of loading, and there seems to be a shipment or two that has not arrived."

"Then your husband means to pay your fine? That is generous of him. You will be keeping the warehouse, then."

Evelyn had serious doubts that Alex had any such intention concerning the exorbitant fine, but she kept her tongue still. She had until Friday, the first of November, to find the money or go to jail. If she were on a ship on the way to England, she could not do either. She rather thought that was Alex's opinion of the matter.

"The warehouse will go to Jacob when he comes of age. That has always been understood," she said firmly and calmly, sipping her tea. Further discussion of the warehouse would not be beneficial to her emotional health.

"Then you will need someone to manage it in your absence. The fellow you have down there may be a fine bookkeeper, but those types are useless in acquiring new business and expanding investments. You would do better to trust it to family. I'll be happy to recommend someone for the position."

Oh, lud, she didn't need to start the day like this. Setting her cup aside, Evelyn rose and gracefully rearranged the folds of her skirt. "You were in such a hurry to see me married, Uncle George, that you should have realized my husband would be the one to deal with such matters. He hired Mr. Johnson. You will have to speak with Alex if you're not pleased with his choice. Now, if you will excuse me, I have some other calls to make."

Sweeping out in a grand flutter of feminine finery, Evelyn succeeded in convincing her uncle she was no longer the one in charge of the dratted warehouse. At the moment, she was almost convinced that Thomas Henderson had been right when he had urged her to sell and reinvest in something more profitable. Had it not been for the warehouse, she would never have met Alex, never been arrested, and wouldn't be worrying herself sick over how the Stamp Act would harm the business. Maybe it was time to sell.

Had Alex been available to ask, she would have consulted him, but he was busy pretending he wasn't married, so she hurried down the street to her lawyer's office. She might find Henderson's ubiquitous flattery personally offensive, but there was no question that he was a good lawyer and that her father had relied on him. If the growing signs of his wealth were any evidence, he had good investment sense. It wouldn't hurt to ask.

Henderson greeted her effusively, as usual. When he heard her question, he looked vaguely startled but quickly recovered to tap his fingers thoughtfully against his desk.

"Then I assume either your husband has agreed to pay the fine or he has provided the court with sufficient evidence to prove your innocence. I know he has been trying to locate the owners of the contraband stored in your warehouse. Has he succeeded?"

"If he has, he has not informed me, Mr. Henderson. You must discuss that with him. He realizes that under no circumstances will my father's trust be touched for any purpose but my dowry and Jacob's future. I assume he has discussed the dowry with you. The sale of the warehouse would free the cash immediately for my portion, and thus partially reimburse him for the cost of the fine if he so wishes. Other than that, the bulk of the sale would need be reinvested so Jacob would be able to start his own business when he is ready."

"I shall give the matter careful thought, Evelyn. The warehouse might not sell for so much as it would in prosperous times, and there is the matter of your debts to be paid from the proceeds. I think your husband would be agreeable to reducing the dowry to increase Jacob's investment were it not for the enormity of the impending fine. If there is any chance that the fine will be commuted due to additional evidence, I would recommend that you discover it. It's a definite factor in the decision."

"Thank you, Thomas." Evelyn escaped as quickly as possible and hurried on to the warehouse. How would she ever persuade Alex to tell her what was in that packet of information that he and the earl had argued over? Was there some way to find the packet and discover it herself?

She had to make some decision, but it need not be immediately. She hoped. November 1 loomed ever closer. Her gaze swept out to the harbor, where the *Neptune* anchored. She could wish she were on it right now. She had bravely claimed she would go to jail rather than bankrupt her family, but the truth was, she was terrified of being paraded through the streets like a common criminal and locked behind bars for years of her life. She would do almost anything to avoid such a fate.

Even marry Alex. That thought came unbidden from the recesses of her mind. She had married a man who couldn't love her simply to avoid the necessity of jail. Not simply. She had to be fair with herself. She loved him, and the thought of letting him return to England without her had caused great anguish, but it would have been better for both of them had she suffered in silence. Alex had told her plainly enough that he had no wish to marry. His actions these last two days had proved his meaning well enough. Even married, he intended to go on as before. Could she endure that better than jail?

She would have to for her family's sake. It was too late to turn back now. But the fear of finally coming face-to-face with Alex after these past two nights of being alone was rapidly becoming overwhelming. She didn't think she could simply fall in his bed when the notion took him, as if she were some bought-and-paid-for trollop. They had to come to some understanding.

Exhausted and thoroughly disgruntled, Alex wove his way back to the Wellington house through the unlighted streets of Boston later that night. The cold north wind sweeping through the alleys and gusting leaves around his feet warned it was time to weigh anchor before winter's ice began to form in the rigging. If he had his way, he would merely fling his wife over his shoulder and ship out now. These damn stubborn Yankees had worn his patience to the bone.

The earl was cozily warming his toes at Hutchinson's fire tonight, but now that the stamps were safely in hands that would dispose of them without warfare, Alex was ready for his own bed. Evelyn had sent him on this wild-goose chase; now that he'd bagged the bird, he hoped she would be suitably grateful. He had the nagging feeling that she would not.

The house was dark and cold when he entered, the kitchen fire being long since banked. He had no appetite for food, however. The desire for sleep had even overcome his ever-present lust. All he wanted was to be in the peace of his bed with the warmth of his wife cuddled against him. He had never bothered to set up a mistress whose favors he could enjoy all night, but he rather liked the notion of waking to a warm and willing woman—sometime tomorrow afternoon, preferably.

Wearily but with a wariness developed over many years of unpleasant situations, Alex pushed open Evelyn's bedroom door. He breathed a sigh of relief that it was not bolted against him. He wouldn't have been responsible for his actions if it had.

His eyes searched the darkened room, settling on the massive shadow of the hand-carved poster bed by the window. Before he could determine if the bed were occupied, a swift movement caught his eye, and he stepped backward in surprise. A light flared and Evelyn's pale face emerged from the darkness as the candle wick caught.

She was wearing her hair in a single thick braid, but light wisps escaped to dance in the candlelight as she reached for her robe. The high-necked flannel gown she wore was not at all to Alex's liking, but without benefit of stays and petticoats and bulky chemises, her slender figure could be detected easily beneath the soft cloth. He stayed her hand to prevent her reaching for the robe.

"You don't need that. Get under the covers and I will join you shortly." He began shrugging out of his coat, damning the tailor for sizing him so correctly that the cloth had to be peeled like a second skin from his back.

"No, not until we talk." Evelyn snatched her hand away as if his touch burnt, and reached again for the robe.

"Don't, Evelyn. I'm too tired to talk." Alex felt the weariness descend like a heavy weight upon his shoulders as he threw his coat aside. The intimacies of the marriage chamber were new to him too—not the physical intimacies, but the emotional ones. He had opened himself to this woman more than to any other person in his life. He wasn't ready to increase that vulnerability yet. The emotions she stirred in him were as yet strange and uneasy ones. He preferred just to keep this on a rational basis, and knew of a certainty that his preference was about to be denied.

"Very well, then, don't talk. Tell me when you are ready. I will be downstairs on the sofa." Evelyn wrapped her robe around her and searched for her slippers with her feet. The room was icy and the front parlor would be no better, but she would freeze before she allowed this man into her bed without a word of excuse or explanation.

"Dammit, Evelyn, I've been up for three days and two

nights and I can scarcely think, much less talk. I just want to sleep. Can you not be reasonable about this?"

"I am being reasonable. I told you to sleep. I am simply unwilling to go to bed with a man who has not been home in three days and two nights after marrying me. You did not even send a note or a message or give a thought to my feelings in the matter. I thought you would at least wait until you tired of me before returning to your previous self-indulgent ways, but it seems that now that everyone's honor has been preserved, our marriage is of little consequence. Good night, Alex." Forcibly holding back her anger and tears after days of rioting emotions, Evelyn tried to get around Alex to reach the door.

He didn't touch her, but he refused to step away. Crossing his arms over his chest, he glared at her with growing fury. "*My* self-indulgent ways? Had you not been busy indulging yourself in your usual disgraceful pastimes, you would not only have received my message but also have been here when I came back to explain my delay! Would you care to tell me where you went in the middle of our wedding night? What scrape were you determined to get into that you sent me galloping off on fool's errands the same night we were wedded?"

"Disgraceful pastimes? Fool's errands? Is that all you think of what we are fighting for? If that is so, it seems passing strange that you would concern yourself at all. Why did you not just drag me home by the hair, take what you wanted, and then go join your drunken cronies in some tavern? Would that not have been more to your taste?"

"While I'm at it, why don't I turn my shrew of a wife over my knee and beat some sense into her thick head? Did you think to stay here and continue playing at being a man once we were married and I had paid your fines? Let me disabuse you of that notion now, dear wife. I have no intention of paying that fine. You will come with me or go to jail!"

"Bastard! I knew that's what you had planned. Why me? Why must I be the one forced to suffer the cruelty of being your wife? Were all the others too timid to linger in your presence long enough? Damn you, Alex

Hampton, you will see how little afraid I am! I will find those smugglers and turn them over to the court, and I will be free. You can go to hell!"

Evelyn shoved past him, racing for the door, but Alex grabbed her arm and flung her backward to the bed. Her words had pierced him more cruelly than she would ever know, more cruelly than he had ever anticipated, because they came too close to truth. He had used his size often enough to intimidate, to keep people at their distance. Women feared him. His manners were not gentle, nor did he make any attempt to gentle them for their sake. His distaste for their sex was evident, even when his need for them was great, perhaps more so because of it. Evelyn was the only one to look at who he was, to stand up to him when he was wrong, to come to him with the same need he had for her. And now she had seen him as he truly was, a villain.

She did not cower against the bed where he had thrown her. She merely threw her legs over the end and attempted to get away in that direction. Alex almost let her go, but he could not. Instinct made him reach for her again, and weariness made him throw her back to the bed rather than crush her in his arms and force her to surrender. Perhaps it was more than weariness that kept him from forcing her. He could force any woman he willed. There was no challenge in that. The challenge was in forcing a woman as strong as Evelyn to come to him in need. He had thought he had accomplished it. Instead, he had proved his own weakness.

"I will not disturb your slumber any longer. I will leave." Alex towered over her recumbent form as she rose to her elbows to fight him again. In the candlelight he could see the soft outline of her breasts against the worn material, could almost feel the tininess of her waist between his hands. Something in her face gave away her realization that he could tear her in two if he so desired, and he clenched his fists against his feelings of rage and helplessness. "But understand this"—he rested his hands on his hips as he glared down at her—"you are going with me. Your mother deserves better than a daughter in jail and a son-in-law who departs and leaves his wife behind. She is eager for this journey and she is going with us, whether you will or not."

That was the strangest argument she had ever heard. Perhaps he was too tired to think. Obviously he was too tired to be sensible. Alex was immensely large looming over her like that, and Evelyn was intensely aware of what he could do to her if he tried. She wished she could see his face, but he stood above the candle's light. Still, it was not fear she felt when he stood so close. The knowledge of his weariness made her want to reach out and urge him to rest beside her. She didn't think Alex would harm her, but she would undoubtedly harm herself. Her gaze was on a level with his hips, and the candle was close enough to that height to reveal the effect she had on him. She forced her gaze back in the direction of his face.

Before she could utter a word, he was gone. Suddenly realizing she was freezing, Evelyn pulled the covers around her, and in heart-rending dismay she watched out the bedroom window for the sight of Alex leaving to ease his needs with his tavern doxy. When no familiar masculine figure stormed out the door as expected, she frowned anxiously. She had felt certain he would head straight for the tavern and a willing barmaid to unleash his lust, just to get even with her. Her stomach clenched a little tighter when he did not leave. Did he mean to come back? Should she bar the door or have some words of apology ready?

She listened and heard his footsteps echo through the carpetless hallway. The sofa she had offered to sleep on was swathed in covers, and there would be no fire in the hearth. She heard the rattle of kindling in the bin and imagined the spark of flint on stone. He was lighting a fire.

Curling down between the covers, she listened as he made the fire and sought cushions for his head. The sofa was a large one, but she did not think it over six feet long. He would spend an uncomfortable night in such a bed.

He'd made that bed. Let him sleep in it. Spitefully Evelyn turned over and clenched her eyes shut. He had forced her into this marriage for reasons of his own. Let him learn to live with it.

The loneliness of the cold bed made her want to weep for what could have been, but she was beginning to see how wrong she had been in choosing a man who could not love her. There would never be any understanding between them. The promise she had felt in that brief dance before their wedding was a myth of her own wishful thinking. She had imagined happiness where there was none.

She drifted off to sleep, to dream of dark eyes and a laughing smile that suddenly turned cold and grim and shouted "Guilty as charged!"

In the morning she rose and dressed quietly and slipped to the kitchen to prepare breakfast. She could hear Alex's heavy breathing in the front room but she dared not look in upon him. Whatever he felt or didn't feel, her own emotions were too close to the surface to react sensibly to the picture of her husband deep in sleep.

If she were lucky, he would sleep right through breakfast, and she could go on to the wharf without further argument. She ought to be looking for that packet with the names in it, but she was hesitant about searching Alex's personal belongings. She still had some pride and honor left. She didn't know what good they did her, but she clung to what few remnants of herself remained after Alex's devastating force had entered her life.

Despite her desire to escape to the warehouse, she fed the fire and started coffee brewing. She cut strips from what was left of the salted bacon in the cold pantry and set them over the fire to cook. They had let supplies run low in the anticipation of leaving shortly, but there were still eggs and her mother had made fresh bread just yesterday. She would have a proper meal made and not be accused of neglecting her wifely duties, even if her dear husband were too exhausted to rise to eat it.

As the coffee boiled, she heard footsteps in the hall. Nervously she reached to remove the pot from its rack, burning her fingers when the holder slipped. Cursing, she set the pot down and sucked on her singed fingers, listening to the movement in the other room. She had not brought fresh water or towels to the room he had used upstairs, but there was plenty to be had in the room they were meant to share. Why did she not think of these things in advance? The thought of Alex muddling about in her personal belongings made her bite her lip, and she forced her thoughts away as she heard his feet going up the stairs.

With no one in the house but themselves to act as buffer or diversion, Evelyn was uncannily aware of Alex's every movement. She tried singing softly to herself to disguise the distant sounds of Alex's ablutions in the other end of the house, but she had no heart for singing. She clattered the dishes onto the kitchen table and rattled the pots and pans over the fire as she fried eggs and toasted bread. If she could just pretend she was alone, she would be fine.

Still, she heard him when he approached the kitchen door, knew when he stood there watching her. She tried not to envision him in her mind, but she could not stay bent over the fire forever. Removing the frying pan, she turned slowly to look up into his newly shaven face.

He had changed into clean shirt and breeches and used water to slick his unruly hair into some semblance of order. The ribbon at his nape was slightly askew, as if he had hurried, but the expression in his dark, deepset eyes was cautious.

"I didn't wish to be accused of starving you," Evelyn said mildly as she lifted the eggs from the pan to the plate.

"I couldn't sleep. I spent most of the night thinking." Alex took the heavy coffeepot from her and filled their cups, then pulled a chair out for her to sit upon.

Trying to hide her nervousness, Evelyn arranged her skirts and sat down, holding her breath until his hand moved away from the back of her chair. The kitchen table was small, and Alex did not take his place at the other end but sat next to her. His long legs brushed her skirts as he sat down. She made no reply to his comment. She could not.

Alex sipped at the strong coffee while Evelyn poured cream and sugar into hers. The dark shadows beneath her eyes spoke of nights as sleepless as his. He had put those circles there, and he didn't know how to remove them. He had spent a companionless childhood and his tutor had taught him little about developing personal relationships. He fitted well into large parties, where the conversation was meaningless and actions counted more than words. He had spent a lifetime dealing with servants and employees and had no difficulty giving orders. But he felt helpless dealing with an intimate situation with an equal.

"What you said last night was partially true," he blurted out. "I didn't mean to force you into marriage, but that's the way it looks, doesn't it?"

Violet eyes widened in surprise as Evelyn turned to him, and the coffee in her cup sloshed as her hand jerked. Hastily she lowered it. He had certainly caught her attention, if nothing else. Alex hurriedly took advantage of this fair beginning. "I don't know who sent us to that inn and stole our horses, but I cannot hold you responsible for the deed any longer. I thought I was doing what you wanted, but I suppose it was what I wanted too. I know if the opportunity occurred again, I would do the same."

Evelyn had to smile at that. She still did not dare look at him too closely for fear he would see how deeply she had fallen. He was attempting to be reasonable. The least she could do was try to be the same. "I don't think I care to comment on that," she replied carefully, if a little unsteadily.

Caught in his own train of thoughts and determined to carry them to the end at whatever cost, Alex let this slip by without wondering at it. "If there were any way I could pay your fine, I would, but the court has refused my notes. We seldom carry that amount of cash on our ships. We could go back with a less-than-full load and use the profits on the sale of the *Neptune*'s cargo, but much of our trading is done in merchandise and bills of sale and not cash. Before Cranville arrived I had meant to demand coins for our cargo, but it didn't seem so necessary once you agreed to marry me, and the opportunity is lost now. I had thought that we could sail without anyone daring to stop us. My cousin has already agreed to look into the matter and have your case set aside once we reach England, but that will take months. Right now, I simply don't have any choices left in the matter. You must go with me until the case is settled and closed."

His intensity seemed directed inward, and Evelyn hated to disturb his momentum, but she could not let that piece of logic go unchallenged. Gently she intruded. "What of the packet the earl possesses? If he has the names of the smugglers, could we not simply give them to the court and demand an appeal?"

That was a matter Alex had struggled over all night, and his solution was no clearer or more logical by morning. His protective instincts had taken over and would not allow him to do what reason said was best. He shook his head. "To do so would cause more harm than good, Evelyn. Trust me on just this one point, please. I know how to use the information to prevent the warehouse and my ships from being involved again, but there is nothing there to prove your innocence. The fact will still stand that the contraband was found on your premises. That, and the fact that you have a judge who is undoubtedly aware of your seditious activities, will preclude any release of the charges from his court. It will have to come from a higher authority."

Evelyn felt the eggs congeal in her stomach and nodded miserably. "Then there really is no choice. I must go with you or go to jail. It's rather too late for anything else in all events. I said the vows willingly enough. You did not even have to hold a gun to my head."

Alex avoided her small attempt at humor. The enormity of what he must say prevailed. Clenching one fist around his cup and the other in his lap, he revealed the conclusion he had reached last night, in the wee hours when everything looked its worst. "The threat of jail was better than a gun. I saw how you were when you came out after just a few hours in confinement. I knew you could never go back again. I didn't need a gun. I'm sorry, Evelyn. I didn't plan it that way, but I let it happen to get what I wanted. I can see now that it won't work. I am not accustomed to obeying any wishes but my own, and have little understanding of a woman's ways. You were never meant to play the part of docile, uncomplaining wife to a rake like me. Neither of us seems capable or desirous of changing. I think our best solution . . ." Alex stopped before saying the final words that would dissolve their marriage in all but name. There was one more important point he must ascertain before continuing. "Has there been time enough to know if you are breeding?"

A bright blush of color flooded her cheeks as Evelyn stared down at her coffee cup. "There has not been enough time," she admitted softly.

There was hope left, then, but not enough to keep the words from being said. Taking a deep breath, Alex offered her the only choice he knew how to give her. "You must come with me in any event, so there will be time enough to know before we reach England. If there is no child, we can petition for an annulment. The marriage has never been legally consummated, and the situation in which you were forced to marry should be sufficient grounds to dissolve the bonds. Somehow, I will see that you are housed with your mother on board ship so there can be no question of our intent."

There, he had said it. Alex closed his eyes and waited for the pain to wash over and engulf him. He hadn't yet decided whether this was the most courageous or damn-fool thing that he had ever done, but either way, it felt like hell. He had just condemned himself to six weeks or more of abstinence when the woman he wanted more than any other was within arm's reach and taunting his senses. Hell couldn't be worse.

Evelyn sat stunned by Alex's revelation. She had wanted to talk, to reason things out, to come to some sort of mutual agreement about her place in his life. She had never dreamed it would come to this. Annulment! They had been married but three days and he was ready to cast her aside. Misery twisted her stomach and burst through her veins and filled her with such anguish she could not think. Her head beat with the pain of it, and she dared not meet his eyes as he waited for her agreement. She could scarcely disagree, once he phrased it that way. He had no intention of changing his ways, and she could not live knowing he was in the arms of other women.

Slowly she nodded her agreement. "Whatever you say, Alex," she murmured. Even the tears wouldn't come. The pain was too great.

22

"I talked to Thomas about selling the warehouse." Evelyn finally broke the thick silence that had fallen around them.

Alex looked up with a start. "You what?"

A hint of defiance returned to her eyes as she finally dared look upon him again. "If you have not noticed, trade is dropping drastically. The tax will cut it even more. I thought there might be a wiser investment for Jacob's money. I told Thomas to think about it."

Alex growled into his coffee. "Leave Henderson out of this. We can discuss selling later. Now is definitely not the time to look for investors. I have a feeling all hell will break loose Friday."

That distracted Evelyn from her ire at his peremptory dismissal of her decision. "Why? What has happened? Has the governor not given up the stamps?"

"He gave them up. I did not question where they went, but of a certainty they will not be available when the law goes into effect Friday. I wonder if they have taken into consideration what will happen then."

Evelyn shrugged. "They will get no money from us."

"It will be illegal to print a paper, load or unload a ship, or issue a legal document without a stamp. With no stamps, the whole damn town will have to close down or be subject to arrest."

Evelyn stared at him in interest, her eyes widening as she caught his meaning and carried it further. "No ships, no warehouses, no work, no money. Lud, Alex, we'll all starve!"

"You will not starve. You're going with me, remember?" With a grim expression Alex pushed away from the table and stood up. "I've got to get down to the wharf and make sure everything's loaded. We're getting out of here as soon as the last shipment is tied down. Warn your mother that there is no time left."

He strode out without giving her time to question. Grabbing the coat and cloak he had left hanging on a chair, feeling strangely hollow, Alex turned his feet in the direction of the lawyer's offices.

Henderson had only just arrived when Alex entered the office without warning. The lawyer's powdered wig was neatly in place and tied scrupulously in a tidy knot at his nape. His clothes, while not as stylish as Alex's London-tailored garments, were richly elegant for this time and place. Alex scarcely gave them a second glance as his harsh gaze focused on the man's handsome visage. The young lawyer had a reputation with women, wooing them easily with his ready smile and pleasant features. Alex had seen his type before and had no use for it. But Evelyn trusted the cad. He would have to warn him off.

"I understand my wife discussed selling the warehouse with you," he began innocuously enough.

Henderson shrugged and indicated that Alex take a seat. He settled in his own comfortable chair behind the desk and waited until his visitor lowered himself to a similar level. Alex's size could occasionally be overwhelming, particularly in a small office like this one.

"I believe I have mentioned to her before that her uncle knows some investors willing to purchase the business. Under the circumstances, I think it the wisest choice."

"Fine." Alex stretched out his long legs and contemplated the tarnish on his silver buckles. His valet would have a stroke when he returned. He tapped his fingers idly on the arm of his chair. "I agree the warehouse should be sold. I have already talked to my senior partner about buying it. Cranville Enterprises cannot afford the taint of crimes against his majesty's trade laws. We are suspending all dealing with anyone suspected of tampering with the laws. The purchase of the warehouse should ensure fair dealings on this end." He looked up with a dark gleam in his eye to pin the lawyer with his stare. "I will personally ensure that any other companies attempting to ship contraband from England will find themselves before judges. I have the evidence and I will use it, if necessary. As long as we understand each other, I would prefer to avoid scandal."

Alex rose to his full height and smiled unpleasantly at the lawyer, who regarded him with a faint trace of an uneasy smile.

"I have little knowledge of the trade, Mr. Hampton," Henderson replied smoothly. "I only wish to see the Wellington trust handled in the best possible manner. If Evelyn trusts your judgment, I have no quarrel with that."

"Very good. You may send your bill to her uncle. The two of you should be able to agree on what the cost to Evelyn has been. I bid you good day." No longer smiling, Alex made no effort at a polite bow, but swung on his heel and strode out.

He was letting the bounder off too easy. There wasn't a doubt in his mind that between them Henderson and Upton had cooked up this whole scheme to get Evelyn out of the warehouse and claim it for their own. Had she simply sold it from the outset, she could be happily sitting in her own home entertaining a swarm of suitors now. His decision to start asking questions and tracking smugglers had forced their dirty hands. Damn, but he wished there were some way to get even with them, but they held all the cards. Exposing them now would only cause greater scandal and harm Evelyn's family more. Besides, he had already learned how closely these men worked with the local judge. There would be no justice here. Not yet, anyway.

As Alex walked toward the harbor, Henderson hurriedly closed his office and strode briskly down the street to Upton's.

George Upton greeted his lawyer's early-morning appearance with surprise. "You do not look as if you've come to share breakfast."

Henderson nodded toward the open door to the breakfast room. "Are you alone?"

The older man took his arm and steered him toward the closed door of the library. "My sister-in-law and

Cranville are here. What is wrong? Yesterday you were bragging we had the warehouse in our hands. Has the stubborn baggage changed her mind yet again?"

They entered the library, closing the door behind them as they spoke. Henderson paced to the newly repaired windows.

"That interfering dandified husband of hers knows about us. That packet you heard them discuss must contain damning evidence. He was at my office first thing this morning threatening me. If the warehouse is sold, it will be into his hands."

Upton issued a pithy curse and sought out the brandy decanter. "We've got everything out of there now except what was left to be used for evidence. They can prove nothing from this end. They may have traced the shipments, but there is nothing they can hold us on."

Henderson turned fiercely on the older man. "He's looking for blood. He has something or he would not threaten us as he did. He wants us to end the smuggling. We will no longer be able to use his ships or warehouses. He's cutting our throats."

Upton settled in a leather chair, his face suddenly betraying its age beneath the gray wig. "To tell the truth, I am growing weary of it. It does not seem worth the effort any longer."

The young lawyer practically snarled as he stalked the room. "That is fine for you to say. You're an old man with wealth enough to last the remainder of your days. What about me? Had you not insisted on getting rid of your niece by marrying her off to that damned Englishman, none of this would have happened. Why should I pay for your mistakes? Do you know how many lawyers there are in this damn town? Do you know how hard I must work and study just to make a pittance? Not worth the effort any longer!" he mocked, throwing up his hand in a vicious gesture. "You may as well say my life is not worth the effort any longer! There is money to be made here, and I will not give it up just to please that lofty niece of yours."

Upton pinched the bridge of his nose between his fingers in weariness. "She will be in England and out of your hair. It is her husband and the evidence you must worry about. It seems to me if he has not turned us over to the court yet, he will not later, unless he suspects we're continuing to use his ships. There are other lines available besides his."

"I will not feel safe until that evidence is in my hands." Henderson threw himself around to face his tired partner. "In any event, I will have to go to England to set up new supply lines while you find us a new warehouse. We can be back in business shortly."

Upton gave him a look of disgust. "It is nearly November. Do you think there will be another ship out of here before spring? It's over. Let it go at that."

Henderson curved his lips upward in a smile that would not be recognized by his lady friends. "There is a ship in the harbor right now, is there not? I'll be on it, and I'll have that packet before we land. Take care, Upton, or it will be only your name left in evidence."

Upton appeared ashen as his partner left the room. Draining his glass of brandy and setting it aside with shaking hand, he stared at the glittering new glass in his windows. There was no way out of it now. Rising to return to his guests, he wondered idly if he would ever see his wife and daughter again. For their sakes, he hoped Alex meant to hold his silence.

Evelyn bent over the last of the trunks to be packed. There was still the mattress Alex had slept on last night to be rolled up and put away again. She was waiting for word on whether they would be forced to spend yet another night on land while the last of the ship's cargo was loaded. She didn't at all like the idea of postponing their departure until tomorrow. That was just daring the fates.

She glanced nervously out the upper-story window to the street below. Any untoward noise made her start and shiver like a frightened rabbit. She kept hearing those soldiers marching, coming for her, hauling her away. She had nightmares about it, but she couldn't tell Alex that. She couldn't let him know her weakness. She couldn't let him see that she craved his arms around her to keep the nightmares away.

It was early morning yet. Surely by tonight they would

be on the ship and sailing away. She needn't worry about soldiers anymore then. She would be safe.

The street seemed ominously quiet. Alex had kept her from going down to the wharf these last two days, and she felt somehow isolated from events. Alex had dutifully reported the latest closings, the number of men looking for work, the quiet fear and desperation taking a grip on the city as the day of reckoning came closer. On the morrow, the town would virtually have to close down or collectively break the law. She wouldn't be here to see how it ended.

Outside, she could see a tall broad-shouldered figure braving the wind, one gloved hand holding his cocked hat to his head and the other gripping the edges of his cloak as it whipped in the wind. Evelyn's heart lodged in her throat as she recognized his hasty strides. Alex had sold his horse to Mr. Johnson yesterday. He was obviously regretting it now.

Raising her hand to tuck a straying strand of hair behind her ear and making certain the pins had not loosened from the braid coiled about her head, Evelyn hurried down the stairs to let Alex in. Maybe the ship was ready to sail.

He burst through the door before she reached the bottom of the steps and looked around wildly, as if fearful she had gone. As she hurried toward him, his thin lips relaxed slightly with relief, but the tension did not leave his shoulders. He produced a newspaper from beneath his cloak.

"Look at this! I don't know what I've been thinking. I've got to get you out of here now."

Evelyn froze, and Alex had to wave the newspaper beneath her nose. A skull and crossbones decorated the masthead like some eerie All Hallows' Eve demon, and she stared at it in horror and confusion. "What does it mean?"

"It means the newspapers are going out of business today. They cannot sell them without stamps tomorrow. It means the courts will close *today*, because they can issue no legal documents tomorrow. It means we have to get you the hell out of here before the judge realizes the same damn thing and comes after you now!"

"Oh, no! They would not!" Evelyn's face went white in horror. She had feared they might be at her door by morning, but she did not expect them a day early despite her nightmares.

"I'm taking no chances. There are mobs already forming in the streets. Sailors and farmers are still pouring into town, waiting to see what happens tomorrow. Right now they're satisfying themselves with heckling your uncle and others of his ilk, preventing them from carrying out their duties, but reinforcements have been called for. There will be troops on the street shortly. Do you still have your boy's clothes?"

"In the armoire. I did not think I would be needing them." She turned and started running up the stairs, with Alex in close pursuit. "What are we going to do?"

"Get you on that ship without anyone knowing. Let me see what you have. It's freezing out there."

Evelyn produced the breeches, shirt, and jerkin that she kept in the drawer, then pulled the faded broadcloth coat and fringed hat from the armoire. "I don't have any man's gloves, but I will be fine. It's broad daylight, though. Are you sure this will work?"

Looking at her reed-thin figure in the glare of the morning sun, Alex shook his head. Light glinted off burnished braids and softened her pale cheeks to satin. In silhouette, the curve of breast and hip were distinctly feminine despite her height and slenderness, and he remembered all too well the devastating effect of rounded buttocks and thighs in breeches. He groaned inwardly and stripped off his gloves.

"It's a damn good thing that's a long coat," he answered enigmatically. "Take these. Have you got a wheelbarrow or cart?"

Evelyn took the soft leather gloves, still warm from his hands, and clenched them tightly. "A wheelbarrow? I suppose, in the shed out back. What are you going to do with it?"

"Haul trunks." He left before she could inquire further.

Closing the door after him, she hastily divested herself of her gown and petticoats. It seemed strange to be donning breeches again. These last two days with Alex in and out, playing at man and wife, had created some subtle change in her thinking. She liked wearing feminine gowns and having men look at her as if she were attractive, but by necessity she had forgone those pleasures too much. With Alex around, it had been easy to rely on him to take care of the business world while she indulged in housemaking, or unmaking, as the case might be. She shook her head grimly at her stupidity. Once the marriage was annulled, she would once again be in the position of supporting the family. She had better not grow too accustomed to relying on anyone else.

Buttoning her coat snugly and pulling the loose-fitting hat down over her ears so it wouldn't blow off easily, Evelyn clattered down the stairs to find out what Alex planned.

He came in the kitchen door rubbing dirt and cobwebs from his frozen hands. Giving her attire a cursory inspection, he grimaced. "I can't imagine how in hell you ever thought you would pass for a boy. But with any luck, no one will be paying close attention."

Evelyn glanced down at her loose cotton shirt and brown buttoned coat and breeches and thought she had done very well. Her woolen stockings sagged to a nice degree, disguising her legs, and her hat hid her hair. What more could he want?

Reading the mutinous look in her violet eyes, Alex couldn't resist drawing his bare finger over the delicate collarbone revealed by the open shirt. One button less and the curve of her breast would be revealed, and he contemplated that fact with satisfaction as his finger hesitated near the crucial fastening. Her frozen stance warned of the dangerous game he played, and he raised mocking eyes to hers. "Next time, we'll have to find you a neckcloth."

He said nothing more, but strode past her toward the stairs. Evelyn remained where she was, feeling the path of Alex's touch burning against her skin, and acknowledging the heated sensation of her breast brushing against the soft cotton that she knew had been his goal. He could see beyond her crude disguise to the woman beneath, and she felt suddenly naked at the thought. Even though they would not remain man and wife, he knew her as a husband would, and she could never erase the memories of those nights.

Her heated blush carried out into the cold as Alex threw the larger trunk into the wheelbarrow and balanced a small one on his shoulder. She had not finished packing the big trunk, so it weighed less than the little one. She eyed her husband with skepticism as she drew on his gloves and watched his ease of handling the heavy boxes. "Would it not be wiser to put both in the barrow?"

Alex gave a brief grin and nodded toward the wooden handle of the heavy cart. "I have my doubts that you can push that much, but we'll have to give it a try. No one in his right mind would expect to see Mrs. Evelyn Hampton pushing a grubby wheelbarrow."

As his audacious plan finally struck her, Evelyn stared at him in anger and frustration. Push a wheelbarrow! Of course no one would expect a lady to push that heavy monstrosity through the street. Only a villain of the first degree would think of it! Refusing to buckle under his mocking stare, she wrapped her gloved fingers around the splintery wood and lifted.

The wheel was loose and wobbled hither and yon as she tried to balance the awkward load. If she tilted it up comfortably to stand, the nose dived toward the ground. If she bent over to level it, her back and arms strained to keep it balanced and moving. Cursing whatever madmen had invented this demented instrument of torture, Evelyn shoved her unwieldy cargo toward the street. Alex's chuckle behind her only spurred her on.

Easily balancing his own burden on one shoulder, Alex walked beside her, whistling as if it were a sunny day in June. Bent over the barrow as she was, watching her load lest it tilt and spill, Evelyn relied on him for directions. Occasionally Alex juggled his burden to reach out and push her hat down more firmly against the rising wind. Avoiding the main streets, he took the narrower alleys whenever he could, but their rutted surfaces were no easier for Evelyn to manage than cobblestones. She bit back her curses as Alex's whistling suddenly halted.

"I see uniforms ahead, little tyrant. We're almost there. Are you willing to take a chance?"

She felt as if her arms would fall off, and her legs shook so badly that she wasn't certain they would traverse the distance of the wharf without collapsing. But freedom lay at the end of that street. She had to do it. "I'll pay you back for this someday," she gritted out between clenched teeth as she once more heaved the heavy load forward.

"And here I thought I was being helpful. I had every expectation of vast rewards for my kindness in rescuing you this day. If you do not appreciate my thoughtfulness, you can leave the trunk here and saunter on down to the loading dock alone."

"Viper," she muttered, trundling the cart out toward the wharf. "Devil. Bastard. Villain." Each new bump of the wheel brought forth another curse.

Beside her, Alex hailed one of the soldiers with whom he was apparently acquainted. While he stopped to converse, Evelyn kept on trundling. She dared not stop her momentum now for fear she would never pick up her burden again. The wind off the water whipped painfully at her cheeks, and she prayed the overlarge hat would remain in place.

She found a sailor in a dinghy waiting for her. The man gave her a startled glance, then hopped up the steps to lift the trunk from the barrow. Behind them, Alex's voice could be heard approaching, to the accompaniment of more than one pair of footsteps. Not daring to look, Evelyn hastily clambered into the dinghy in a pretense of aiding the sailor to load the trunk.

"I daresay we'll take the evening tide. Don't want to risk not carrying a legal load, you know. Evelyn's at her uncle's saying her farewells. She's been a damned good sport about all of this."

"I suppose the earl took care of the fines? It's a shame to treat a lady like that. You know, she must have been tricked by some bounder. I never did believe she was guilty."

The stranger's voice seemed falsely sympathetic to Evelyn, and she kept her head down as they drew closer.

"You had a fine way of showing it, Captain."

Evelyn recognized the voice of Sam Adams and

gulped. He would know her clothes if nothing else. She prayed he would have the wisdom to remain silent.

"It's water under the bridge, gentlemen. I wish I were able to stay and see how all this turns out, but I must own I'm eager to be home again. In case I do not see you again before we sail, it's been a pleasure knowing you." Alex spoke lightly but with an undertone of tension that Evelyn recognized as he attempted to dismiss his companions.

"Are you taking that lad with you?" the captain asked in puzzlement as he noted the wheelbarrow left on the dock and the boy in the boat.

Adams replied, "Mr. Hampton kindly offered to give me a few books he brought with him from London. The lad's to fetch them back for me. These bones grow too old to take that icy wind out there. Alex, I expect you and your wife to keep in touch. You'll be sorely missed hereabouts." After glancing into the dinghy, he clapped Alex on the back and took his leave. Grabbing the elbow of the red-coated officer watching with suspicion, Adams steered him in the direction of the nearest tavern. "Let us get in out of the cold and leave the gentleman to his last-minute preparations. I do not envy him a voyage at this time of year."

His voice trailed off as they moved away, and Alex finally climbed into the dinghy with the second trunk. He didn't dare look closely at Evelyn's averted face, but his hand brushed briefly over her hunched shoulders. "I'm going for the others now. Toby will see you to your cabin. Will you be all right?"

Her silent nod had to be sufficient answer. Alex returned to the dock and watched the tiny boat row out toward the great ship anchored in the harbor. His heart still beat erratically and his stomach clenched with tension from the encounter with the damned suspicious officer. He dared not chance docking the *Neptune* for any more loads. There was still one of his majesty's navy frigates in the harbor that could give chase if necessary, but he would worry about that eventuality later. Right now, he had to get the rest of his passengers on board before the troops discovered Evelyn was nowhere to be found.

23

Noon came and went before the *Neptune* was prepared to sail. Alex came on board last and waited at the rail as the canvas opened and the anchor was weighed. The soldiers were no longer on the wharf, and the activity of earlier had dwindled to nothing as the clouds overhead grew heavier with the passing of the hours. The chilling north wind now brought spitting snow. The idlers would have transferred their presence to the taverns and the mob to their homes. Alex wondered where the troops went.

As the wind caught in the canvas and the *Neptune* moved out, he heaved an immense sigh of relief. He felt like Gulliver escaping yet another strange land. He was ready to return to the sanity of home.

The thought of home brought other problems immediately to mind. He had spent foolish hours imagining what it would be like to have Evelyn to come home to, to have her laughing gaze and no-nonsense manner sweeping out the ghosts of the old hall, warming the rooms with life. He could almost imagine enjoying living in that isolated abode under those conditions, but there was little sense in thinking about it now. An annulment would have to be sought in London, not Cornwall. They would be in each other's pocket constantly in the earl's town house, but at least there were other amusements to distract them until the deed was done.

Wondering if the time had come to set up a mistress to take care of this aching need he could not rid himself of, Alex started for the cabin. He would see his passengers settled, then find a suitable bunk and drink himself under the table for the rest of the voyage. He could think of no other way of surviving these next six weeks.

Entering the passageway leading past the smaller cabins to the captain's dining hall and larger cabin, Alex encountered his first obstacle. Amanda Wellington hurried toward him, a determined look upon her square face. Alex bit back a prayer for mercy. Beneath all her gentle, ladylike ways, Amanda Wellington had nerves of steel and the flexibility of a fine-honed rapier. He had the distinct feeling he was about to be skewered.

"There has been some mistake, Alex," she began inauspiciously enough.

Gently taking her elbow, he led her toward the larger space of the main cabin. "I've been known to make a few in my time, Mrs. Wellington. Is there anything I can do to correct it?"

To his chagrin, Alex found his noble cousin propped in one of the chairs at the table, his feet up, and a bowl of shelled walnuts in his lap as he listened to their conversation with obvious interest and a hint of amusement. Mrs. Wellington ignored this audience in pursuit of her goal.

"I certainly hope so. Your foolish captain has Evelyn sharing a room with me. I know the accommodations are limited, but there must be some way of managing this a little better. Perhaps he did not know you were married?" she asked hopefully, not being able to state the matter any plainer.

Alex held his temper at the earl's chuckle and tried his best to placate this woman he admired and respected. "I told Captain Oliver to give you and Evelyn the most comfortable cabin since you are the only ladies on board, and the voyage is quite likely to be an unpleasantly cold one. I do not wish to risk your health or Evelyn's. That is my uppermost concern."

Amanda smiled and touched her large son-in-law's arm. "I feared it was some such nonsense as that. I am happy to know that Evelyn has chosen such a considerate husband, but you do not need to make such sacrifices for me. I am healthy as a horse. If you will just have them move my things to your room, you can move in with Evelyn, where you should be. A young couple needs to have time alone together to cement the bonds that make a happy marriage."

Alex contemplated telling her he bunked with the crew, but he did not like lying to this woman. Besides, he greatly suspected she had already surveyed the situation and knew precisely where his belongings were. Before he could say anything, Cranville brought his feet to the floor and stood up.

"I'll go find someone to make the necessary transfer, Alex. I believe your bride is looking a little peaked and may need some consoling. I take it this is the first time she has ever been away from home." This last was meant to be an admonishment, and Alex accepted it with a painful bow.

Amanda patted his arm again. "I must find Jacob and try to keep him out of trouble. Someday I hope I can thank you enough for what you have done for us."

She slipped away, leaving Alex standing there feeling like the greatest cad in existence. He had done nothing but take what he wanted from the first. Now that he was trying to mend his errors, he found himself tripping over lies and deceptions everywhere he turned. To share a cabin for six weeks with a woman he wanted more than life itself and not be able to touch her would be a living hell. Surely his sins were not so great as to deserve such punishment.

Cautiously approaching the door to the cabin the captain had sacrificed for the ladies, Alex gave it a hesitant knock. The rustle of skirts from within told him Evelyn had had time to change her attire. When the door flew open, he could scarcely keep his gaze from drinking in the beauty revealed. Knowing that he was to be trapped in this dangerous company for nearly two months, he attempted to inoculate himself against temptation by studying her closely now.

She had donned a warm, high-necked gown of tightly fitted rust-colored wool. The ruffles of her chemise emerged from the elbow-length sleeves to spill over her wrists, and a white linen fichu gathered at her throat kept her modestly covered from all eyes but his. He knew the creamy satin skin hidden beneath that flimsy cloth. He could almost feel the weight and warmth of her breasts in his palms as he traced their shape beneath the bodice. Dragging his gaze upward, Alex felt the full effect of those devastating eyes as they watched him with wariness. He wanted to catch his fingers in her irritating braids and loose the lovely silken waterfall of her hair. He clenched his fingers into his palms to prevent any such impulsive madness.

"It seems we have a small problem, my love. May I come in?"

Evelyn stepped back so he might enter. Alex carried with him the brisk, fresh sea scent of the cold air outside, and his hair was still tousled from its encounter with the wind. He discarded his cloak as he entered, and gazed around the cabin as if judging its suitability. His head nearly brushed the timbers overhead, and his shoulders filled the doorway, blocking any possible retreat. Evelyn gulped at the rippling pain of desire passing through her as she watched his thick-lashed eyes return to her. She felt as if those dark eyes could see right through her, and at this moment she prayed they would.

"Problem?" she prompted him when he seemed in no hurry to speak again.

"Your mother objects to sharing a room with you. Do you have some unspeakable habits that I should know about?" He tried to make a jest of it, but he could see her pale before his eyes.

"I thought you would talk her out of it. Surely there cannot be too many other places she can sleep. We brought no maids with us. She would be quite alone."

"That does not seem to bother your mother overmuch. She has already coerced Everett into helping her move her trunks. They will be back here shortly to begin the transfer."

"You call this a small problem?" Evelyn glanced frantically at the wide bed bolted to the floor in the room's center. Evidently Cranville Enterprises provided the comforts of home for their trusted captains. There was easily room enough for two, even if one were as large as Alex. "What are we going to do?"

"We can tell her we have agreed on an annulment," he suggested with a trace of distaste. "Or we can make do as best we can. I leave the decision up to you."

She could not tell her mother that Alex wanted this marriage annulled. She could scarcely bring herself to consider the concept. The whole idea seemed dreadfully sordid somehow. But then, there was the small matter of the bed. Fighting back a blush as she tried not to look in that direction again, Evelyn nervously wound her fingers together. He seemed as uncomfortable with the decision as she. Recalling all the angry words she had flung at him this morning, she realized he must be dreading this proximity too. It would be just punishment to make him suffer a bit.

"I don't think I can tell her, Alex. I haven't seen her this happy since before my father died. Is there no other solution?"

Alex drew a deep breath and regarded her bent head with a mixture of anguish and hope. Six weeks was a long time. Almost anything could happen in six weeks. Trying to crush a ridiculous flood of elation, he kept his voice neutral. "We've muddled along this far, my love. We'll manage somehow. I hear them coming. Shall we give them a picture of marital bliss?"

Before Evelyn could protest that that was a foolish thing to do if they were to ask for an annulment when they reached London, Alex wrapped her in his arms and silenced her complaint with his kiss. The sudden shock of his heat and strength encompassing her after all these days drove out any thought at all. Evelyn closed her eyes and drank in the heady liquor of his mobile mouth against hers, felt the burning brand of his tongue invading her senses, and knew that only his arms kept her from falling.

The partially open door flew open before a well-placed kick as a sailor hauled in Alex's trunk under the earl's direction. Cranville's cough brought the embrace to a reluctant end, and Alex turned to glare at the sailor's grinning expression.

"I can see privacy will be a rare commodity around here." Seeing Amanda Wellington hovering in the room behind, Alex kept a possessive hand on Evelyn's arm and moved her aside so the others could enter. "Mrs. Wellington, if you would tell this scoundrel what to take, he can begin moving it for you."

"Why don't you call me Mother, Alex? Or Amanda, if you prefer. I don't think the formalities are necessary any longer." She swept in and pointed out her unpacked trunk for removal, then turned approvingly to the young couple. "I'm so happy for the two of you. Every time I look at you I think of John and myself when we were young, and it gives me a warm feeling inside. Do you mind terribly if I kiss you?" She gave Alex little time to answer, but stood on her toes and planted a solid buss to his cheek when he leaned over to embrace her.

Righting herself and gazing at them proudly, she nodded. "I think this shall be a most pleasant journey, if only I can keep Jacob out of the rigging. I'll leave you two alone now."

Cranville had leaned his slender frame against the door to watch this scene. At Amanda's departure, he straightened and gave his young heir a wink. "I guess that means I must go amuse myself also. You wouldn't happen to know who our other passenger is, would you? Perhaps I can strike up a game of cards."

Alex scarcely heard the question, but frowned briefly as it sank in. "Other passenger? Didn't know we had one. Ask Oliver. It could be one of his old cronies."

The earl nodded and backed out, closing the door behind him. Alex glanced down at the quivering woman in his hands and wondered what she would do if he carried her to the bed and threw her skirts up. The sudden rush of boiling blood to his loins warned that was not the proper direction for his thoughts, and he hastily dropped Evelyn's arm.

"We might as well unpack and make ourselves at home. It's going to be a long trip. Do you by any chance play cards?"

Relieved at his release, Evelyn replied carefully, "I am willing to learn. Will you teach me?"

Thinking of the hours they would have to while away in each other's company, Alex nodded. He was going to make one lousy teacher when all he could think of was getting his student into bed, but it would keep his hands occupied for a time. Sighing, he turned to unpacking his trunks.

* * *

Their mysterious passenger did not appear that night at the dinner table, but, wrapped up in other concerns, no one gave him much thought.

The earl complained of a chill and retired early without seeking a card-playing partner. Amanda Wellington learned that Jacob had some intention of sleeping in the crew's quarters and, horrified, remanded the care of the boy to Captain Oliver and his officers, who offered to keep an eye on him. Satisfied with this arrangement, she, too, retired early.

Unable to leave Evelyn in the rough company of the ship's officers, Alex escorted her back to their cabin. Leaving her to prepare for bed, he donned his cloak and went out on deck, hoping the cutting cold would chill his overheated blood.

Oliver wasn't the kind of man Alex preferred to converse with, but he sought him out for the sheer sake of company. A few minutes of the captain's obsequiousness was sufficient to send him in other directions.

He strode out to the railing and stared up at the cloud-covered sky. He had been brought up to the life of an idle gentleman, but he had learned to enjoy the exhilaration of earning his own way these past few years. There were those who would scorn him for dabbling in trade instead of the more genteel investment funds, but he had learned to live with scorn long ago. Gradually he was beginning to learn that it was his own scorn that he feared. The more disgusted he became with himself, the worse he behaved. Cranville had given him an opportunity to reform, and Alex had accepted it with little enough gratitude at the time. Feeling the ship rolling beneath his feet now, knowing he was the one responsible for seeing that it made a profit, that lives other than his own relied on his decisions, he had to acknowledge the enormity of the differences in this life that the earl had given him.

Still, there were the personal parts left untouched. Alienated from his only parent, uncertain how to develop a relationship with a younger cousin he had nearly ruined, and with only the older earl to call friend, he was returning to a loneliness that had driven him to dangerous straits more than once before. London wasn't Boston. His reputation as rake and bankrupt preceded him. He was shunned by genteel society and feared by the lesser sorts. He didn't know how to fit in, and had never really tried. It wasn't difficult to find someone to gamble and drink with. He had his fair share of invitations to dubious entertainments, but they weren't conducive to close relationships. Boston had been a revelation to him, a world where he could move about and be heard in any society with respect. They were a tough people to get to know, but he thought he had done a creditable job on the whole. Was there any possibility that he could do the same in London if he tried?

Thinking of the woman waiting below, Alex was willing to try anything. He couldn't induce her to stay for long with a man who spent his nights in brothels and gaming hells and whose closest friend was a brandy bottle. She was accustomed to a close-knit circle of friends and relatives who respected and admired her intelligence and independence. Somehow, he would have to find a replacement for that circle if he were to make her happy.

Acknowledging for the first time that what had brought on this train of thought was a desire to keep Evelyn with him, Alex shoved his hands in his coat pockets and lifted his head to scan the sky for some trace of the moon. Moon dreams, be damned. They were deuced rebellious, traitorous dreams, for all he could see.

He didn't know his own heart anymore, and he assuredly didn't know hers.

Evelyn had fallen into an exhausted sleep by the time Alex returned to the cabin. Moving about quietly so as not to disturb her, he stripped to breeches and shirt, found a spare blanket, and rolled up beside her. It was a hell of a way to spend a wedding journey, but he had come to a few conclusions this night. One of them was that he wanted this woman free and clear of all guilt and encumbrances.

He knew he could seduce her and cancel all chance of any annulment. He knew he could make her pregnant and bind her to him for the rest of their lives. But for the first time in his life he was bound and determined to do this the honorable way. She was his wife in name only. If he wanted to make the arrangement permanent, he would work for it.

There was time enough yet to decide whether he wanted to make the arrangement permanent. Closing his eyes, he finally slept.

When Evelyn woke the next morning, Alex was already up and gone. Growing used to the mixed feelings that all thought of him engendered, she hastily rose and dressed. He had apparently decided to play the part of gentleman. The best she could do was pretend to be a lady.

She found only Lord Cranville and her mother at the table. The earl looked a trifle pale and coughed frequently as he informed her that Alex had taken Jacob to explore the ship. Between Evelyn and Amanda, they persuaded Everett to tend to his cough by returning to his bunk with warm blankets and hot rum to take away the phlegm. Pampered by their attentions, he eventually slept again.

With the threat of meeting fashionable London shortly, the two women brought out their mending kits and began sorting through their clothes. It served to pass the time constructively and gave them the opportunity to catch up on the talking that had gone neglected these last hectic weeks.

When Alex returned and found them cozily ensconced in the main room, he turned to find some other occupation, but Evelyn's call brought him around. She tossed him a colorful skein of yarn to which she held one end.

"Make yourself useful, my husband. If I am to spend these hours in ladylike knitting and sewing, you must needs attend me and keep us amused."

He could think of worse occupations. Propping his feet up on a nearby chair, Alex set about making himself agreeable. He had never intentionally attempted such a thing before, but the reward would be well worth it if he could win Evelyn's favor. Giving her enticing figure a wicked leer, he began a half-naughty tale to return a blush to her cheeks.

Two days out and the icy north wind already freezing the lanyards, their mysterious passenger finally presented himself at the dinner table. Caught up in his plans for Evelyn and concerned about his cousin's health, Alex had neglected to interrogate Oliver on the occupant of the one remaining cabin. He swore vigorously to himself as Thomas Henderson sauntered into the main cabin in time for the evening meal.

The lawyer made a polite bow before the ladies and gave Alex only a hint of a lifted eyebrow. "I fear it takes some time before I acquire a stomach for this kind of travel, but I was eager to have your lovely companionship, ladies. Forgive my delay in presenting myself. I trust everyone has fared better than I?"

Evelyn discreetly removed her hand from Henderson's polished grip. Catching a glimpse of Alex's grim frown at the appearance of her handsome lawyer, she felt a moment's inexplicable joy at the possibility that her husband might be jealous. Sweetly pressing her advantage, she offered Thomas a seat beside herself.

"You never mentioned you intended to journey to England, Thomas. What brings you to join us?" Evelyn smiled into the man's face and was rewarded by Alex angrily rising to his feet to join them.

"I have numerous investments there that must be tended to, and I hoped to persuade some old friends to hear your case and perhaps have the appeal transferred to more neutral courts. I cannot bear to have your name sullied wrongly."

"My cousin and I are well able to look after my wife's concerns, Henderson. You would do well to take your reports to your Tory friends and leave Evelyn out of them." Alex pulled a chair to Evelyn's other side and casually rested his arm across the back of hers as he leaned over to speak with the intruder.

Deciding she had no desire to be the topic of argument, Evelyn diverted the subject. "How is Lord Cranville, Alex? Will he be well enough to come to dinner?"

Alex frowned his concern. "He said he felt a trifle feverish and thought it would be wiser to stay abed. I fear he caught cold with those long, chilling hours on the island. I forget that he is not accustomed to these colder climes."

"Then we must do everything to keep him warm. Have they put a brazier in his cabin yet?"

"They have, and he's resting nicely. I'm sure it will pass soon enough. Deirdre would quite literally have my head should I bring him home in less than the best of health. It has been nearly five years since they were married, but they still behave as newlyweds."

Alex spoke with fondness of the countess, but Evelyn heard the worry in his voice and lifted her gaze to meet his. He had so very little family that she understood his concern, but the look he gave her held other fears also. He had said the earl would live forever and they need not worry over such things as titles and estates. This first hint that his cousin might be as mortal as anyone else cast doubt upon his assurances.

What would happen to their plans if they arrived in London as the Earl and Countess of Cranville?

24

Alex's fears were justified by the end of the first week of their journey. The prevailing cold and damp worsened Everett's cough and fever until there was no longer any question of his rising from his bed. Alex had a hammock hung in the earl's cabin and slept there during the night. Amanda and Evelyn took turns during the day waiting on him.

He wasn't a difficult patient, but his illness annoyed him. He quite willingly drank hot broths and submitted to cold compresses in hopes of a quick cure, but the congestion seemed to settle in his chest and he could not get rid of it.

When Alex came in one evening during the second week of their voyage to discover Everett fevered and barely conscious, he hastily sought out Evelyn and Amanda. "The brazier isn't enough when he lies against the cold damp of the bulkhead. We are going to have to move him."

Evelyn knew instantly what he meant. They had scarcely shared the wide double bed in the captain's cabin since those first nights. Alex had somehow contrived to sleep only when she wasn't there or simply napped in the hammock in the earl's cabin. He had done everything humanly possible to keep their agreement. The possibility that the earl might die on this voyage made it imperative that he do so. She was not a fitting countess in her mind, and obviously Alex had come to the same conclusion. His worried countenance now was evidence of that.

"Let us move him to our cabin, Alex. We can nurse him better there in any case, and he will be away from the worst of the damp." Evelyn gave him the permission he sought.

Alex winced inwardly at how easily she surrendered their marriage bed, but it was scarcely unexpected. The brief hopes he had savored at the beginning of their journey had crumbled into dust quickly enough with his cousin's illness. He had hoped for years in which to persuade her that titles were meaningless and harmless enough. He read the fear in her eyes now quite clearly.

The earl was too ill to protest the transfer. When he was conscious, he consumed as much liquid as his racking coughs allowed him, but he spent more and more time in the semiconscious state of his fever. Alex paced the decks when he was not at his cousin's side. He disliked this feeling of helplessness at the hands of fate. His only relief was Evelyn's new cooperativeness. Instead of opposing him at every turn, she stood beside him and together they worked to keep the shadows of death at bay. Healing the sick diverted the energies they had once devoted to the passion that had brought them together. They had no need to argue.

Still, Alex felt a vague uneasiness every time he stepped from the sickroom for a breath of air to find Evelyn entertaining the glib lawyer in the main cabin. The weariness and worry that lined her face when they worked together over the earl's bed disappeared to some degree when she was with Henderson. She spoke easily with him, occasionally laughing and nodding in agreement to some lighthearted chatter. Alex was jealous of their ability to converse with such ease when all his conversations with his wife anymore were conducted under a strain not conducive to a mutual exchange of thoughts. He wished the lawyer to the devil and imagined ways of shoving him overboard.

Henderson noted Alex's scowl as he donned a cloak and went on deck for air, but he gave no sign of it as he returned to Evelyn's conversation. He had hoped for an opportunity to search for the packet with the damning evidence, but the state of chaos around him made it difficult to ever be alone in any place that it might be. He had found a new path for his hopes, though. The strained relationship between husband and wife was evident even to him. It would be much easier if Evelyn could be persuaded to search for the information. She did not seem at all averse to his company. It would be quite amusing to seduce the arrogant Hampton's wife right beneath his nose. And if Evelyn were caught searching for the packet, she would bear the brunt of her husband's fury, not he. It made much more sense that way.

Evelyn's mind was far from smugglers and evidence, however. She watched Alex leave the cabin with a sinking heart. She had thought to stir his jealousy with Thomas' attentions, but Alex's hardened heart couldn't be stirred by anything she did. She might as well reconcile herself to the fact that he truly wished this annulment. She had quit fooling herself long ago that she desired any such thing. Her arms felt heavy and empty knowing they would never feel Alex's embrace again. She knew now that she did not bear his child, and that fact brought hot tears to her eyes. Desolation filled her soul as he departed without a word.

"Has he ever told you the names of the smugglers his investigation uncovered?" Henderson asked idly, throwing a card down on the solitaire game he had begun some time before.

Evelyn scarcely heard his question, but shook her head numbly in reply. Perhaps she ought to go in and relieve her mother of nursing duty for a while. It must be her turn by now.

"It seems odd that he would keep such information a secret. Do you think the evidence might in any way incriminate himself?"

Evelyn gave him a blank look. "He would be a trifle foolish to investigate himself, wouldn't he?"

At least she was listening. Henderson gave a casual shrug. "Perhaps there isn't any evidence. He's just aroused my curiosity. I fully understood him to say he had sufficient information to free you from all charges. It seems odd that he has not presented it."

Evelyn vaguely remembered her own worries on that subject, but the matter did not seem so pressing as before. She watched the passageway for some sign of Alex's return. "It scarcely matters now, does it?"

Thomas favored her with a look of surprise. "You

could very well be a countess before long. If this smuggling scandal comes to light and others know the details, you could be pressed for blackmail to keep it quiet. I should think it would be in your best interest to destroy anything connected with the scandal, or at least give me the information to protect you. That packet could be essential to your defense."

Evelyn frowned and tried to draw her attention back to the conversation. He wasn't making any sense, but his urgency stirred a vague uneasiness in her. Could the contents of that packet be used against her? Surely Alex would not do that. The annulment would be sufficient to buy his freedom. He need not seek ways to destroy her.

Shaking her head, she dismissed the subject, but her curiosity was whetted. What could Alex hope to do by keeping the evidence secret? He had called it explosive material. She didn't like the sound of that at all.

The earl continued to battle the illness that drained his strength and left him helpless. By the end of November, with the worst of the journey behind them, he was no better, however. His constant attendants bordered on exhaustion themselves. The voyage had not been a pleasant one, and the winter storms had brought chills and sickness of varying degrees to all of them.

Alex found that a brandy bottle eased the anxious hours as he sat at his cousin's bedside waiting for the fever to break. Everett regained consciousness occasionally to frown at his heir's occupation, but he had little strength to scold him. Alex seldom showed any sign of overindulgence, and his solicitousness relieved the earl's fears.

"Where's Evelyn?"

Startled from his reveries by this croak from the bed, Alex set aside his glass and bent to check the compress on his cousin's forehead. "Sleeping. It is that time of night."

"You should be sleeping with her. It is your responsibility to produce heirs now. Or can you tell me there is one already on the way?"

Alex kept his frown to himself. He knew there was not. His one single flickering hope had been doused when he came upon his wife washing out the cloths proving their coupling had borne no fruit.

"Produce your own heirs, Everett. That ought to be incentive enough to get you out of this bed. I have no need of a weeping plump wife and sniveling brats to entertain me," he said callously as he helped his cousin to sit up and drink from the cup at his bedside.

"Deirdre might be a trifle annoyed should I try." The earl took a drink, coughed, and leaned back upon the pillows. "She is past childbearing age, and well you know it. The title and the responsibility will be yours. You cannot have one without the other."

"You never seemed overly concerned about the matter. It took you how many years to come back to see if the estate still existed?" Alex wasn't certain what made him taunt his cousin, but he regretted it instantly. Cranville suddenly appeared older and grayer as his thoughts turned to those lost years.

"Divided loyalties make life difficult sometimes. You do not have that problem. You have a lovely wife and the entire future ahead of you. Make the best of it, Alex. Someday you will be old like me. Make your memories pleasant ones."

There was deep sorrow in his voice, and Alex had to turn his head away to hide the sudden wetness behind his eyes. Cranville had been lost from his home and family for twenty years by a twist of fate that married him to one woman while the one he loved bore his child half a world away. Not until both women were dead did he learn of his daughter Alyson or know that he was heir to an earldom. The loss of so many loved ones and so much time grieved him, although he seldom spoke of it to any. Alex wondered how his own life might have turned out had his cousin been there to claim his estates all along. There was no point in speculation, but he liked to think they might have been friends.

The earl slept again, leaving Alex to his brandy and his own morose thoughts. The title meant very little to him anymore. He had no lust for power, nor did he need men fawning at his feet because of an accident of birth. But after Everett, he was the last of the Hamptons, and it obviously meant something to his cousin not to let the line die out. It meant something to him too, more than he had ever thought about. If nothing else, he had a responsibility to the people on their estate. The lands would be forfeited to the crown if he died without heirs.

The weight of all these responsibilities sat uneasily on his shoulders. He had taken much into his hands these last five years or so since the earl had come into his life, but business was an impersonal responsibility. Wives and children and estates and titles were responsibilities that he alone could fill. He had thought he had chosen Evelyn out of lust more than anything else, but as he considered his marriage in this new light, he realized he had chosen a woman with the strength to stand by his side and share this burden. He needed her a great deal more than he had realized.

And he had given her permission to leave him. Damn, but he was a bigger fool than he had thought! The one woman in the world who would stand up to him and call him fool when he needed it, and he would be rid of her. Why? She had the right to call him fool. He had acted the part. Of course they fought. They would probably always fight. But they were not battles of hatred or lack of respect, but genuine differences of opinion that could be worked out did they but take the time to try.

They had not fought once since coming aboard because they worked for a common goal. Evelyn had stood by his side as they changed linens and fed broth and bathed their semiconscious patient. She had held his hand, understood his fear, and said nothing when he ignored her, shunned her, and tried to cut her out of his life. Did she know he could cut off his arm easier than he could be rid of her? Just imagining a future without Evelyn left him empty and aching.

When in hell had that happened? He had never needed anybody. He had learned that lesson long ago, at his darling mother's knee. Love meant pain. So perhaps he didn't love her, but he sure as hell wanted her. And he'd be damned if he would let her go.

Making certain that his cousin slept easily, Alex quietly left the captain's cabin. Knocking at Amanda's cabin door to signal their change of shifts, he listened with surprise to voices coming down the corridor and the snapping shut of a door. Advancing across the open main cabin, he saw Henderson just returning to his own bed. Suspicion born of long years of hard experience immediately rushed to his head. With fury in his eyes, Alex stalked to the cabin Evelyn now used.

The lamp still flickered on the washstand as he entered, giving him light enough to note she had just come in from outside. The cramped space of the tiny cabin scarcely had room for both of them to stand when she swung to meet him, and Alex found himself staring down into terrified violet eyes at close range. His gaze scornfully swept over the cloak she was just discarding and the dinner gown beneath. He had not been able to keep his eyes off the revealing décolletage of that gown all evening. Apparently Henderson had not only shared his fascination but also taken advantage of it.

Alex's lips turned up in a snarl. "At least you are still dressed, my dear. I'm surprised you still cling to your Puritan modesty. Haven't I taught you that a lover's caress is much more satisfactory without the hindrance of clothing?"

At his rude stare, Evelyn moved to pull the cloak back over her shoulders. Alex stayed her hand, catching the heavy material and flinging it to the bunk behind her.

"Have you gone mad? What is wrong? Is it Lord Cranville? Has something happened to your cousin? Alex, don't scare me this way. Let me go to him. He shouldn't be left alone." She tried to edge around him, but Alex's greater size was unmovable as he blocked the door.

"Everett is sleeping peacefully. Your mother agreed earlier to look in on him so I could get some rest. Didn't she tell you? That's a pity. Had you known, you might not have risked my wrath by seeing Henderson behind my back. It's too late for regrets now, isn't it?" Dark eyes regarded her insolently as Alex began to shrug out of his coat.

Evelyn retreated a step until her legs came in contact with the bunk. She raised a hand to her mouth as she read the fury emblazoned across his face, and a shiver shook through her. "I don't know what you're talking about. Captain Oliver wanted us to see the school of whales playing in the moonlight. There is nothing improper in Thomas escorting me to the deck."

"How often in this last month has he escorted you on deck? How often have you come back down to be warmed in his embrace? The two of you always have your heads together. Do you think I am a blind fool? Whatever the case may be between us, you are still my wife. I will not be cuckolded by a lying scoundrel like Henderson."

"Alex!" Horrified by his accusations, Evelyn attempted to avoid the strong arm whipping out of the darkness to encircle her waist. "You cannot believe this of me! What have I ever done to make you think—"

Her words were cut off by the force of his mouth across hers. Her fingers instinctively closed around the rich brocade of his vest as Alex's strength bent her backward, threatening to unbalance them both as her knees buckled. His sudden suffocating proximity overwhelmed her, and the fire of his demanding kiss burned like flames across her lips until she succumbed to his pressure.

Evelyn gave a tormented cry as Alex lifted her against him, stealing her breath away with the harsh demands of tongue and lips until she had no choice but to respond. And respond she did, whether willingly or no, it did not matter. The complete joy of having his arms around her again filled her with excitement, erasing all the doubts and fears, easing the emptiness of these long, lonely weeks. Her hands slid to his shoulders and she offered no protest as he pushed her back against the bed and crushed her beneath his heavier masculine weight.

"I'll have you bearing no bastards with my name, madam. If it is heirs I must have, then they will be my heirs, born of my loins. I have been a fool before, but no longer. Open for me, my wife, and we shall begin our dynasty."

Evelyn heard him with horror, smelled the liquor on his breath, and knew he labored under some drunken misapprehension. Had she room to fight him, she might have, but the bunk was narrow and Alex had all the strength and leverage. There was nowhere to turn to or flee. Her screams would bring her mother and Jacob and Henderson running to her door, and the embarrassment of such a scene was greater than the humiliation of being accused a whore. In truth, she wanted him too much to fight him, however he wished to take her.

Alex's hands forced her bodice down and he suckled at her breast as his roving fingers found her skirt and hiked it up. Evelyn clung to his shoulders and rose hungrily to the heat of his mouth and denied the shame as he ripped open her petticoat ties and cast them to the floor. She was open to him now, just as he had wanted, and she buried her face against his wide shoulder as she felt the heat of desire rise up in her.

He wasn't long in unfastening his own clothing, nor did he waste time in preparing her more. Evelyn muffled her cry against his shoulder as he plunged in, stretching and filling her and then retreating just as she felt she would surely burst.

In her ear he murmured, "Nine-hundred and ninety-eight," and then he plunged again.

She gave in to his haste, felt her muscles tightening urgently around him, and wished to scream her need aloud when a quick rap on the door and her mother's voice outside interrupted them.

"Alex! Come quickly! He's calling for you. Hurry, please."

Alex closed his eyes and cursed and tore himself away before Evelyn's welcoming softness could destroy his mind and will and make more a fool of him than it already had. Evelyn gasped as he left her cold and uncovered while he stood to adjust his breeches to decency.

Without a word to her, he strode out.

25

They avoided each other for days. Alex had his hammock hung in the captain's cabin, where he could hear his cousin's slightest call throughout the night. He slept little, ate less, and sought solace in the brandy bottle until supplies were gone.

During the day, Alex sat broodingly in the main cabin while Evelyn retreated to the sickroom. There he could be certain Henderson stayed away from her. The nights were what ate at his innards.

Drink and anger and lust were a fatal combination, Alex finally concluded by the third day without a brandy. Instead of sealing his marriage, he had cut his own throat. He hadn't even done a very good job of that because he seemed to be slowly bleeding to death instead of dying outright. Every time Evelyn averted her face and hid in her room at the sight of him caused him another stab of anguish.

The worst of it was that they had no place to fight it out, no privacy to air their griefs and shout and scream until they understood the extent of the damage and might try to mend it. Their argument was too private to be aired in front of a crew of sailors on deck or within hearing of family and friends below. They could only put a lid on their accusations and let them simmer to a boil.

Everett's health did not improve with time and devotion. They took solace in the fact that it did not worsen either. Alex privately decided that his cousin was clinging tenaciously to consciousness just to see Deirdre and his daughter again, but to admit that aloud would be to recognize the other side of the coin. Once he had achieved this one goal, would the earl then give up the fight and slip away from them forever?

Evelyn watched the grim sadness of Alex's expression as he left the sickroom early one morning, and marveled at the changes carved into his once haughty, cold face. The lamplight caught on a streak of silver in his thick dark hair, and the lines about his mouth were those of grief. She longed to take him in her arms and hold him, but she understood his pride prevented that. She did not blame him for what had happened that night, but he blamed himself. She questioned her own sanity in believing that he could change, that with time and love he would learn to trust and return the feelings she had for him. She didn't know what drove him to these impulsive, rash actions that hurt him as much as anyone, but she was willing to try to understand, if only he would let her.

As it was, she could scarcely meet Alex's eyes without revealing her need or blushing with the memory of that night between them. Better that she avoid him and keep him from knowing how foolishly she had fallen. He didn't need any more pressures in his life right now. Let him think he was still free if he wished. He was free. She was the one who was bound and chained by her own heart.

They arrived in London in mid-December and a collective sigh of relief must have blown the winter clouds away for one brief moment as the *Neptune* sailed up the Thames. Evelyn pulled her cloak tighter against the whipping wind and watched as the sunbeam caught at the Tower of London along the bank before disappearing into the overall gray of the day again. Farther down the river would be the Houses of Parliament, where the future of their home would be decided. She prayed the sunbeam was a good omen.

Beside her, Jacob was staring in awe at the towers and spires in the distance. His head swiveled to marvel at the huge bridge ahead and the towering sailing ships all around. As they neared the dock, his eyes grew round at the massive brick warehouses stretching as far as the eye could see. Clouds of smoke hovered over buildings far into the distance, without relief of trees or countryside. This was London, and it was just as frightening to Evelyn as to her little brother.

Alex came down from his discussion with the captain on the quarterdeck to join them. Amanda had remained below with the earl, and Henderson had apparently found it necessary to take this time to repack his trunks. Alex read the fear plainly in violet eyes and rested his hand reassuringly on Jacob's shoulder, though he dared not touch Evelyn's.

"It is like a dozen different towns all built together. Once you know which one is which, it won't be so overwhelming. You'll learn Fleet Street is our publishing district, and banking is done around Cheapside in old London. The theaters are found near Drury Lane between the old districts and the newer ones. We will be going to St. James, which is one of the newer suburbs and has quite a large park similar to your Common, although we don't graze sheep there."

Evelyn heard the reassurance in his voice and knew it was for Jacob. The buildings and the streets didn't frighten her. It was the people she feared, and he could give her no reassurance on that point. Evidently he meant to take them home with him. How would his family accept a Yankee wife who was not a wife? Would Alex tell them that he meant to have their marriage annulled as soon as possible? How would she face their scorn, if so?

His hand came to rest lightly on her collar, and one finger stroked a straying strand at her nape. "We will be going to Cranville House, Evelyn. Everett and his wife reside there and keep a suite of rooms for me. There is quite sufficient room to house your mother and brother also, but not in the same suite that we must share. Deirdre will be distraught at Everett's illness. I don't wish to disturb her with our problems. She would find it odd if you did not stay with me."

He had read her mind. A shiver, not from the cold, went through her, but Evelyn nodded her understanding. She stared out at the dirty water and wished Alex would wrap her in his arms and hold her close against him and prove that everything would be all right. As it was, she must be satisfied that he had come to her at all and take pleasure in his proximity for whatever short time remained to them. She would let her ears freeze rather than draw up the hood of her cloak and disturb the placement of her husband's hand.

A carriage was sent for when they docked, and Evelyn hastened below to help her mother with last-minute preparations. Alex had insisted that his cousin would wish to be appropriately garbed when he arrived home, and he had enlisted several crewmen to aid in the process. By the time the carriage arrived, Lord Cranville was fully roused and coughing harshly, but alert to the fact that he was going home.

The highly polished, elegant landau with its glass windows and gleaming brass lanterns and discreet coat of arms on the side would have impressed Evelyn thoroughly at any other time. As it was, she was more concerned with helping Alex to get the weakened earl inside and resting comfortably on the plush cushions. Jacob willingly accepted a seat beside the liveried driver, and a footman in immaculate black uniform assisted Amanda and Evelyn inside.

As she settled on the seat across from him, the earl opened his eyes and gave her a solemn wink. His voice cracking and barely audible, he commented, "Not quite the same as the colonies, eh?"

"It would be quite dull if everyone lived alike," Evelyn agreed. She saw the flame of hope leap to Alex's eyes at this sign that his cousin had improved, but soon after, the earl closed his eyes and drifted off again. They rode the remainder of the way in silence.

Warned in advance of their return, Deirdre and a host of servants swarmed down the steps to greet them as the carriage arrived. Evelyn stared in awe at the immense facade of cut stone that was Cranville House. The carriage had pulled through towering iron gates and driven up a semicircular drive to halt at the foot of a wide expanse of steps that led up to a building grander than any she had ever seen. She had rather thought Westminster might look something like this. The State House in Boston could fit in one corner of this palace.

Her attention was caught by the necessity of helping Lord Cranville from the carriage. From the window Evelyn could see a petite woman with charming smile and laughing eyes who had come to greet them suddenly turn pale and cold as Alex spoke to her and the footmen ran to aid Lord Cranville from the carriage and up the steps. The earl appeared to waken sufficiently to wrap an arm around his wife's shoulders as she flew to his side, but she could not hold him steady and a servant hastened to carry him up the stairs. The lovely countess seemed very human and vulnerable as she ran after them.

Alex's return to the carriage cut off the rest of this scene. He helped Amanda down, then reached for Evelyn's hand. Their gazes met in wordless speech, hers fearful, his both worried and reassuring. He kept his fingers firmly around hers as she stepped down and an awestruck Jacob leapt down to join them.

"Please excuse Deirdre for not greeting you properly. She is usually the sole of propriety, but . . ." Alex shrugged his shoulders in helpless explanation of the bonds between the countess and the earl.

"I would have done the same," Amanda assured him calmly. "Perhaps it would be best if Jacob and I found lodging elsewhere. Lady Cranville is going to be very occupied until the earl recovers. We will only distract her."

"You are my guests. Deirdre will be glad of your company once she realizes there is nothing she can do but wait for time to tell. The housekeeper will show you to your rooms. You'll want to rest until tea. By then the physicians will have been here and Deirdre may be a little more coherent."

Alex led them inside the magnificent open foyer, where a circular staircase led the eye upward to towering murals and a brilliant skylight that cast the hall in a warm glow. At Evelyn's gasp he smiled slightly. "I have heard the classicists murmur 'Palladian' and 'Jones' when describing this monstrosity, but the truth is that the first earl was too cheap to hire any architect at all. He just stole the ideas from the best ones he could find, and then threw in a few of his own."

"I don't suppose he also housed a bank, a church, and a village in here while he was at it?" Evelyn inquired a trifle dubiously as they turned toward the stairs, where the housekeeper waited.

"My great-great-grandfather was a bit of a rascal. He

was a bank of sorts, and undoubtedly thought of himself as God once the king traded him a title in payment of the huge debts owed to my ancestor's coffers. I'll show you his stateroom sometime if you wish to see his idea of a church. And it takes a village of servants to run this place, so you're not far wrong."

The housekeeper waited stoically through these irreverent explanations. Alex gave her grim face an amused look before making his introductions. "Evelyn, this is Mrs. Green. She hates me because I'm more like the first earl than anyone dares to admit out loud. Mrs. Green, this is my wife and her family. You will show Mrs. Wellington and Jacob to the blue guest rooms. I think I can still find my way to my own rooms, unless you've boarded them up and had them exorcised?"

The stout woman regarded this nonsense without expression. "Yes, sir. As you wish, sir." Then she directed her gaze to the weary lady in drab colonial attire, and her expression surprisingly softened. "Come this way, ma'am."

Evelyn watched as her mother and brother were led away into the depths of a far hall while Alex steered her in the opposite direction. She had been terrified of meeting Alex's family. She should have spent more time worrying about how to deal with an army of formidable servants. At home, Molly counted more as family than maid. She was no example at all to judge by.

A woven carpet muffled their steps as they passed bronze statues in windowed recesses and beautifully polished elongated tables with elaborate inlays to draw the eye. Alex's suite apparently consisted of the entire corridor, for there were only three doors leading from it, and they were at the far end, secluded from the public rooms and the remainder of the household.

He opened the left-hand door and led her into a sitting room that would have occupied the entire first floor of her home. Tall pedimented windows looked out over a small garden at the side of the house. Heavy silver-gray brocade draperies shimmered in the remains of the late-afternoon sun breaking through the clouds. Marvelously wrought Persian carpets with the jewel colors of rubies and sapphires blended with threads of silver and gold accented the floors. Graceful sofas in shades of blue and gray were interspersed with comfortable chairs in pale gold. The effect was both gracious and overwhelming. Evelyn lifted an inquisitive eyebrow to her silent husband. "Do you do much entertaining?"

At this unexpected response to his home, Alex hesitated, uncertain he followed her train of thought. As he looked around the room through her eyes, however, he began to grin. "I doubt that Deirdre would have heart failure if we held a reel or two in here, but there are other rooms better used for dancing. I believe you're supposed to bring your closest lady friends here for tea and gossip. Otherwise, it's just a place to while away our evenings if we tire of the social whirl. I have a desk in my chamber, so the secretary over there can be yours. I expect you will wear it out writing to all your Yankee friends about our ostentatious way of life."

The trace of that rare smile on his lips did not relieve all Evelyn's uncertainties, but it gave her something steady to hold on to. Realizing she was still clinging to his hand, she released him and took a few steps on her own into the room. Her gaze caught the door at the far end of the room, and she lifted her head inquiringly to Alex. "Our chambers?" she asked more boldly than she felt.

This time, he took her arm to lead the way. The polite gesture was not so intimate and thus less threatening to her composure than holding hands as he guided her toward the bedroom.

The sapphire blue carried over to this chamber, with more of the saffron and accents of the deeper blue in the carpet and occasional chairs scattered about. The canopied bed provided the centerpiece, its posts draped with transparent veils of gossamer yellow obviously not intended to keep out cold drafts. A deeper gold silk comforter covered the wide bed, and pillows in shades of blue and gold were stacked decadently at one end. The draperies were of sumptuous gold velvet, and Evelyn had to wonder how many lovely dinner gowns she could have made of such luxury. She would have to stop thinking like that if she were to stay married to Alex. She sent him a sidelong glance as she walked toward the draperies and pulled them back to look out. His features were expressionless, and she could not fathom his thoughts as he introduced her to the room he meant for his wife. Had that one night on the ship meant an end to his plans for annulment? Her insides clenched in apprehension as she tried to imagine spending the rest of her life in a chamber such as this. Could she do it?

She could do anything if she knew Alex was with her. The real question was, would Alex stay by her side or go his own way? He had not made that very clear, and she feared any answer he might give.

Feeling his silence, she offered a slightly quavery smile. "It is lovely, Alex, like an enchanted fantasy world. Do you ever grow accustomed to living like this?"

He shook his head. "I spent too many years on the edge of poverty to fail to appreciate it." He gave another of his lopsided grins. "I should have taken you to Cornwall first. You would have felt at home there. This is a palace meant to impress. The estate from which the wealth was obtained is a working farmhouse, glorified by turrets from medieval times, perhaps, but destitute of this extravagance. I think you would like it."

She didn't know if she would ever see it, so a reply did not come readily. She bent her head in acknowledgment and wandered to the massive rosewood armoire. She wondered if he kept his clothes in there, and she did not dare to open it.

"Would you care to see the rest of the suite?"

"There is more?" In astonishment she turned to see him gesturing toward still another door.

Alex gave her a curious look. "Perhaps I should not tell you, if you are satisfied with these arrangements."

Her gaze went to the wide bed she had thought they would share and then back to him. There was something in his dark eyes she wished she could read, but she felt only the heat of embarrassment as she realized he had never intended that they share the bed. "Let us see the rest of this palace," she replied stiffly.

"Actually, palaces are royal residences. 'Mansion' will have to suffice for commoners like us." Brushing over the loaded exchange that had just passed between them, Alex stalked to the door at the side of the room and threw it open. "Your dressing room, madam. Your maid's chamber is behind this. The first earl didn't think highly of having servants close at hand, but the second earl's wife insisted it was less than civilized to have to ring for her maid. She had the dressing rooms cut up with partitions for the servants."

Evelyn slipped past him to a room larger than her old bedroom. A discreet door at the rear indicated where some stranger would sleep if she had to employ a maid. Another massive armoire filled one wall, and a lovely dressing table occupied the wall next to it. Her glance fell on yet another door, similar to the one she had just come through.

Following her gaze, Alex stoically crossed this smaller room and opened the door opposite. "My dressing room."

"Oh." Evelyn held back. The rooms they had just come through were as impersonal as a museum because no one had actually lived in them. She had a feeling that would not be the case in these next ones.

"Come along. I have seen your home. You must learn mine." Impatiently he caught her elbow and led her to the next room.

The dressing rooms were fairly identical, hers being more silver and gold and his blue and gray. The exception lay in the fact that there were brushes and combs and wig stands scattered about his dressing table. A rack in the corner held a jumble of walking sticks, umbrellas, what appeared to be a discarded golf club, and a pair of tall leather boots. On the wall hung pistols intricately carved about the long barrel, with beautifully polished wood handles. Dueling pistols. Her heart sank a little further.

Alex was waiting for her to enter what she hoped was the final chamber. Steeling herself, she strode bravely through this next door, to find herself at last in Alex's home.

There was no mistaking that this was where he lived. Despite servants' attempts to tidy all personal belongings into their proper places, they could not hide the open liquor cabinet with the marvelously ornate decanters and crystal goblets. Nor would they take away the lovely matched paintings of ships at sea on either side of the massive tester bed. Dark blues dominated here, in the heavy comforter and bed hangings, accenting the tapestried draperies. The feel was almost medieval, and the crossed swords on one wall added to the feeling.

She knew the armoire would conceal his expensive frock coats and linen. She doubted that he wore nightshirts or caps, but if he did, they would be in those drawers over there. The stand beside the bed held a lamp for reading the jumble of volumes stacked beside it. The massive bookcase desk between the windows held more leatherbound books and an organized chaos of papers and pens and ink. She recognized ledgers behind the shelf windows and knew he used this room as much for an office as anything else. She felt Alex's presence here so strongly that she had to force the erratic beat of her heart into control before turning to face him.

There was almost a vulnerability behind those normally impenetrable black eyes as they met hers, and Evelyn's attempt at controlling her emotions slipped disgracefully. She reached out to touch his arm, and wished desperately that he would wrap it around her and hold her close and carry her to that bed they ought to share. Instead, he went rigid, and she hastily removed the offending hand.

"I like this room best," she offered simply, then turned and left for the coldly formal chambers that were to be hers.

Alex simply stood there watching her leave. He had thought he could manage this. He had had some odd notion that he could remain polite and aloof and treat her as any female daring enough to invade his chambers. Lord only knew, he had many years' experience in keeping women at an emotional distance, even when they shared his bed. Why, then, was this one so different?

Perhaps because he had no right to keep her against her will and no wish to give her up.

That made a damned knotty problem he had little time to contemplate. He'd better go check with Deirdre about the physicians and then send a message to Rory and their solicitor. Cranville Enterprises had been neglected too long, and there was still the matter of Evelyn's charges to be appealed or dismissed. It was time he returned to work.

26

"Alex has terrified me for years." The petite young woman smoothed her skirts out across the settee and smiled warmly at the gentleman who had just released her hand. Her words seemed to have no connection with her demeanor. When she returned her attention to Evelyn, she gestured airily with her hands. "He looks at me with those forbidding dark eyes of his as if I were some particularly repulsive henwit, and waits patiently for me to be gone so he can go about his business. He is so . . ." She threw her hands up and wide expressively. "He is so very large and intimidating that I feared him on sight, which is always a mistake with Alex. He takes advantage of fear and plays it against you. Do you know, he actually threatened me with physical violence? Horrible man. But of course, I know now what you must have learned from the first. He's quite incapable of harming a soul."

The gentleman behind her coughed at this sweeping and absurd generalization of Alex's supposed docility, and Evelyn had difficulty hiding her amusement. She had fallen in love with Alex's cousin Alyson the first time they met, and the relationship between this fey female and her overtly masculine and decidedly practical Scots husband held her enthralled. Alyson was capable of flights of fancy beyond the bounds of reason; Rory simply held her on a silver chain and brought her down when she flew too high. Obviously Alyson was treading clouds now, but not dangerously enough that her husband wished to disturb her.

"Alex can be a trifle intimidating," Evelyn agreed with a polite murmur.

"A *trifle* understates the fact. Alex *cultivates* intimidating," Deirdre announced decisively. "Many's the time I have contemplated taking a fire iron to his head. I cannot imagine how you got close enough to him to even consider marriage."

From behind her, Evelyn heard the clink of a glass and Alex's deep rumble. "Perhaps she neglected to use Alyson's boiling water or your fire irons to entice me." His hand came to rest on Evelyn's shoulder, and she could sense his hidden amusement even though she knew he would keep his face poker straight. She looked up to test her judgment, and he lifted his glass in a slight salute. "Would you believe that faint creature over there once dumped boiling water down my leg?" he said to her, indicating Alyson. "I still have the scars to prove it. Very odd idea of terror, I must say."

Just the sound of his voice sent tremors to Evelyn's toes, and the look on his face now pierced her with quiet joy. Here with his family Alex was relaxed and at ease with himself, and she felt the closeness they once had shared. She smiled easily and touched his hand with her fingers. "I am not even going to ask what you did to cause a lady as gentle as Alyson to act so. I'm certain you deserved every minute of your agony."

"He did, but at least he displayed uncommon good taste if not good sense. There's some hope that the lad has grown up since then." The lilting roll of Rory's R's gave hint of some strong emotion, and Evelyn glanced quickly between the two men.

Alex's hand tightened on her shoulder, but there was no anger in his voice as he replied. "You are still jealous that I might have married her first, Maclean. Letting Alyson get away may have been one of my worst moments of stupidity, but it seems to have worked out very well. Evelyn, at least, doesn't faint at just the sight of me."

A hint of humor twisted Rory's lips as his wife grew as puffy as a pigeon with her feathers ruffled. Soothingly he rubbed a knuckle against her cheek. There did not seem to be need of any further communication between them, Evelyn noted jealously. Again her eyes lifted to Alex. So Alyson was another of the women who had rejected his suit. For a man who despised marriage, he certainly had a talent for asking for it.

"I might not faint at sight of you," Evelyn spoke for herself, "but I am quite inclined to do so should you ever say a pleasant word without prompting. Will you please sit down and quit towering over me? I'm likely to strain my neck if you persist in standing."

Laughter rippled around the room and Deirdre murmured a soft "Brava!" as Alex's expression went from surprise to amused abashment. When he sat down on the chair beside hers and took Evelyn's hand, a splattering of applause broke out.

In her corner, Amanda Wellington watched this scene with a mixture of love and amazement. She had much experience in the cruelty of society and had feared for her daughter's ability to be accepted by Alex's aristocratic relatives, but she could see now that her fears were for naught. They had taken her in as one of their own without question. They were all good people, and she nodded her relief as she continued her needlework.

"As you can see, the tyrant has nagged me into this marriage. She apparently prefers timid, easily browbeaten men," Alex teased, refusing to let Evelyn's hand go as she tried to jerk it away.

That inane remark brought more laughter, and Alyson quickly jumped to her new cousin-in-law's defense. "That is not at all as I understand it, monster. You must know that Father tells tales. You had best treat Evelyn with all due respect, or I shall repeat them to everyone."

Alex grimaced and Evelyn shook her head in embarrassment as she hastily replied, "Do not take all Lord Cranville says with seriousness. He is not privy to all that has gone between Alex and me. We are not always on our best behavior."

"I would say Alex never is, but admittedly, he has his uses," Rory said, easing the rising tension. "Have you got that Weatherford contract yet, Hampton? We need to act on it with all due haste."

Alyson made a wry moue of distaste as Rory turned the topic to business. Alex immediately swam for these safer shores, and the two men retreated to another room, leaving the women to share confidences without interruption. Evelyn felt suddenly abandoned. She was accustomed to being consulted about business and included in the men's arguments. Finding herself in this all-female company left her mildly uneasy, and she was surprised when Deirdre picked up her embroidery and took the chair that Alex vacated.

"As much as I love my husband's sole heir, he can be very daunting at times. Tell me, Evelyn, are all women in the colonies as courageous as you?"

Evelyn exchanged a glance with her mother, shook her head, and laughed. "Not any more than all the women in London are as lovely as you and Alyson."

Deirdre accepted this reply complacently. "All the women in London are cowards, then. Everett does not speak much of his fears, but he has been worried that Alex would never settle down. That is one of the main reasons he sailed off as soon as he learned Alex had fallen headfirst into woman trouble as soon as he set foot in Boston. He was quite determined to whip Alex into line this time."

Embarrassed, Evelyn didn't quite know what to say to this forthrightness. It seemed she and Alex had nothing secret between them. Did his family know, too, that they did not sleep together? Apparently such a situation was not unusual in society, since she had learned most married couples kept separate bedrooms, but it still felt most wrong to her.

Alyson softly chided her husband's aunt. "Come, Deirdre, you know Father could never make Alex do anything against his wishes. Like Alex, he gets restless and looks for trouble sometimes. He has only himself to blame for his illness now. It sounds as if he enjoyed every minute of his stay in Boston. With smugglers and rebels thrown into the picture, I am quite surprised Rory did not join them."

"That is probably because he knew you were breeding again," Deirdre replied airily before tossing the ball to the woman in the corner. "Amanda, do you think all men are as trouble-prone as ours?"

Amanda lifted her gaze from her sewing and tilted her head thoughtfully, quite at ease with the discussion that left her daughter's head spinning. "Men crave action more than do women, I suspect. We have been trained to stay home and tend to our tasks dutifully, so we make our trouble in less active ways."

"Like talk," Evelyn interrupted. "That is why they say that behind every good man you'll find a good woman. We twist their arms verbally instead of physically, so no one sees it. I had never quite thought of it like that."

"You almost have it," Deirdre laughed. "If it were not for women plotting and planning as we do here tonight, men would never get things straight. They would take swords to each other and be done with it. Alex and Rory have come that close to blows, but look how much better it is when they work together. Do you think that would ever have happened if Alyson had not been there whispering soft words in Rory's ear?"

A dreamy smile drifted across Alyson's face as she sought some memory and lifted her rounded chin to speak her piece. Evelyn watched her with fascination, knowing Alex considered her half-mad.

"Not always words, Deirdre. We take action too, but we're more limited in the kind of action we can take. We are not as big and strong as they, so we cannot beat them physically."

"But we can join them physically." Deirdre laughed as she completed out loud what Alyson would have left unsaid. "We are all married ladies here, cherub, we need not be shy." She turned her attention to the newest married member of the company. "I think Evelyn already knows the power we can wield without saying a word. I don't think Alex's gaze left you all evening."

Evelyn blushed and wished she had something to occupy her hands as all eyes turned toward her. She had no power over Alex. He controlled her heart, her soul, her life. She was helpless. Perhaps it was different when a husband loved his wife, but these women did not know that Alex was incapable of love. She shrugged diffidently at their continued silence. "Alex is his own man. I have no desire to control him," she responded simply.

Alyson smiled affectionately at her and Deirdre reached over to pat her hand. "With Alex, that's probably the wisest way of looking at it. Nevertheless, there are some things you must teach him. A little sugar always makes it easier." She rose and straightened her skirts with a graceful gesture. "Everett should be awake by now. Will you go up to see him before you go home, Alys?"

"Rory and I both will. You go on now. I know he'll wish to see you first." Alyson sadly watched her stepmother hurry away.

The unspoken truth lay between them with these simple words. The physicians came and went on a daily basis with pills and nostrums and advice, but the earl's health still did not improve. Rory and Alyson stayed in Deirdre's old home with their two rambunctious youngsters when in London, but this last week Alyson had practically lived at her father's side. The strain was beginning to tell despite the evening's light chatter.

"I wish there were something I could do," Evelyn said morosely, gazing at her hands. "When my father was ill, I managed to keep busy and felt useful to him, even if I could not make him well. Here I can do nothing, and I feel guilty that Lord Cranville's illness is partially my fault."

"That is nonsense." Alyson threw her threads and needles in a nearby basket. "Father had this same inflammation of the lungs last year. His physician advised that he return to warmer climes, but he was enjoying himself too much here. The decision to stay was his alone. Marrying Alex is the best thing you could have done for either of them."

Evelyn said nothing and Alyson gave her a curious glance, but unlike Deirdre, she kept her thoughts to herself. "I suspect if you mention to Deirdre that you have a talent for business, she will most happily unload the household finances on you. She detests bookwork, and with Father ill and Alex so busy, there is no one to help her."

That was something Evelyn could do with ease, and she glanced up gratefully, only to suddenly remember that Alex had never mentioned to his family that she had operated a warehouse and knew bookkeeping. Perhaps Lord Cranville had said something to his daughter about it. She was surprised that Lady Alyson did not frown upon such a plebeian occupation, but the earl's daughter tossed the matter out as if she spoke the price of butter. Evelyn nodded her relief.

"Thank you, I will do that. Alex is gone so much of the time that I seldom have time to talk with him about such things."

Alyson gave a breezy wave of her hand as she rose to capture her straying husband so they might leave at a reasonable hour. "Should you find yourself less than occupied, you need only visit my home. I have two little rogues who wear out more nursemaids and governesses than any ten children. They would be happy to do the same for anyone else foolish enough to volunteer to care for them a little while."

The family gathering broke up shortly afterward, but Alex remained in the downstairs study while Evelyn made her way to bed. The huge suite seemed icy, though warm fires burned in the grates. The maid Deirdre had assigned her hastened to remove the lovely gown the dressmaker had brought just that day. Deirdre had been the one to hire a mantua-maker to see that Evelyn was adequately gowned, and Deirdre had been the one to introduce her to servants and family these past days. Alex had remained aloof and remote, and she felt his distance as much as the icy chill of these rooms.

If she only knew why he avoided her, perhaps she could deal with the problem more readily. Surely he did not think she had encouraged Thomas Henderson? Her solicitor had called to leave his new address and visit for a few minutes, but there was nothing wrong in that. But then, there had been nothing wrong in viewing the whales the night that Alex had practically attacked her. She had thought it had only been the liquor and his fears for the earl speaking that night. Perhaps she was wrong. It wouldn't be the first time.

There was such a distance between their rooms that she did not even know when Alex finally retired. He entered through his own door, avoiding hers as he had every night since they arrived.

Henderson called again a second time the next day to see if Evelyn would care to drive in the park or view the sights of London, since her husband was too busy to escort her. Christmas was a week away, and she had done no shopping. She consented without a second thought.

When they returned laughing, their arms full of packages, Alex was waiting for them. Evelyn caught sight of his black glare first but blithely ignored it, surrendering her packages to a maid and her pelisse to a footman. Henderson had no such options. Once the packages were safely on their way upstairs, he had to face Alex.

"Good evening, Hampton. Home a little early for a change?" A hint of a challenge tinged his voice as he held his tricorne in front of him. Not a hair of his immaculate wig was out of place, and his expensive redingote sat his shoulders well.

"I needed to see about a few papers Cranville was holding for me," Alex replied smoothly. "I need to make some decision as to how to use them. Perhaps you and I might discuss them sometime."

Though pleasantly said so as not to cause raised ears among the servants, Alex's words hid a silky threat that Evelyn heard plainly enough. She glanced between the two men and felt their scowls without needing to see them. Without wishing to know what inane game they played, she lifted her skirts and took her leave of them.

"I am off to brush the icicles out of my hair, gentlemen, if you will excuse me." She sidestepped the massive obstruction of her husband and gracefully ascended the stairs after the maid.

Alex waited for the other man to take up his offer or leave. Already having a good idea what papers Alex spoke of, Henderson was in no hurry to discuss their contents or their potential use. He gave Alex's icy glare a respectfully wide berth as he returned his hat to his head. "Your wife has my address. Call on me sometime if you wish," he replied with equal suavity.

Alex cursed as the man escaped under the protection of the servants. Swinging on his heel and starting after Evelyn, he halted abruptly, remembering the last time he had tried to warn her away from Henderson. That fiasco flared large in his mind, forcing him to retreat into the study. He reached for a brandy, caught himself, and shoved his hands back in his pockets. Somehow he had to sort out this mess he had made of their lives, but he couldn't do it with drink.

He had no idea if he had ruined their chances of an annulment. He had meant to persuade Evelyn that she didn't want to end their marriage at all, but after that night he feared her hatred too much to confront her with his wishes. With the threat of the earl's illness hanging over them, he had no position at all with which to argue his case. The future looked bleak, and it seemed easiest to immerse himself in work. Perhaps if he could arrange to have her charges dropped, Evelyn might speak to him without scorn again.

Not that he had given her much chance to speak to him at all except in the company of others. She was making a coward of him. Everyone seemed pleased with his choice of wife, and Evelyn appeared to be adjusting nicely to his home. Alex didn't wish to disturb the peace with his usual rash words that always brought the ceiling crashing down upon his head. Perhaps he was just learning caution. Sighing, he picked up a pen and started to work on the stack of papers waiting for him.

Upstairs, Evelyn waited for Alex to follow her and vent his anger. It had been exciting to get out of the house and meet a new world for those brief hours today. Henderson was as obsequious as always, but she could easily ignore him as she perused all the enticing curiosities that London's shops had to offer. Thomas had assured her that her dowry was sufficient to make her purchases inconsequential. She disliked charging things to Alex, but her lawyer's words had assuaged her conscience. Now she wasn't at all sure she had done the right thing, but Alex did not come to chastise her for it at all.

On the ship she had wished for the privacy to exchange all the angry words that needed to be said. Now that they had the privacy, they seemed to be avoiding each other, treating each other with the delicacy of fragile porcelain. It wasn't natural to either of their natures, and she greatly feared Alex had truly lost interest in her, but she didn't know what to do about it.

Alyson descended upon the household with her tribe the next evening. The ensuing screams from the nursery brought Evelyn to investigate. She found Jacob on the floor with two wild Indians threatening to scalp him and all three making enough noise to scare off banshees. She looked around for some sign of the nursemaid that should be attending the younger two or the tutor assigned to her brother.

At the sound of the gradually increasing racket, Alyson hastened in from her father's room, but by then Jacob had spotted his sister and was in the process of disentangling himself. He glanced at Lady Alyson with a slightly shamed face and futilely tried to hush the toddlers.

Alex's black-haired cousin gave the scene a distracted look and turned absently to Evelyn. "Have I misplaced a maid somewhere?"

Evelyn couldn't help smiling at her dazed expression, and she reached to lift the younger toddler. A cherub of barely two, he crowed with delight and buried his little fists in Evelyn's loosely looped hair. "Perhaps she eloped with Jacob's tutor."

"One can only hope."

The deep voice came from behind them, and Evelyn swung around so quickly the child in her arms squealed with delight.

Alex admired the sight of his wife with a child in her arms, hair tumbling in dishevelment about her shoulders. He hated to tear his gaze away from her wide violet eyes and moist lips parted in surprise, but he could see the other toddler launching a frontal assault. Deftly he bent and scooped the plump armful up before he could be knocked to the floor by an exuberant hug about the knees. Alyson's little demon let out a war cry suitable for a Highland warrior, nearly deafening him, and Alyson looked even more bemused. He laughed and tickled a bare tummy beneath a shirt hanging from dusty breeches.

"Confess, Jacob, how did you get rid of your wardens?" Alex lifted his laughing burden to his shoulder.

Jacob grinned as he realized he wasn't about to be read a lecture by his sister. Alex understood these things, and he shrugged inelegantly. "I was done with my lessons and Millie promised the boys a treat and Mr. Harrison said I might have one too if I waited here while they went to get it. You'll probably find them spooning on the back steps. I expect a double helping of Cook's tarts for this."

"Oh, my. Millie's really too young. I'll have to send her back to her mother." Alyson drifted out in a flutter of petticoats and ribbons, leaving Alex and Evelyn holding the deserted culprits.

Alex turned his eager gaze back to his flustered wife. "You quite see what I mean about howling brats, don't you?"

As the one on his shoulder was systematically untying Alex's queue and demolishing his jabot without a word said in reprimand, Evelyn gravely returned his gaze. "Yes, I most certainly do. They shouldn't be allowed in public until they're safely out of Oxford, and not even then until they're firmly under the influence of some genteel young woman."

"Right. They're heathens without fear of God until then," Alex agreed solemnly. "Do you think Cook will give us all tarts if Jacob goes down to help carry them?" Well aware that the kitchen was the favorite haunt of starving young boys, Alex watched the boy's eyes light with eagerness. He was gone before Evelyn could raise any objections.

Evelyn watched this defection with exasperation. The toddlers were already squirming for the freedom of the floor and new delights, and she let her armful down, only to quickly block his escape route when he decided to follow Jacob.

Alex laughed and put the Maclean heir on top of a dresser where he could grab at several carefully arranged toys on a wall shelf. "Now what, wife? Have you any experience at minding children?"

"I rather thought they were supposed to mind us. I don't suppose they will sit and play quietly with a toy apiece?"

Alex brought down a large wooden soldier for the tot on the floor and lifted the older brother down with both fists wrapped around a stick horse. The younger immediately set up a cry for the elder's toy.

Alex leaned his wide shoulders against the wall,

crossed his arms, and waited for Evelyn to resolve the battle. She gave him a scathing look, grabbed a ball from another shelf, and sat down in front of the crying lad. His tears instantly came to a halt as the ball bounced in front of him.

"Stalling tactics, very effective, my dear. Do you wish to spend your life that way?"

That blunt question brought color to her cheeks, and she refused to look at him. The other boy dropped his horse and rushed to join the game, and both were squealing with glee as a chastened nursemaid hurried in, saving her from reply.

As Jacob and Alyson returned and tarts were distributed all around, Alex took his treat and made his excuses. "I am keeping Farnley waiting, I fear. As much as I would enjoy helping you smear jam across your chins, business calls. My regards, Alyson." He bowed slightly and spun around to stalk out, his back stiff and his stride long.

Evelyn watched him go with such a wistful look on her face that Alyson couldn't help commenting. "He's all splendid show, you know. He calls the boys all kinds of terrible names and pretends he detests children, but the children adore him. Children aren't fools. They know when they're loved. You'll notice how quickly he appeared when the commotion began. A man who hated children would have walked out and found the solitude of his club."

Evelyn turned her attention to the tot in her lap, who had decided two jam tarts were better than one. "I think I knew that, but it's nice to hear one's opinions confirmed. He denounces all of you as if pretending he doesn't care will save him from hurt, but he does care, far more than he'll ever show."

"So you know that." Alyson absently wiped at a sticky hand. "I was wondering if you did. Alex is truly an enigma sometimes."

Evelyn laughed as the two-year-old went after an escaping dab of jam with his tongue. Perhaps she wasn't suited to spending her days in a nursery as Alex had implied, but she rather enjoyed these few precious moments of it. When the jam was caught, she returned her attention to the lovely Lady Alyson across the table. "He had me convinced you were half-mad, but I see now that is a mark of his esteem. He really does admire you."

"Moon dreams," Alyson murmured in the same tone another would have said "Fustian." "He thinks impossible dreams are impractical. He is very much a man of the world. But everyone has dreams. We cannot live otherwise. That is why he thinks I'm mad. I'm a dreamer."

"Perhaps, then, so am I." Evelyn set her tyke down for the nursemaid to wash and rose from the table. "Do you think your husband would mind very much if I asked to speak with him and the family solicitor?"

Alyson didn't appear particularly perturbed by this request. Wiping the hands of her son, she answered without hesitation, "I will tell him that you have asked. I'm sorry Father isn't well enough to help you, but Rory will gladly lend his hand."

It had taken every ounce of courage Evelyn possessed to make that request. She hadn't known she would do it until the words were out. Alyson's total lack of surprise made her wonder, but she did not stop to question.

It was time one of them quit stalling.

27

Christmas Eve Alex returned home early, only to find Henderson just stepping into a carriage and pulling away. Alex's hand wrapped around the package in his coat pocket as if he could take his wrath out on the object. Somehow he would have to warn Evelyn away from her lawyer. He had thought warning Henderson away would be sufficient, but the man seemed particularly dense. Perhaps he ought to turn the evidence over to the authorities and devil take the Upton family. Trying to do the honorable thing didn't seem to be reaping many rewards.

The trouble was that he had too many pressing concerns to involve himself with smugglers again. He'd put an end to their use of his ships and Evelyn's warehouse. That had been his first responsibility. Now he had the problem of the charges against Evelyn plus the situation in the colonies to deal with, along with the day-to-day concerns of an organization as large as Cranville Enterprises. There just wasn't time in one day for everything that needed to be done.

He had taken the time from his busy schedule to make a few personal purchases for Christmas, but he could see the time would have been better used guarding his own front door. Containing his anger, Alex entered the house just as Rory and the family solicitor came into the hall.

The expressions on their faces as they saw him betrayed more than a hint of guilt, as if he had just been the topic of conversation. Cursing to himself for not being able to go directly to Evelyn, Alex awaited their approach.

Rory was seldom given to physical expressions of

affection toward his partner, but he slapped Alex soundly on the back now. "Decided no work can be done when the whole town is closed for the holiday?"

"Something like that. What brings you here? Shouldn't you be home singing carols with your wife? And I should think Mr. Farnley serves us well enough to deserve a holiday too."

"I'm going home directly," Farnley assured his employer. "I must tell you that it is a pleasure knowing your wife. A fine, sound mind she has. I congratulate you on your choice. Many another in your place would not have noticed her quality."

Meaning anyone else expecting to hold the title of earl would have sought among the nobility for a bride, Alex translated wryly to himself. But then, very few of the nobility would be interested in a man engaged in what under any cover was trade. Cranville called it "investing," and for him, perhaps, it was. He had made his fortune and had no need to earn more. Alex's position was considerably more precarious. The bulk of the Cranville wealth had gone to Alyson on the death of Everett's father. Everett's wealth would go to Deirdre and a daughter in Barbados. Alex had only what he earned. He didn't find it in the least strange that he had chosen a wife who knew what it meant to earn money.

"Evelyn and I are well suited," he agreed stiffly. He didn't know what Rory and Farnley were up to or why Evelyn's name had come into the conversation, but he had other thoughts on his mind and was anxious to see these two gone.

They, too, seemed particularly eager to be off. As soon as they left, Alex took quick strides up the stairs to their suite. It seemed the logical place to look for a woman who had just been out with her *cicisbeo*.

He entered through the sitting room, catching Evelyn by surprise. She swung around with a guilty start, still holding the papers she was about to put in the secretary. Seeing him, she hastily shoved the papers in and closed the drawer.

Alex stared from the flushed expression on her face to the secretary, put them together with the coincidence of meeting Rory and Farnley below and Henderson leaving, noted Evelyn did not appear to have been out in the cold, and felt his heart sink into his boots. How many reasons could a woman have to consult with family solicitors and lawyers? He had made no further mention of the annulment. Evelyn had obviously grown impatient.

"Is there something I can do for you?" Her husky voice broke the silence stretching between them.

Alex had an easy reply for that one. "You can stop seeing Thomas Henderson." He began to cross the room with a lazy grace that disguised his fury and despair.

"He's my friend. He's the only person I know in this town besides your family. You cannot forbid me to see him." Evelyn held her ground. She could have told him that she had not even seen Henderson, that she had sent him away when his card was presented because she was busy talking with Rory and Mr. Farnley, but he wouldn't have believed her. And he would have wanted to know what she was talking about that had been so important she couldn't be interrupted. She was afraid he wouldn't like the answer.

"I've told you before that I won't be a cuckold, Evelyn. As long as you are my wife, you will conduct yourself with the discretion the position deserves. I will have Henderson forbidden the door if you persist in your defiance."

Alex loomed terrifyingly over her, his hands on his hips as his black eyes glared down at her not inches from her face. They stood toe to toe and Evelyn considered lifting her foot and kicking him in the shin, but she didn't think that would ameliorate his anger. Instead, she smiled sweetly, though her gaze filled with venom.

"Very well, my lord and master, I will ask that Thomas not come to the house any longer. No thanks to you, I am beginning to learn my way around the city quite well. I'll simply meet him elsewhere. Is there anything else I might do to please you, sir?"

She was so close he could smell the faint perfume of her violet-scented bathing soap, and the odor twisted his guts around a burning brand. He could reach out and crush her easily, take her right here on the carpet, and no one would hear her screams, but he didn't want her that way. Damning himself for a fool worse than his half-mad cousin, Alex swung on his heel and stalked to the far side of the room.

"What do you want from me, Evelyn?" He tried to keep the anguish from his voice as he stared over the winter-bare garden below. "I have given you freedom and respected your privacy. I have tried to make you comfortable. I told Deirdre to spare no expense in seeing that you were adequately clothed. I don't believe you find my family too objectionable. What else can I do to make you happy and keep you away from that scoundrel?"

He could give of himself and she would be happier than with mansions and silks, but she knew she could not say this to him. In his eyes, he had given her all that he had to offer. No fault lay in the fact that he had no love to share. Sadly she ran her fingers over the satin finish of the mahogany desk.

"Give me something to do, Alex," she finally answered. "I am not accustomed to being waited on hand and foot and have no resources to draw on to fill idle hours. Deirdre has said I may keep the household accounts, but they are child's play. I am not needed to help nurse Lord Cranville. I am useless."

Alex took a deep shuddering breath and tried not to let relief make a fool of him. With hands behind his back and still looking out the window, he replied slowly, "All right. I will see what I can do. Cranville Enterprises has its own accountants, and I will not have you working in our warehouses, but perhaps there are some of my daily tasks that you can share. I hadn't realized that in a house the size of this one there would be nothing to keep you occupied."

Evelyn wanted to scream at him, "Of course you didn't realize, you don't even know I'm here!" but her emotions were too ambivalent for anger. She wanted to make this marriage work; she just didn't know where to begin. "Your housekeeper manages very efficiently and consults only with Deirdre. I did not think it my place to interfere," she answered quietly.

Chastising himself for not realizing that boredom would be the greatest sin of all for Evelyn, Alex finally turned to face her. "When Everett is better, perhaps we can remove to Cornwall for a while. Deirdre has no position there as she has here. The estate has been sadly neglected for some time. Perhaps you would find more to keep you occupied there."

The thought of removing to still another strange place where she would not even have the company of Alex's family did not ease her misery, but she nodded obediently. "I would like to try it. Do you think Lord Cranville might be well by spring?"

Alex tried to fit this question into the conclusion he had just drawn about her meeting with Farnley, but it didn't fit quite so neatly. Perhaps it was only the question of the title that worried her, and she sought reassurance that she would not be named countess before she could make her escape.

"We can only pray. I had best go change for dinner. I cannot find tasks for you immediately, but tomorrow being Christmas, I think you'll find yourself well occupied. Much of society is out of town, but all those that remain behind will be here sometime during the day. With Everett's illness, Deirdre hasn't been accepting callers, but she plans to open the house tomorrow. You stand forewarned."

Evelyn offered a bleak smile. "I will welcome the company, thank you."

Her look of loneliness startled him. In Boston she had always been surrounded by friends and family, and Alex had never thought of her as being lonely. It was a state he was accustomed to for himself, but it did not come naturally to Evelyn. No wonder she sought to be rid of him. He had no friends to whom he could introduce her, and his family was limited at best. Damn, but he made no fit husband. Why had he ever thought he would?

Vowing to correct the situation somehow, Alex made a brief bow and left the salon for his own chambers, using the hall doors rather than the ones through her room. He did not feel he had the right to intrude upon the small privacy she possessed.

The gaiety and laughter Evelyn knew as Christmas at home did not fit so well into the formality of Cranville House's best salons. The servants had strung some evergreen roping decorated with sprigs of holly and the conservatory provided bouquets of brilliant flowers, but in the magnificence of velvets and gold and the ancient graciousness of furniture from the beginning of the century, these poor symbols of the holiday appeared more intrusive than merry.

However, the parade of visitors proved amusing, and with Alex constantly at her side to keep all the names and titles and relationships straight, Evelyn bore the long day well enough. Alex hovered solicitously at her shoulder while she sat in the salon exchanging social commentaries with their company. When the buffet was opened for the evening open house, he quickly filled their plates with the choicest delicacies and found a more or less secluded corner where they could eat and relax for a few brief moments. Rory and Alyson soon found them, and they made a merry party until Deirdre arrived to chase them out to entertain the guests.

Alex held Evelyn's hand as they circulated through what rapidly had become a crush, and she was physically conscious of his presence in the way that an expensive silk clings sensuously to bare skin. She knew his breath, his stride, his voice, the texture of his fingers against her wrist. By the end of the evening she was so enwrapped in him that she was scarcely aware when all the guests had left.

Only when Alex's arm slipped around her waist and his head descended to ply her lips with a gentle kiss did Evelyn realize they were practically alone. She responded quickly to this first hint of warmth he had offered her in months, and his arm instantly tightened until she was crushed against him. Only Rory's embarrassed cough reminded them they were not exactly private.

Biting back a groan of frustration, Alex looked up irritably to find both Rory and Alyson waiting to invite them to the family salon. "Go along with you," he responded in annoyance when they made their request. "We'll be there shortly."

"The kissing ball's in there, not here," Rory reminded him with a grin. "We've waited long enough to exchange gifts. We'll not wait any longer."

"Damn you, then be off," Alex growled.

Evelyn wasn't sorry when they left. To be in Alex's

arms again was a gift she hadn't expected, and the intensity of her reaction to this closeness stunned her. She had every right to be furious with him, to shun him as he had done her, but all pride was lost in her need for his kiss again. Just his kiss, she told herself.

When Alex again bent to look on her, his finger traced the hollow beneath her cheekbones, and his expression was vaguely bemused as he regarded the soft parting of her lips. "We need to talk, Evelyn," he murmured, much too aware of the servants scurrying through the rooms behind them.

"That would be the intelligent thing to do," she agreed, although talking was the last thing on her mind when she rested against his hard body as she did now. Her hand came up to rest daringly on the linen of his shirt, absorbing the heat of his chest and the solid rhythm of his heart.

"I'm not certain about that, but we'll try it. Come, the others are waiting." Releasing her waist, Alex formally offered her his arm.

Fresh punch and cakes had been carried to this small parlor where the family gathered. At this late hour, Alyson's brood had been carried to bed, already sated with food and worn out from the excitement of gifts opened earlier that day. Jacob had been allowed to remain, however, and weary with this day's activities, he sat close to his mother. Deirdre had taken a comfortable chair near the fire, while the matching chair on the opposite side of the grate remained empty. Evelyn's fingers closed tightly on Alex's arm as she realized this was where Lord Cranville would sit were he well enough to come down. A tear formed in her eye and she hastily brushed it away. She truly liked the genial gentleman who had blessed their marriage despite the circumstances. She sent a silent prayer winging his way now.

The family gifts ranged from extravagant to nonsensical, Evelyn observed as each person distributed his own. She and her mother had used their small hoard of coin to buy modest gifts for all, limiting their use of Alex's credit, and she felt relief that their gifts would not be conspicuously poor in comparison with the others. Alyson had knit a foolish pair of mittens for Rory that he insisted on wearing as he opened the rest of his packages. Alex, in turn, had bought Alyson a tawdry pamphlet on interpreting dreams that brought convulsions of laughter.

He seemed pleased by his cousin's reaction to his jest, but he made no grand flourish as he reached to his stack of gifts to select the one for Evelyn. In fact, he did it while the others were still laughing and passing the pamphlet around.

"Your other gift is apparently snowbound and didn't make it in time," he murmured as he handed the small package to her. "I should have considered the weather, but it is too late now. I hope this one is to your taste. I've never seen you wear the like, but I thought it fitting."

Realizing he meant for her to open it while the others were distracted, Evelyn quickly peeled off the wrappings. Her wide gown practically filled the sofa where they sat, but Alex rested his arm behind her and leaned forward to watch as she pressed open the small box in her hands. Her gasp was hidden by the sounds of laughter around them, and the shadowy light of the corner they had chosen did not reveal her expression to anyone but Alex. He watched in satisfaction as she gingerly touched the lovely parure of tiny diamonds and sapphires. The base of the necklace spread out in a delicate web of gems from which a single perfect pear-shaped diamond hung. The dangling earrings had much smaller, similar stones.

Evelyn's fingers clutched convulsively around the box, and when she looked up to him, the lamplight danced off the tears in her eyes. "It is too much, Alex," she whispered. "I do not deserve such as this. They're fit for a queen. How could I—"

He placed a finger beneath her chin and brought the words to a halt. "My wife should have jewels. One day, perhaps, they will become family heirlooms. For now, I wish you to wear them. Tell me only if the style or color displeases you."

The heat of his dark eyes as much as his words caused Evelyn to gulp back any further protest. Fearing she would shame herself before the company, she hastily looked down to the brilliant sparkle of the rare stones in her lap. "I have never seen anything lovelier, Alex," she admitted softly. "My gift to you seems paltry in comparison."

"I did not expect you to give me anything at all." Inordinately pleased that she had thought of him, Alex took her offering with one hand, reluctant to remove the other from its proximity to her shoulders. He had spent considerable sums on gifts for women in his salad days, using them to buy their brief affections. None had ever thought to return the favor.

Finally admitting the need to use both hands to unwrap the tiny box, Alex sat up and tore at the wrappings, unaware that they finally had an audience. With surprise and amusement he lifted the intricate silver watch fob from its velvet bed. Holding it to the lamplight, he exclaimed, "It's the *Minerva*! Right down to the figurehead! By Jove, how did you do it?"

"Rory found the architect's drawing for me, and Deirdre recommended the jeweler. It is not much, but . . ." Evelyn's words straggled off as she realized they were the center of attention. Alex continued studying the detail with great concentration, oblivious of their audience.

"Let's see how well the man did," Rory demanded, holding out his hand for the miniature ship that Alex studied so closely.

"He did too well." Refusing Rory's hand, Alex pulled out his watch chain and fastened the fob to the end, safely tucking it out of sight.

Evelyn stared at this rude behavior in bewilderment. "Is there something wrong with the design? I will take it back and make it right."

Alex stretched out his long legs and smiled his satisfaction while keeping his hand protectively over his watch pocket. He ignored the protests coming from around the room. "I'm not certain whether to reward the man or challenge him, but he made it right."

His smug expression brought instant suspicion, and Evelyn hastily reached around him to try to remove the fob for a closer look. He held it close, refusing access, and she beat his hand with frustration.

Across from them, Rory began to grin. "Complete with figurehead, you say? A truly creative jeweler."

The women turned to him for explanation, but meeting Alex's gaze, Rory shook his head. Both men grinned at each other in understanding, but before they could be slaughtered by a room full of curious women, a confusion in the foyer caught their attention. The parlor was too distant to hear the pounding on the front door, but the sounds of several animated voices carried easily through the spacious marble halls.

Alex was instantly on his feet and hurrying toward the noise. Uncertain whether she should follow, Evelyn hesitated, until something familiar in the cadence of the voices caught her attention. She leapt to her feet at the same time as her mother and rushed after Alex.

Alex stepped back from his welcoming of Matilda and Frances Upton as Evelyn and Amanda flew to embrace them. The rest of the small party joined them in curiosity, and quickly taking in the situation, Deirdre began giving orders for trunks and rooms and fires. Chattering happily, the group made their way back to the warmth of the parlor.

Frances seemed unusually silent as she gazed in awe at their gracious surroundings, then settled on Evelyn in her fashionable attire. Accustomed to seeing her skinny cousin in boy's garments with her hair uncoiffed or wearing dowdy cotton, she could scarcely believe the change. For the occasion, Evelyn wore her hair in powdered ringlets that emphasized the cream and rose of her complexion and the hollowed shadows of her cheeks. Her dark brows and flashing eyes seemed to hold the man beside her entranced, even if the daring décolleté gown did not. The rich maroon velvet of the bodice barely cupped her bosom and fitted like a glove to her rounded curves before belling out over wide panniers and a rose-and-cream-striped satin underskirt. The creamy lace at throat and wrists completed the elegance, and Frances sighed in envy. She had underestimated many things, but most of all she had underestimated Evelyn.

Somewhat subdued by this revelation and the knowledge that her own attire sadly lacked for fashion in these exalted circles, Frances hugged her aunt and cousin with more fervency than previously. In the months since leaving Boston she had learned it was much more difficult to be the center of attention outside her own environs. Her mother's family treated them practically as dependent relatives and scarcely took notice of her. It felt good to be recognized again. She hugged Evelyn enthusiastically, then held her hand out to Alex.

"I think we owe much to you, Mr. Hampton. I don't think we have thanked you enough."

Surprised, Alex took her hand and bowed politely over it. Then, straightening, he looked down into the fair face of the beauty of the family. Golden hair and pale blue eyes and exquisite complexion marked her as lovely in any setting, but he preferred Evelyn's more vivid coloring. He smiled indulgently. "You need not thank me for anything. I'm selfish enough to have done it all for Evelyn."

Evelyn watched her husband with her beautiful cousin and her heart skipped a beat, but she refused to let herself consider such thoughts. Alex had always looked at Frances with disdain before, but he looked at most women in that manner. That did not keep him from their beds. Surely he would not consider her younger cousin in such a light. It was just the season and he was feeling pleasant. In a little while they would go up to their rooms and perhaps Alex would explain himself and all would be well. She could not have imagined the heat of his kisses.

The lateness of the hour and the weariness of the new arrivals quickly broke up the family gathering. Rory and Alyson disappeared first, making their excuses, although the way they were looking at each other gave all the explanation they needed. Jealously Evelyn watched them go, wishing she and Alex could learn to live that way. She turned back into the room to catch his gaze on her, and she blushed under the intensity of his stare. Maybe this night would put an end to their stalemate.

As her mother and Deirdre offered to accompany the new arrivals to their rooms, the butler arrived carrying a salver with a letter upon it. Discreetly standing out of the way of the departing ladies, he held the missive out to Alex.

Evelyn watched in dismay as her husband hastily read the letter, turned a shade whiter, and shoved the paper into his pocket. She hurried to catch up with him as he started for the door.

"Alex? Is anything wrong?" She caught his arm, forcing him to recognize that she was still present.

"A little trouble, nothing more. Go on up to bed. Make certain your maid puts your necklace in a safe place."

He seemed distracted and without memory that he had promised to talk with her this night. Evelyn released his arm, belatedly recovering some of her pride. "What kind of trouble? Is there anything I can do?"

"Not a thing. It's business. I have to go out for a little while." As if suddenly remembering this was a holiday and he had a wife, Alex bent and gave her a small peck on the cheek. "Merry Christmas, little tyrant, and thank you. You could not have found a better gift."

She wanted to thank him too, to throw her arms around him and kiss him thoroughly and show how much she appreciated all he had done to make her Christmas happy. But he was already on his way down the hall and reaching for the cloak the footman held out to him.

Brokenhearted, she watched his tall masculine frame stride out without another look back. Damn the man, every time she imagined he was developing some feeling behind that icy facade of his, he slapped her in the face. When was she going to learn to hate him?

28

Alex didn't come to her that night, and he was conspicuously absent from the breakfast table the next morning. Rory looked grim as his meal was interrupted by a message similar to the one Alex had received, and he hastily made his excuses and departed. He made no explanation to his wife, and Evelyn looked to Alyson to see how she had taken this abrupt departure.

Alex's lovely cousin stirred her tea absently, a distant look on her face. Feeling Evelyn's gaze on her, she looked up but only shook her head with an oddly bleak look. It was that look that made Evelyn's stomach clench with foreboding.

By evening the news had filtered down to them. One of Cranville Enterprises' smaller ships had gone down at sea with all hands aboard. Evelyn gave an inadvertent cry at hearing this, then bit her tongue as Deirdre left to tell Alyson. Alex hadn't returned, but the news carried word of his whereabouts at the shipping office.

While the contents of the ship were insured against the loss of cargo, there were no means of protecting against the loss of human life. The families of all the sailors aboard had to be notified. Evelyn had lived too close to the sea all her life not to know what that meant. The captain's widow and children would need to be personally notified, and the other families would receive heartbreaking letters of regret. She turned around and left the salon, hastily wiping her eyes with the back of her hand. This holiday would not be blessed for some any longer.

Evelyn wished there were something she could do, but Alex had effectively closed her out again. Instead of turning to her in this time of need, he had turned inside himself, shutting all else out. She was beginning to recognize the symptoms. Now he would bury himself again in overwork and deny the pain that surely he must be feeling. Even Alex could not be so callous as to ignore the human tragedy of something so devastating as a shipwreck.

If he returned that night, she didn't know of it. When she rose the next day, he was already gone. That he could not come to her with his pain or his problems made her want to scream, but she held her tongue and wandered through the house like a ghost, waiting for his return.

That she had married a man with a problem greater than she could combat was beginning to sink in. Alex had spent his childhood virtually alone, with only a selfish, demanding mother to turn to. The next years of his life he had spent in challenging everyone and everything he encountered to reject him as the first two women in his life had done. Now that he had a wall around him so thick no one could pierce it, he no longer sought rejection, but he could not open up the barrier either. He was as thoroughly trapped on the inside as she was on the outside, and she could see no means of ever reaching him.

There had been moments when she thought she had found the secret entrance. Those rare smiles he cast upon her had to count for something, and she did not think he opened up to others as he had to her that first night they spent together. There were other times, precious fleeting moments that had brought her to the altar against all common sense, but looking back, they were few and far between. The only times she really felt as if she had touched some part of him were when they were making love. She dared say it was only lust that had caused those few brief moments of pleasure.

They were gathering in the salon after dinner when Alex finally appeared. The stormy look on his face brooked no interference, his irritated bellow at the servants as he entered warned of his mood, but Deirdre ignored the signs and foolhardily approached him.

"Have you had any further word of survivors, Alex? Sometimes there—"

"They are dead, my lady, all of them. One cannot run aground on an iceberg and swim to safety. Now, if you will excuse me . . ." He rudely pushed around her and stalked toward the liquor cabinet.

Alyson drifted into his path before he could reach his goal, her white hand lifting to his chest to forestall him, her misty eyes turned up to him worriedly. "Alex, you cannot blame yourself. The captain chose his route wrongly. Sit down awhile and let one of the maids bring you some warm punch."

Alex coldly wrenched her wrist away. "Tell me you've read a dead man's mind to reach that conclusion, Cousin. Now, out of my way. I have more work to do, and the lazy maids we have about here haven't restocked my brandy."

Rory materialized at Alyson's side, holding out a snifter of his favorite drink. "Have this and sit down, Hampton. You cannot bring back the dead by working yourself to your own grave."

"By damn, will you get out of my way! Next time, I'll send someone to fetch the damned bottle for me." Flinging open the cabinet, Alex removed a newly filled decanter of brandy, and without looking at anyone, strode out of the room.

The silence that descends after a tempest filled the room. The roar and the thunder echoed in the distance as some unfortunate servant entered Alex's path. Evelyn felt her aunt and cousin look away from her in embarrassment, but more than that, she felt the sympathy and curiosity in other eyes as they awaited her reaction. She was not accountable for Alex's behavior, but they seemed to be waiting for her to do something. She clasped her hands and stared at them. How could she tell them that she was the last person in the world to persuade her husband to reason?

The chatter slowly returned as Frances agreed to play the spinet and tea was brought in. Rory made some excuse and departed, but Alyson came to sit beside Evelyn. She made no pretense of drinking her tea, but stared idly in the direction of the draped windows.

"At least I am not afraid of him anymore." She offered that comment without any prelude or explanation. "His vile temper is dangerous, but usually only to himself. After our first child was born, Rory and Alex and all the men had a drinking contest. I could not blame them. That was a terrible time and they deserved a night of oblivion, but Alex was still awake when all else had fallen under the table. He kept shouting for more, but the maids were too terrified to bring it to him. The house was practically barren of food and drink, and he nearly demolished several cabinets before he found what he sought, and by that time his hands were bleeding so profusely he could scarce lift the bottle. There is a madness in him sometimes that he does not recognize. I hope you do not mind, but Rory has told me of the child he lost. I think that night, with the birth of my child, Alex was reminded of what he preferred to forget."

Evelyn squeezed her nails into her palms and willed herself to be calm. She knew of the madness of which Alyson spoke, knew the anger inside Alex ate at him, but he had shut her out. There was nothing she could do. "He will not listen to me," she replied softly to Alyson's expectant silence.

"It is not words he needs, Evelyn. It is love. He does not think he's deserving of love. Did you know that his father died when Alex was but three? His mother took him away from his rightful family, from the men who might have taught him a man's world, because she hated his father. James Hampton was an undisciplined rake, but most of all, he was a drunkard. He died of a broken neck after drinking too hard and making a wager to race to Yorkminster. Despite his mother's interference, Alex spent many years trying to follow in his father's footsteps."

There was no accusation in Alyson's voice, only sad understanding. Evelyn clenched her hands and mourned those wasted years. His father had died of drink. There was a good chance Alex might do the same if he returned to his reckless days, or if he were left alone long enough to discover there is no oblivion in a bottle. He needs love, Alyson said. Could she be right? Every time Evelyn got close to Alex, he pulled away, but if just once she could break through that wall and hang on . . .

Without a word to Alyson, indeed, with little recognition that any others were in the room, Evelyn rose to follow her husband. If she thought about it, she would realize this was madness, so she stopped thinking and acted on instinct. Someone had to dissolve this barrier between them if they were to have a true marriage. She had forgotten her objections to marrying. Perhaps they had been valid once. Perhaps they still were. But what mattered most was the lonely man upstairs and her love for him.

She had to believe that. Only the strength of her love could carry her into the lion's den. Finding herself in her own chambers, Evelyn came awake long enough to carefully remove her clothing. If she had only one way to reach Alex, she would use it. Acres of velvet and silk would only get in the way.

In one of the many drawers of her armoire she found the lovely lace-and-lawn nightgown that Deirdre had given her for Christmas. It was an extravagant confection unlike anything she had ever owned before. The gossamer softness slid over her skin like cool water. Without corsets or garters or petticoats to hinder her, she felt free and unfettered. The lace dripping from elbow-length sleeve to wrist floated daintily with every movement. The wide ruff of lace at her throat moved with every breath, revealing the valley between her breasts. If she looked too closely in the mirror, she knew the material covering the rest of her would be nearly transparent. She didn't have the bravery to look that closely. The sheerness of the fabric as it clung to her skin provided an alarmingly erotic sensation she could scarcely bear to credit.

Taking the pins out of her hair, Evelyn brushed it to a satin gleam. She was grateful she had given her maid the day off to visit her family. She didn't want anybody to know the seduction she embarked upon. Or the rejection she would almost certainly suffer.

Not willing to think of either, she set the brush aside and stared at the door to Alex's dressing room. It wouldn't hurt to go into his dressing room. If he were there, she could always ask to borrow something. But she knew he wouldn't be in the dressing room.

She turned the knob and silently let herself in. The room was empty and unlit, and she had to cross it with only a candle and memory to guide her. Perhaps she should have brought a lamp, but she distrusted throwing any more light on what she was about to do.

Her fingers hesitated over the knob to Alex's chamber. Once open, there would be no turning back. She would seal her future with this next step. Did she dare make it?

Her choice was laid out before her. She could go back to her room and to her bed and to the life she had led these last weeks. It wasn't an unpleasant life. She would be sheltered, entertained, clothed, and given the keys to the city with the Cranville title behind her. Or she could go forward into the unknown, almost certainly destroying any chance of annulment, binding her marriage forever to a man who could not love and did not need a wife. The choice was hers, and in his own enigmatic way, Alex had given it to her.

It was that realization that made her turn the knob until it clicked, signaling her presence to anyone on the far side. Still, he did not call to her or give any sign that she was wanted. Setting her lips, Evelyn pushed the door inward. She was damned tired of being shut out of his life. He had promised they would talk. So they would talk. Now.

The room was in darkness. She hesitated, trying to remember the furniture arrangement. The huge bed she recalled from her one visit here should be directly in the center of the far wall across from the door. The form looming there now did not seem so massive as she remembered, but she walked toward it anyway. With all the lights out, surely he had retired to bed. He couldn't be working in the dark.

For a brief moment Evelyn feared Alex had not even come to his room. Perhaps he had gone to the library, or worse yet, to some maid's room. He could be anywhere. What had made her think he would come here?

Because this was his home. This was where Alex would come when he was hurting. Evelyn raised her candle slightly as she approached the bed, illuminating the pale lace over her creamy satin skin, sending her slender figure into graceful silhouette, heightening the fiery strands of color in waist-length hair. The light and movement brought a sharp intake of breath from the bed.

"Have you come to strangle me in my sleep? If so, I warn you that sleep avoids me. You will have to try poison."

She could see his masculine shape rise up from the pillows where he had been reclining. A glass clinked as he set it aside. From what she could tell from the gray light of the windows, Alex had discarded his coat but not bothered to undress more.

"You are doing a fair job of poisoning yourself, sir. I need not do it for you." Bravely, or foolishly, Evelyn set the candle down on the table and sat down upon the edge of the bed near his hip.

As she had hoped, Alex reached for her. His hand caught in the silky lengths of her hair and he pulled her backward until she leaned against his shoulder. His fingers found her throat, and he caressed the bare flesh there. "Have you come as the sacrificial virgin, then? Did the others send you up to appease the angry gods?"

"That would be like sending my soul to the devil. Your family is too considerate for that." Evelyn pulled her legs up to the bed and curled beside him. Her toes were frozen, but Alex's fingers were skillfully drawing heat as they skimmed over her collarbone and slid to the neck of her bodice. Daringly she raised her hand to his chest and found his shirt partially open. Her fingers briefly caressed the heat emanating from his flesh. When he tensed beneath her touch, she began unfastening the rest of his shirt.

"So you're sending yourself to the devil. Why?" Alex's voice hissed the words almost threateningly.

Again she hesitated, but the time for denials was gone. Drawing her hand up his chest to his neck, curling her fingers about his nape, Evelyn drew him down to her. "Because I love you," she whispered as his lips descended to cover hers.

Alex's arms closed convulsively around her, pulling her hard against him as his mouth bruisingly plundered hers. She felt his shudders as she gave of herself freely, circling his shoulders with her arms, pressing her breasts against his chest, and opening her kisses to him with a passion neither could deny.

There was a cry in his voice as Alex twisted to push

her back against the pillows. "Tell me you want me, Evelyn. That's something I can understand. Lie to me if you must, but say you'll never leave me."

He still wouldn't accept her love, but this time she wouldn't back away. "I won't lie to you," Evelyn promised softly. "I'll never leave you because I love you. Alex, couldn't you love me just a little?"

Evelyn felt his groan as much as heard it when Alex's heavy weight moved over her, pressing her downward. Her fingers sought his face, encountering tears streaming down his rough cheeks, and she gave a distraught cry of love and anguish. Throwing her arms around him, Evelyn pulled him close, and their lips met in promises their voices could not.

The pain of these past days found escape in violent action; Evelyn's fragile gown gave way beneath Alex's fingers. Unable to help himself, unable to stop the desperate need he felt for her, Alex freed his wife's breast from the hampering material. Evelyn moaned as he played her flesh urgently, pressing the peak to an aching hunger demanding satisfaction. When Alex's mouth moved from her lips to fill this new need, closing moist and warm over her eager flesh, Evelyn knew she had won this first battle. She arched against him joyously, giving her body as a gift of her love, and he took it with a hunger that came from the soul.

That first time, they wasted no precious minutes on the nicety of undressing. Alex pulled Evelyn's gown above her hips, and finding her as ready as he, unfastened his breeches and took what she offered before she had time to think better of it. He plunged deeply, satisfyingly, forcing Evelyn to take all of him before realizing she encouraged instead of fought him. That notion was like an aphrodisiac to his senses, and he lost himself in the welcoming softness sheathing him. Evelyn arched into him eagerly and moved with the same demanding hunger that drove him.

When she came as quickly as he, Alex knew there had been no others for her, as there had been none for him. He had thought himself half-dead when he could not find the desire to seek out those women he had frequented before journeying to Boston. Now he knew he was fully alive only in her arms. He was not particularly grateful for that knowledge, but he felt only relief as he rolled over and Evelyn snuggled into his arms, refusing to leave his side.

"You are as mad as Alyson," he whispered wonderingly against her hair.

"Everyone should be as mad as Alyson," Evelyn agreed sleepily. His large hand found her breast and stroked it gently. The tension had gone out of him, and she smiled to herself. "Are you sorry that you are shackled to a madwoman?" she asked suddenly, belatedly aware of one of the factors that had kept them apart—not her madness, but the finality of what they had just done.

Alex stayed silent for a moment, kissing her brow and exploring her flesh with growing purpose. When he spoke, it was with the firmness that characterized his dealings with the rest of the world. "I was only sorry that I gave you no choice. I am not sorry that you chose to stay."

Such cold, formal words. Evelyn turned her nose up, and pressing a hand against Alex's chest, pushed him back into the pillows. Leaning over him, her hair forming a heavy veil around them, she began kissing every inch of him that she could find. The tears that she had found on his face earlier were gone, but she tasted their traces with her tongue, wondering that a man as strong as Alex could still have the compassion to cry. Between kisses, she replied brokenly, "You are an insufferable prig, Alex Hampton. I think I liked you better in Boston."

Alex's hands caught in the hem of her gown and jerked it upward, exposing the nakedness of Evelyn's back and buttocks to the cold air where she leaned over him. When she gasped and tried to cover herself, he wrapped his arm about her waist and pulled the hampering material over her head and flung it aside. "I'll do better next time, tyrant, and even better the time after that. And all the times in all the nights and days to come. You have bound yourself to a harsh taskmaster, my dear."

Heat flooded through her at the seductive thoughts his words engendered, and the memories of the past faded with anticipation for the future. Hours they would have together. Hours when they could teach each other the ways of love. He might have more experience, but there were things she could teach him that he had never known. Love, for example.

Feeling his maleness rise against her again, Evelyn slid her hands into Alex's unfastened breeches and pushed the cloth downward. The soft, downy hair that covered him startled her, and the hard narrowness of his hips and buttocks was an erotic sensation she had not dared imagine before, but she managed to remove the garment with only a little help. When he was freed from this confinement, Alex lifted her on top of him.

"If you are going to be brazen, my love, let me show you how. Where were we? At nine hundred and ninety-seven?"

That was the Alex she knew. Straddling his waist, Evelyn bent to kiss him. Just the feel of flesh against flesh inflamed her senses. She could smell the brandy of his breath as he captured and invaded her mouth with his tongue. His jaw was rough with unshaven beard, but she rubbed her fingers over it anyway. She kissed his eyelids and felt the ripple of muscle beneath her as he reached for her and pulled her down to suckle at her breast.

She needed his hunger, needed to know he wanted her. It was the fragile line that bound them, and she wanted to increase its strength until love had time to grow. Wantonly Evelyn followed his dictates, discovering desires of her own as Alex's hands roamed over her. She learned the boldness of her position when he pushed her toward his hips and she was already open and vulnerable to him.

When Alex lifted her so he could enter, Evelyn welcomed him with a cry of surprise. She heard him chuckle as she sank deep around him and discovered her own power in this position, and she seized the opportunity with an eagerness that left Alex breathless. When her inexperienced motions quickly taught her more exciting movements, he growled deep in his throat and flung her over, plying her more rapidly.

"Wanton tyrant," he whispered in her ear as she clasped his neck and arched against him. "You learn too fast."

"I will be your equal in all things," Evelyn gasped as he plunged deeper. "Almost all things," she admitted as he repeated his action with swift, sure strokes.

It wasn't a game any longer. He was part of her, so much a part that she didn't think they could ever be separated. She clung to his strong arms as they strained to find that final fulfillment that would merge them totally, blend them into one. When it came, it wasn't blinding stars or noisy rockets but a sweet song and gentle paradise as their bodies rocked together and the seed of his life poured into her, and the bonds were sealed. Perhaps physically they might part again, but part of him would always remain with her. To be complete, they would need to be together.

Evelyn wrapped her arms around Alex's broad shoulders and felt his weight engulf her, and she slept.

29

Evelyn woke sometime in the middle of the night when Alex pulled her into his arms again. He was on his side, and his kisses were urgent as they covered her face. Before she was quite aware of where she was, he lifted her leg over him to ease his entrance and came into her.

He took her with a force that surprised her, but his urgency incited her to meet his demands with an excitement of her own. They found satisfaction quickly, with a pleasure that had naught to do with need or hunger but a pleasure of their own bodies.

Evelyn murmured incoherent protests when Alex started to move away, and he obligingly remained, stroking her hair, holding her close, pulling the covers around them.

"I want you in here every night. Will you do that? Even if I am not yet home, will you sleep in my bed?" The relaxed satisfaction in his voice barely concealed the anxiousness of his demands.

"I had never thought to sleep elsewhere." Evelyn pressed a sleepy kiss to his shoulder. "You're the one with houses so big you cannot think what to do with the space except create two chambers where there need be only one."

Alex smiled in the darkness and smoothed his hand over her flanks, reveling in the satin softness of her. "We'll make a billiard parlor of the other."

Evelyn giggled softly and they slept again, this time until past dawn.

Alex had forbidden the servants to enter his room unless called, and he was paying for this privacy the next morning with the iciness of a dead fire. Hugging the slender warmth beside him closer, he nuzzled at her ear with his rough chin. Evelyn murmured with pleasure and squirmed closer, her rounded bottom fitting neatly into the curve of his body as he curled around her.

When Alex began to play with her breasts, her murmurs became a sensuous purr. Heat rose between them as his hand continued to roam where it would without any protest from his sleeping wife. When his fingers finally plied the moist heat between her thighs, she shivered and shifted to meet his need and he knew she no longer slept. Gently he rode into her, and a sigh of pleasure greeted his ears. He needed no more encouragement, and his arm wrapped around her waist and guided her until they rode together to sweet bliss.

Evelyn groaned when he left her, and Alex gently pushed her back against the pillows to chafe her with his bristly kisses. Her eyes opened and she caught his hair in both hands and held him looking down on her. "You need a shave," she informed him solemnly.

Grinning, he eluded her hold and buried his scratchy face against the vulnerable curve of her throat. She squealed and tore at his hair, and they went tumbling through the covers until Evelyn happened to get a glance at the bed they were thoroughly demolishing.

Pushing him away, she pulled the sheet up to her chin and stared at the hand-carved posters she had last seen in Boston. "Our bed. I thought you had forgotten it. You've been sleeping in our bed!"

Her tone was accusatory, and Alex laughed, pulling her down into his arms. "You could have been sleeping here too, if you'd wanted. All you had to do was ask. I am eager to please."

"The deuce you are!" She pounded the hard bulge of his biceps with her fist, but he didn't flinch. "You have been an insufferable cad for months. I don't know why I even speak to you. You don't deserve so much as the time of day from me."

"But you gave me a lot more than that last night," Alex reminded her wickedly, holding her securely against him. "Several times, in fact. You must have a strange affinity for insufferable cads."

"Only in bed, I assure you," Evelyn replied huffily.

"Out of bed, I demand explanations and apologies. You have been not only insufferable but also rude and intolerable and cold and arrogant. I demand reparations."

"To my holy saint of a wife, I humbly apologize. I was not aware of her affinity for insufferable cads. I intend to make full amends for my neglect by being as insufferable as she can desire. Will that do?" Alex nibbled at her ear and pressed suggestively against her hip.

"Bah, you are a dolt who will never learn. I am starving. Am I allowed breakfast?"

Leaning over her, Alex pressed his mouth to hers and filled her with his tongue until her arms circled him and she arched voluptuously against him. Then he released her and smiled down into glorious violet eyes. "I'll feed all your hungers, my love. What kind of breakfast would you like?" he inquired suggestively.

"You cannot possibly," Evelyn whispered, half in fear that he would follow through on the promise in his voice. "I am sore in places I did not know existed. Have some mercy on me."

Alex kissed her cheek, pushed himself off her and out of bed, and strode in splendid masculine nakedness across the daylight streaming in the windows. "I have quite decided this house is too antiquated for our needs. We need running water up here, and a tub big enough for two." He pulled a robe from the armoire and wrapped it around him before turning to admire his wife in the bed. "I'll be back in a minute."

Evelyn could not quite believe all that had happened. Gathering Alex's covers around her, she gazed at the lovely poster bed, then discovered the scattering of their garments across the bottom of the bed and the floor. His shirt lay atop her gown in the same abandonment their owners had engaged in the night before. Her cheeks flamed in memory of what they had done. Had she really been that brazen? Could Alex truly have enjoyed such unladylike behavior from his wife? It did not seem possible, but he had not seemed displeased when he left.

He returned with a contingent of servants, a huge tub, and buckets of hot water. Another maid hurried to light the fire, and still another carried a tray of steaming hot chocolate and crumpets. Evelyn discovered a ravenous hunger for all four: water, food, fire, and, most of all, the man garbed only in a long robe waiting for the servants to be gone. He turned and caught her gaze, and his dark eyes gleamed like hot coals in return.

When the servants departed, Alex strode purposefully across the room. Before she knew his intentions, he pulled back the covers, lifted her into his arms, and carried her toward the tub. Evelyn squealed and wriggled and protested, but his arms were unmoved by her feeble actions. Standing over the tub, he halted and took the time to thoroughly observe her glorious nudity with a lascivious stare.

"Just think of all this time I've wasted in darkness. It's a sin. From now on, I wish to see you like this in light." Alex unceremoniously dropped her into the tub, but joined her within the few seconds it took to doff his robe.

"Alex!" Fire ignited Evelyn's face as she discovered herself facing that broad hair-covered chest in full daylight and at such intimate proximity. His long legs raised around hers, and after last night, she could not help her thoughts drifting to the erotic position that posed. "You cannot."

Solemnly he reached for the soap on the low table beside them. "I can and I have. Do you need some help? Come over here and I'll wash your back."

"You are an odious lecher," she informed him, without the ire he deserved. "Had you but waited your turn, I would have washed your back. I'll not go splashing about like a duck in a puddle for your amusement."

Alex laughed, a sound so deep and joyful that Evelyn would almost have agreed to present her back to him if he asked again. The rumble of his laughter vibrated her heartstrings, and she would have readily agreed to anything he proposed. Instead, as he began soaping himself, she reached for the delicate porcelain cup of hot chocolate on the silver tray beside them and sipped from it as if accustomed to sitting in a bath with a naked man and drinking chocolate every day.

"You are a sybarite, my dear. We'll need to feed your pleasures more often. We'll convert one of the dressing rooms to a bathing room, with a tub big enough for both of us and running hot water."

Evelyn almost forgot to act elegant as she stared at him in curiosity. "Running hot water? Can you do that?"

"If Chatsworth can do it, I can," he assured her pompously, then spoiled the effect by leaning forward to smear soapsuds across her breasts.

She nearly dropped her cup and hastily set it aside to return the favor. In moments, breakfast was forgotten and the floor was soaked from splashing as they tussled with soap, cloths, and each other, until Alex finally had her where he wanted her. Evelyn cried out at the liquid smoothness of his invasion, but his gentleness returned the urgent throbbing she had learned too well this past night. Wrapped closely in his strong arms, the steam of the bath rising around them, she felt her insides melt and blend with him until there seemed no more natural place to be.

As the water began to cool, Alex kissed her cheek and ear and rubbed his hands along the length of her slender back. "You belong in my arms," he said with a trace of wonder. "There's no me and you but only us. How is that?"

Evelyn opened one eye and looked at him with a tilt of her head to keep the hair from her face. "No moon. That ruins Alyson's theory."

Alex chuckled and lifted her gently back to her end of the tub. "No moon dreams for my little rebel. It wouldn't be fitting."

Soaping herself boldly beneath his interested gaze, she continued as if they were at the breakfast table, "Have you spoken to any of your cousin's associates about the state of affairs in Boston?"

Alex grinned at her sudden defiance but allowed her this small rebellion. "I have. I've met a countryman of yours, Benjamin Franklin, from Philadelphia, who was caught as much by surprise at the uprising as our celebrated government. The matter is to come up in the next session in January."

"I wish I knew what was happening." Frowning, Evelyn rinsed herself and stood to reach for the towel warming by the fire. Water trailed off her in rivulets, and Alex admired the glorious sight with full enjoyment. "Do you think they've decided to ignore the law and gone about business as usual?"

Alex reluctantly rose from the tub. "I cannot see how they could do otherwise. How long could the courts last without trying cases? They would need stamps for all the paperwork. I should think that would be quite a dilemma for the judges."

"Good." Evelyn finished drying herself, then, glancing around and remembering she had no clothes in Alex's room, hastily wrapped the towel around herself, though it scarcely covered more than her middle.

Alex admired the figure she cut: long slender legs leading to neatly curved hips and small waist and to the rise of firm breasts that were neither too big nor too small, but just the size they ought to be.

His grin at this thought caused Evelyn to glare at him suspiciously. "There is something humorous in the situation?"

"Forgive me. My thoughts strayed." There was nothing repentant in his grin. Taking a towel for himself, he offered her his robe. "I was thinking of figureheads."

Evelyn wrapped the long robe around her, but though she was totally concealed behind the lengths of satin, she did not feel hidden from his gaze. Her skin still burned with the memory of his touch. "Figureheads? You and Rory laughed at some such at Christmas. If my gift was funny, I would know the jest." Distracted by this new subject, she momentarily set aside the more important one.

"Your gift was perfect. I may have to cut your jeweler's throat for his forwardness, but it seems a shame to deprive the world of his eye for beauty."

Evelyn flung a soapy cloth at him. "You are a horrid beast. If all you will do is laugh and not tell me the jest, then I'll take it back."

Alex caught the cloth easily and flung it back to the tub. Fastening the towel about his hips, he stalked toward her. Evelyn whirled about and raced for the door. Alex trapped her there, one hand on either side of her head, his body an invincible barrier. "I must remember you suffer insufferable cads only in bed. We may do better never to get up."

Breathless from the nearness of his overwhelming near-nudity, Evelyn tried to focus on Alex's face and not the breadth of his shoulders or the bulge of muscle there. "That could become a trifle awkward after a while, I suspect. Wouldn't it be easier just to tell me of figureheads?"

His gaze drifted down to the deep V gaping open from her loosely wrapped robe. "There weren't any."

"I beg your pardon?" Evelyn tried to close the gap but felt the slippery belt loosening as she did.

"The architect's plans you gave your jeweler would not have included the figurehead. That came later." Alex dropped one hand casually and caught the belt between his fingers.

Evelyn grabbed the belt as it gave, but holding the belt did not ensure the placement of the slippery satin. The gap widened. "But all your ships have figureheads. There's one on the fob. Are you saying it isn't correct?"

"I'm saying it's perfect. Perhaps a little more well-endowed than the original model"—he ran his finger beneath the gaping satin, finding her breast with intimate accuracy—"but excellent craftsmanship. Minerva was a bit of a dowd anyway; all that armor is rather repugnant."

Evelyn closed her eyes and tried to make her mind function as his hand closed warmly around her breast. "You are saying that the jeweler didn't put Minerva on the fob."

"No, madam, he did not. Your jeweler does not know his classics. No armor, no olive branches, no toga, no curls. He invented a new Minerva, a much more satisfactory one."

She had a vague remembrance of the warrior goddess on Alex's ship. Her cheeks flamed as Alex bent his head to kiss her. His lips trailed along her cheek to her ear while his hand played seductive games with her person. The figure on the watch fob had long flowing hair, she suddenly remembered. As Alex lifted her breast to meet his kiss, she remembered the other endowments of which he spoke, endowments which were hidden by armor on the original, and she groaned her dismay.

Regretfully Alex released this tender temptation. The chafing of his unshaven beard had already reddened Evelyn's skin, and he knew he had not treated her with the consideration a new bride deserved. He smiled ruefully into her embarrassed face. "I had best let you get dressed or we shall both starve to skin and bones. I think I'll not cut your jeweler's throat today. He couldn't help but immortalize such loveliness. I trust he knew it was for your husband."

"He did." Evelyn leaned against the door, more for support than escape now as he removed the temptation of his hand. "Is it really like? How could it be? It is so small."

Alex grinned and released her. "Not the parts that count. You are definitely well-fed in his imagination. You really are going to have to start hiding your hair in some civilized fashion, my dear."

He knew her tendency to wear it only looped or pulled back, and Evelyn grimaced in embarrassment. "If you show that thing to anyone else, I'll cut *your* throat."

"There's no fear of that, tyrant. I'd prefer keeping my wife concealed from the eyes of others, even if only her graven image. I realize it is a hopeless task to keep you in an ivory tower, but the fob stays hidden."

"Thank you." Realizing he must be freezing standing there only in a towel, Evelyn stood up and reached for the doorknob. She hated to be parted from him for even a few minutes, and she glanced back at him wistfully. "I don't suppose you would have time later to tell me if anything has been done about the charges against me? I would hate to think I remain a criminal in my own home."

Alex's expression tightened a shade. "This is your home now. I have not forgotten the charges, and I am doing what I can, but they are meaningless over here. No one is going to arrest my wife for some trivial disagreement in the colonies."

This was the Alex that made her want to scream and stomp her feet. He was shutting her out again. As soon as the door closed, he would forget all that had gone between them and become the forbidding statue again. She glared at him in frustration. "Trivial disagreement," she mocked. "Years of my life or everything I'm worth is too trivial to notice, assuredly. I'm sorry to have disturbed your time with such trivialities."

She slammed out of the room, leaving Alex to stare in black fury at the carved panel that protected her. He heard no lock click or bolt thrown, but it was the same as if he had. He knew the futility of arguing with angry women. He would not dignify her rage with notice. He turned to his wardrobe and began searching for a shirt.

Alex arrived in time to escort her to the breakfast table. A bit pale from lack of sleep, emphasizing the shadows beneath her eyes, Evelyn took his arm without looking too closely at him. She knew what she would find, the shuttered stranger, so she comforted herself with the strength of the arm beneath her hand. She knew where that arm had been during the night. That was something no one could steal from her.

Those early risers there before them gaped in astonishment as Alex gallantly led his wife to the table and touched her shoulders intimately as he seated her. Alex hadn't been seen at the breakfast table since he arrived home, and his accompaniment of Evelyn at any time seemed to happen only by accident. When Alex actually greeted his family with some semblance of geniality, a round of applause spontaneously erupted around the table.

Alex glared at the instigator of this noise. "Why aren't you on the way back to the heathen hills?"

Rory grinned unabashedly and reached for a muffin. "I wouldn't miss this for a fortune." He sent Evelyn a glittering look that very much spoke of hidden laughter. "I know where I can find a good whip if you should require one, Mrs. Hampton. His bite really is every bit as fierce as his bark."

Evelyn couldn't help but meet this sally with a smile, and a slight blush colored her cheeks as Alyson sent her a knowing glance. "I would prefer to keep all weapons a safe distance from his hands. I value my life too dearly."

Alex snorted at this facetiousness, but seated himself beside his wife and proceeded to fill her plate along with his own. "I didn't marry a fool. A termagant, yes, but never a fool."

The look Evelyn gave him caused her own relatives to erupt in laughter, and Alex finally had to admit to a smile as he glanced down at her. "But then, I'm an insufferable cad," he whispered so only she could hear him.

Evelyn grinned at that, and, awed at how the lamb had tamed the lion, the others held their peace. An Alex who didn't roar or brood or disappear in company was a rare creature indeed. It seemed wisest not to question motives or tactics.

Alex and Rory left together after breakfast, and, the holiday over, Alyson prepared her youngsters to return to their own home. While everyone else was otherwise engaged, Evelyn slipped up to Lord Cranville's room. She made this visit every day, though frequently he slept and was not conscious of her presence.

This day he was awake and offered a frail smile as she entered. His cough as he sat up was so deep and painful that she almost regretted disturbing him, but he motioned her to the chair beside his bed. With an inborn authority that illness could not rob him of, he dismissed the nurse to the outer chamber.

"You look as if you have not slept," he said faintly as she settled beside him. "I trust my heir is treating you with his idea of kindness."

"Ummm, I'm not certain 'kindness' is the word, but Alex would never abuse me." Evelyn smiled reassuringly and watched the twinkle of understanding leap to the earl's eye.

"I keep waiting for some announcement of the next heir. What is delaying you?" The earl's voice was gruff, but there was nothing harsh in his frail demeanor. He had always been a slender man. That slightness had faded to skin and bones with illness, and the skin seemed wrinkled and gray, as if aging before its time.

"Alex and I are too alike in some things, and too stubborn for our own good. Be patient with us. I have no doubt that there will be children soon enough."

"I'm not a doddering old fool, my dear. You and Alex would be at each other's throats or in each other's beds with no happy in-between if left to your natural inclinations. I trust you will both become a little more civilized with time. Until then, try the bed for a while. It becomes you, and I would know that all is well before I go."

There was no doubt as to his meaning. Both startled and alarmed at his tone, Evelyn reached for his hand. "You will see half a dozen more heirs to your throne before you go, if we all have to move to Barbados to accomplish it. I've always wondered what the West Indies was like."

The earl squeezed her hand gently. "Have Alex take you someday. I have a daughter there who would love to meet you. I fear I have wronged her in not returning once since I left, but there was so much to require my time . . ."

"I will have Alex make the arrangements as soon as you are well, or perhaps a little later. You will want to see if Alyson has a daughter this time."

Everett smiled sympathetically at her denial of the truth and closed his eyes. He had lived a long and full life. He had regrets, but they were not such as to keep him here. If anything, they called him to another world, where the first woman he had loved awaited him. If he traveled anywhere, it would be to her. He rather anticipated the meeting with growing excitement.

30

Everett Hampton, fourth Earl of Cranville, died peacefully in his sleep during the first week of January while a howling snowstorm whirled about the chimneys.

The first Evelyn and Alex learned of it came with a wild knocking on the door to Alex's chamber. Evelyn stirred sleepily, curling closer to the heat of her husband's nakedness. His tension brought her abruptly awake.

He pulled Evelyn into his arms and kissed her head as the servant cried again, "Lord Cranville, please, her ladyship says to come quickly."

Evelyn clung to him in sudden uncertainty as still another rap sounded on the door from the dressing room. Her maid's voice rang out from behind the panel. "My lady, wake up, please. Her ladyship needs you. Hurry, please."

The color had left Alex's face and his expression was bleak when Evelyn looked to him for some explanation of this intrusion. The servants' loyalty to Deirdre was notorious, but there was more than just loyalty behind this summons. She refused to acknowledge what their words were saying, but looked to Alex for confirmation. His expression gave it, but still she wouldn't believe. "Alex?"

His mouth tightened as he saw the fear and disbelief in her eyes. He felt a rending pain in the area of his heart at submitting her to this, but death was not a matter within his control. He kissed her long and hard, then set her aside as he swung his legs out of the bed.

"I'm coming," he shouted at the door. Then, holding

his hand out to Evelyn, he brought her to her feet beside him. Neither of them wore a stitch of clothing, and the icy drafts from the wind outside whirled around them. Alex caught her robe from a chair beside the bed and wrapped it around her. "Deirdre will need you, love. Hurry and dress." As an afterthought, he added with odd regret, "I'm sorry."

The kiss he brushed against her hair as he sent her toward the dressing room did nothing to soothe Evelyn's jangled nerves. Her maid greeted her with relief, and Alex's valet brushed silently past them as they left the master's chambers. The valet had no expression at all, but the maid was in tears. If Evelyn had any doubt at all as to what had happened, the servant's next words crushed it.

"You will be needing the gray today, my lady. We'll send for the seamstress to have mourning gowns made when the shops open. Her ladyship is that distraught, she will listen to no one. You must hurry."

The shock of being pulled from Alex's arms into the icy dawn must have befuddled her brain. In a daze, Evelyn allowed the maid to dress her, something she had never bothered to do before. The maid must have needed the distraction of this commonplace task as much as Evelyn needed it done, for she quieted and the tears dried as she fastened the last of the hooks and laces and proudly smoothed the elegant silk over Evelyn's petticoats.

"There, now, we can dress your hair better later. 'Twill do for now." She pushed a straying pin into the thick chestnut tresses, making certain no strands escaped. "You'll make his lordship a lovely countess."

The words were said soothingly, but they sent shards of fear piercing Evelyn's soul. Her fingers clenched into her palms, and she rose hurriedly. She must get to Deirdre. She had delayed too long over this silliness.

She flew down passageways to the far wing of the house where the earl and his wife had their rooms. The rustle of stiff cottons and the clatter of heavy shoes sounded throughout the halls, but she scarcely saw any of the servants running about on a myriad of errands at this unusual hour. They were there to be commanded, but they remained invisible until called.

A worried maid in stiff white apron and black gown opened the door immediately at Evelyn's scratch. The Cranvilles' sitting room was identical to Alex's except that the decor had been converted to two separate lifetimes of memories. A painting of the earl's foreign daughter hung with a painting of Deirdre's ancestral home in the Highlands. The bagpipes, Evelyn knew, were a jest from Alyson to both of them. But the magnificent collection of shells came from Barbados and the enormous claymores over the grate belonged to Deirdre's father. The room spilled over with these remembrances of days past, and her heart swelled with sorrow as she found the small woman huddled on the sofa with an emerald satin robe in her hands.

She looked up as Evelyn approached, and Evelyn could see the ravages of tears in reddened eyes and stained cheeks. Deirdre had always seemed ageless, her petite stature and proud stance disguising her years, but the disguise was lost in the tide of anguish. She hugged the luxurious robe closer as Evelyn came to sit beside her.

"He hasn't had time to wear his Christmas gift," Deirdre murmured brokenly as Evelyn sat down.

Deirdre had lovingly embroidered the earl's initials and crest on the robe for months before the holiday. Evelyn smoothed the fabric across both of their laps and fought back tears. "But he loved it. He showed it to me at Christmas and hung it where he could see it. He loved you so much, and he was so proud of you. That's what counts, isn't it?"

Deirdre began sobbing again, and Evelyn wrapped her arms around the woman who had showed her such kindness since she had arrived. She didn't know what to say, but stayed silent as tears rolled down her cheeks to mix with Deirdre's.

Alex entered from the earl's chamber, and the grim tiredness of his face chased Evelyn's fears into hiding. Tomorrow she would worry about titles. Today her husband needed her calm and reasonable. She gave Deirdre a handkerchief and helped her compose herself.

"We've sent for Alyson and a physician, but in this storm it will be a while before they can arrive." Alex stoically removed his own handkerchief and offered it to Evelyn to mend her tear-streaked face. "The solicitors and the newspapers and a number of others will have to be notified. Will you be all right here?"

Evelyn nodded. "Have someone go to my mother. She has some sleeping powders that we might need. I'd like to have her here."

That seemed sensible, and Alex nodded absently. As Deirdre composed herself, Alex awkwardly offered his condolences. "You've known him as long as I, Deirdre. I wish he could have been my father. He was the closest I ever had to one. He loved you dearly. He wouldn't want you to grieve."

"I know. I know." Deirdre held the handkerchief to her nose for a minute. "I'll be all right in a while, Alex. It's just . . . I didn't expect it!" This last came out as almost a wail, and Evelyn hastily caught her in her arms again.

"Neither did I," Alex said harshly, as if blaming his cousin for these unforeseen circumstances. Unable to say more, he stalked out.

"I'm making it harder for him, I know," Deirdre whispered into her handkerchief. "He can't cope with emotional outbursts, but I know he loved Everett in his own way. They fought all the time, but they respected each other. Everett was so proud of how well Alex has been doing, and he was thrilled with your marriage. He said Alex couldn't have made a better choice."

Evelyn let her wander on. It seemed the wisest thing to do. There was a gaping emptiness in her own life, knowing the charming man in the next room was no longer there. She didn't even want to try to imagine what Deirdre must feel. Picturing Alex out of her life was beyond her capacity, and they had known each other only a few short months. Deirdre had years of memories to recall.

Amanda came hurrying in a while later, worry and concern lining her brow as she looked first to her daughter. What she saw there didn't seem to ease her anxiety, but she quickly took charge, sending maids for tea and ordering Deirdre back to bed. With relief, Evelyn let her take over. Her own emotions were too raw and aching to be reasonable for any length of time.

Alyson arrived on Rory's arm and broke into tears at sight of Evelyn. Again Evelyn opened her arms and cried silently as her new friend poured out her heart. Rory looked embarrassed and ill-at-ease, and Evelyn sent him in search of Alex. Alex needed someone with him, but she could see that she might not be the right person at the moment. She wished there were someone to console her, but her pain was of a different sort and not so great as that of those who had loved the earl for these years past. Better that Alex have someone practical and less emotional at his side.

The physician arrived, and various solicitors, and soon Alyson was led away to get some rest, and Evelyn found herself abandoned. The cold breakfast in the dining room didn't appeal to her, and she flinched every time a servant addressed her as "milady." She contemplated searching Alex out but decided it might be better if she waited until he was ready to come to her. They might both break into tears right now, and that wouldn't be conducive to intelligent thought.

A butler already wearing mourning black entered the salon where Evelyn sat morosely contemplating a cabinet of curios. He made a slight bow and waited patiently for a signal from the new countess that she would hear him.

At Evelyn's nod, he announced, "A gentleman to see you, milady. Lord Cranville was too busy, but the gentleman asked if he might have a word with you before he departed."

"Who is it, Burton?"

"A Mr. Franklin, milady. An American, I believe."

The name seemed familiar, and she nodded acquiescence. Anyone braving the icy streets outside deserved some recognition. The snow had stopped, but she could see from the window that the world was coated with an icy frosting of white.

A stout plain-clothed gentleman in old-fashioned bob wig and carrying a walking stick was introduced to the salon a few moments later. Evelyn sat on the sofa beside the velvet draperies at the window, and he approached with a definite gleam of masculine appreciation in his eyes.

"Mrs. Hampton, I'm Benjamin Franklin, from Philadelphia. I hope I do not intrude."

"You have caught me at an unhappy moment, I fear, sir, but your journey out into the snow should not go unrewarded. I have sent for some tea and coffee. Would you have a seat?" Evelyn regarded him with curiosity. She remembered Alex mentioning him now, and she studied him as the maid laid out the table. He had a kindly face, with extremely intelligent eyes that seemed to smile at some private joke. She rather liked what she saw.

"I will not stay long if it's inconvenient, but Mr. Hampton mentioned that you were from Boston and concerned about events there. I've just received a letter from a friend in that city, and I thought you might wish to hear what he had to say."

Evidently no one had seen fit to inform him of the earl's death and Alex's new status, but Evelyn was in no hurry to correct the omission. The mention of Boston brought her head up eagerly. "When was the letter written? After the Stamp Act went into effect? What is happening now?"

He smiled and sipped at his steaming coffee. "Your husband called you a flaming rebel. Will you be pleased to hear that the courts have, indeed, been closed down? That much business has come to a halt and ships are trapped in port with no legal means of loading or unloading?"

"I know we will suffer in the short term, but in the long term, is it not for the better? Surely Parliament will see that we cannot be forced to give up our rights. Tell me more." Evelyn sat forward eagerly.

"Well, the situation becomes a little complicated. Without courts, a man cannot sue for payment of debts, so there are those who do not pay simply because they know they can't be made to. On the other hand, those nearly ruined by this economic crisis can't be sent to jail. Many ports are allowing ships to leave with letters to the effect that no stamps were available to franchise the cargo, but the owners risk imprisonment if they try to sell their goods in England or the West Indies without the proper stamps. Those who refuse the risk have laid off their crews, and Boston is rapidly filling with unemployed, disgruntled sailors. It is the same in many other cities. I fear it will be a cruel winter for many."

Evelyn sighed and closed her hands around her cup as she stared into it. "I stand to lose all that my father made, but it would be no different if we had accepted the stamps. There was no cash to pay such a tax. I wish there were some way to help. If Parliament would only act swiftly, some end could be brought to this tragedy."

Franklin heard her words with approval. She made no apologies for her beliefs or her husband's wealth, but looked at the situation with clear and open eyes. Hampton might insist that he was a businessman and not a politician, but his wife might have other ideas.

"Perhaps you can help. Parliament is made up of men with minds that can be swayed by numerous events. What is happening in the colonies has them concerned. Now they need to hear the voice of reason. What better way than to have you whispering in their ears at their homes while people like me bellow at them in their offices?"

Evelyn gave him a slight smile that showed she understood, but she shook her head. "You have found the wrong person for that. Even if I knew any of these men or was invited into society, they would not listen to such speech from a woman. But you see before you a house of mourning. Lord Cranville died last night. There will be no society for me for some time to come."

Franklin became instantly apologetic. "I'm sorry. I had not realized his illness was so serious." His mind moved quickly, remembering briefings on the various influential members of government, bringing up the fact that Hampton was the earl's sole heir, and this slight woman now before him was the new countess. His eyes narrowed shrewdly. "If you would forgive me my presumption, I believe you are underestimating the situation. You may not engage in the frivolities of the season, but in the days to come, you will be called upon by some of the most influential families in the country. Politics might not be an appropriate subject in a house of mourning, but it will give you an opportunity to meet the people who most need influencing. All that I ask is that you keep that in mind."

Evelyn pondered what Franklin had said after he left. She disliked being useless, and she had felt worse than that these last months. She didn't see how Franklin's suggestions would be very effective, but he had given her something to think about, and she badly needed that over the next few days.

Caught up in his own grief, pressed by the numerous demands required of him as the new earl, Alex retreated behind his wall again, and Evelyn saw little of him. She spent her days with a grief-stricken widow and daughter, greeting their visitors with them, maintaining a flow of conversation when Deirdre stopped in mid-sentence or Alyson drifted off to another world. She learned to order the servants to bring tea, to announce when they weren't accepting calls, to answer their questions when Deirdre retreated to her chambers. If she pretended she was home running the warehouse, it wasn't too difficult, and it occupied many of her hours. The evenings were worst. No one called then. Alyson went home to her husband and children. Deirdre was little or no company. And Alex was seldom there. Gratefully Evelyn turned to her mother, aunt, and cousin for company, but they were beginning to feel uncomfortable as guests in a house of grief. Increasingly they spoke of returning to Surrey to visit relatives.

Late at night Alex would come to their bed, but if Evelyn allowed herself to fall asleep before he came, he didn't disturb her, and he would be off again before she woke. Most nights she tried sitting up and reading until he arrived, but he was inclined to be surly and uncommunicative. Their lovemaking was often frantic, as if they poured out their fears and frustrations in this physical act rather than spoke of them. Alex fell into the sleep of exhaustion soon after, leaving Evelyn to stare at the ceiling.

Lying beside him, she wondered if she had made the right decision for her life. She closed her eyes and tried to remember those times when they had laughed and loved together and she had known she had done the right thing. But that was before the responsibilities of an earldom had come upon them, and she greatly feared she would never see that Alex again.

Having abjured all responsibility for the greater part of his life, he took it all too seriously now. Evelyn ran her hand across his broad back and wished she could relieve some of the burden he carried there. She felt certain she could if only he would let her, but she didn't have the heart to start one of their soul-crushing arguments now. He had to be made to see without the need for harsh words.

Franklin's suggestions kept coming back to her. She had feared and deplored being called countess, but Franklin had been right about the number of influential people crossing their doorstep. Alex was seldom home to greet them, but Evelyn had accepted condolences from men and women she had never dreamed would be more than vague names to her. Perhaps some fitted her notions of idle, effete aristocracy, but there were many who were genuinely grieved at the late earl's loss and were interested in the new heir's Yankee wife. Some disdained her colonial accent, but the truly well-bred among them greeted her with more curiosity and politeness than disdain. She had a chance with them, if she tried.

Did she dare try? Would Alex appreciate her turning the gracious salons of Cranville House into tea parties for Whigs and Tories? She seriously suspected he wouldn't, but she could not make the idea go away. Although her beliefs were pure Whig, there was little sense in preaching to the converted. Alex's title put him in a position to be coveted by the influential Tory party, and it was there that she must lay her groundwork. Plans kept coming to mind even when she had almost convinced herself she couldn't do it. She became obsessed with the idea.

Thomas Henderson came to express his sympathy and ask if there were anything he could do. Again he pressed for the details in the packet about the smugglers, and Evelyn uneasily remembered she had promised to look for it, but that problem seemed too distant from this immediate one. She distracted him with talk of the people she had met and asked about all those he knew. By the time he left, he had learned nothing but Evelyn possessed a few more valuable pieces of information for her collection. If she were going to make her scheme work, she needed to know these people as well as they knew each other. It wouldn't be easy.

Alyson was of no use. She had never cultivated society and spent most of her time in Scotland. Evelyn doubted that she knew the difference between Whig and Tory or even cared. Rory was shrewd enough to have connections in the political world, but asking him questions was tantamount to asking Alex, and she wasn't ready for that yet. Deirdre was her best hope.

After that first emotional week, Deirdre managed to regain some semblance of control, but Evelyn often found her lost and drifting down some empty hall with no notion where she was going or why. She needed some focus as much as Evelyn, and tentatively Evelyn tried to find it.

Entertaining to any extent was out of the question, and they could not be expected to begin their round of visiting yet, but Evelyn had urged some of their more sympathetic callers to come again, and to her surprise, many of them did. She started with these people, asking Deirdre questions after they left, learning of their lives and relations.

When Franklin called again, Evelyn made certain Deirdre was there to talk with him too. One of his quips actually brought a ghost of a smile to the older woman's face, and she appeared vaguely amused by this colonial's attempt to cultivate society. Afterward Deirdre was the one asking questions.

A comment from Rory at dinner one evening brought the realization that Alex actually meant to take his seat in the House of Lords, and Evelyn's hopes soared. Alex should have been the one to tell her, but she would respect his need for privacy as long as he came home to her every night. And he did.

When he began bringing home some of the men who thought as he did to drink and talk and map out strategy in the comforts of his study, Evelyn felt triumphant. If Alex was making this step, he couldn't object if she did the same. If only they could work together, she would be in heaven.

Progress was slow, and other than Deirdre, Evelyn had little support from those around her. Her mother decided it would be best if she and the rest of the family went to stay with her family for a while rather than impose on newlyweds and a grief-stricken widow any longer. Evelyn protested, but her mother was immovable. By the time Parliament came into session, they were gone.

Soon after that, one of the partnership's smaller ships arrived in port, and Rory decided it would be better if Alyson traveled home before her pregnancy was too advanced for comfort. At this desertion, Evelyn wanted to cry for them to take her with them, but she bit her lip and reached for Alex's hand instead. He was home early for a change, and he too seemed stunned by this departure, but he merely squeezed Evelyn's hand and wished them a safe journey.

Later that night, when Evelyn prepared to retire to their chamber, Alex left his study to join her. He remained silent as they ascended the stairs and traversed the upper hall. Instead of going directly to their bedroom, he threw open the door to the sitting room and led her in. That made her uneasy, but Evelyn held her peace as he poured them both some wine.

She didn't know whether to sit or stand, and she took her clues from Alex. When he began to pace, she remained standing. If he wasn't going to relax, neither was she. Tensely she watched his elegantly garbed figure stride back and forth. His thick black hair was pulled back in a plain queue, his lace had been discarded for immaculate linen, and while his dark coat and white vest sported golden buttons, they had none of the elaborate embroidery and trim that he had once worn. It seemed now that he was lord in truth, he need not dress the part any longer.

But his clothes weren't what she had seen in Alex. What she loved in his appearance was the determination of his square jaw, the occasional flashes of vulnerability in his dark eyes, the strength of his muscled shoulders, and the grace with which he carried himself. He could be naked and she would still be attracted to him. Even more attracted than with clothes, she admitted to herself wryly as he came to rest before the fire and turned to face her, legs spread as if on the deck of a rolling ship.

He took a deep breath and his dark eyes glittered as he observed her tense stance and untouched wine. "Have I made you very unhappy, Evelyn?"

The unexpectedness of the question left her temporarily speechless. She gasped, set the wine aside, and fiddled with the draping of her black velvet gown while she tried to compose some sensible reply. None came. Then she looked up to the pained look in his eyes and knew there was only one reply she could make.

Crossing the room, she lifted her arms around his neck and pulled his head down so that she could brush featherlight kisses across the taut muscle of his cheek. "Events might make me unhappy, but you have given me more happiness than I ever dared expect. My only regret is that we have so little time to share together."

Evelyn felt him set aside his glass, but Alex's mouth had already found hers, and her concentration was entirely on the elation generated by his kiss. A shudder swept through her as Alex gathered her into his arms, and she pressed eagerly into him, clinging tightly to his shoulders as he lifted her from the floor, and their lips melted together with the sweetness of joy as much as need.

"Oh, God, Evelyn, I'm so afraid of losing you. I don't know what you see in me or why you stay, but help me understand what I need to do to keep you."

His arms held her so close that his buttons pressed into her breast. His lips trailed fire along her cheek, and Evelyn turned her head to seek them once again before replying.

"Love me, Alex," she whispered. "I need you to love me. You don't have to say the words, just show me. Hold me like this, make love to me, and talk to me. I need you to talk to. I'm so alone sometimes, and I need you. Don't shut me out, Alex, please." She was pleading with him. She knew she was pleading with him. She had never meant to beg, but he had opened a door and she wanted in, and she would use everything in her power to gain entry. His kisses were the fire in her hearth, and she would freeze to death without them. Eagerly she sought his mouth once more.

To her surprise, he didn't take the opportunity she offered to undress her or carry her off to bed as usual when they were physically intimate. Instead, Alex carried her to a chair beside the fire and pulled her into his lap as he sat down. His kisses were soft and gentle as they brushed against her face, and his hand merely came up to cup her breast and occasionally caress it as he spoke.

"I promised you wouldn't have to be a countess for many years. I didn't mean to lie. I miss him. There's this huge hole that he's left behind, and I don't know how to fill it. I wanted the title once. I thought I deserved it. I thought people would have to start listening to me then. I was a damned arrogant pup. Everett showed me what it took to be a Cranville. He did it with such ease. He was always so genial to everyone, but he commanded respect. I don't know how he did it. I haven't got the knack. He was always there when we needed him, but he had enormous responsibilities. How did he do it? How did he manage to seem idle and accomplish so much?"

"Fifty years' experience might have helped," Evelyn offered dryly. Then apologetically she pressed a kiss to his cheek. "You're not your cousin, Alex, and weren't meant to be. Yes, he was charming and genial and probably idle because he delegated his duties to everyone else. That's the way he was and he was loved in spite of it as much as because of it. You're too intense, too determined, to live as he did, and I love you in spite of it as well as because of it. I wouldn't want you any other way. But it would help ease the long, lonely hours if I knew you would come to me like this at the end of the day."

Alex looked down at his wife's flushed face with a growing sense of discovery. He traced her cheek with his finger and brushed a wisp of hair behind her ear. The room was well-lit, but here beside the fire there were shadows to dance across her features. He focused on each one, outlining them with his touch, memorizing the feel of her as well as the scent and taste. He was just beginning to realize that what they had wasn't temporary. She was going to stay. The thought terrified as well as thrilled him.

"I'm not used to having anyone to talk to," he admitted. "It's not an easy habit to break. Couldn't I just seduce you? I have a lot more experience at that."

The rakish quirk of his lips warmed her to the bones, but Evelyn placed an admonishing finger across them. "I scarcely need seducing, I'm afraid. I'm no challenge at all. All you need do is look at me and I'll fall into your arms. You need more challenge than that. You'll have to seduce me while talking to me. I promise to put up a good fight then."

Alex chuckled and moved his hand to the hard tip of her breast pushing through layers of clothing, giving evidence to her words. He played that sensitive crest as he pressed a tempting kiss to her parted lips. "Don't you think we would talk better in bed?" he whispered as he drew his mouth away to caress the line of her jaw.

"Perhaps we've talked enough for one night. I have a thousand questions I wish to ask you, but I cannot seem to recall even one of them right now."

Alex smiled down into violet eyes. "I'll wager you remember them soon enough. Come, my little termagant, tonight it is just thee and me against the world. Let us see what we can make of it."

Holding her easily in his arms, he rose from the chair, and instead of going through their dressing rooms, where their servants waited, he carried her across the hall and directly into his chamber. A fire burned warmly in the grate and a single lamp lit the bed, but they needed no more than that.

As Alex returned her feet to the floor, Evelyn raised her arms to begin unfastening his jabot, and a pleased grin crossed his face. He held her by the waist and savored the pleasure of knowing she wanted him. As her fingers reached the bare skin of his chest, he bent to whisper against her ear, "I'm yours to command, little rebel. How would you like the forces employed tonight?"

"On me," she announced firmly, reaching for the fastenings of his breeches. "You'll need full artillery and a cavalry charge or two, I suspect. Are you prepared?"

His laughter echoed through the chamber and out into the hall. In their small rooms, the valet and lady's maid heard the laughter and resignedly withdrew to their own separate beds. The earl and his countess wouldn't be needing them anymore this night.

31

The workmen and the plumbers began tearing apart the dressing rooms the next morning. The commotion of collapsing walls, pounding hammers, and a constant stream of noisy boots stomping up and down the back stairs disrupted much of the household, and the noise even carried to the front salons, where the guests looked questioningly for explanation.

Evelyn's attempt to explain Alex's decision to install a bathing room brought such blushes to her cheeks that Deirdre laughed clearly for the first time in weeks and took over the discussion of that particular topic. Evelyn gratefully left her in charge when a servant appeared in the doorway to announce that Mr. Farnley would like to see her for a few minutes. She excused herself and hurried to the study.

The elderly solicitor greeted her with more excitement than she had ever seen him display. There was even the trace of a smile on his lips as he bowed over her hand and assisted her to a seat. Evelyn clasped her hands in her lap and watched him expectantly.

He didn't disappoint. He took a seat in front of her, removed his spectacles to clean them, and launched into his subject. "I have found the individual you requested we look for, Lady Cranville."

Evelyn didn't dare display her hopes or fears. Reining in any display of emotion, she watched him intently to judge his feelings about this news. "What have you found out?"

"The girl is approximately fourteen years of age, in good health, apparently well-thought-of in the commu nity. She has attended the village school taught by the local clergyman and his wife and has shown a remarkable intelligence in all her studies. They speak well of her but say they have taught her all that they know. She is currently helping them teach the younger students."

Evelyn gave the first hint of her relief by leaning back in her chair. "Please go on."

Farnley nodded approvingly. "The roads are poor this time of year, so I have not gone to see her myself. My correspondent tells me she is quite attractive in a wild sort of way. Hampton blood will tell, you know. She has the dark hair, the dark eyes, and unfortunately, the temper. I don't think there's any mistaking her parentage. Her mother and her adopted father were both fair. There is little doubt among the villagers as to whose child she actually is."

Evelyn put her hand to her face in a futile attempt to hold back the tears. When Mr. Farnley halted in his recitation, she shook her head. "I am fine. Please continue."

"Her mother is a bit simpleminded, but her adopted ather apparently doted on her. He died last spring and eft his entire holdings to the child. The girl has wisely ented out much of the land, since she cannot possibly vork it herself, but she does oversee a few small plots ear the house. She's quite comfortably off, actually."

"But she's only fourteen," Evelyn whispered between er fingers. "What a terrible age for a girl not to have a ather to protect her. She will be a victim to every forune hunter in the county."

"That's quite possibly so. There were hints of such in y correspondence with the vicar. He displayed some ar for her well-being and asked if I could use my influnce with Lord Cranville. I have not answered him." arnley stated that firmly, waiting for Lady Cranville's sponse to this challenge.

"I must tell him, mustn't I?" Clenching her hands gether, Evelyn met the solicitor's gaze fearfully.

"Immediately, if I may be so bold," Mr. Farnley suggested with a hint of gentleness.

"But he is likely to be angry, and then he will do thing. I have to find the right time, but I cannot bear to think what might happen to that child. She is too young yet for such responsibility. Is there nothing we can do until Alex can be brought around?"

Farnley understood her hesitation. He had been the Hampton family solicitor for over two score years. He knew their tempers well. A subject as explosive as this one was like live ammunition. He had already considered the problem, but there was no good solution without the earl's knowledge. He shook his head.

"I would suggest she be sent to a proper girls' school, but I cannot justify such an expense without Cranville's approval. I see no hope for it but to tell him."

Evelyn lifted her head and met his gaze with defiance. "Then I shall tell him, but first you must write to your correspondent and arrange for appropriate transportation. I want the child informed and on her way here before I tell Alex. If you are quite confident that this is Alex's daughter, I will not have her left in ignorance and danger any longer. He may throw as many tantrums as he likes after the fact, but the child will be safe. Can you do that?"

"You would bring the child here?" The obvious incredulity in his voice revealed he had not even considered that solution.

Evelyn rose and applied the full weight of her newly acquired authority. "Would you send her off to school without even the opportunity of meeting her father? I daresay they will not get along. Hamptons seldom do, from what I have seen of them. Do not think I'm being foolish and romantic about this. The child is old enough to be offered choices rather than moved about as a pawn in some adult game. She should be informed of her parentage if her mother has not already done so, and then she should be politely asked if she would like to make the journey to London to meet her father. If she is any kind of Hampton at all, she will have the intelligence to recognize what is best for her and the fury to wish to confront her neglectful parent. I would rather have your task than mine."

Unable to remain in the room any longer, Evelyn left the solicitor standing there with his mouth open. Her heart beat so fiercely she did not think she could stand still. Alex would never forgive her for this interference. What had she done? Just as they were coming to some closer understanding, she had to throw fireworks between them. He would hate her for dredging up the past.

But she could not leave Alex's daughter to the whims of a cruel world. Even with her father's protection behind her, Evelyn had known the pressures men could apply. What chance did a young girl have against deliberate seduction by charming liars, or brutal rape by less subtle suitors, without that protection? Those were the ones who would apply to her first. The more honest ones would not even consider courting a child that age. The girl had to be made safe. Alex could sulk all he liked.

She was afraid to tell Deirdre, and she was terrified of keeping secrets from Alex. She wished Alyson and Rory had stayed awhile longer. She needed good sound advice at the moment, but she had no one to turn to.

When Alex came home early again that night, Evelyn almost collapsed into his arms and babbled out the whole story to him. Only the fact that he was still immersed in his own world and paying little attention to her kept her from revealing all. When he asked if she could put together a small dinner for some friends and their wives, she forgot her fears and stared at him in astonishment. When he looked up impatiently at her lack of reply, she nodded.

"Of course, Alex. It is not as if I have to cook it myself. Deirdre will help me with the menus and invitations. Just give us a list."

Alex frowned at the barest hint of hesitation in her demeanor. "Are you certain? I can arrange to entertain the men at my club if you prefer."

Evelyn felt as if she were walking on eggshells. She wanted so much to please him and to avoid the hideous arguments that so easily came between them that she tried not to say anything that might set them off. Yet she could not stand here and say nothing.

"I would be happy to entertain your friends, Alex. I'm just uncertain that they will be happy to meet me. I have met a few who are hostile to the idea of a Yankee countess."

Alex looked thunderstruck, then grim. "Who? Who

have not treated you as your name deserves? I will have them hounded out of town by sunrise."

Evelyn sighed at this flare of temper. "I do not want retribution, Alex, only your recognition of the facts. I am a stranger and an outsider to these people. I do not know your objective for this dinner, but I do not want it harmed by my presence. I only wish for you to consider that possibility."

Alex made a gesture of irritation. "You are protecting me again, Evelyn. If they are such fools as to object to your background, then I do not need their support anyway. I am not an utter idiot."

"If my attempting to help makes you an idiot, then I shall refrain from doing so again. Heaven forbid that a woman should interfere in a man's world!" Evelyn could not hold her tongue any longer. "Just give me your list and I will worry about my gown and the menu and other such feminine things and leave the important issues to those masculine minds better equipped to deal with them."

"Evelyn, by all that's holy, you would drive a man to madness for a simple request! You may speak your mind as you will, but just stay out of my way while you're doing it. I have too much to do to leave myself victim to your tongue."

"You insufferable ingrate!" Lifting her skirts, Evelyn swept from the room with head held high, losing her dignity only when she slammed the door behind her. Chandeliers throughout the house shook at the blow.

Before she could so much as reach the hall stairs, Alex stuck his head out for the last word. "Cad! The word is 'cad.' And this insufferable cad will be up to warm your bed as soon as you cool down!"

Evelyn mounted the stairs and glanced back over her shoulder to the arrogant man below. "I'll cool down when hell has snowballs, Hampton."

"Good, then I won't have to waste time warming you up." He grinned, then slammed the door behind him again as he retreated into the study.

Evelyn flounced down in the middle of the stairs and burst into tears.

* * *

It wouldn't do. She would never be able to tell him. The tension of these last few days had her nerves twisted in such balls that she could not untangle one emotion from another. Everything she said seemed to cause an argument. And every argument seemed to lead straight to bed. She had no objection to that. Alex in bed was as volatile as his temperament. He could be both fierce and gentle, but most of all, he was loving. Their need for each other did not diminish with the tensions tearing them apart, but increased. It was rather like living on the edge of a volcano. It was no place to discuss lost daughters.

After the days of tension, the dinner was mere child's play. The service went well, the food inspired praise, and the company was congenial. Afterward the ladies retired to the salon, leaving the men to their politics. Many of the ladies had been to one or more of Evelyn's tea parties, and they were eager to take up the enlightening discussions that had ensued there. Evelyn obligingly provided them with more stories of her home.

After their guests left and they were left alone in the privacy of their chambers, Alex drew his wife backward against him and began to remove the pins from her hair. Instantly suspicious at this solicitousness, Evelyn tilted her head back to better judge his expression.

"Your discussion went well?" she asked tentatively.

"Swimmingly," he agreed, carelessly casting aside the pins and tumbling her hair over her shoulders. His hands closed about her upper arms and held her against him as he brushed a kiss against her ear. "There seemed much talk of starving children. You wouldn't know aught of that, would you?"

His fingers drifted to the low-cut neckline of her gown, and Evelyn could scarcely think at all, much less find the direction of his question. She waited for the moment when Alex's hand would slide beneath the silk and satin to find the aching point of her desire. Her breasts strained upward, eager for his touch.

"Starving children? What was the topic of your discussion?" she asked breathlessly.

His hand finally stole beneath bodice and chemise to locate the sensitive crest that removed all her inhibitions.

He smiled as she arched into his palm. "Do you have some doubt, my ıady? The revocation of the Stamp Act, of course. We will be forcing it to a vote shortly. Now, why were my guests discussing starving children in relation to a tax law?"

"Do you have to ask?" Evelyn reached behind her to struggle out of the hooks preventing his full access to her flesh. Alex willingly obliged by releasing her breast and setting his fingers to nimbly unfastening everything in sight. "The act has halted trade, destroyed the economy," she informed him. "We are not rural landholders. We live in cities, just as you do. We don't grow all our own food. We have to buy it. Where there is no money, there is no food. Of course children are starving."

The bodice slipped from her shoulders and Evelyn could feel Alex's fingers tugging impatiently at the ties of her stays. The excitement building between them did not affect his speech, however.

"I never mentioned such to them. Do you think they took it into their own heads to come to those conclusions?"

"Any sensible man ought to be able to divine the results of his actions," Evelyn replied tartly. The stays were loosening. Any minute now the ties to her hoops would fall victim to his impatient fingers. She took a deep breath as his warm hand slid between whalebone and cambric to cover her belly.

His voice whispered huskily in her ear, "But it was their wives that brought it to their attention. How is that, my love? How did those good ladies know of starving children in the colonies?"

"I can't imagine." Smiling, she leaned back into him as her panniers and gown slid past her hips to the floor. Once all the padding and material were removed from between them, she could feel his arousal. She rubbed suggestively against him.

"I can." He lifted her from the puddle of fabric and turned her around to face him. Kicking the gown aside, Alex still did not allow her toes to touch the floor as he met her fearless eyes. "You've been interfering again, my lady. What am I going to have to do about it?"

Evelyn curled her brow up thoughtfully as she wriggled closer into his grasp, skillfully finding his shirt fastenings.

"We could argue about it, I suppose. I would say I'm helping, not interfering, and you could roar something appropriate. And then we could fall into bed and make violent love. Or you could thank me for my helpfulness and I could kiss you all over and we could fall into bed and make violent love. Or . . ."

Alex laughed, a slow laugh that started as a chuckle somewhere deep down in his chest and grew over the time and distance it took to reach his throat. By the time it came roaring out full force, he had her sprawled across the bed, trapped beneath his weight, and wriggling ecstatically to the rain of kisses upon her face and neck.

"Let us skip the preliminaries then and go directly to the main event. Take me in, wife. I want to be reminded who is master here."

"I'll grant you supremacy in this, husband," Evelyn agreed easily, lifting her legs to wrap around his hips as he leaned over her. "You're bigger than I am."

She giggled as he bit at her ear, then drew his head down to taste her kisses. She still wore her chemise, and he was fully clothed, but the rough brush of his clothing between her legs was as erotic as his nakedness. She rose against him and felt him groan between her lips. She wriggled, and his imprisoning hands left her shoulders to unfasten his breeches.

He might be bigger, but there were one or two things she could still do to keep them equal. Deirdre's explanations of months ago had never rung truer, and she smiled happily as she felt Alex suddenly naked against her.

When he lifted her hips and plunged in, she gave a cry of sheer joy. There were still some things she preferred that he be master in.

When they lay in each other's arms later, Evelyn knew the time had come to reveal her secret. Alex was nearly asleep, and so content that she hated to disturb him, but it had to be done. Mr. Farnley had already informed her that the girl was on her way.

She twisted her fingers in the dark mat of curls on his chest and kissed his bare shoulder. "Alex? Are you awake?"

"No." He settled her more comfortably against his side and moved his hand to stroke her breast.

"Good. Then I don't have to tell you that Mr. Farnley found your daughter."

Alex lay still, his fingers absently playing with the tempting nipple rising to his caresses.

She feared he hadn't heard her, but she did not dare repeat herself. "Her adopted father is dead, and the local vicar fears she might be in some danger from overeager suitors. She is only fourteen, Alex, but her father's lands—"

His hand moved from caressing Evelyn's breast to harshly clenching her arms. He jerked her over him until she could stare down into the black fury of his eyes. "What father? What have you done now, Evelyn? Did I ask you to dabble in my life? Did I say, 'Evelyn, be my wife and interfere in everything I do and dig up the secrets of my past while you're at it'? Did I?"

He didn't shake her, but his fingers were pressed so cruelly into her arms that he didn't need to. His face was contorted with fury, but the small bedside lamp gave enough light to reveal the pain there too. Evelyn braced one hand against his shoulder to steady herself, then caressed his jaw with the other.

"Scream at me if you must. I know I have trespassed where I shouldn't, but I love you too much to leave you always hurting for what was done so long ago. I know you didn't want a wife, Alex, and I know I should be meek and obedient and grateful for all you have given me, but I cannot. I cannot be any less than I am, any more than you can be. And I know the man you are will not blame a child for the sins of her parents."

"You know a damn lot, don't you?" Alex wrapped her more gently in his arms and felt her hair cascading over his arms as she rested her head against his shoulder. Soft kisses burned gently against his throat where her lips could reach, and he crushed her tightly, trying not to let his rampaging emotions get out of control. Since first he'd laid eyes on this witch she'd had this effect on him, and he had resented it from the start. Life had been much easier before she came into it and turned him inside out, exposing all his feelings for the world to see.

But it had been a miserable excuse for a life just the same. "Is she well?" he whispered hoarsely.

Hot tears dripped on his bare shoulder, and he felt Evelyn's head move up and down in a nod.

"According to Mr. Farnley's spies, she is fine and happy. They say she very much resembles you. She's very intelligent and has learned all the local school has to offer. Mr. Farnley thinks she ought to be sent to a girls' school."

"Does he now?" Alex growled. "And has he asked the girl if she wishes to go? What is her name?"

Evelyn began to relax and allowed herself a small smile. "You will have to ask Mr. Farnley that. Alex, I was worried about her. I know what it's like to be left alone in charge of wealth, and she's so young. She will have no experience in dealing with fortune hunters."

"The old goat left her all his land? I'm not certain whether that proves his stupidity or his intelligence. Surely he must have known the child wasn't his." Alex sighed and ran his hand through his hair as he contemplated all the complications involved. "I can't go after her right now, Evelyn. It's imperative that I keep battering away at some of these hardheaded Tories until they see the light."

"I know," Evelyn whispered against his ear, twining her long leg with his. "And I love you for that too. See how fickle I am? I even love you when you're contrary. According to Mr. Farnley, the vicar and his wife broke the news to her already. She trusts them, and he thought that would be best. She agreed that it might be in her best interests to leave the farm for a while. They're already on their way here."

"Oh, God." He groaned and closed his eyes and tried not to imagine this new invasion into his hitherto quiet life. "What in hell am I going to say to her? 'Hello, bastard, where've you been all these years?' Evelyn, this is an impossible situation."

"Nothing is impossible," she announced firmly, slithering off him and returning contentedly to her own pillow. "She is halfway between an adult and a child and frightened out of her wits. If I am any judge of Hampton behavior at all, she will react with anger. That covers a multitude of sins."

Alex caught her hand and held it. "People respect anger. They don't respect the weaker emotions."

"People are fools. Love is the strongest emotion of all. Those who dare to love risk everything. Only people strong enough to take such risks can afford to show love. Even an infant can show anger. There is simply no comparison as far as I can see."

"And how are you going to tell that to a fourteen-year-old child who has just discovered that her father isn't her father, that her real father is a self-centered bastard who's ignored her all these years?"

"*Very* gently."

Alex snorted, rolled over, and buried his face against the sweet scent of her hair. "Tell me again, love. Tell me how strong I must be so I don't resort to anger and strangle you in your sleep. And say it gently."

Evelyn laughed low in her throat and wrapped her arms reassuringly around him. "I love you, and you may strangle me all you want, after you make love to me. If you have the strength."

32

The carriage arrived in the afternoon while Alex was still out. Already informed of the impending new arrival, Deirdre clasped Evelyn's hand reassuringly at the announcement.

"You have done the right thing, Evelyn. Let us not stand on ceremony but go to meet them. It will have been a difficult journey."

"Do you think we should send word to Alex? I know he is eager to see her even if he is terrified of her hatred. Tell me, Deirdre, I am all a-dither and cannot think."

Deirdre smiled affectionately at her lovely young relative. Since arriving in London, Evelyn had adapted many of the fashions. Her long hair was pinned skillfully in curls, and she wore an elegant morning gown of gray satin that far outshone anything she had owned in Boston. There was little outer difference to identify her as a stranger to London, but the inner Evelyn would never quite be a society matron. Her interests were far too different, and Deirdre approved of the difference. Alex would never have been happy with a woman whose only concern was gossip and balls.

"I'll send someone to look for Alex while you greet our guests. He can do as he wishes when he hears the news."

"Let us hope he does not wish to get drunk," Evelyn responded grimly as she started for the hallway. "Right now I can understand the temptation."

Deirdre's laugh followed her into the confusion of the wide entry hall. Servants were scurrying about carrying bags and parcels and icy cloaks and hats while the newcomers gaped at their surroundings and reluctantly surrendered the protection of their outer garments piece by piece.

While their attention was distracted, Evelyn grasped this opportunity to study her newly discovered stepdaughter. The girl stood aside from the nervous vicar and his wife, staring up at the murals ascending the stairway to the magnificent skylight. She was tall, nearly as tall as Evelyn already, and she wore her thick black hair unbound and cascading down her back. Her complexion had more color than her cousin Alyson's, but it was not the ruddy, weathered look of a farmer's daughter so much as a golden hue of striking attractiveness. When she finally realized she was observed and turned to meet Evelyn's gaze, Evelyn nearly gasped at the beauty of the long-lashed dark eyes greeting her. Alex's eyes.

Evelyn loved her instantly, if only for the eyes. Hurrying forward, Evelyn clasped the girl's cold fingers between her own. She could scarcely be considered a child any longer. Both face and body revealed a maturity unusual for one of such a tender age. No wonder the vicar worried for her safety. There was still a certain awkward grace to her movements, as if she were yet unaccustomed to her new status as woman and not child, and her eyes flickered briefly with childish uncertainty, but she quickly masked it with indifference as she removed her hand.

Evelyn made no fuss, but turned to greet the girl's elderly chaperons. "I am Lady Cranville, and you must be the Granthams. I'm so happy to meet you at last. Won't you please come in by the fire? It must have been a terribly tedious journey, but we are so grateful that you could make it."

Talking to disguise her nervousness, she led their guests to the small family parlor where Deirdre waited. The Granthams made small, polite noises in reply to her steady stream of questions. Their protégée said nothing.

Evelyn introduced their guests to Deirdre. When she came to Alex's daughter, she caught her hand and drew her forward. "And this, of course is Elizabeth Margaret. How are you called at home, Elizabeth? Beth? Bess?"

"Margaret, just like my Grandmother Hampton, but

she's not a Hampton any longer, is she? They call her Lady Barton now."

The girl's cool address left Evelyn momentarily nonplussed, but Deirdre seemed to take it in stride. She gestured regally for their guests to take seats. "Your father's mother never was a Hampton except briefly by name. It was considerate of your mother to share part of your heritage with you. Lady Barton still resides in the area, then?"

The vicar replied when the girl did not. "Oh, yes, my lady. She has been the baronet's wife these many years past, and a strong supporter of the church. She is an invalid, however. We seldom see her in the village."

Evelyn had not considered the possibility that Alex's mother was still alive. He had never mentioned her since that night at the inn, and no one else had ever offered any indication of her existence. What a strange family this was. No wonder Alex was reluctant to divulge much of his past.

Tea and hot chocolate were brought in with a selection of tempting biscuits and cakes meant to appease the appetite until a proper meal could be prepared. Evelyn watched as Margaret sipped approvingly at the rich chocolate. The girl's eyes continued to study her surroundings, occasionally coming back to flicker briefly over Evelyn as the difficulty of travel in winter was discussed.

"When you are warm, perhaps I could show you to your room." Evelyn spoke quietly to the girl while the others were engaged in polite conversation. "A few months ago I was as much a stranger here as you are now, and I still find the place a little overwhelming at times. I tried to find a room you might feel comfortable in, but we can always look for a better one when we explore the house."

The girl turned dark, hostile eyes toward her. "You are the one who sent for me, aren't you? Why? Can you not have children of your own?"

The question was brutally direct and all Hampton. Evelyn's lips quirked upward in the corners. "If your father were in your place, he would have asked the same thing. I think Hamptons are born suspicious, except your cousin Alyson, of course. I cannot answer your questions as easily as they are asked, and I will warn you now that while your father can be just as blunt, he also takes offense as easily as you. Your questions would have offended him."

"Then he shall just have to send me back where I came from. I've done without him quite nicely all these years."

Margaret gave the outward appearance of being unperturbed, but Evelyn could see how tightly she clenched the fragile porcelain cup in her hand as she set it back on the tray.

"That is because you had another father who loved you all these years. He would not have given you up to a stranger's claim. How is your mother taking this?"

The girl shrugged. "She is warm and happy and already entertaining other gentleman callers. She never argued when Reverend Grantham named me a bastard, although he did it in much politer terms," she answered honestly.

"You have a name. You're not a bastard. Someday, perhaps your father will tell you the story, but in the meantime I will not allow anyone, not even you, to call you by that term. If you are done, let us go see your bedroom."

Evelyn rose and held out her hand. The others turned to watch in anxiety as the girl hesitated, but a child's curiosity won out over the more adult bitterness. Scorning the offered hand, she rose and followed Evelyn from the room. Behind them, the others exchanged glances of relief.

They were coming back down the stairs when the furor in the front hall reached their ears. Evelyn halted and glanced over the banister to catch some glimpse of the combatants. Alex's booming, furious voice was unmistakable. The woman's high-pitched whining was not so easily placeable. Evelyn frowned.

"You cannot do this to me, Alexander! It's a public disgrace. How could you? All these years we've ignored the embarrassing rumors until they were all but forgotten. And now you do this! You cannot publicly acknowledge a bastard, Alexander! It is simply not done. I will be the laughingstock of the community. How will I hold my head up when I go out?"

"My daughter is not a bastard, madam!" Even though Alex kept his voice low, the words thundered through the hall like fireworks. "If you should so name her again, I will forbid you this house or any other that belongs to me or mine. You chose your life, and I have made what I could of mine without you. I do not need your commands at this late date."

Evelyn felt the girl come to stand beside her, her fingers gripping the banister with such force her knuckles whitened. It wasn't the manner in which Evelyn would prefer to introduce father and daughter, but it was typical. Placing her hand gently on the girl's shoulder, she gestured toward the stairs. They couldn't remain here to eavesdrop.

"Oh, my, I don't think I can bear it! Alexander, I feel faint. Help me to the sofa. That my own son should speak to me so . . ." the voice wailed upward as Evelyn and Margaret proceeded down.

"Burton, help my mother to that chair. She will be leaving shortly. Where is my wife?" Alex spoke briskly, callously dismissing his mother's vapors.

Evelyn came into view, her arm still across Margaret's shoulders as the two of them took in the scene in the entry below. The small woman garbed in flowing fur-lined cloak and muff held the back of her hand to her forehead in a dramatic gesture that was quickly arrested as she swirled around at the sound of Evelyn's voice.

"I am here, husband." The smile in Evelyn's words was evident, and Alex's head jerked upwards to meet her gaze. "I do so love happy family reunions, Alex. Would you introduce me to your mother? And I would like to make you acquainted with your daughter, Margaret."

The silence was deafening as they descended to the hall. Evelyn could feel the girl holding back as she met the gaze of the large, furious man staring up to her, but she did not run and flee. Grateful for that, Evelyn squeezed her shoulders reassuringly.

Alex didn't take his gaze off his daughter as he spoke. "Mother, Lady Barton, this is my wife, Evelyn, and my daughter, Margaret, who for some odd reason has been named after you. Her mother never did have much sense."

"Alex!" Evelyn remonstrated without rancor. She released Margaret to hold out her hand to Lady Barton. "So pleased to meet you, my lady. Would you come in and have some tea? Lady Cranville and the Granthams are there, and we will be much cozier by the fire."

"I will not come anywhere where that . . . that urchin is welcome." Lady Barton withheld her hand, turning her glare to her son and ignoring her daughter-in-law and granddaughter. "I am not at all well, Alexander. I demand to be shown a room at once."

Alex and his daughter were still regarding each other warily. At his mother's whining demands, he sent her a brief look of irritation. "Say hello to my wife and daughter first. Then I will send someone to help you to a room."

Evelyn gave the girl beside her a quick glance and noted the ghost of a smile as she stared up at the woman who must have scorned her all her life. It seemed odd to Evelyn that grandmother and granddaughter could live in the same small village all their lives and never meet on equal terms, but the terms had changed now. The girl's chin lifted an inch higher when her grandmother stared at her in horror.

The older woman took the only way out. She gave a faint moan, closed her eyes, and swooned.

Alex inelegantly caught her with one arm and passed her to a footman. "Find a dungeon somewhere to keep her in. She'll recover soon enough." Then he turned to wife and daughter and offered both arms. "It's damn cold out here. Shall we?"

Delight danced in Margaret's dark eyes as she took her awesome father's arm. Amusement lighting hers, Evelyn took the other, sending only a faint look of concern to the woman stoically being carried away to the upper stories. The lady had made her choice. So be it.

Deirdre and the Granthams exclaimed with happiness as Alex entered with wife and daughter on either arm. The truce might be a temporary one brought about by a common enemy, but it was a much better start than could have been anticipated. Beaming with relief, the Granthams reassured themselves of their charge's well-being, and hastily exited.

Evelyn filled in the awkwardness of their departure by discussing the changes Margaret might prefer in the bedchamber she had just seen. Alex sat quietly in his chair, watching his only child with an unreadable expression. The two were so obviously father and daughter that Evelyn had to swallow a lump in her throat several times while she spoke.

When a lull finally fell in this feminine conversation, Alex intruded cautiously. "Margaret, we were led to believe that you would prefer going to a finishing school for your education. Is this so?"

Twisting her glove nervously, Margaret looked up to her handsome father. He appeared every inch the authoritative earl she had imagined him to be, much grander than the local nobles she had seen in the rural countryside. She had never known fear before, but his imposing figure could easily inspire fear. The only thing that she knew for certain that she wanted was not to be forgotten again. She had very little idea how to arrange that.

"I had thought to learn to be a governess, but with Papa gone, I suppose that's not necessary. Are there schools to teach me how to run a farm?"

Alex didn't manage a smile, but continued studying her with all seriousness. "I would be better off if there were. Somehow, I have to learn to run my estates in Cornwall now that my cousin is gone. The task looks quite formidable. Perhaps by the time you are old enough to operate the farm on your own, I will know enough to teach you. In the meantime, perhaps you would like to attend a school where you might learn French and etiquette and whatever it is that they teach in those places."

Evelyn rather suspected the girl's mention of running the farm had been thrown out as something of a challenge. The fact that Alex didn't dismiss it out of hand as so many men probably already had left Margaret gaping, but she quickly recovered. Before she could say something spiteful as to the necessity of conversing in French with cows, Evelyn intervened.

"Of course, your home will be here, Margaret. We could hire a tutor if you would prefer, but there aren't many girls your age in the vicinity, and neither of us is very familiar with the neighbors in Cornwall. It might be nice to meet other girls your age so you can have friends to bring home with you on the holidays. You don't need to decide immediately. We just wish to see you safe and happy."

Margaret stared pensively at her hands, not looking at either of them. "Why are you doing this?" she finally whispered.

Evelyn sat back and waited for Alex to answer. He gave her a helpless glare, but seeing his wife's obdurate look, he gave in and took on the task of explaining.

"I wanted to do this from the very beginning, Meg. I never meant to deny you. You will need to ask your mother about her decision to choose another father for you. Perhaps she made the right choice at the time. I was very young when you were born and couldn't have cared for you as I ought. In case no one has informed you, I have not exactly been a model of exemplary behavior in the past. Let us just say it is past time that we got to know each other. I am quite proud of how well you've turned out, but I'd like to have a small part in helping you become all that you can be. Perhaps someday, when you become a parent, you'll understand that."

The girl raised her head defiantly. "I don't intend to marry and have babies. I'll teach other people's children and run my life the way I want to do it!"

Alex and Evelyn exchanged glances of mutual understanding and a hint of laughter. It was Alex who replied. "Fine with me, chit. Now, let's go dress before I starve to death."

There were at least ten thousand other subjects to be addressed sometime in the near future, but the most important had been settled. Margaret would be staying. Evelyn took the girl's hand and bent and kissed Alex's cheek.

"I love you," she whispered, and he looked quite pleased with himself as he watched them go. Evelyn felt her heart pounding with the small pleasure of knowing she had done something right, even if she were an interfering shrew.

That night when they prepared for bed, Alex was unusually inattentive, and Evelyn watched him with worry. When he came to her and drew his hand through her hair, she rested her palm against his chest and looked up to him inquiringly.

He responded to the question in her eyes almost wistfully. "She is very lovely, is she not?"

Evelyn's heart skipped a beat. She began unfastening his shirt for him. "She looks just like you, Alex. She is so beautiful, I think I'm jealous."

"Jealous?" He tugged her hair back to gaze down into her face. "What has got into your head now?"

Evelyn wrinkled her nose up and looked away. "She's lovely and intelligent and in a few years she can do all the things for you that I can do: hostess your dinner parties, entertain the wives and daughters of your friends, and run the household and probably your estates. You won't need me at all."

Alex began to grin as he pulled her head back around to meet his gaze. He brushed a kiss beside her mouth, traced another along her lips, and located the drawstring of her chemise. "Is that what I need you for? I didn't know. I knew there must be some reason I took you for wife. I know I can't sleep without you. And I have great difficulty breathing without you. And eating is quite out of the question if you're not by my side. So I rather thought you were an aid to my health. And there is the matter of the great discomfort that occurs when I think of you wearing only a thin chemise, or a revealing ball gown, or a modest day dress, or only the bubbles in your bath. I have discovered you are the only relief for that discomfort, little tyrant. So I rather need you around a lot because I think of you a lot. And I suspect that means we may have a dozen daughters even more lovely than our Meg because you will be their mother, and I'd hoped you would stay long enough to help me bring them up. They're bound to be a handful, I fear."

The chemise fell to the floor and Evelyn found herself in strong arms being transported to the bed. She tried to remember if she had ever needed a nightgown since gracing her husband's bed, but that thought went the way of all others as he began to kiss her all over. His words had succeeded in producing an aura of enchantment that was too beautiful to dispel, and she floated in ecstasy as he came down beside her.

"Do you really think you might need me just a little?" she asked breathlessly as his lips found a particularly vulnerable spot.

"I really think I need you a whole lot. I really think I have needed you all my life. I really think you had better stop doing that or our dozen daughters will spill all over the sheets." He moaned this last against her hair as her hand stroked him.

Evelyn laughed huskily. "One at a time is quite sufficient. And I believe the prospects of the next being a son are quite good."

"The Cranville heir, of course. We will need two or three or half a dozen of those also," Alex said contentedly as he knelt between her legs and found his goal. Her welcome momentarily robbed him of the power of speech.

"A daughter now, a son in September, and maybe another daughter—" Evelyn gasped as she was caught up in the sudden frantic rhythm of his movement, and only the outpouring of murmured words and small cries was heard for some minutes.

Not until he had achieved satisfaction for both of them did Alex feel the import of her words sink in. Bracing himself on both arms above her, their bodies still joined in the melting heat of their lovemaking, he stared down into his wife's contented expression. "A son when?"

Evelyn's eyes flew open, and a worried look briefly crossed her brow. "In September. Is there something wrong?"

"September." Alex did mental gymnastics. This was mid-February. By September. That meant . . . He gave a sudden whoop of joy and rolled over to release her from his heavy weight, forgetting that he had been too impatient to seek the center of the bed earlier.

His cry as he tumbled to the floor with a crash brought worried calls from behind the doors, and it was Evelyn who whooped as she bent over the edge of the bed to observe her lordly husband sprawled across the cold floor, grinning.

33

The debates in Parliament over the colonial Stamp Act reached furious proportions, and Alex was gone most of every day and night, twisting arms and pleading his case. Franklin stopped by a time or two to congratulate Evelyn on her husband's valiant efforts, but he could offer no assurances that past wrongs would be righted. The prospect of war with the colonies seemed to tickle the fancies of the more militant members of the government.

Evelyn carried her pregnancy easily, with a golden glow that brought smiles to the faces of all around her. Alex's whoops of joy the night he had received the news had been proudly explained to all who would listen, and all of London now knew of his impending fatherhood. The heart-stopping smile that only Evelyn knew her husband was capable of appeared on his face more frequently now, even when he returned tired and frustrated to his home to find it in an uproar.

And uproars were more common than not. The plumbers were still piecing together the bathing room in Alex's suite, while carpenters began to tear apart a room in Deirdre's suite to provide the same for her. Evelyn discreetly entertained politicians and their families throughout the confusion, providing a forum to discuss the issues at stake that often lasted into the wee hours. And in and around this mass confusion, Margaret made her presence felt, volubly protesting the stays required for her fashionable new attire, exuberantly racing through the halls after a stray cat she acquired, and throwing a tantrum to match Alex's when confronted with Lady Barton's spiteful ill humor.

Alex rolled his eyes heavenward and clutched his walking stick like a weapon when entering one evening to the less-than-musical harmonies of grandmother and granddaughter sharpening their tongues on each other. But a smile soon bent his lips as Evelyn came hurrying toward him, her arms outstretched to take the hug he offered. He wrapped her soundly in his embrace, and ignoring the stares of servants, his weariness, and the harsh sounds of discord, he began to ply her face with kisses.

"Let's go hide upstairs where no one will find us. I want to see how baby tyrant is growing, and then I want to take mama tyrant and . . ." He whispered several suggestive phrases in her ear that caused Evelyn to blush furiously and whisk from his grasp.

She headed for the steps, however, and threw a knowing smile over her shoulder as she started upward. "You're no gentleman, Alexander Hampton. I'll have your dinner brought to your room, but I'll not be on the menu."

With black fires in his eyes, he strode after her, swinging her up in his arms. "That's 'Lord Cranville' to you, wench. Has no one warned you that we noble dragons devour saucy Yankees for supper? You will be nothing more than a pleasant memory and a full stomach by morning."

His growl brought shrieks of laughter as he ran up the stairs with her. The argument in the upstairs library came to a sudden halt, and downstairs, Deirdre entered the hall to smile contentedly at the sounds of merriment. Servants once terrified of Alex's uncertain moods now grinned at each other and returned to their tasks. On another such night, his lordship might have lashed all within sight and sound with his tongue before returning morosely to his chambers with a brandy bottle. That was behind them now. Even his nagging witch of a mother only brought impatience to the master's expression now. And she would be gone as soon as the roads had cleared to her satisfaction.

Alex ignored the urgent knock at the front door as he reached the second-floor landing. The naughty creature in his arms had already pushed aside his vest, unfastened his jabot and part of his shirt, and was tweaking the hairs on his chest with slender fingers. His weariness had fled beneath a surge of lust, and he had only one thing on his mind as he turned determinedly in the direction of their bedroom.

The sound of the door opening, the shout of the butler as he ordered the footman to follow, and Deirdre's anxious voice did not penetrate Alex's fixed intentions. Only the feel of Evelyn going tense in his arms distracted him enough to realize that a footman had dared to stand in his way. His black glare would have sent the man scurrying at another time. Evelyn's presence gave the servant courage to stand resolutely at attention before the earl's most forbidding stare.

"By Jove, I'll have you hanged from the chandelier, Ames, if this is not important." Alex reluctantly lowered his wife to her feet but kept a possessive arm about her waist. His shirt gaped open and the servant stared at this dishevelment in fear and confusion.

"The messenger said it was urgent, my lord," he finally stuttered. "It just came from the colonies. He carried it from Plymouth direct from the captain of some colonial ship."

Evelyn caught her breath as Alex took the folded and sealed paper from the platter. Urgent messages seldom carried good news.

"Is a reply requested?" Alex didn't open the letter, but waited for an answer.

"No, my lord. The messenger has already gone."

"Thank you." Dismissing the footman by simply walking past him, Alex steered Evelyn toward their chambers.

"Are you not going to open it?" Evelyn demanded as he seemed undistracted from his original purpose.

"You are so eager to hear bad news that you would deny me the comforts of my home to have it? Fie on you, my lady. What can a few more hours matter when it has already taken weeks to reach here?"

Alex threw open the door to their chamber, pushed Evelyn through, and bolted it behind them. He threw the letter on his desk and began to divest himself of coat and vest. The heat of his gaze made Evelyn step backward. Torn between her fear of the letter and the need for her husband, she made no move in either direction.

Alex stalked across the carpet and located the lacing of her bodice. In a few short minutes he had the velvet off her shoulders and was untying the tiers of skirts and petticoats and hoops. His fingers grazed her stays impatiently. "You will have to stop wearing that damned contraption, my dear. I'll not have my child born with his head bent in the middle to please your vanity."

"I do not even have a belly yet, Alex. There is time before I have to hide myself behind closed doors." His impatience was winning out over her fears. She wanted him touching her, and her hands quickly took over the task of unhooking and untying.

"I'll not hide you behind closed doors. I want you in the gallery when the vote comes on the Stamp Act tomorrow or the next day. I want you by my side when we go to Cornwall to direct the spring planting. I am quite prepared to display you before half the population of England between now and September. That's my child you're carrying, and I'm damned proud of the fact. I had imagined it would take rape, bribery, and other forms of coercion to ever see this day."

He accompanied his words with the hasty shedding of his own clothes while Evelyn delicately extracted herself from the complexities of hers. Throwing aside his boots, Alex rose and swept her unencumbered figure into his arms again. Only his breeches and her chemise protected their decency, and he knew from experience how quickly these last impediments would disappear.

Evelyn wrapped her arms around his shoulders as he lifted her from the ground, and laughed low in her throat. "I should be a pretty sight walking the fields with my stomach protruding past my feet. Perhaps I should have forced you to rape, bribery, and coercion just to make you earn the profit I so readily give you."

"I have a feeling I'll spend the rest of my life earning it." Alex laid her gently back against the sheets. Sprawling beside her, he propped his head on one arm and ran a proprietary hand over the still-slender curves beneath him. Dark eyes searched violet ones cautiously. "Do you have any regrets, Evelyn? I tried to offer you a choice, but I fear my need for you did not make that very clear."

Evelyn stroked the dark shock of hair from his forehead with one hand while holding his palm over her belly with the other. The spread of his fingers encompassed the whole of her abdomen and the life within, and she felt the warmth of him seeping through her. She would give him what others had not, and she smiled up at him.

"I have no regrets. I'm no fool, Alex. I knew my choices. My only concern was that I make the right one for you. I didn't want you saddled with a wife you didn't want. There never was any question of your being the husband I have always desired. I just didn't know if I could be strong enough to make you love me too."

No smile crossed Alex's face as he continued to study her expression as if he could discern the truth or lie to her words there. He wanted to believe her with every pore in his body. He wanted to believe she had chosen him above all others, that she would have continued to refuse him against all odds had she not loved him. This was what she was saying to him, and softened by the knowledge that she had come to him first, his heart opened enough to trust her words. Their nights together could not be a lie. The child between them might be proof of his prowess in bed, but Evelyn's promises of a life together were the proof of her love. He needed no more than that.

Bending over, Alex kissed her cheek, then her brow, then nuzzled softly at her ear. "Heaven help me, but I think I believe you, little tyrant. I cannot imagine what you see in an ogre like me, but for what it's worth, I love you too much to ever believe otherwise. Make a fool of me as you will, my lady, you have the power. My love is too mad to believe any ill of you."

Evelyn had never thought to hear him say it. She had thought him too badly wounded by the past ever to admit a weakness like love. The shock of his admission coursed through her, and her gaze traveled wonderingly across Alex's strong visage, finding the vulnerability there behind the challenge in his dark eyes. A small smile began to form on her lips as she gently touched the square line of his jaw.

They succumbed to temptation then, no longer fighting the love and the need that had brought them together, but savoring them to their fullest. It was a long time before either one of them remembered the unopened letter on the desk.

Lying with one hand behind his head and the other around his wife, Alex stared up at the posts of his Yankee bed and wondered if there were any necessity in opening the letter before morning. For the first time in his life, he felt complete, and he had no desire to disturb this sense of belonging by moving from its source. His hand idly rubbed at the side of Evelyn's soft breast, and she sighed and snuggled closer to him.

Only the memory of the charges against her and the retribution they had defied by running away kept him uneasy. Justice was slow, and he had not yet succeeded in bringing the matter before a court of appeal. What if the letter were some kind of warning? He could not let it wait any longer.

Evelyn grumbled when Alex gently extricated himself from the covers wrapped about them. Forcing herself awake, she watched him cross the room to the desk. Only then did she remember the urgent message waiting there. Pulling the cover to her chin, she propped herself on one arm and watched as he lit a branch of candles with the flame from the bedside. His expression revealed nothing as he calmly perused the letter and turned to carry it back to her.

Setting the candles down beside the bed, he passed the letter to her shaking fingers. "I'm sorry, Evelyn," was all he said.

The words blurred and jumbled together at first, but as she reread the warehouse manager's meticulous penmanship, the sense began to seep through. She folded the letter carefully and laid it beside the candles.

"Why, Alex? My uncle never liked me. Why would he stand before a troop of his majesty's soldiers and refuse to let them confiscate my warehouse?"

Alex replied by crossing the room to the desk again, pushing a hidden mechanism, and opening a concealed panel beneath the bookshelves. Producing a packet of papers, he returned to the bed and handed them to her before climbing back in bed and adjusting the covers around them. He wanted her in his arms while she read the damning evidence.

"Guilt, I imagine, love. He knew he was responsible for your being arrested. He didn't wish you to lose the one thing that belonged to your father after all he had done to you. Perhaps loneliness gave him a conscience at the last. I'm here to admit that it can gnaw at a man's insides."

Evelyn opened the packet and glanced at the cursory summary of the contents, then at the names and signatures on the contracts and certificates that proved the ownership of the companies shipping the illegal goods. "My uncle and my lawyer. They did this to me. Why?"

Alex gently removed the evidence from her hands. "I don't think they meant for you to get involved. They just wanted you out of the way. But you proved more intransigent than they anticipated. Unfortunately, we made it easy for them. With you married to me and out of the country, they thought they would gain the control they needed. I am fairly certain they're the ones responsible for tricking us into the inn."

"And for having me arrested," she added bitterly. "I'll never forgive the humiliation. Why did you not tell me sooner? I thought Thomas was my friend. Why didn't you warn me?"

Alex slid an arm behind her shoulders and pulled her down against the pillows with him. "I tried to warn you, but I didn't want to turn you against your family. I know what it's like to be without family. I think I had convinced your uncle to get out of the business. There seemed no point in involving your aunt and cousin in scandal and possibly losing all that they possessed. And I knew Everett had the power to have your charges dismissed eventually. Just holding the evidence seemed a strong-enough deterrent to further illegal activity. I didn't foresee the Admiralty going so far beyond its authority as to confiscate a child's trust."

"And Uncle George died trying to prevent that? I can scarcely credit it. What can we do now?" Weary, sleepy beyond measure, Evelyn curled into her husband's embrace and accepted his high-handed methods.

"The apoplexy could have taken him anytime. I think your aunt will be proud to know that he died trying to protect your interests. We'll not tell her the rest. But the evidence in that packet should be sufficient to convince any court in the land of your innocence, or at least establish reasonable doubt as to your guilt. The warehouse may be tied up in legalities for some time to come, but it will belong to Jacob one day. You need not fear that."

"They will go after Thomas and the rest of the men on that list," she murmured thoughtfully as she slipped down beside him.

"They're not our concern. Go to sleep, love." Alex pressed a kiss to her brow as her eyes closed. "I will send messages to your mother and aunt in the morning."

"Will you send someone for me too when the time comes for the vote? I want to be there." Sleepily she kissed his shoulder.

"I shall hire a stable of message boys to gallop about all day. Go to sleep or we'll wake junior."

"Alexander Hampton II," she whispered.

"Brat."

A soft giggle was his only reply.

Alex was gone before Evelyn woke the next day. She felt none of the nausea that she had been warned would be her fate for carrying a child, but she felt an odd lethargy that she indulged until remembering the letter brought her fully awake. She had better write to her mother with more details than any message of Alex's would contain.

Alex had left the packet with the evidence lying beside the letter. Remembering how she had once promised to search for these papers, Evelyn wondered if Thomas had really thought her so lacking in sense that she would not read them before handing them over to him. Or did he not believe his guilt was traceable? Pulling out the papers, Evelyn read them over again. The name Thomas Henderson appeared in several places, usually with her uncle's name. As her uncle's attorney, Thomas would be expected to draw up and witness many of these papers. That didn't mean he necessarily knew that the operations of these companies were illegal. He was partial owner of several of the businesses, but there were many other names on those lists. If her uncle directed them, as she suspected he would, then it was possible his attorney was innocent. Her uncle the customs officer and the various ship owners and captains represented here would of necessity know the illegality of the goods coming through. A lawyer would be expected to be left innocent of such nefarious dealings. Her father had trusted Thomas, and she had never seen him commit a dishonest act in all the years they had worked together. She owed him some warning.

Carefully replacing the packet in its secret hiding place, Evelyn dressed and went down to breakfast. To Deirdre she explained the contents of Alex's urgent correspondence. She agreed a letter needed to be sent to Mrs. Wellington, but Evelyn mentioned nothing of the note to Thomas Henderson. If he were innocent, he might call on Alex for further information. If he were guilty, well, he had stood by her side in too many black moments not to give him a fair chance. It was more than she had been given, but she had room in her heart to be indulgent these days.

It did not occur to her that Thomas would plead for an audience. Now that she understood Alex's objection to the man, she could not in all good conscience allow Henderson back into the house. Evelyn stared with dismay at his note begging to talk with her. She couldn't be the type of person to ignore a friend's pleas or judge him guilty before a court did so. She could not consider herself above him or place him beyond contempt. Smuggling was practically considered a legitimate trade in the colonies. As a friend and countryman, she simply couldn't ignore Henderson's request to see her.

Sighing, she penned a reply assigning a place and time that they might meet. She would bring Margaret. They could have tea and some of those delightful bakery cakes the girl loved, and when Thomas arrived, she would ask Margaret to run across the street to the lending library for that new volume by Walpole. It would take but a minute to explain she could be of no further help. She hoped whatever Thomas had to say wouldn't take much more than that.

Margaret was eager for the outing. The weather was still cold, but there was a hint of sun to dispel the dreariness of old snow and the gray clouds of chimney smoke.

Gradually families were returning to the city for the season of parties and routs that marked the parliamentary sessions. The streets weren't yet crowded at this hour of the morning, however, and they reached the appointed spot without difficulty.

The Hampton carriage with its noble crest emblazoned on the side came to a halt behind a black hackney stopped before the bakery. Assuming Thomas must already be inside, Evelyn instructed the coachman to return within the half-hour. Margaret looked disappointed that they would not linger longer, but Evelyn preferred the means for a hasty escape should Thomas prove difficult. If everything went smoothly, they could always tell the carriage driver to leave again.

When the landau pulled away, Evelyn took a deep breath to steady her nerves and started toward the bakery. The scents of fresh-baked cakes kindled her appetite more than breakfast had earlier that morning. She was beginning to enjoy having the leisure to come and go as she pleased. The work Alex had brought home for her was interesting but undemanding. She could work at it whenever she willed, and go out to tea or shop when the mood took her. Feeling strangely content despite the unpleasant news from Boston, Evelyn gave Margaret a smile.

In the next instant a strong arm wrapped around her waist and she was yanked backward toward the hackney. Margaret let out a screech and attacked Evelyn's captor with reticule and parasol, but the man seemed impervious to her trifling blows. A hard hand closed over Evelyn's mouth as she prepared to scream, and the jerk backward made her fear for the safety of her neck. An arm like a steel bar clamped her middle, and she could see only Margaret's terrified face as she was lifted from her feet. Caught entirely off-guard, she could only kick futilely at her petticoats and skirts as she was pulled into the dark interior of the curtained carriage. Another man inside shoved Margaret's screaming, clinging form to the ground when she tried to follow, and the door slammed between them, plunging the interior into full darkness.

While one man pounded frantically for the driver to hurry, the other grabbed at Evelyn's flaying arms. Her hand connected with a jaw, but that small slap didn't deter her assailant. He merely caught her wrist and twisted it backward until she screamed. A handkerchief was shoved between her teeth then, and with both hands captive, she could do little more than kick and squirm and cause as much trouble as possible before they trussed her like a prize sow.

The jouncing of the racing coach threw her about as much as the man holding her. This fashionable part of town had almost no traffic this early in the morning, and there would be little to hinder their escape. Evelyn wildly considered throwing herself against the door, but even if she could escape the strong hands now binding her wrists, she didn't dare risk the child within her by a bruising fall.

As her eyes grew accustomed to the darkness, she searched frantically for the identity of her captor. She recognized his voice at the same time that she found the familiar seductive smile.

"You weren't supposed to bring company, Lady Cranville, but you always were one to make life difficult, weren't you?"

Evelyn stared at Thomas Henderson's handsome face with loathing. The only reply she could make was a swift kick to his shins.

34

The man behind her tightened the knots and shoved her into a corner. Evelyn turned her glare to ascertain his identity, but his gap-toothed grin and bulkily bland face could be any one of a hundred sailors down at the docks. She returned her venom to the handsome lawyer now safely out of reach of her vicious pattens.

Henderson closed his hands over the head of his cane and regarded her studiously. "I had planned to persuade you away more gently than that, Evelyn, but you've become the fashionable lady now, haven't you? Traveling unescorted through the streets is beneath your dignity, I suppose. That's a shame. Hampton will be notified soon this way, so we'll have to race against time. You won't be too comfortable under the circumstances."

He checked beneath the curtain to discern their location, then shook his head at Evelyn's warder. "It will be a while before we reach the outskirts of the city. You'll have to keep her gagged."

He sat back against the poorly padded seat and smiled pleasantly. "You always did talk too much, Evelyn. It should be much more pleasant this way. I may just keep you gagged for the entire journey."

As Evelyn's thoughts raced frantically over all the possible places he could be taking her and why, Henderson's smile grew less pleasant, and he answered her thoughts.

"I mean to be in Plymouth by tomorrow night, my dear. A ship has been waiting there to take me back to Boston for some time now. All I need is that packet of evidence you were supposed to provide me. I don't suppose you have it on you?" At her stony glare, he clucked his tongue sympathetically. "It would have saved you and your husband a lot of anguish if you had. Well, it can't be helped, I suppose. It's you or the evidence. We'll just have to wait and see which he chooses."

Henderson's chuckle didn't bode well for either choice, and Evelyn closed her eyes in fury and helplessness. The first chance she got, she would tear the villain's eyes out.

Margaret's hysterical screams brought the proprietors of nearby shops running into the street to watch whatever show was taking place. An elderly gentleman stopped to inquire helpfully if he could be of assistance, but when Margaret pushed away his encroaching arm and demanded someone follow the departing hackney, he lost interest. There wasn't another vehicle in sight beyond a few sedan chairs, a farm cart, and an ancient equipage occupied by an equally ancient dowager who turned up a frosty nose at the plight of the blatant beauty intermittently screaming curses and sobbing. Not until the Cranville carriage returned could Margaret find sympathetic ears for her story.

Deirdre felt disinclined to believe anyone could be abducted in Bond Street in broad daylight, but Margaret's hysteria and Evelyn's absence left little choice in the natter. She sent footmen fleeing through the city in earch of Alex.

When Alex's message came later that day urging Eveyn to hurry if she wished to hear the vote on the Stamp Act, it became clear that none of the footmen had suceeded in reaching him. Panic-stricken, Deirdre wished esperately for Everett's advice. Evelyn had been gone ɔr hours. How would they ever trace her?

Rory was in Scotland, too far away to be of any use. he had to reach Alex. As a precaution, she sent word › Mr. Farnley asking for his help; then, donning pelisse ıd bonnet, Deirdre set out to take Westminster by orm.

Alex returned home a few hours later, at almost the me time as a disheartened Deirdre. The frantic mesges hadn't reached him until after he'd left the floor of e House. His soaring happiness at defeating the nefarius act crumbled into nothing when he read Deirdre's words. Months of hard work, the welfare of thousands, and it all meant naught when faced with the loss of Evelyn. He tore across town on a horse borrowed from a sympathizer and met Deirdre's carriage rumbling down the drive after letting its passenger out at the front door.

Flying up the stairs and into the foyer, he nearly bowled over the butler and two footmen as they helped Deirdre from her pelisse. The excess of servants in the front hall bespoke the eagerness of all concerned to hear the lady's news. Alex's sudden appearance set them back. A very real fear filled their eyes at the sight of his lordship's black anguish and rage.

"What does this mean!" Alex flung the crumpled message on the entry table as Deirdre's frozen face turned toward him. "By Jove, you don't turn a man gray by sending mad missives like that to his office! Where's Evelyn?"

By this time Alex was aware that Margaret had come racing down the stairs, and even his mother had timidly set a foot outside the salon where she had been waiting. But Deirdre was closest, and he focused his fury on her.

Alex's tempers had always terrified the tiny countess, but she had faced worse in her lifetime and learned to stand up in the face of adversity. She didn't quake before the flash of black fires now, but spoke as calmly as she was able.

"If what Margaret tells is true, Evelyn was abducted this morning. We have spent the day trying to reach you."

"That's preposterous! It's some kind of hoax. Margaret . . ." Alex held out his hand to his frightene daughter, but before she could approach, the butler tentatively held out a sealed letter.

"This came while my lady was out. Ames has the messenger in the kitchen in case you wish to talk with him."

Alex ripped open the seal and hastily scanned th words inside. He didn't need to recognize the writing The demands told him instantly with whom he dealt Turning a shade grayer than before, he stalked silentl toward the kitchen, oblivious of the entourage followin behind.

The messenger provided no useful information. Th

man who had paid him to deliver the note resembled no one of Alex's acquaintance. The messenger had been hired off the street simply for his knowledge of the whereabouts of Cranville House. Alex dismissed him wearily and turned, to be met with almost the entirety of his household at his heels.

He wiped a trembling hand across his brow in hopes of steadying his thoughts, but only silent screams of fear and rage and desolation filled his mind. These people, his family and servants and friends, needed to be told what was happening, but he didn't have it in him to explain. The only one who could have spoken for him was in the hands of an immoral bastard whose promises couldn't be trusted for even a moment.

Silently Alex handed the letter to Deirdre and walked out. A path opened before him, but he was scarcely aware of the deference and the sympathy that opened it. He found the study blindly and reached for the decanter of brandy.

Deirdre read the letter to herself but could make no more of it than a demand for a packet of papers and a large sum of cash. The note was written as if Evelyn had gone willingly and the writer meant only to notify her husband of her whereabouts in exchange for payment. Obviously it had been written before Evelyn was forcibly dragged off before witnesses.

She hurried after Alex and found him draining a glass of brandy while staring morosely at the fire. When Deirdre threw the letter on the desk, Margaret unabashedly snatched it up, but Deirdre didn't care. She took the glass from Alex's hand and flung it at the fire.

"If you believe that letter, you're a greater fool than I ever dared conceive. Evelyn would not willingly leave without letting you know where or why. She was *abducted*. What are you going to do about it?"

Alex managed a wry smile at the sight of dainty Deirdre's ire getting the better of her noble demeanor. Awkwardly he wrapped an arm around her shoulder to comfort her.

"I believe you, my lady. Evelyn is not the type to sneak away. If she wished to disclaim me, she would do it to my face, with both barrels. No, this is the work of a desperate snake who has hidden beneath rocks for too long. I have no choice but to do what he says for now."

He didn't add that he didn't believe Henderson's promises to release Evelyn for a minute. By now the bastard surely must realize he would be a hunted man. He would need Evelyn to ensure his safety and his escape. What he would do with her after he left the shores of England did not bear thought. Alex had to make certain he didn't leave England.

Driving everyone out of the room, he began to write. Before dawn, that stable of messengers he had promised Evelyn would be on their way to every port in the kingdom. It was only a matter of delaying payment and waiting.

By midmorning of the next day, Alex was still at it. He hadn't stopped to rest or change or shave. His dinner had gone untouched and only his morning coffee showed any evidence of consumption. His once-immaculate lace was ink-stained and gray at the wrist, and unfastened and disheveled at the throat. The fire had died, but only the servants coming in with his breakfast noticed. The messengers going to and fro were too terrified and awed by the earl's harsh commands to see anything but the ogre behind the desk.

He had written to every man in every port that he ever knew. Every Cranville ship crew would be on the alert. Tavernkeepers, customs officials, warehousemen, and all the sailors they came in contact with would be on the lookout. Pride had at first prevented asking help of the powerful men Alex dealt with here in London, but by dawn pride had flown with the desolation of knowing he had not yet done enough. He wanted Evelyn back regardless of the consequences.

He started on another series of letters. By noon, every hackney driver in the city would be questioned and men would be on every road out of London asking at coaching houses and inns. Men with Yankee accents weren't so prevalent as to escape notice, and Evelyn didn't exactly blend in with the woodwork. Someone had to have seen them. If every man Alex knew in London would send out every available servant to notify others of the search, they could cover England in a few days' time.

Alex buried his face in his hands and groaned at the thought of days of this hell. Evelyn in the hands of Henderson for untold days and nights was a nightmare worse than any he had ever encountered in a life pockmarked with nightmares. She could be bound and gagged and suffocating in a trunk somewhere. Henderson could be forcing her into his bed, and with the child to think of, Evelyn would be powerless to fight. The humiliation would destroy his proud-and-proper Evelyn. He couldn't bear it.

Throwing back his chair and standing abruptly, Alex slammed a stack of books to the floor and crossed the study in jerky strides. He couldn't just sit here and do nothing. He had meant to wait for the message dictating the delivery of the packet, but he couldn't just sit here until he had word. He would go mad. There had to be something else he could do, some stone yet unturned.

The noisy arrival of a carriage outside turned Alex's frantic gaze eagerly to the front hall. Perhaps Evelyn had escaped. Perhaps it was all a mistake. His strides carried him rapidly toward the opening door.

Alyson burst through in a flurry of flowing capes and loose long black hair that made her appear the witch she had been accused more than once of being. Anxious pale gray eyes found Alex instantly, and she flew down the marble corridor toward him, Rory running close behind.

"Alyson, dammit! You'll terrify the household! Wait . . ." Rory's words halted as he caught sight of Alex's drawn visage. The once-elegant earl garbed in clothes wrinkled from a day's and night's wear spoke volumes. Rory bit his tongue and once again acknowledged the truth of his wife's premonitions.

"Alex, she's on a ship! There's a great gray wall around the harbor, and a hideous stone fort on a hill. I see two rivers coming together. She's terrified, Alex. You've got to find her!"

Alex took his fey cousin in his arms and hugged her fearful figure close while he raised his gaze to meet Rory's over her head. He didn't even want to know how Alyson had known or how they had got here so quickly.

With Alyson, it was better not to know. But her description of Evelyn's whereabouts sent gooseflesh creeping down his arms. He knew at once where she meant. The question remained, how in hell did Alyson know?

Rory's Scots burr was heavy as he replied to a part of Alex's questions. "She made us turn around and sail right back. It was either risk the babe and her health on the sea or lock her in the tower. She's right, isn't she?"

"Evelyn was abducted yesterday morning. It makes some sort of insane sense. Alys just described Plymouth. That would be the most likely place for a Boston-bound ship to leave."

Rory nodded curtly. "I'll trust Alyson's vision. Want me to go for you?"

"I want you to go with me. Now." Alex's dark face was rigid as he released Alyson into Deirdre's comforting arms and began shouting commands. Whether Alyson's quirky second sight was true or not, he could no longer sit here and wait to find out. A mad flight to Plymouth suited his needs better than waiting.

He agreed to a change of clothes and a hasty meal, but they were on the road within the half-hour, the miles disappearing beneath the thunder of the horse's hooves. With the icy wind whistling through Alex's hair and numbing his fingers and toes, he could freeze all thought and pour all energy into action. He needed that, or he would be forced to face the images of Evelyn being tormented by her captors, and all because of him. He had made the wrong decisions, acted too slowly, not taken all the possibilities into account. If he had only done . . .

Alex froze his thoughts again, concentrating only on keeping his mount safely in the center of the road, where the ruts and holes and patches of ice weren't so numerous. He was aware of Rory racing close behind, but they had left the army of grooms and stablehands far in the distance. At such short notice, it had been difficult to find enough men who could ride.

Finding good horses at posting houses proved nigh on to impossible, but Alex's title opened the doors of stables up and down the highways and byways. Friends he hadn't known he possessed offered their best mounts, and his army of followers began to swell and improve in quality as the men of his acquaintance came out to join him. Word spread rapidly of the Earl of Cranville's desperate flight, and Alex didn't even have to ask for horses by the time they reached Devonshire.

His followers wouldn't let him cross the moors by night. Half-frozen, half-mad, Alex allowed Rory to drag him from his horse and into the noble halls of some marquess who had ridden out to greet them. He didn't make it to a bed, but fell asleep in the chair they pushed under him when he stopped pacing long enough to sit. By dawn Alex was grabbing handfuls of provisions from the breakfast table and starting out the door before the rest of the company had stirred.

Rory forgot breakfast and ran out after him, notifying the servants of their departure. Behind him, grooms and stablehands and members of the aristocracy groaned and hurried for their mounts. Plymouth was only a morning's ride away.

Alyson's vision hadn't specified which ship held Evelyn, but lack of this information did not deter Alex's rage. The gray, spitting snow of the previous day had changed to a balmier southern wind by the time he rode into Plymouth, and his thoughts were rapidly defrosting also. Fire burned through his veins as he approached the harbor. He no longer considered the possibility that Evelyn might not be here. He intended to dismantle the harbor until he found her.

On a day like this, the docks teemed with life. The fishing boats and their crews had left at daybreak, but there were still ships in dry dock crawling with sailors and workmen, men mending nets, vendors hawking their wares, passengers crowding around waiting their turn to board, goods being loaded and unloaded with the accompanying cacophony of carts and curses. Undisturbed by this familiar milieu, Alex strode without hesitation in the direction of his majesty's coast patrol. Rory, on the other hand, went directly to a weathered ship manned by a definitely rough-looking crew.

Between them they covered both the legal and the illegal levels of this world and came up with the same piece of information. The schooner bobbing up and down farther out in the harbor was a Yankee ship. It had docked briefly yesterday to allow passengers on board. One of those passengers had been a heavily cloaked and hooded female who had to be carried on board. Alex's jaw drew so tight at this news that the speaker backed away as if he had seen a specter of death.

Rory clapped a hand on Alex's shoulder. "You didn't think Evelyn would willingly walk that plank, did you? She's probably given them royal hell ever since they snatched her. They ought to be ready to give her up by now."

"She's carrying my child, Maclean," Alex responded heavily. "She'll not do anything to harm the child. The bastards would not have got this far with her if not for that."

That did put a different face on the matter, and Rory stared stonily out to sea at the ship bobbing so effortlessly there. He had been where Alex stood now and knew the man's agony. Alex had stayed at his side throughout that hellish nightmare. He could do no less for Alex. His hand gripped the hilt of the sword at his side. This southern port wasn't his Scottish homeland, but there had to be a way to breach the castle walls, or the ship's bulwark, as the case might be.

By this time their entourage had caught up with them, and Alex grimly observed the motley army of inexperienced sailors at his command. With resolution he turned to Rory and in low tones discussed the only plan that immediately came to mind. Rory nodded once or twice, made a suggestion or two, and soon the ill-assorted band of men dispersed on various assignments.

Shortly after noon, a suspiciously low-lying and heavily armed sloop slipped from the harbor bearing twice the number of ruffians it had entered with. Not long after that, a navy vessel followed in pursuit. The only oddity to these departures was that they occurred in the broad light of day, not the dark of night.

A smattering of fishing boats, private yachts, and any other boat that could lift sail gradually followed in the wake of the larger ships. Had Evelyn been on deck to see this flotilla, she might easily have recognized the battle plan that had once attempted to turn the Earl of Cranville away from Boston harbor. No one waited aboard the deck of the Yankee schooner to observe this, however.

Alex had not been raised to be a warrior. He had learned the techniques of shooting and swordfighting at gentlemanly schools for the pleasure of possessing the skills. Other than an absurd marksmanship at bagging game, he had never used those skills in actual combat. That was Rory's career, not his. But he stood on the navy vessel with loaded pistols in hand and a sword at his side now. Never before had he kept his boiling anger curbed with such control. Never before had he been so dangerous.

Recognizing the deadly look in his noble passenger's eye, the navy captain stayed at his side. With a marquess, an earl, and an assortment of viscounts and baronets and gentry aboard his vessel and the others scattered around it, the captain couldn't afford the devastation that would be wreaked should actual fighting break out. He was equally certain the man beside him had no such concerns.

A woman's screams galvanized them all into action. The sloop bumped along the starboard of the Yankee ship while the navy vessel took to the port side. All eyes turned to the large man waiting tensely for the opportunity to make that crossing. The grim look that had darkened Alex's face all the way out into the harbor had suddenly taken on an odd aura of triumph. Unlike everyone else, Alex recognized those screams. They weren't ones of pain or fear. They were the screams of a woman hell-bent on ripping a man to shreds. A smile began to turn the corners of his lips as he heard the staccato curses in between the screeches. The termagant had learned one or two things from him, after all.

Evelyn looked up briefly in surprise at the sudden jarring of the ship, but she quickly returned her full attention to the no-longer-obsequious man in the cabin with her. He had ordered her unbound and the gag removed, but whatever his reasons had been, they'd been thwarted by Evelyn's lack of gratefulness.

"Lay one more hand on me and I'll rip your eyes out, Henderson! Are you really fool enough to think you'll get away with this? Alex will hunt you down for the rest of your life." She lifted the heavy ceramic water pitcher in her hand to a height matching the level of the lawyer's head.

"Don't be too damn certain of that. These lofty British peers have strange notions sometimes. Spoiled Yankee wives are easily dispensable. By the time we reach Boston you may even be bearing my brat. Do you think your noble husband will want you back then?"

Thomas grabbed for the pitcher and Evelyn screamed again, pumping all her fury into it in the hopes that someone somewhere would hear her. She swung the pitcher with all her might, but days of being bound by ropes had sapped her strength. Thomas easily blocked the blow and the pitcher bounced off his arm to crash into pieces upon the floor.

He caught her wrist and she went after him tooth and nail. The wooden pattens she had worn to protect her shoes when she set out for the bakery days ago connected resoundingly with his shin once again, and she felt his wince of pain with satisfaction. Screeching curses, Evelyn clawed his face with her free hand and battered mercilessly at his legs as he shoved her back toward the bunk. Her screams pierced the air, nearly obliterating the onslaught of booted feet on the deck above.

Shouts of anger and the pounding of feet down the companionway finally woke them to the fact that something was happening outside this tiny cabin. Thomas cursed and flung her hand aside to tear open the door. He blanched and instantly jerked Evelyn in front of him as Alex in a black fury loomed before him, pistol in hand.

They had reached an instant stalemate. Evelyn felt Henderson's strong arm crushing her waist as she gazed rapturously beyond the barrel of the pistol into the miracle of her husband's dark face. She didn't know how Alex could possibly have found her, but she was ecstatic that he had. Now all she had to do was rid herself of the worm holding a knife to her side. She hadn't known Thomas had a knife. She didn't wish to imagine what he meant to do with it.

"I trust you brought the papers, Hampton." The lawyer reacted smoothly, with his usual air of cool control.

"You'll get nothing while you have my wife in your hands, Henderson. Let her go."

Evelyn recognized the barely leashed fury in Alex's voice, but Thomas seemed impervious to it. He spoke as if he had complete control of the situation. "Just keep out of my way, Hampton, and you can have her back. She's a shrew of the worst sort, always has been. You deserve her. All I ask is a fair exchange, my freedom for your wife."

"You don't honestly believe I'll let you get away with this?" Alex growled, his gaze shifting rapidly from the position of the knife at Evelyn's belly to the man's bland face. The lawyer even wore his damned wig. Mayhap he was bald beneath it.

Rory came to stand beside Alex, his gaze rapidly assessing the situation. "Stand back, Alex, and let the man pass," he said gruffly.

To everyone's surprise, Alex did as told. Henderson glanced suspiciously at Alex's position on the side of the door opposite the companionway, then took in the number of hostile faces surrounding him. For the first time, he began to understand the precariousness of his predicament.

"I think not, Hampton. Clear your cronies out of here. Bring me the papers and a pardon for any additional charges. I'll keep your wife until I have the papers in my hand and the ship is granted free passage from these waters. Then you can have her back."

Evelyn impatiently jerked her head around to give Henderson a scathing glare. "This is ridiculous. You'd do better to face the charges of smuggling than kidnapping. The evidence isn't all that damning or I would never have agreed to see you in the first place. You'd quite likely get off free. Now, put that knife down and let me go. You're hurting my arm."

Her sharp tones brought a chuckle from several of the onlookers. Although looking pale and lovely with her disheveled tresses spilling about her fair shoulders, Lady Cranville did not present the expected picture of a lady in distress. Several were inclined to wonder why Alex had gone to this much trouble for the return of such a sharp-tongued creature, but the earl's temper was notorious, and they kept their countenance.

"Talk to your husband, not to me. I'm perfectly willing to release you. But I have no desire to get my head blown off in the course of things. Tell them to go away, and you'll be fine."

Alex gestured for the others to go above. Rory hesitated, giving Alex's dark face a look askance, but someone needed to keep an eye on the explosive situation above. The combination of British and Yankee smugglers mingling with Navy officers and British noblemen made him shudder. Someone had better find a solution to this stalemate, and fast.

"Give me my wife, Henderson, and we'll leave. You can rot in hell for all I care. You can steal the whole damn country blind. I don't care what you do. But I'm not taking my eyes off of you until you release Evelyn."

Sensing he would never be free unless he acted now, Henderson desperately made one last offer. "Go in front of me and I'll follow. When we get up on deck, clear your men off the ship, bring me the packet and a pardon, and I'll release her. We'll all be in plain view. No one will come to any harm."

"Put that knife away and I'll agree." Alex clamped his teeth and clenched his fists and held himself still while Henderson wavered.

"Get over on that side where you can lead the way, and I'll do it," he finally agreed.

Alex nodded curtly, stepped toward the companionway, and turned to make certain Henderson kept his word. The lawyer returned the knife to its sheath, and holding Evelyn's arm behind her back, pushed her along in front of him as a shield against Alex's weapons.

They climbed up into the bright light of day. Evelyn shut her eyes briefly against the glare and wished for the cloak she had left behind in the cabin. The wind blowing off the water sent a chill through layers of velvet and petticoats. When she opened her eyes again, she was amazed at the assortment of ships and boats bobbing about them, and she stared awestruck at the odd army Alex commanded. A blinding smile began to replace her fear as she met these friendly gazes, and she couldn't resist greeting the friends Alex had found.

"Welcome, gentlemen. I wish Alex and I could entertain you more nobly, but you have caught us unprepared. Perhaps if you'll stop by Cranville House sometime, we'll better entertain you, but I do thank you for coming." She smiled mischievously as the solemn faces around her broke into grins of surprise and delight. They might be afraid, but she wasn't. Not any longer. Alex was here. Evelyn turned her expectant gaze up to her husband.

Alex felt the full burden of her trust in that look. Independent brat that she was, she would never have surrendered her ability to act on her own did she not trust his ability more in this situation. That knowledge swelled him with a pride he had lost long ago, and the love in his eyes blazed boldly for all to see.

"Rory, take the men back to the ships. Write out the pardon he requests, have the captain witness it; Summerville and I will sign it." Alex kept his gaze focused on his foe. "I'll not leave until Evelyn is released, so you'll need bring the paper here for me to sign."

As the men began to scramble back to their respective boats, Henderson suggested, "Tell them to take your weapons, Hampton, and I'll be a good deal more comfortable. Your wife might appreciate the benefit of that."

Since he had twisted Evelyn's arm so tightly in his nervousness that she was pale with pain, Alex saw the wisdom of compliance. His weapons were useless until she was released in any case. He signaled for the Marquess of Summerville to take his weapons, then held out his hand to Henderson. "To be fair about this, your knife too."

Henderson surrendered it reluctantly. The marquess glanced hesitantly at Alex, but at Alex's nod, he too departed. They had worked well together in the Lords, and Summerville trusted the earl's judgment. Unaccustomed to giving his trust or his friendship easily, Alex accepted his peer's unquestioning agreement with gratitude. The man had an ally for life, should he ever get himself out of this mess.

Henderson's hold on Evelyn relaxed, but he refused

to release her completely. She still provided a shield and a shelter from Alex's fury.

Evelyn had the urge to yank her arm away and kick painfully at her captor, but she read the warning in Alex's eyes well enough. He planned something. She would wait. It was much better working with him than against him or on her own. She liked knowing he was there. Perhaps her husband's business and political interests would keep him occupied and busy for most of their days, but she knew now she could always rely on him when she needed him. And she could rely on him not to interfere when she did not. Evelyn felt a sudden sense of freedom in this thought, and her elation filled her eyes as she met his gaze.

Quietly Alex held out his hand, his gaze not veering from hers. "Now, Evelyn."

At his word, she jerked abruptly forward, catching Henderson by surprise and upsetting his balance. Alex pulled her behind him, and Henderson immediately surrendered his fragile hold on her wrist when suddenly confronted with Alex's ominously large frame.

Evelyn fled to the safety of the railing when Alex lifted his fist and brought it with a satisfactory crunch against the lawyer's jaw. She felt Rory instantly clambering down beside her, sword in hand to keep Henderson's crew away from her, but she had no fear of those men while Alex battered their leader into submission. Her fear was that Alex would go too far.

Henderson narrowly missed stumbling back down the companionway. He caught himself against the bulwark and slid to the side before regaining his feet. Alex was upon him in an instant, his massive fist slamming into Henderson's narrow abdomen with a force sufficient to send his opponent rolling toward the railing.

More men hurriedly scrambled back to the deck, forming a protective wall around the combatants. All and sundry seemed to agree this was a private fight and that no other quarrel need intervene. Navy officers stood beside smugglers without regard to occupation. A fight over a woman was neutral ground for all but the combatants.

Evelyn clung to Rory's arm as Thomas grasped a barrel and heaved it at Alex, then grabbed for an ax hung against the bulwark. Alex stopped the barrel's roll with his foot and shoved it back at his opponent, catching Thomas and hurling him backward before he could reach the weapon.

It was obvious to all that the smaller man was no match for Alex's greater strength and that trickery would be his only escape. Alex's rage had reached full steam now, and he bore down on his victim with the violence of hurricane winds. His blows sent Thomas sliding closer to the railing. Someone cried a warning as Thomas rolled with a blow and grabbed a length of rope connected to the rigging, pulling it taut across Alex's path. Alex tripped but caught himself, flinging his large body to the side rather than overboard. Swiftly he grabbed at Henderson's foot and jerked as they both slid across the deck.

Henderson kicked, gave a mighty shove, and gained his feet. Before Alex could lift his larger frame, Thomas grabbed a barrel lid and swung it viciously at his head. Alex dodged forward, and the force of Henderson's swing and Alex's maneuver sent the lawyer stumbling backward into the railing.

The splintering railing of the neglected smuggling sloop cracked with a snap that caught everyone by surprise. Henderson tried to throw himself forward, but the ship lurched, keeping him off-balance, and the weathered wood split beneath his weight. With a cry, he sprawled backward into the depths of the water below.

Alex wasn't among those who rushed to the railing to throw out ropes and lower dinghies to rescue the man overboard. With a look of purpose, he stalked toward his wife.

Evelyn released Rory's arm and waited, her heart in her throat. He had told her not to see Henderson again. He had shown her the reason why. And still she had defied him. Whatever punishment he meted out, she deserved, but more than anything, she wanted to be in his arms again.

She held herself straight and proudly as he came to her, but Alex took no notice of her haughty stance. With a single groan he caught her up in his embrace and buried his face in her hair and held her tight against him.

"Damned Yankee rebel, I'll have you clamped in

chains for this," he growled against her hair as her hands locked behind his neck.

Without reply, Evelyn turned her face up to his and caught his lips with a fierceness that denied the existence of all around them. With wonder, she felt the hot moisture of his tears blend with hers, and she clung to him as if she were drowning.

Only Rory's cough at their side eventually intruded upon their reunion, and reluctantly Alex settled his wife on her feet again, while keeping her close against him.

"They've hauled Henderson out and the navy has him in custody. I don't think he'll be causing any more problems in the immediate future. Do you wish to go ashore by way of the navy or my friends down there?" Rory nodded in the direction of the small vessel preparing to disembark.

Alex raised a languid eyebrow at his cousin-in-law. "I'll refrain from telling Alyson of your choice of friends if you'll find me the first ship bound for Boston. The Yankee and I are taking a little voyage—sans family. Deal?"

Rory began to grin. "Deal. I know just the ship. Would you be visiting the West Indies while you're there?"

"Wait a minute!" Wide-eyed, Evelyn jerked around to face both men. "Why Boston? Are you trying to get rid of me, Alexander Hampton? Because it won't work, you know."

Dark eyes gleamed as they stared down into her lovely but irate countenance. "I thought you would wish to be the first to give your rebel friends the news. They won. The tax is dead. There will be months of circumlocutions yet, but for all intents and purposes, your colonial hotheads won the war without a battle."

Joy spread rapidly across her face as Evelyn met his gaze. "You did it! You really did it! Oh, Alex, I love you!" She flung her arms around his neck and kissed him soundly. Before Rory could be embarrassed again, she promptly released her stunned husband and, hands on hips, announced, "We had better leave immediately before I am too large to travel."

Rory's whoop of laughter at Alex's mixed look of pride

and embarrassment brought stares and yells of encouragement from all around them. When the earl swung his Yankee countess into his arms and marched her toward the waiting ship, a roar of approval rocked the motley flotilla in Plymouth harbor.

Epilogue

April 1766

The round of cannon shot echoed through the spring-evening air, followed by a tumult of screams, shouts, ringing bells, and shotgun fire. The crowd beneath the Liberty Tree surged with a wave of motion that soon flooded into the street in a continuous cacophony.

Alex drew his wife back into the safety of a nearby doorway, his arm clamped snugly beneath her breasts, his other hand resting protectively over the slight rounding of her abdomen. Evelyn had abandoned stays, panniers, heavy petticoats, and silks in favor of simple cotton and chemise this night, and he could feel every curve of her lithe figure leaning into him.

"I suppose you wish to follow them too," he murmured against her ear as the crowd streamed toward the State House.

"They say they've built a huge pyramid covered with all kinds of figures, even the king and queen, although I hear Sam Adams ranks higher. And there are hundreds of lamps all over it, and fireworks up on top. You'll never see anything like it in London."

"There are many things I've never seen in London, but I'm not disposed to battle mobs to find them. Those are guns they are firing out there. And do you have any idea what happens to fireworks when they come in contact with hundreds of lamps? Do all Yankees like to celebrate dangerously?"

Evelyn laughed softly and rubbed suggestively against him. "We do everything dangerously. That's the kind of world we live in."

"I shall remember that." Alex turned her around and wrapped his hand in the thick wave of hair pouring over her shoulder. Her eyes sparkled with delight, and the parade of flags, people, and illuminations behind her provided the ideal setting for her young, vibrant figure. She belonged here in this simple and half-savage world. Silks and lace and powdered hair had no place in this country. Wistfully he wrapped his hand in her loosely bound hair. "You are happy now?"

She knew his question had naught to do with the joyous riot that had erupted at word of the Stamp Act's repeal. Nor did it have anything to do with the fact that with the help of the marquess, the navy, and Henderson's arrest, he had been able to bring her case to appeal so she might return to her home. It was another kind of happiness he questioned. Pressing her hands against his chest, she reached up to kiss his bristly jaw. "Happier than I have ever been in my whole life. And you?"

"I don't think you need to ask that." Alex lifted her until their lips met and the electricity flowed between them, and only the jeering encouragement of passersby reminded them they were not in a private place. Reluctantly he set her down. "Would you be happiest if we stayed here? This is your home. I never meant to rob you of it."

Evelyn linked her arm through his and lightly pulled him toward the velvet darkness of the narrow alley beside their hiding place. The clamor of the mob was rapidly moving toward the center of town. She turned her feet in the direction of the Common and her home. Every house had candles in the windows to celebrate their joy at the news. It was almost like Christmas, but in spring. She took a deep breath of the crisp night air.

"You are my home. Wherever you are, I am happy. I never imagined it could be this way."

Somewhere in the distance premature fireworks went off, and screams of delighted laughter permeated the night. Alex didn't need to see the display of colored light. He felt it going off inside of him as he lifted Evelyn into his arms and hugged her close, burying his face against her silken hair.

"I never imagined it either, tyrant. But then, I never

imagined being led around by a pint-sized termagant with a knife for a tongue either." Before she could pull his hair out by the handful, Alex added, "Nor did I imagine I would be so lucky as to fall in love with a beautiful woman stubborn enough to endure my multitudinous faults. Can we go home now? I can think of better ways of celebrating than with shotguns and flags."

Evelyn dug her fingers more fully into Alex's thick hair and pulled his head down to meet her kiss once more. She needed no words for her reply; her tongue said it all as it slipped between his lips to seek his response.

Alex groaned and crushed her against him briefly; then, half-carrying, half-pulling her, he guided her hurriedly toward the privacy of the empty house on Treamount.

Molly had lit candles in the windows and left to join the rest of the celebrants in town. Alex pushed open the door, then swept his wife into his arms and carried her up the stairs to the feather bed that had been laid out for them. It wasn't their elegantly carved bed in London, but it was better than the narrow ship's berth they had shared for the voyage. Alex gently laid his wife across the covers and fell down beside her.

He pulled the ribbon from Evelyn's hair and spread the silken tresses across the pillow as he bent to ply her lips with kisses. Evelyn responded with such enthusiasm that his hand quickly found the fastenings of her bodice and strayed inside to better caress the soft swells of flesh pressing temptingly into him. Evelyn moaned contentedly and arched against his palm, and Alex succumbed to the familiar surge of heat in his loins.

By the time the noise outside had disappeared into the distance, they were lying naked in each other's arms, their bodies covered with a fine sheen of sweat from their exertions. Alex pulled the covers over them, carefully keeping the chill night air away.

"I love you," she whispered, making the flesh on his arms rise in excitement as if the words had feathered along his skin.

Gathering her in his arms, Alex rested her head against his shoulder and succumbed to the seductive pleasure of Evelyn's softness pressed up and down his side, her slender legs wrapped about his thigh while her kisses occasionally licked along his skin.

"You're so much a part of me now, I cannot imagine a life without you. Your happiness is mine, Evelyn. I want you always to be happy. What do I have to do to ensure it?"

The old insecurities lingered, but Evelyn brushed them away with her fingers and replaced them with her kisses. "Never leave me, and I'll always be happy. I know I'll soon be too fat to be seen with you, and I'll have to find some way of occupying my time while you are out and about, but I will not mind so long as I know you will be coming home to me."

Alex let his hand drift down her side to play idly with the delights her body offered. Her breasts were heavier now, and the slight swell of her abdomen gave him pleasure to touch. He smiled to himself as she wriggled closer into his hand, and his fingers slid downward to stroke another favorite place.

"I don't think I dare let you out of my sight for the next few months, tyrant. I want my heir born in my bed and not on a smuggling ship or a London street. I think you're about to see more of me than you will ever want again. By the time we sail to Barbados to meet Everett's daughter and return to England, you should be nicely plump. Then I shall install you in that pile of rocks in Cornwall where you cannot escape and put you to work at making a home of it. I doubt that there will be sufficient time for you to complete the job before the child is born, so we will linger for some months after. I don't foresee leaving our splendid isolation until . . . Oh, let us say after the third or fourth child has reached an age for schooling."

Warm all over from his words and growing warmer with his touch, Evelyn curled around him, twining her fingers through the curls on his chest and pressing her kisses into his throat and shoulders. She had no doubt that before the night was over they would be one again, with Alex inside of her and as much a part of her body as the child growing within. But the anticipation was almost as good as the actuality. Her fingers began a casual caress of his hard body beneath her.

"You lie, you know. There will be some issue in Parliament that will call down your wrath, and you will be off to London. And there will be opportunities to expand your shipping enterprises, and you will be off talking men out of their wealth. And there are all the other investments that must be looked after personally, since Alyson and Rory will not. You will be lucky if you have time to breed three or four children. And what makes you think this one is your heir? I rather fancy a daughter myself."

"Shrew." Alex pressed a kiss to her cheek. Her caresses were working their magic, but he wanted her gentleness now. In a few minutes, perhaps, he would indulge in her passion. "Alyson tells me hers is to be the only girl in the family, besides Margaret. You will have to be satisfied with a houseful of rough-and-tumble boys. And I will be there with you every night to ensure that fate, never fear. After a while you may wish I would go off to London and leave you alone."

Evelyn laughed and moved over him, pressing kisses against his jaw while tempting him with the brush of her breasts. "I will go to London with you and let our three or four junior Hamptons loose upon the civilized world. You will come home to me quickly enough."

Laughter rumbled from deep in Alex's chest as he pulled her down to ravage her saucy mouth. "I will learn to carry a whip and a chain. Come here, little rebel. I will give you something more pleasant to dream about."

Swiftly Evelyn took him between her legs, capturing him by surprise. Alex's shout of pleasure filled her heart with joy. She had no illusions about the future. They would fight often enough, and she would lose battles and skirmishes, but the war could have only one peaceful solution. Their love would win every time.

About the Author

Patricia Rice was born in Newburgh, New York, and attended the University of Kentucky. She now lives in Mayfield, Kentucky, with her husband and her two children, Corinna and Derek, in a rambling Tudor house. Ms. Rice has a degree in accounting and her hobbies include history, travel and antique collecting.